THE REED

JORDAN MUSEN

BLACKBIRD BOOKS
NEW YORK · LOS ANGELES

A Blackbird Original, November 2024

Manufactured in the United States of America.

Cataloging-in-Publication Data

Musen, Jordan.
The Reed / Jordan Musen.
p. cm.
I. Title.
1. Ancient Israel—Fiction. 2. Bible—Authorship—Fiction.
3. Women—Fiction. 4. Historical fiction. I. Title.
PS3613.U35 S44 2024 813′.6—dc23 2024949021

Blackbird Books
www.bbirdbooks.com
email us at editor@bbirdbooks.com

ISBN 978-1-61053-054-5

First Edition

10 9 8 7 6 5 4 3 2 1

To my mother, Delly.
She would have enjoyed this.

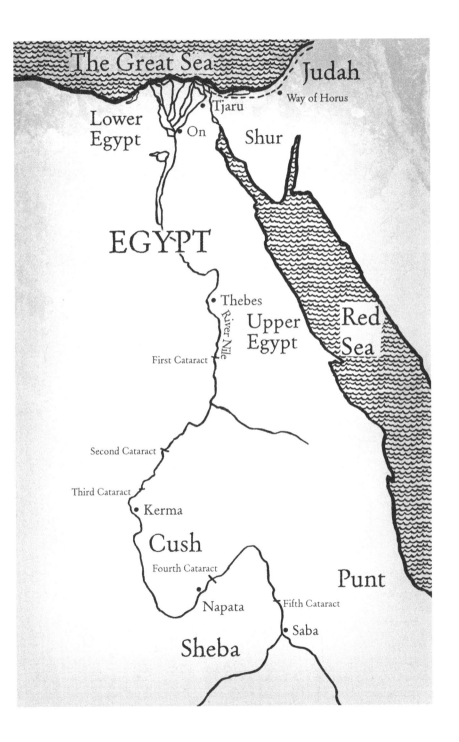

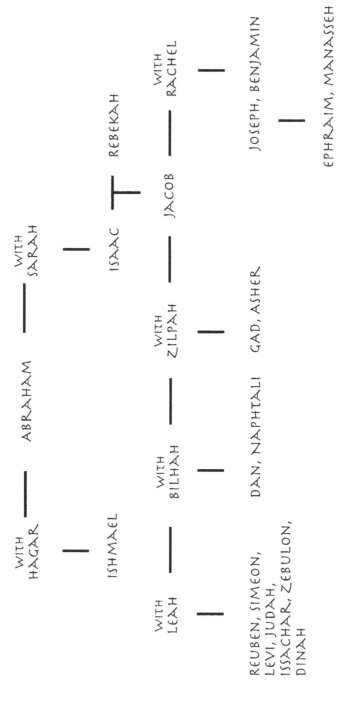

WITH HAGAR

ABRAHAM — WITH SARAH

ISHMAEL

ISAAC ┬ REBEKAH

WITH LEAH

WITH BILHAH

JACOB — WITH ZILPAH

WITH RACHEL

REUBEN, SIMEON, LEVI, JUDAH, ISSACHAR, ZEBULON, DINAH

DAN, NAPHTALI

GAD, ASHER

JOSEPH, BENJAMIN

EPHRAIM, MANASSEH

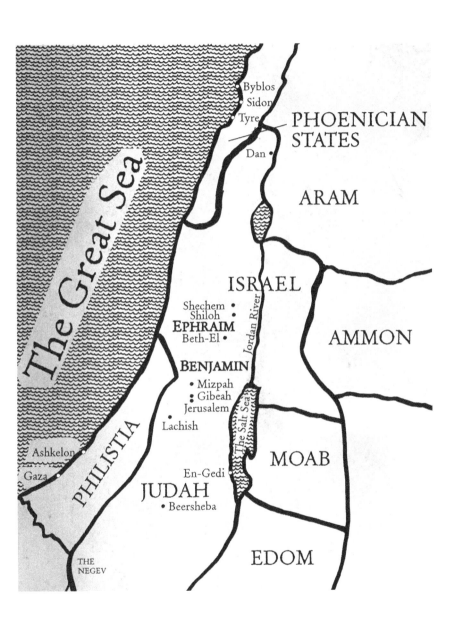

PART I
LEVITICUS

CHAPTER ONE

On the limestone wall, Hannah's unmistakable shadow descends the stairs, her shape reminding me of the Hebrew letter tet, so fat, so pregnant. Her blackness expands, consuming my thin, cursed silhouette.

"Praying to Astarte?" I ask, with my slight stammer, in the fluttering light.

"The incense is that strong?" my sister-wife responds as she steps onto the mosaic floor, decorated with amethyst, topaz, and rubies, joining me at our cooking room's hearth. "What are you preparing?" Hannah bends her head into my creation; her thick, braided hair dangles above the dish. "Pigeon and raisins?" Dipping her fingertip in the bowl, she gives it a taste, making a face. "Too much coriander."

"Do you think?" I say, pretending this evening is just like any other, that our conversation is like any other.

"I really shouldn't be eating the seeds." Hannah touches her belly. Deliberately. "If you don't want to take your meals in the banquet hall, then let one of the servants cook for you. Who in the palace cooks for themselves, anyway?" She lumbers back

3

toward the cedar stairs. "When you're done, why don't you pray with me? It'll be something we can do together."

I picture myself, skinnier than a tent peg, kneeling at the fertility table to the idol's overly large breasts and wide hips, while praying ardently by my side is Hannah and her growing abdomen.

"Maybe," I say, picking up the mixing stick to stir the dish. I am so tired. She has no idea how tired I am. Go up the steps, Hannah. Go.

"Trust me, you want to get pregnant again, don't you? Let's pray to Astarte."

All my life I've never warmed to the goddess. Why would Astarte suddenly pay me any attention now? Maybe I expect too much from Hannah, but she should know that I'm not ready to try for another child. Yet even if I were willing, my husband Raddai would have to lie with me. But it's Hannah he wants now, the choicest wheat, not me, the gleanings after the harvest.

"Astarte's the one you should be asking for help, not your god," she says. "He's obviously not listening to you."

I wonder how many guards I'll be facing in a few minutes. And once I'm in the great hallway, what if I have one of my blackouts, and collapse on the floor, my head slamming into the pigeon and raisins only to wake up later to a ceiling of horrified faces? *Stop it, Keb. Calm yourself. You have to or it will all fall apart.*

I can't let it fall apart. I have to do this for him.

"Did you hear me?"

"Hannah, we've discussed this—"

"What does your male god know about the inner workings of a woman? Trust me, you need a fertility goddess behind you. You're the only woman I know who doesn't ask Astarte to open her womb. You could still have children. You're not *that* old."

4

You're not *that* tactless, I want to tell her. But I can't muster the words. To *sheol* with her and her growing belly, to *sheol* with Raddai who hasn't looked at me in two years, to *sheol* with Astarte and her exaggerated breasts.

"After I'm done, I'll come upstairs," I say to end it.

"Good." She smiles and I force a grin. As she leaves, and as the oil lamps flicker, I add cucumbers to the stew that no one will ever eat, on my hearth, which I might never light again.

א

Carrying the dish, I pass by the servants' quarters, all so small and barren. Hannah's youngest and her wet nurse are fast asleep. How an infant can sleep through all the billowy smoke and ash from the burning incense is beyond me. Even my own eyes, well accustomed to the sooty gum, are watering up.

I peek into the shrine room. Praying with her back to me, Hannah is fertile as the Nile Valley, her vagina, the lush Delta. Her dress is large and loose fitting. Underneath it all, she's supporting that new weight on her thickening thighs. I assume she feels what I felt years ago, that mix of emotions: the euphoria that soon she will see the birthing stool, the annoyance of dealing with such an awkward body, the dread that she might not survive the ordeal.

She's chanting softly so as not to wake her children, kneeling, overdoing the frankincense on the small clay-brick altar, her idol standing farther back on the sandstone slab. Hannah serves a fig cake and a goblet of wine to her Queen of Heaven. Then my sister-wife holds her hands out, palms toward the ceiling, hoping to get a gift for a gift. I leave her.

The goddess is obviously watching over her, even if Hannah hasn't produced a son yet, for she has two healthy girls with one

5

more child on the way. Still, I can't let myself believe that I've been a fool to rely on my god Yahweh. He once answered old prayers; he will answer them again.

In my dressing room, I can hear Hannah's muffled voice singing, coming through the thin plaster. "Children are a gift from Astarte . . ." I set the dish aside for the moment and open my clothing chest. Sifting through my dresses, I find my dark red tunic. I dig inside the sleeve and find the scroll. My greatest fear these last few months has been Raddai discovering the writing. My heart has clenched a hundred times just imagining him shouting his predictable, "Recognize this?"

I stow the papyrus in my goatskin satchel, loop the bag around my shoulder, and search for my sandals. Where are they? I haven't had them on for the longest time, since right before the olive harvest. Raddai's nagging has been so tiring these past months. *Stop your mourning. Put your sandals back on.* I find them behind the chest. It feels so odd slipping my toes in; my feet feel strangely confined and heavy. I pick up my bowl and once again pass by the household gods, giving a final glance at Hannah. I walk by unnoticed as she continues praying, so focused and determined.

I place my free hand flat against the cedar door that leads into the great hallway, and I tell myself that it's just one push. In my heart I recall the words from the harp song:

I do not aspire to great things,
Or what is beyond me,
But have been taught to be contented in Jerusalem,
Like a weaned child with its mother.

Did my grandfather David or one of his minions compose the ballad to keep the lowly in place? It works on me in this moment. I ask myself if I can go through with this. All I know is that there's an earthquake rattling inside me. I feel as though the floor below is about to cave in, swallowing me up, my trembling hands intent on spilling the stew I worked on all day. *Breathe and relax.* Recall when you were a child, running away in Thebes, knowing what you might face—what you *did* face. You weren't fearful then. Don't fear now. You can do this. Just concentrate on the first leg of the plan, and the easiest. Take the scroll and walk right into the King's chamber.

Remember a piece of old wisdom you once heard as a young girl: to send an arrow forward, you have to pull back the bow.

א

The great hallway stretches so long that the end disappears into a stony darkness. When I had younger eyes, I could just make out Solomon's chamber from this distance, but age and time spent on tablets and papyrus have taken their toll. A baby cries out.

My little Ariah, I think for the shortest moment. Then I realize that's impossible.

Now I see it's just a scrawny palace cat, indistinguishable from the ones outside that plague the city. Unnerving how it can sound so human. This one's as black as obsidian, no splotches of white or gray; the two of us are grapes off the same dark vine. Toddling over and purring, it eyes me, or more likely the plate I'm carrying. I swipe my finger into the dish, kneel down, offering a little pigeon to the animal, who quickly licks it up.

Passing the row of high officials' apartments, I walk on the tiled mosaic, in dim lamplight, the cat following me. Ah, I made a friend.

There is heavy thumping behind me.

A crescendo of giggles. "Eve! Eve, come here and let me taste your fruit," a deep masculine voice begs. Spinning around, I make out three figures rushing toward me. I hold tight to my dish, placing it between the wall and myself.

"If you let me taste them, I have something for you!" shouts an emerald-colored man. "Something you'll enjoy. Just you wait!"

They gallop past. First, a topless and fig-leafed Eve, holding two late-winter dates. Then the man: naked, his body dyed in malachite, his member erect. He's playing the snake. I recognize him. Joash, Fourth Priest. After him, another teenage girl, also leafed. I glimpse her loincloth—fig leaves glued to a priest's ephod. Although it's one small piece, she's wearing men's clothing. Still, *she* gets to break a law without incurring any punishment.

"Excuse me," Second Eve says, laughing, as she nearly barges into me, causing a few drops of my stew to spill out. Joash herds the girls into his apartment, then slams the door.

I pass his chamber and then my brother's, the Prince Regent, and the row that makes up his harem. The mix of perfumes and incense doesn't blend well, but I've long since adjusted to that kind of stink, which is at least better than the smells outside the palace. A guard's on duty and we trade nods. He doesn't stop me, and I relax as much as I can.

A purr comes from my ankles and I look down. The furry face pleads like a beggar. No, I've given you enough dinner, little cat, I'm sorry. It stays with me as I make my way past the hall of Solomon's harem. There won't be any Eden portrayals here. My father's dying, and his wives and concubines are getting up in age; most are much older than me. In fact, my father's harem used to take up more of the hallway, but he has outlived so many of them, and in recent years, there's been no need to restock the pen. Plus my brother Rehoboam needs the space for his own women. He couldn't touch the King's even if he wanted to—and knowing his depravity he might just be tempted to dip his glory into that old, skin-cracked, decaying pool.

My heart is in full grind again, and now my mouth goes dry as I approach the dead end of the King's chamber and the four sentries posted by the door. They're dressed in white tunics under tan leather plates. Their skin borders on alabaster. There is one with red hair and another with blue-gray eyes. By the look of them, they must all be Philistines.

I know one of them: a graying soldier in some kind of deep conversation with the redheaded mercenary, the two standing off to the side. I remember him when his hair was darker, when I would tramp around the palace as a young girl. I recall him occasionally shouting at my sisters when they teased me for too long. *What's his name? What is it?* As I'm thinking, the cat sprints back toward my apartment. I'm friendless again.

Staring down at the dish, I think of the Jacob story in *The Chronicles*, the one where his mother Rebekah tells the future patriarch that she'll make a similar stew to help dupe old, blind Isaac into giving Jacob his blessing.

I'll make the kind of delicacies that your father loves.

"Hey, woman, that for us?" asks a guard, pointing to my pigeon. His fat face and squinty eyes remind me of a plow ox.

My mouth becomes so sand dry I feel like I can't speak.

"Now why don't more of you palace-types think of your hard-working protectors, thanking them with a meal?"

"This . . ." That's all I can manage to squeak out.

"This? Yes?" Plow Ox says, smiling, enjoying himself.

"This, this is for the King."

"You know he can't eat," chimes in the blue-eyed guard, looking me up and down, his tunic hanging without a single, frivolous wrinkle.

"Wouldn't you rather give it to us?" Plow Ox asks.

"It's his favorite—"

"Leave it here then," Blue Eyes says, reaching for the clay. I keep the dish locked in my arms, pressing it tight against my chest. My fear says I should hand it over and slink back to the apartment. Then try my luck again later with a different set of guards.

But it's getting late, and if I were to come back in an hour or two, they would think it odd that I would visit in the middle of the night. It has to be now, not tomorrow or the next day when Raddai will be home. Lately it's been rare that he actually travels with my brother instead of sending one of his underling scribes. It's one thing to do this behind Hannah's back, but with my husband watching me in the apartment? And then what if my father were to die tonight or within the next few days and my brother were to take his room? No, now is the time. This has to be it.

"I'd like to feed it to him myself," I say, as I try to will control over my hands.

Blue Eyes cocks his head, and his cheeks tighten. "Who are you?"

"I'm Keb."

"Who?"

"Keb. His daughter, Keb."

"The King has a lot of daughters," Plow Ox says. "He's one," pointing to Blue Eyes, who doesn't laugh.

"The Master of the Palace would have to approve," Blue Eyes interjects. "And he's made no report."

"This, this is the King's favorite dish, and I was, am, one of his favorite daughters."

"Daughter?" Plow Ox repeats. "You're a bit dark for that, don't you think?"

"This lion," I say, holding up my amulet, trying to calm my shaking hand. "Symbol of the House of David."

The two study the silver. What is the name of that other guard who is still talking to the redhead? The one I know. Dagon something, like their Philistine fish god.

"Looks more like a sick baby cub." Plow Ox laughs at his own stupid remark.

"Dagonil!" I shout, causing the middle-aged sentry to abruptly break from his conversation. He stares, trying to recognize me. "It's me, Keb."

"You know her?" Blue Eyes asks.

Dagonil comes over, taking me in. His face has a few more wrinkles, and his neck is larger than I remember. "It's been a long while."

"She claims she's one of the King's daughters."

"So she is. Adopted or something." *Adopted or something*—he's being kind.

"I've never seen her," Blue Eyes says.

"Dagonil, please let me feed my father. Who knows how much time he has—" My words stop as I look at him through wet eyes.

The middle-aged guard gives me a sympathetic look.

"How do you know her?" Blue Eyes asks.

"She was at the court a lot as a kid. For a while she was the center of it all. The King would have her harp, tell stories, all that shit."

"You any good?" Plow Ox asks me. "With the harp and all." He pantomimes strumming one.

"The stew's getting cold." I say, desperate to move this forward. "Please, let me see him one last time."

"Ba'al's ass," Dagonil says, shaking his head.

"Give me your skin," Blue Eyes says, reaching for my satchel.

I hand over my goat pack, and he opens it, finding the papyrus. He takes it out and unrolls it. He fixes his eyes on the writing, but I'm sure it's all just meaningless black markings. Looking up, his face waits for an explanation.

"His favorite songs. I thought I'd sing to him."

"You can read this?" Blue Eyes asks.

"No, it's a present. I learned the songs by heart."

Blue Eyes points to the stew. "I want you to taste the dish first." I move to stick my finger into it, and he stops me, pointing again. "This part here."

I comply and swallow. Hannah was right. I did overdo on the coriander.

The guards wait a few moments to make sure that blood isn't dripping out of the corners of my mouth.

Then Blue Eyes nods, handing me back my scroll and skin. He motions to the young, redheaded guard that Dagonil was talking to. "Take her in, but watch her close."

As we walk forward, Dagonil says, "You can sing, but he won't hear you. He hasn't heard shit in a long time."

CHAPTER TWO

Ivory tables, cedar paneling, an ornate gold and silver ceiling. Palms and sycamores on linen tapestries, fabrics that could only be dyed by the most skilled Tyrian craftsmen. Even poor lighting from the few lit lamps can't dim the evidence that my father knew how to live and how to spend. To have all these adornments loaded and carried on muleback from the Phoenician coast, through the Jezreel Valley, over the northern hill country, and all for what now? I take in the tragic figure lying there, on the bed, more bone than man.

King Solomon, ruler of the Two Kingdoms, Judah and Israel, emaciated, gaunt, his skin yellow, buried in a coma he'll never wake from. And so bald, not the thick mane I remember. His face is now lined like the driest fig left on the vine. His throat gulping his breaths. Unconscious and unaware. The room could be filled with sword-drawn Edomites, dancing sphinxes, and a herd of goring oxen, and he wouldn't know.

As I kneel by his side, I have a rush of a memory. I picture myself as a young girl sitting next to him on the cedar-paneled portico in the Hall of the Throne. He had just finished hearing a tiring case.

"More pomegranate," he said to his wine steward and then turned to me. "Sing and harp for us, Keb."

"Your Majesty, you don't really want to hear me. My voice, my voice is no better than a frog's."

"Nonsense, I love your voice. And you'll have to perform alone as I don't think there are any frogs performing at court today." He signaled the Master of the Palace. "Ahishar, do we have any frogs scheduled?"

My father's high official looked down at his papyrus, grinning. "No, Your Highness, I'm sorry to report there are none."

"We've no frogs. Sorry, Keb, you'll have to be our entertainment. Everyone, gather round. Play the 'Song of the Sea' for us."

With my father's wave, two slaves carried over a harp. I stood there for a moment, my face appealing his decision, but I was forced over to the instrument by Solomon's unbending stare. Kneeling down, I sighed, then gave in, placing my tiny, shaking fingers on big strings. After a few strums of an introduction, my quivering, twelve-year old voice sang,

> *Pharaoh's chariots and his army,*
> *He has cast into the sea,*
> *And the pick of his officers,*
> *Are drowned in the Sea of Reeds.*

As I performed, a couple dozen of my brothers and sisters ignored me—they were the kind ones. Then there were scores more, snickering and laughing as always. But Solomon just sat there, eyes wide, seemingly enjoying every off-key note, every misplucked chord, every contortion of my jerking body.

I glance up now at the young, redheaded mercenary who brought me in, his eyes on me, standing at the entrance. Then I stare back at old Solomon, wondering if I will look like this someday. As I put my finger in the bowl, raise it to his lips, I immediately realize how useless the act is. His mouth, teeth, and tongue are all failing organs. I try to think if I could do something to make him feel more comfortable. Then again, can he even feel?

What if he were to open his eyes and see that I'm here, to have one moment together, to know that someone cares for him? And if he could see not just me, but my son. Yes, what would it have been like to introduce the King, in his prime, to his grandson? To Ariah, my shy, naked little boy, hiding behind—my eyes search the chamber—maybe that taupe paneled door. I let my unyoked imagination concoct something I wished had happened:

"Ariah, come meet your grandfather," I'd say.

His puffy, brown face pokes out.

"Come, Little Lion." Ariah retreats again behind the cedar. "Don't you want to meet your King? He wants to know his grandson." Nothing but little fingers clutching the door's edge. "Ariah, don't make Your Lord wait." He steps out and shyly smiles, then brings his hands up to hide his face. Then he ducks behind the door again.

"It's all right, don't force it," I picture Solomon, at his best, saying to me. "Our lion will make his appearance when he's fit and ready. And then, watch out!" He gives a loud feline roar, then laughs.

There were times, like this scene in my mind, when he was as kind as they come. Then there were times when he was utterly cruel. Not to mention hedonistic, lecherous, vicious, even a monster.

But those descriptions are all past. None apply now. Soon he'll be gathered to his people, lying with the remains of David, Jesse, Obed, and Boaz, in the burial cave cut deep in the bedrock. When he's placed in his tomb, I imagine it will look and feel a lot like this very chamber: ornate, dark, musty, the air thick and weighted like a shroud. Then there's the silence—a horrible silence that must prick at the ears.

"I forgive you," I mouth.

Collecting myself, I remember why I'm here. With the bed and Solomon acting as a shield, I remove from my satchel the thin scroll tucked inside the larger one, the text containing the notations of five harp songs, and leave it by his bed. I keep the meatier papyrus, the writing I've labored on these past months, in the goatskin.

Looking up, I notice two slaves, wearing nothing but their loincloths, standing perfectly still, waiting should the King suddenly awake and beckon. That has to be an art, to spend most of your life as human furniture.

The redheaded guard stares at me, waiting.

I pretend to wince and let out a moan.

"Can I use the chamber closet?" I ask, as I stand up.

"You want to use the closet?" The guard takes a quick glance behind him, perhaps wondering if he should check with Blue Eyes on the other side of the wall. He faces me again.

"Womanly matter," I say, doubling over. Then I moan again, this time much louder.

"Um—"

"My apartment, it's all the way at the other end of the hallway. I don't think I can make it. Please."

He nods yes.

"Where is it?"

"There." His finger directs me to a door at the room's end.

Leaving the pigeon and sliding the satchel over my shoulder, I start to walk the long chamber. "I, I may be a while."

I find a lamp in a wall niche, grab it, and close the closet door. In front of me there it is: the King's seat on the ebony-paneled platform. I picture my father sitting there, in his old age, constipated, straining, and I shudder. Creeping up to the seat, I reluctantly, slowly bring my nose to the hole and breathe it in. I grimace. Yet, I'm relieved to only detect a trace of excrement, if that. And I'm pleased to see that the space should be big enough. I bring the lamp closer and look down. From this angle, the floor several feet below actually looks quite clean. I can make out individual floor stones, jagged, rough, but free of royal droppings and soiled wiping strips. Bedridden Solomon probably hasn't used the closet in weeks, and the servants seem to have done their jobs, thoroughly cleaning the bottom. In forming this plan, I've also counted on the slaves being too scared to help themselves to the hole.

Opening my satchel, I search the inside pocket, the one that Blue Eyes overlooked, and grab the flax rope tucked inside. I tie it to the end of the oil lamp, then carefully lower the lamp down the hole, toward the rocky floor below. The bottom illuminates. It's pristine, scrubbed well with lime. *Thank the heavens.* But now a problem. Not enough rope. Even with my arm extending as far as it will go, the lamp dangles a couple of feet from the surface. I have no other choice but to drop the lamp and wince. It smacks and bounces a little on the stone. But it remains lit. Thank you, Yahweh.

Up in the closet it's almost completely dark, the lamp keeping most of its light underneath the stall. I feel for my satchel and, with my eyes adjusting to the darkness, I grab, then lower it through the hole. I swing the skin, and it lands a few feet away from the lamp.

I'm next.

The space should be just large enough for thin Keb to squeeze through. In the dimness, I step on the platform and place my legs in the hole, my behind perched on the ebony bench. I take a breath, then I let my feet drop until my forearms rest on the wood. I drop more, nearly all of me now under the seat, except my hands, which are still grabbing onto the edges of the wood. In my mind I imagine I'm falling just like his excrement. I swing and thump down onto the ground.

Grabbing the lamp, I stand and examine my linen dress. From what I see, still white, and I relax a little.

I attempt to orient myself: I am now in the sewer underneath the palace. With the exception of my father and myself, the rest of the city assumes this cramped tunnel leads out in only one direction, west, to a locked entrance door that I'm guessing is manned by a soldier or two on the other side. That the passageway exists for the sole purpose of having the royal servants enter through that door and walk thirty yards to remove the King's waste.

But if a childhood memory holds true, there is another reason for this underground walkway. Alone with my father, sitting on his lap, we studied the plans for the palace and Temple grounds.

"Can you keep a secret?" Solomon asked.

"I can."

"Are you sure?" he asked, this time with an eyebrow pitched high.

And I have, I've kept it. All these years.

Now with my back to the entrance door, I face east and find the sewer continuing several yards, but tapering into a dead end. I collect my goatskin and creep toward the narrowing. At first glance, it looks walled off, but at a sharp angle there is a space guarded by a few jagged stones. I turn sideways, breathe in, wrap my arms tight around my tunic, and squeeze through. Thankfully, I don't feel anything pinching and scraping. Passing this threshold, I make out a rock-cut corridor in front of me, a corridor that should lead to my destination. The Temple.

I do another check with the lamp. No dirt that I can make out. I double check. Gods! My tunic is torn just a tiny bit on my left sleeve. I shut my eyes, wincing and swallowing. When I open them, the rip and the frayed threads are still there. *Have I just become impure?* After a minute of going back and forth in my mind, I decide I have to chance it. So I continue onward, the rough ceiling not more than two feet above me, my long, thin shadow creeping on dark, graven walls.

It's cold. The air's thick with moisture and my exposed right shoulder really feels the chill. As I shake from the draft, I wonder if the soldiers have figured out yet that I am no longer in the closet. Their shift is about to end, and I hope I'll be forgotten with the changing of the guard, but I know this thinking is more wishful than realistic.

At the sound of scratching noises, I jump a little. Ahead a rat disappears into limestone. I could have used my feline protector, my friend from the hallway, not only to keep away rodents, but for some trusty companionship down here, because I'm scared to face this all by myself. How odd it is to not have another person in sight, as I've seldom been by myself. Even when I've felt alone, which is most of the time, I'm not really alone. Someone was always nearby, a servant, Hannah.

There is my god, Yahweh, I remind myself. But it's not as it was. In the Golden Age, he had walked with men, but where does he walk now? Not here underground, not upstairs in my apartment. *Where the heavens was he when my boy was taken from me? Where were you?* And so why my steadfast loyalty? Could Hannah be right? Should I be praying to Astarte? Have I been an idiot? Have I only stuck with my god because I believe everything I've been taught? Because it has been pressed into me: the notion that turning to other deities would be a treachery to the Kingdoms, is that it? I cheer for Judah and

Israel to subdue other nations, so shouldn't I be cheering for our god to pummel theirs?

I know that partly it comes down to nostalgia. Younger, happier days. When I call out to Yahweh, I'm sitting on my father's lap.

Or maybe it is simply that promise I made as a young woman, an agreement I can never go back on. He kept his end of the bargain on stopping Solomon when he went too far. And Yahweh gave me a boy. So I must keep mine.

The shaft has been winding for a few minutes; the circuitous walkway has to navigate around the palace cistern and a long patch of some hard granite. But this is new—I'm hunching just a little as the area is narrowing. I see chiseled marks in the rock and visualize the Tyrian laborers, the ones my father hired, banging away with their pickaxes, crawling in tiny spaces, working in dim lamplight, breathing in all that heavy dust, always under the threat of being crushed in a cave-in. Maybe it was all worth it if, when arriving at the Temple foundation, they secretly pocketed flakes of the carved-out limestone, only to later present them as souvenirs to their children, who rushed at them with hugs and kisses at the door.

I move forward and my lamp shines on a stony protrusion from the wall. Without warning it sends my thoughts to the cold, hard, rock bench Ariah's body lies on. What does my son's corpse look like now? I don't want to think about it, but I can't stop my mind. Decaying tissue shrinking, revealing bone. Horrible, ugly colors. I shake my head wildly to stop the images.

I hear them singing, *"The voice of Yahweh kindles flames of fire . . ."*

A soft clanking noise spins me around with the lamp, but I don't see anything human or animal. There is nothing except scattered dust and the resting rock. More banging comes, but the sound is from above. I turn, walking forward again a few more paces. On the ground ahead, a giant pile of ash blocks me. I hear more of that muffled clanking and banging. Putting it together, I know now exactly where I am: the dumping ground for the animal remains or what's left of them after they have been cooked on the altar. So I'm under the Temple's inner courtyard.

I find my watery eyes lost in the charred debris of all that sacrifice. I'm frozen for a few moments and then force myself out of it. I have to figure out how to pass through this ash without getting the profane gray all over me. It looks to be close to waist high, from the first animal burned some twenty years ago to the present, and who knows how many sheep, goats, oxen, and what else the priests incinerate a day.

There is more clattering and I envision them boiling, scrubbing, and rinsing out the ten bronze basins; mopping up and scouring away the blood from the courtyard floor; ensuring the requisite purity for tomorrow's arrivals, to be ready for a whole new day of slaughtering. I envision them cutting necks and plunging hands deep in carcass, of drenching the altar in animal gore. Do they have any idea of the unholiness lurking below them down in these depths? That this tunnel turns into a sewer? My father's dark joke.

Shining the lamp, I notice that the ash tapers toward the walls, so that's my path. I gingerly take small steps, trying hard not to kick up the cinders, hugging the sides and stooping, managing tiny strides, like an infant. After several yards, I clear the heap and examine myself again. Only my sandals are gray and soiled, but I think my feet and the rest of me came out unscathed. Still, there's that torn sleeve.

I press on, sensing the floor slanting upward. After traveling a little more than fifty yards, I find myself facing a wall. *Where is it?* I scrutinize the rocks. *Where the sheol is the entrance stone?* I frantically point the lamp everywhere, searching, feeling the rough with my hand. Nothing but dead-end limestone. Is that it? All this for nothing? Did they never finish the job or was the entrance later discovered and sealed?

Still, I keep searching, my hands inching, and then, yes, I locate it toward the ground: an iron handle attached to a large block, set inside a groove.

One pull and I'll be in the Middle Sanctuary.

Countless times I've been told that only the holy priests and Levites can enter Yahweh's Temple. To the impure rest of us, it is out of bounds. If caught, the penalty is stoning. Your witnesses throwing the first rocks. I only know one instance of such a transgression. An unstable man somehow pushed his way past the priests and the doorkeepers, up the Temple steps, to the portico by the two columns. He couldn't enter, because the main door was shut as it always is. But that violation was enough. As the sentence was carried out, families, men with little children on their shoulders, everyone in the city watched on, most cheering, like it was some grand entertainment. Then again, I was there watching too.

The priests also, who come near Yahweh, must stay pure, lest Yahweh break out against them.

Purity. My profane monthly bleeding is two weeks behind me, and I haven't lain with my husband in ages. And earlier this evening, while the pigeon was cooking, I removed my bracelets, my nose ring, bathed, oiled my body and frizzy hair, doing everything I could so as to not defile the Temple with my presence. Why can't that be enough? Because I'm not from the tribe of Levi? Because I'm a woman? That my skin is the brownest brown, that I'm a burnt face? I shine the lamp and do one last check for filth. Everything seems fine, except that tear. Will that be enough to contaminate me if the rest of me is clean? Something so minor?

Even if I am impure, and if Yahweh were to smite me, could I end up any worse than the walking netherworld I'm living in? How can I turn back now and live with myself—knowing that when given the opportunity to stop them, I chose not to act?

My conflicting thoughts do nothing to stop the fear. Because I find myself trembling as I wrap my hand around the handle, my insides clamoring, like chariots pounding the vanguard. When I open the door, what will I find? Looking down at my amulet, I grab it tight.

I close my eyes and tug, but nothing moves. I grab the handle again, and I pull hard this time. It still doesn't budge. I try it again, with both hands, forcing my legs, my back, my whole body into it, wincing, and straining nearly every muscle. This time the rock slides a hair and a sliver of bright light winks in. I pull again with everything I can muster and hear something in the groove crack. The stone finally gives. But I lose balance and land on my side.

I frantically check my dress in the lamplight. I'm half covered with gravel and dust.

Panic fills me. I can only stare at the darkness behind me, contemplating the distance I traveled since the chamber closet. It is the distance that finally turns me around. I locate the stone resting in the same place where I first found it. Then like a stubborn child, one knowing full well the punishment that waits, but foolishly disobeying anyway, I pull on the handle once more. This time, with just the slightest effort, the block glides smoothly on its track, filling the tunnel with light.

Stooping down, I look straight ahead and gaze into the sacred.

CHAPTER THREE

I am startled by what I don't see. No gold, no imported cedar panels, no images of palm trees, no rosettes, no cherubs. None of the things listed on the inventory tablet I had found long ago in the library. Only pinkish-gray, undecorated blocks of limestone. This can't be the Temple, can it? I stare at the plain stone for a couple minutes, then brave it enough to extend my head inside a few inches. I turn and see, through the incense smoke, thick and porridgy, the back of a bald-headed priest. My heart pounds and I pull my head back in the tunnel. My lungs grab bags of dusty air. Relaxing a little, I reflect on what I just saw. The priest: naked except for his tiny loincloth, necessary so that his genitals are kept hidden from the divine, attending to the lit and crackling perfume altar, there to provide my god a sweet smell and to drive away flies.

I wait a long while and then slowly stick my head back in. The priest is gone, at least from my vantage point. There's the altar: the stand, the hearth, and the four ornamental horns protruding out from each of its corners, all of it gold. The table for the bread to feed Yahweh, gold as well. But the side and front walls that I can make out are as plain and uninteresting as the city's gate. So, this is the Holy Place. And while the incense altar and the table are what I expect, why are the Temple sides so unadorned? Did my father have only enough Tyrian cedar and Ophirian gold for his palace?

I start to creep in. But then I remember my profane sandals. Yes, my tunic is dirtied and torn, but still, I should be as clean as possible. I unstrap them, wiggling my toes, my feet once again liberated from the leather. I place my footwear on the tunnel side and hope to the heavens that in a few short minutes I'll return here to strap them back on.

I crawl in. Although smoky, it's hearthy warm, especially compared to where I've been. Carefully getting up, I realize *I'm still alive. And the Middle Sanctuary is empty.* Breathing, I check where I came from: the right side of the ramp that becomes the stairway leading to the Holy of Holies. I take in more of the Temple. The Middle Sanctuary itself is small, maybe twice the size of the first floor of my apartment. I missed the mark about there being no decoration. I see it all high up on the north and south walls that make up the longer sides of the Temple, and up on the east wall, the one leading out to the portico and the entrance. Triptych frescos of the highest quality showcase the creation of the world. Beginning on the south wall, there is Yahweh in his guise as the sun, carried in his horse chariot, his arms extend from his solar disc, one arm holds a javelin, the other a net; he battles the seven-headed Leviathan against a backdrop of Yam, the tumultuous sea. On the wall above the portico, the solar Yahweh turns Leviathan inside out with his javelin, dividing him, the monster's skin becoming the firmament, his guts and belly, the earth. The north wall concludes the action with Yahweh enthroned, his hand grasping a scepter, sitting on top of his winged sphinx, holding court with the lesser gods.

What am I doing gazing at the walls?

But I don't start searching quite yet. Because I find myself taking in the purple and blue curtain made of yarn and fine linen, the curtain separating this middle room from the Holy of Holies, where my god sits enthroned above the ark and sphinxes. There he is, creator of the earth and heaven, up a short flight of steps, on the other side of the thin fabric.

You cannot see my face, because no one shall see me and live.

I start running, nearly tripping over my tunic. I hike my dress up and rush to the first of ten lamp tables, the one on the south side, closest to the curtain. There I pull back the royal blue linen tablecloth. Just as I surmised, I find a storage shelf underneath. Thank you, Raddai, for talking in your sleep. This has in it jars of frankincense and galbanum for the altar. Not what I'm looking for.

I scamper to the shelf of the next lamp table, which houses several golden cups and ladles. Under the third table, tucked in linen, there's a bronze cast, luminous, in the shape of a serpent. The one Moses made? Supposedly anyone who was bitten by a snake out in the ancient wilderness and who looked at this would live. The 500-year-old artifact looks to be in pristine condition.

Glancing up, I find I'm still alone. But seven more tables.

Frantically inventorying the two remaining tables on the south side, I'm not finding it. Then I rush to the ones against the north wall, and start at the sixth table. But again, it's not there, and I'm awash in sweat, as if Mot himself rose from the depths of Sheol to cast his hottest heat. Table seven—nothing. Table eight—nothing. Where is it? Did they move it out of the sanctuary?

At table number nine, I finally locate it. The papyrus. I grab my scroll, the one inside my bag, and shove it on the shelf. The writing that had been there, well, I snatch that and toss it onto the incense altar. It burns into oblivion.

With the substitution complete, I run back to the right side of the ramp, and hunt for the opening I came through. But I don't see it. My hands are all over the rock, feeling. My fingernails scratching, clawing, pounding madly on the limestone.

Where is the wretched block? Where is it? Gods, what am I to do?

Keb, think. The block must have slid back in and I'm not going back that way. Accept it, the tunnel was only a one-way arrangement, like descending into the underworld.

I arrow forward to the massive entrance door past the portico. Of course, shut as it always is, and I can't figure out how to get by the pinewood. I speed back into the Middle Sanctuary. There's the stairway to the Holy of Holies—no, I don't think so. But there are several small closed doors on the north and south walls, where the priests must enter and leave. So choose one: the center door on the north side. I gazelle toward it. But as I do, I check that ninth table and see the tip of my scroll sticking out from the tablecloth. *What if I'm discovered and they notice this?* I dive back to the table, pushing the papyrus all the way in.

"Who are you?"

Spinning around, I see him. A priest.

"What are you doing here?" he demands.

Gods! I was so close.

"A woman's in here!" he screams to the walls.

"Please, I'm the King's daughter, you don't, please, please don't call to them."

"A woman's in here! There's a woman in the Temple! A woman's in the Temple!"

The altar. I run for it. I grab onto the hot, golden horns, my face feeling waves of heat from the fire. My fingers burning.

Doors burst open. They stream in like the flooding of the Nile.

I'm circled by a dozen bald men wearing only the tiniest of loincloths.

"I want asylum!" I shout, still gripping tightly. "I want asylum!"

I keep screaming these three words over and over as a tall, husky priest tears me from the altar and carries me away.

אָ

The two doorkeepers guarding me in a room in the Temple annex won't let up on their glares. It's not every day an intruder gets by them, and perhaps there'll be a big shakeup in their ranks for allegations of incompetence. I hope no one gets thrown from the city walls, but it's for a greater good. If only the entrance stone by the ramp had remained opened, I would have crawled back into the tunnel and made my way to the King's closet, and it would be as if nothing ever happened. Perhaps I would have run into the palace guard down in the sewer looking for me. If so, I had my story ready. *I got sick on the toilet, lost control, and somehow fell in the hole. When I landed, I cried out for help, but no one heard me. Then I stumbled upon the passageway, following it, hoping it would lead me back into the palace. And now you found me. What rewards can my husband shower on you for saving me?*

But I have concocted no story for being caught in the Temple, for what story could possibly save me? Only Yahweh's priests can be there to feed and attend the deity.

A half-dozen lit sconces illuminate the sparsely furnished room. There's just a basic oak table, containing a carafe and goblet that was brought in a few minutes ago, and a couple of stools behind it. My legs are hurting as I've been upright now for an hour or two, waiting. I keep reminding myself that as long as I don't tell them why I was in the Temple then I accomplished what I wanted, no matter what they end up doing. I've been on this earth thirty-three years, a fair span of time. Still, it's a struggle to ready myself for death, even though I knew this was a likely outcome from the moment I began my preparations months ago.

Stop it heart, stop beating so much.

The doorkeepers remember their posture as Ahimaaz ben Zadok struts past them. The Chief Priest carries his scepter with its pomegranate-shaped head. He is in full garb: a blue robe, belted with linen, his turban bearing a gold flower of Yahweh. But the gaudy centerpiece of it all is his large, jewel-covered breastplate, decorated with several times the number of precious stones I have in my jewel box. On the occasions I've seen Ahimaaz swagger around the palace—filling up the halls with his towering body, each strand of his long, dark beard, disciplined and taut—he was content to simply wear his regular linen tunic. Did he don his full, holy attire tonight just to intimidate, to appear more divine than man?

Following him is his son, the next chief priest in line, who couldn't be more than nine or ten. The boy carries a toy scepter and wears a little-man breastplate. His mother and my half-sister, Basemath, must have fun dressing him. The father takes the table; the son, one of the empty stools behind.

Can he possibly know how much I hate him?

You're spies, and by this you will be tested.

"Who let you into the Temple?" Ahimaaz asks, trying to get comfortable on his seat.

I go back and forth on whether any good will come if I provide an answer. For the time being, I hold my tongue. My throat is drying up too, which all but convinces me to stay mute.

"You understand the Temple has been made unholy because of you, a non-Levite, a woman, blemished even more by your skin's color. You have sinned and sin must be answered by stone. That one who helped you has also sinned, and he should face the consequences too. So, I'll ask you again, who let you in?"

As he talks and as my blood hammers, I try to convince myself that Ahimaaz can do little more to me than he has already done. Would it be so horrible to join my little Ariah in Sheol? And in a little while Solomon? They say you're just stumbling around down there, making your way in an unforgiving fog, the soul nothing more than a shadow, barely aware of anything, except being incredibly hungry all the time. I try hard to convince myself that perhaps the underworld's not as bad as people say and, even if it is, I'd find Ariah and we'd stumble through it together.

"Which priests, which doorkeepers were involved?" Our session is the first time in the twenty years he's known me that he is offering me his eyes, along with those thick, black strokes that hang under. "You paid someone to help you by providing sexual favors no doubt. Whore."

"Don't . . ."

"Don't what—call you what you are?" His voice is in a register worlds lower than mine.

"Don't, don't talk to me like, like that," I manage to blurt out, in a babble reminiscent of the ones toddlers use when first trying to work their tongues. "My husband, the Chief Scribe, Raddai, what would he think of you speaking to me, speaking this way, he—"

"Is miles away in Edom. Your husband?" He snorts. "I understand that your marriage is in name only. Second wife." How does he know what goes on in our apartment? Is Raddai discussing our bed with everyone?

"I am the King's daughter." I speak my first clear sentence, but my voice is still quivering.

"The King has many daughters." He pours some wine into his goblet, gulping it down. If there is anything left in the cup, I need no diviner to know what the patterns tell.

"My brother, the Prince Regent, should be—"

"Rehoboam is away and the Temple is my jurisdiction."

"The Mayor of the City Gate—"

"You're in my court, and I'm your judge. Now I wonder, does Rehoboam even know you? If he does, I assume he only thinks of you as his bastard Cushite sister."

"It's Sheba, not Cush."

"Does it make a difference?"

"I'm royalty, on both sides," I say, searching for a tone that somewhat resembles authority, but my voice sounds fake, like the false beard of a pharaoh.

"That doesn't cure all your imperfections and deformities, whore, and you've caused the Temple to be polluted by your very presence. Why? Why would you want to contaminate it?" So he hasn't figured out the reason I was there, and maybe he'll never know—none of them will know—and that's all that matters.

Shuffling and clumping noises from outside invade the room. The cedar door swings and limping in on his crutch is old Zadok, Ahimaaz's father and the former Chief Priest. Zadok was forced to retire when his purity was blemished by his failing legs. He had quite an effect on me, for when the scroll of my life was closer to its beginning then its end, he brought me to Yahweh.

"Help him," Ahimaaz shouts to the doorkeepers who, in turn, rush over and carry the old man to an empty stool next to his grandson. Three generations of priests versus one generation of me.

32

Ahimaaz shuts then opens his narrow eyes. "Tell me who let you in! If you don't, I'll imprison everyone who was on duty."

"I let myself in. No one helped."

"How then? What magic did you use?"

"I want asylum. I grabbed onto the horns."

"You are in no position to make requests!"

"My temple is a place of asylum—"

"Your temple? The one that you just polluted?"

"What about the workers who built it? They weren't priests. When they were laying the stones, did they soil and contaminate it?" My eyes land on Zadok for support, but he just sits there. It's been many years since I've seen him up close. His remaining teeth are black; his face worn, crinkly, and yellowing, like aged papyrus in the tomb. His beard long, colorless, tangled, neglected. To be old is a blessing, but he doesn't look blessed.

Ahimaaz pours some more wine, drinking half the goblet. "I'll ask you once again. How did you get in?" Receiving no answer, he snorts forcefully like an ox. "Do you want to be cut open before you tell? Is that what you want? My priests in the dungeon are equally skilled with taking a knife to people as they are to animals."

He unsheathes his slaughtering knife and lays it on the table. Similar to the one Zadok showed me as a young girl, Ahimaaz's cutting tool is composed of a simple oak handle and an iron blade—hooked and gleaming and polished and pointed. No more than a day or two off the whetstone. As I study it, I'm doing my very best not to break down, struggling to deny him a triumph. He then grabs the knife and stabs it into the tabletop.

"I want asylum," I say, barely getting the stuttering words out of my mouth, as my eyes dampen. "Isn't the Temple a place of asylum? When my father became King, didn't Joab, commander of the army, who failed to support him, flee to the

33

Tabernacle, grasping the horns of the altar to escape persecution? I grabbed onto those very same horns tonight, deserving Yahweh's protection." As I speak, it dawns on me why my father built the palace-temple access tunnel that I used tonight. Those altar horns could come in handy in the face of an unexpected coup or civil war.

"She knows her history," Zadok finally says, his voice reminding me of old shards, rough and scratchy.

"Father, please," Ahimaaz says, with his eyes never leaving mine. "To answer your question at this very moment you are neither in the Temple, nor in the old Tent—"

"Your priests took me away from the altar when I asked for asylum," I say. "And right now we're on the Temple grounds."

"We're not *in* the Temple. And, as I recall, Joab was struck down in the Tabernacle by order of Solomon."

"You know, Son—" Zadok starts to talk, only to be waved off by Ahimaaz.

"Now as you say, in times of royal succession, with nervous heirs about to take over, the siblings of new kings are in the most precarious of positions, searching for altar horns." He takes another swig of wine, and then rises from his seat. "No one's coming to your rescue. You're alone." He adjusts his breastplate so it dangles free. "You really don't want your black skin and insides marked in any way before your sentence, adding to your deformity. I'll give you a short interval to think, and then we'll have some answers." He yanks the knife out of the table and sheathes it. "Answers always come at the end."

CHAPTER FOUR

Three mercenaries escort me as I descend the swerving thoroughfare down Mount Moriah. Because I left my sandals back in the tunnel, my bare feet sense every rough of the freezing cobblestone. In dim glow of the soldiers' torches, my eyes keep watch for dung, both animal and human, along with the occasional broken pottery shard, but I can't discern everything and my soles already have several cuts. During the past months, when I have walked down the hill barefoot to the Mount of Olives, it's always been in daylight and I had no problem avoiding the debris. But not now. How I crave to oil and bathe my damaged feet, feet that are becoming indistinguishable from those of the slave and the poor. My feet though are the least of my problems.

"Don't dawdle," one of the guards shouts as he shoves his hand on my back, causing my legs to move faster.

A high-pitched wail. What is that? Of course: my father's menagerie behind the wall, which I visited with Ariah a few years back. We saw some amazing peacocks, which my father procured with ships sent beyond Babylon. They were something to look at and I remember thinking it's nice to be born with so much vivid color. We also saw ibex, gazelles, a jackal, ostriches, and a variety of other birds, but many of those were sick and even dead in their cages. But Ariah didn't mind; to him it was all a source of wonder.

"Mommy, can I pet that?"

"No, you can't, Little Lion, that's called a pork-pine, I think, and it has needles that will hurt you." The animal was close to the bars, within reach. "Do you want to see the animal that bears your name?"

He nodded yes, and I took him to the central attraction. The lion was down on the ground, eyes half shut. Then the beast rose to his feet as we neared, looking straight at us.

"Little Lion meet Big Lion." Ariah hid behind me, holding my hand tight. "He's in a cage and can't get past the bars, it's all right. Don't worry."

As Ariah cocked his head a little to peek at the animal, the large feline collapsed, as if something was wrong with him.

"It's all right, Lion," my boy said softly, parroting back my words to the creature. "Don't worry."

Amazingly, his assurances seemed to have a curing effect, the beast kneeled first on its two hind legs, then stood fully up. Ariah's face beamed, as if the two could truly communicate in some kind of magic known only to them. Then the animal roared and licked its lips, causing Ariah to go into a long round of crying, abruptly ending our visit.

My mind races from my boy to Ahimaaz's knife, wondering if that very blade will find its way in me. I try to shake away his cutting iron from my mind, and finally do so by concentrating hard on the sights and sounds of the thoroughfare. I realize flies are circling around me. That there are cats howling for scraps and a man relieving himself, his urine whipping against a muddy wall.

We reach the lower end of the hill before the market, to the slums where I used to live, passing by the dark alleyway leading to the brothels and the wine houses at the city's edge. I spot men creeping toward the coarse and the vulgar, to strong grape and pomegranate or the harder stuff like poppy seed and honey, to women lying in cramped, dusty rooms, waiting to remove the veil.

א

The guards march me down narrow stone steps that lead to a holding cell below the city gate. I cringe. A single small lamp positioned a couple feet above me, and beyond reach, provides just enough light to sicken me. As my eyes adjust, I can make out a space less than the size of my apartment chamber, with none of its comforts. I find a pot half-filled with excrement, a scampering rat, a floor of unpaved rock and puddle, the sides jagged limestone with scratches and clawed marks of unrecognizable graffiti, the markings surrendering to sprawling patches of moist orange and green lichen. All of it more cave than room. And how could such a place be anything but freezing, damp, and moldy, stinking like the primal watery abyss.

Before the guards can throw me in my cell, I voluntarily cross the threshold, but the door pounding shut behind me answers that act of dignity. The oak looks and feels thick and heavy. In the morning, as Jerusalem begins its affairs, will the city elders even know I'm down here? Calling out to them then would make no sense, because even if my scream could be heard through the door, it would have to compete with the unrelenting din of soldiers, traders, city administrators, and the never-ending throng streaming in and out of Jerusalem's gate (that huge acacia door with bronze fittings, strong enough, we all hope, to withstand an Egyptian battering ram), located about five feet above the ceiling.

I look around at my new residence. This is how Joseph must have felt. Well, perhaps not the real Joseph, but the one I imagined. Yet, if only *this* were imagined. How I wish to the heavens that this, and me in this, were only an invention, that I could be a mere character on the sheet. But I have to confront that what's in front of me is real, the bloodstains on the dank ground are real, Ahimaaz's knife or whatever they end up using on me will be real. And yesterday's myrrh and frankincense, that is now something my mind will have to conjure up.

At the moment, though, it's not what is before my eyes, but within my body that is administering pain. My flailing head and gurgling stomach have no shyness, reminding me I'm starving. Will I soon be reduced to eyeing the still scampering rat?

I suppose I could try to lie down on the wet, make a kind of bed with my dress, try to somehow find sleep, as my legs are heavy. But instead I remain standing. To cope against the cold, the stink, the fallow field that is my stomach, I imagine my boy here keeping me company.

"Hey, Little Lion."

I see him mulling around, carefully maneuvering his feet on the stone. "Mommy, I'm missing all the cracks."

"Don't step on one or the Evil Eye will get you."

"Let's do storytelling," Ariah says.

"Do you want to start it?" He shakes his head no. "Alright, I'll begin then. Who should our hero be? A bandit? A crocodile? A monster?"

"Monster."

"Alright. Let's see. The Babylonian gods created Enkidu, half man, half animal, a creature with shaggy hair all over his body who shovels grass in his mouth and laps up water from puddles in the woods, like this, wha, wha, wha . . ." I imitate the wild man, bending down, but avoiding the urine pooling on the floor. "Then he has a life and death battle with a king named Gilgamesh. It's a stalemate—"

"What's stalemate, Mommy?"

"No one wins. It's a tie. They become fast friends. Friends for life. Your turn."

"Then Enkidu and Gilgamesh meet a monster and they turn around and run and run and run. Your turn, Mommy . . ."

I often question if I am somehow responsible for what happened to my little lion. Have my mistakes, like what I did to my sister Irty, resurrected, looping back in a game of "What goes around?" Ariah must have died for a reason, but my sins appear so minimal compared to my punishment—and his.

The door thunders open. What I thought were thick walls of stoic courage are nothing but veneer. I wince, and start to tear up as I imagine terrible, horrible things.

CHAPTER FIVE

I receive four visitors. First is old Zadok, dressed in his turban, tunic, and sash, carried in by a young slave wearing a loincloth dyed red, Ariah's favorite color. A finicky eater, Ariah would sometimes try a new food if we placed it in that bright crimson dish of his—the plate now resting on the tomb floor by his side.

Trailing the former priest and his servant are two lanky guards, each carrying an oak stool and several wool blankets, looking coarse and cheap, but invitingly warm.

"You can leave us," Zadok says to the soldiers and the servant.

"Your son has sent you for his answers?" I say, over the bang of the shutting door. As I set my heavy legs down, I find the hard stool almost billowy soft.

"I came on my own."

"The guards, they just let you in?"

"You don't need to worry about that. But first, this is long overdue. I mourn with you. I know what it's like to entomb a son." He looks tired and almost empty, like a forest felled long ago.

"You mourn with me? Where were you six months ago?" I wrap one of the itchy woolskins around me, keeping in the warmth.

"There's no excuse for that. Still, I mourn." With no response from me, he goes on. "These are strange circumstances that bring us together. It's been a long time since you and I—"

"I don't want to talk about old times." Old times. For a moment, I'm back in the annex again, a shy twelve-year old, swallowing Zadok's every utterance about how, in times of trouble, Yahweh would swoop down from his celestial court, rescuing his people.

"It must be hard these days without . . ." he trails off, glancing at his feet.

"I don't want to discuss that either."

"What shall we discuss then?"

"You tell me."

"Maybe I can help."

Staring away, I watch the rat lap up a urine puddle.

"Keb, I didn't come here to learn how you walked right into the Temple, although I'm curious. But what I'd like to know is why? Why would you risk everything?"

"I tell you and then you tell your son."

"My son has no knowledge that I'm here. This is just between you and me. I swear to Yahweh."

"Ahimaaz seemed annoyed at your presence earlier. Does he think you won't let go of your old post? Are you both two camels, tied tail to tail, wondering who's leading who?" The pair remind me of those gods of the Sea Peoples, how in each generation the son battles the father for supremacy.

"Let me help you. You know what they're capable of. If there were a good reason to explain you being in the sanctuary, maybe I could convince Ahimaaz to lessen your sentence."

I stare at clawings in the rocky limestone left by previous guests. "Are you here out of guilt?"

"Hear me. There are things I can do."

"There are things you can do? What things? Your son's made his decision. When his mind is fixed, it's fixed." I feel the wet starting to build around my eyes.

"You don't have to die."

"And how would you arrange it otherwise, when you couldn't—"

"I got past the guards, I'm here with you now."

"Ahimaaz would—"

"I have my resources."

"Resources? You're not Priest anymore."

"Keb—"

"There were a dozen men who saw me in the Temple," I say, breaking down and giving up on Zadok's futile offer, as if the feeble old man can do anything for me. There's nothing he can do, not a wretched thing. Because, while I know that none of the priests who found me will be a David taking aim with his slingshot, they're not all going to miss with their rocks.

א

With neither outside light nor a timepiece, I have no idea the hour, maybe midday, maybe the last watch of night. I'm half asleep in the wool blankets Zadok brought, as the door bursts open, letting in groans and grunts. My mind begins to clear as I make out shades, with no apparent worry about me, carrying something: a man. Then the figures, who my eyes now discern are two soldiers, dump him a few feet away from me before marching out.

Now fully awake, I creep up to my new cellmate. He's fully naked, his chest and head bleeding profusely with too many scars to count. He just lies there, moaning. I'm unsure what I should do, but I relinquish my blankets and make a bed for him, pushing his head and torso on top of the cloth. I give him a few sips from a jug that Zadok left me, but he struggles to hold it down. I wash his wounds as best I can with a relatively clean end of one of the blankets, then cover him.

As he drifts into sleep, I watch the rise and fall of his ribs toil, his heart not yet breaking ranks and scattering, but each breath seems vexing and hard. Studying these bodily movements, I find it strange that they would pair opposite sexes in the same room. Now I'm not concerned about this lame, butchered man taking advantage of me, but it seems odd that we're forced to share the same horrible space. Is there only one dungeon cell available, or is this intentional? Do my jailors want to scare the color out of me, providing a peek at what's waiting for me tomorrow or in a few short moments?

A ram's horn, soft, but I hear it. Then silence followed by another shrill of the horn. This time it's louder.

After what could be an hour passes, my cellmate opens his eyes. He sees the jug. "Water?" He asks, his voice sounding like broken bedrock. I offer the fired clay, helping him hold it, and he gets a fair amount down. "Thank you." Then he looks up toward the ceiling. "What's that?"

"The ram's horn? It's been blasting for a while now."

"I've never heard anything like it." He says, his voice a tad stronger.

"They play it at the festivals."

"I've never been. But there's one now? I thought the next one, the one for the bread, is not for a while."

I shake my head. "I don't know why it's sounding. Could be we're under attack."

"Someone launching a rescue?"

44

"Any attackers, if they defeated the army, would most likely kill or enslave the entire city, including us." In my mind I'm back in Egypt, learning that the greater the devastation, the more memorable the scene on a temple wall. If we were taken in chains, what would the enemy chisel in stone? *Jerusalem has been made nonexistent; every wife a widow, every son and daughter a slave.*

"But if the attackers were to kill our torturers?" he asks. The horn goes silent. My cellmate and I hold a stare. "They just kill the horn blower?"

"Perhaps, but I don't hear anything now. No shouting, no whooshing of arrows, no battering ram."

"So we stopped them, eh?"

"To be honest, I'm not certain what a real battle, sword to sword, would sound like."

"If they do storm us, then maybe you're the last person I'll ever talk to."

"Maybe," I say.

"I hope your conversation's good then."

I feel the barest pull of a smile. "I'm Keb."

"Nebat. These blankets, I don't remember them." I just give him my eyes. "They were yours, weren't they?"

"I don't need them."

"No, you should have them." He starts to gather them, but then he recoils, groaning.

"Can I do something for you?" Standing over him, I straighten out the wool.

"I'll be all right."

I look at him. I try to see him as he was before they did what they did. Perhaps he's a young man, but who can tell? I think I can make out what might have been a baby-face, but that's been replaced by rows of fresh cuts and rooted scars.

Stepping back to my area, I sit and try to hear what might be going on outside these thick walls. But all I hear are my cell-mate's plodding breaths, interrupted now and then by a succession of jagged coughs. Nebat raises the jug toward me. I wave him off.

After a few moments of hesitation, Nebat drinks, tilting the jug up, and then lifting it higher, gulping it rock dry—until there is nothing left for me. I remind myself that I'm not his host, that I've been too gracious. But I suppose he needs it more than I, and perhaps he can't help himself. And if I do die of thirst, that has to be better than Ahimaaz's knife or the Levites' rocks.

A long silence and then I have to speak something that's been stirring in my mind. "What did they do to you?"

"You don't want to know."

"Probably not."

His eyes search. "They used a sickle and a threshing sledge."

I imagine sharp iron edges and wince.

"It was my sickle and my threshing sledge," He continues, regaining his strength. "They're my tools. Were my tools." He adjusts his body a little on the wet wool. "It worked. I confessed to end it, not that they needed it. They have the two . . ."

"Witnesses," I say, completing his sentence for him, while I notice I've been pulling at the loose threads on my tunic.

"One's my brother, but I think he would prefer not to dirty himself if he doesn't have to. Do you have any more water?"

"There's nothing else."

He surveys the room. "Except the piss on the floor."

"Except that."

"Why are you here?"

"I was in a place I wasn't supposed to be." He looks at me. "The Temple."

46

"What? The one here in Jerusalem? Only priests can go in there, right?"

I nod.

"And you're no priest."

"I'm no priest."

"Breastplates, I hate them. My brother's one."

"I hate them too—at least some of them," I say.

"I'll tell you why I despise the lot of them, and if you want, you can give me your reasons."

"As you like." Under the circumstances, a passable way to sacrifice some time. And how much time is that, I wonder.

"I'm a Levite, but I didn't have to priest as I married a woman who inherited a barley farm near Debir."

"*She* inherited?"

"She had no brothers or male family. But my brother, the priest . . ."—his words turn into a fit of coughs, which eventfully dies down—"he wants the farmland. He knows that I have . . ." He stops, and I wonder should I just leave it. But I don't, I need to hear the story through.

"You have?"

He pauses, but then lets his words roll out, perhaps the very same ones he handed his torturers. Maybe they come easier with each telling. "A weakness for men."

"I see."

"He plants a handsome slave, and he and a fellow breastplate catch me in the act, on the threshing floor. I think that's why they tortured me with my farm tools. Some sort of perverse joke." *What will they use on me?* After a few difficult coughs causing his body to wave, he continues. "With my death, he'll have to marry my wife, inherit, and get what he wants. So much for everyone sitting under his own fucking vine."

I try not to cringe as I see him in my mind, this man doing unnatural acts, groping the slave's member, worshiping it. Then Nebat's putting the slave down on the straw and chaff, penetrating him from behind, or worse, being the submissive and letting the slave do the thrusting. But whatever the abomination, I assume there must be a demon at work, and he should not be blamed.

"I don't understand," I say, "unless you're cheating with a free, married woman, it's not adultery." My mind flashes to Galit, my pretend big sister, guilty of that sin, her husband casting the first stone. How I've missed her.

"It's not adultery," he says. "The crime is, 'Lying with a man as one lies with a woman.'"

"That's what they're calling it now? Hmm. They're saying that warrants death?" There it goes again, the blare of the ram's horn.

"That's what they're saying."

"Since when is that capital? The penalty as I recall has always been beating and banishment. Also, the enforcement's been rather lax."

"All I know is the slave's been executed. And all I've been hearing since I got here is, 'You're going to die,' and 'Haven't you heard of Sodom?'"

"Sodom?"

"Like I know what that is. And they keep mentioning this fellow Lot. Like who the fuck is he?"

Sodom and Lot. I recall what I wrote: that Yahweh sent two angels to Sodom to save Lot, his wife, and their young, virgin daughters. But then a crowd of Sodomites gathered outside Lot's door, wanting to know the two strangers. Lot offered up his daughters instead. But the throng rejected the girls and began breaking down his door. They were only stopped when Yahweh struck them with a blinding light.

"That's not the story's point," I say.

"What story?"

"The one in *The Chronicles*."

"Chronicles? What's that?"

"The scroll read at the last Feast of Tents."

"I wasn't there, I was on my farm. What's this scroll?"

That horn again, screeching.

"This is wrong," I say.

"What is?"

The door opens, and my pulse javelins. Two soldiers. Who are they here for? One stares at me. But then the other motions him over to Nebat.

"The story at Sodom doesn't have a thing to do with one man lying with another!" I shout to the guards as they stoop down and grab my cellmate. "It has to do with, with Lot not mistreating his guests. Especially if his guest is a god!"

"Please don't," Nebat murmurs to the soldiers. "Please. No, no, no. Don't . . ." To shut him up, they punch his mouth dumb.

"It's about a father abusing his daughters!" I continue bellowing, trying to correct the misinterpretation, but now to their backs. "Caring not that they, that they would be raped by the mob . . ."

The one who had glanced at me glances again, as if to give my lips the same treatment he just delivered.

That gods' awful horn, blaring.

"Forget her, help me," the other one says, and the guard complies.

"That you can't, can't have sexual power over Yahweh!"

Ignoring me, they start carrying him out, and I cry, realizing I could be arguing to the urine on the floor for all it will do me; I'm simply howling to instruments, doing only what they're told.

As I well up, I can't shut the onslaught of my thoughts, the ones echoing guilt and responsibility that I just killed that man. It's as if I took my stiff writing rush and drilled it through his heart. *Why did I ever write that stupid thing? Why did I even pick up the papyrus in the first place?*

The bright lines appear again, waving in front of me, creeping across my field of vision, and I know what's going to happen next, as it's happened twice before. No matter what I do, the lines keep plaguing me, whether my eyes are open or closed. Dancing and pulsing. My head throbbing.

You killed him. You killed him. Keb, you killed him . . .

I keep hearing the echoes until the blackness comes.

CHAPTER SIX

A bronze ox of Ba'al dangles in front of my eyes. The amulet is strapped around the neck of a Temple priest, who I can only surmise has divided loyalties. His hands are all over my face, touching me. I shrink back at his hairy fingers, and he steps away. Since I must have passed out, I'm assuming he's been practicing his healing arts. And now that I'm conscious, he probably believes that Yahweh, Ba'al, or both in tandem, working through him, revived me. Maybe the gods drove out a demon or an evil spirit all because of his efforts, but who knows? During the past six months, I've blacked out twice like this and awoke without the benefit of any priestly aid. The first time was the day after Ariah's entombment; I collapsed in my room, awaking sometime later, keeping my secret, as no one found me. Two months later, I fell unconscious a second time. It occurred by my son's tomb in the Mount of Olives when I was feeding him. When I opened my eyes, I found several horrified faces peering down at me and I managed to stumble back to the palace, never saying a word to Raddai, not wanting him to think I was possessed.

The priest whispers something to another bald man, which in turn leads to more whispers. Where my cellmate had been slumped, by a small portable hearth where mild incense now burns, sits Zadok. After muttering something to the old man, the two Temple servants go off to some other priestly business, leaving me alone with my former teacher of the cult.

I hear the ram again. This time, though, it's muffled and soft.

"Why are they blowing the horn?"

Zadok takes a moment to let his tongue shape his words. "I have sad news."

Why is bad information always prefaced and delayed? Why can't people dive right into cold water without feeling the need to first wet a toe?

"Your father is dead," he continues. "Your brother is being rushed home for his anointing."

I'm numb. The impending death of my former cellmate, Nebat, a total stranger, has struck me far worse. I know I should react somehow with this report, but I don't. True, I know I missed my chance to reconcile with Solomon, and there is now one less person on this earth who showed me any kindness. But I feel no tears, no rush of blood, no impulse to rub dirt in my stringy hair or don the coarse sackcloth.

"Since you were among the last to see your father alive, you are a suspect in his death."

"Solomon, he was on his deathbed—"

"I'm just telling you what I know," Zadok says. "Also, you had a fit in here, your hands and legs moving uncontrollably. Those priests believe you are a witch and are planning to tell this to my son."

"Do you think I am?" I grab the blankets, submerging myself in them.

"Some may conclude that only a witch practicing dark magic could have entered the Temple unnoticed. What were you doing there?"

"We're back to that again."

"I spoke to the one who first found you. He said you were poking around one of the lamp tables."

"Is that what he said?"

"I can still help you. But I want to know what you were doing in there."

I listen to the incense snap and crackle, and I sigh. I'm so tired—how much longer until I journey through the Gates?

"Keb, are you listening?"

"If you think you can help me, then help me."

"Why were you in the Temple?"

"Why the need for an examination? The priests, they'll be doing that soon enough."

Zadok takes a long breath. "That particular lamp table has a scroll in it. Do you have any idea what you may have been touching?"

"No, what, what was I touching?"

"You tell me."

"What would I know of it?"

"Years ago, when we had our lessons, you took pains to hide it from me, but I knew you could read." I have a flash of me as a young girl studying a scroll of prayers on Zadok's table while waiting for him. When he caught me, I told him the sheets looked soft, so soft they invited my fingers to caress them.

"Read?" I say. "Women can't read, we're not smart enough."

"Stop it. The scroll in question is *The Chronicles of Moses.* But you know that, don't you? I wonder if you can tell me any of its contents. Humor an old man that no one listens to. At least let me ask you some things about it."

53

"I can't read."

"If you say so. But let's just take a look at it, shall we?" He takes out a crinkly papyrus from his satchel, unraveling it.

"That's not"—I catch myself—"something I can decipher."

"Were you about to say, 'That's not *The Chronicles?*'" The old priest snorts. He unravels it more. What had been an inventory list of Temple supplies turns into blank sheets, but then there are large words:

> *I can help you Keb.*
> *I can get you out of here.*
> *Trust me.*

"Has anyone ever told you that your lips move just a little when you read?" he asks, grinning, his smile tight and small and unsettling, something you would expect to find on a golden sarcophagus of a dead Egyptian.

"No, I think not," Zadok continues, "except perhaps the one who secretly taught you. Your old tutor, Talus, perhaps?"

"I can't read."

"If you say so. At last year's feast the priests read *The Chronicles* to the people for the first time and we all know you were present. Let's assume you can't distinguish an alef from a bet, still let me ask some questions anyway. We'll just say your responses are from your memory of that public reading. So, tell me, what are the four heads of the river flowing out of Eden?"

He's baiting me. If they connect me to that writing . . .

"I can help you," he continues. "But first I need to know if you know what is in that scroll." I just sit motionless. "What you say is correct; no man of weight is going to believe you can read, including my son. So even if I think you literate, I wouldn't be able to convince him or anyone. There's nothing to lose. I think you want to keep your secret, which makes sense. I would too.

Trust me and let me help. If you really believe I can't do anything for you, at least let someone else in the world know how truly smart you are."

Zadok grimaces a little. Maybe the foulness of the cell is getting to him too, as the waft of incense, at least from my direction, has become fairly tepid. With the stink returning, I'm reminded how truly bleak my situation is. I look at the old man. He has no influence. Everything rests with Ahimaaz. Still, he managed to be down here with me, he brought me water and blankets. But water and blankets might be the height of his power.

"During the reading, the scroll mentioned three branches out of Eden," he says. "These names are known to everyone: the Tigris, the Euphrates, our own Gihon spring. But there was one other whose name is unrecognizable; no one I've spoken to can place it. Do you recall the name?"

"What makes you think I read that part of *The Chronicles*—assuming I can read? It was fairly large scroll and I didn't have much time in there before I was discovered."

"I know, but we're assuming this is from your oral memory from the Feast. What was the name of the fourth branch? I know you know it."

"My cellmate, Nebat, is being tortured or worse. I want you to help him."

"Humor me and I'll see what can be done. The fourth branch out of Eden?"

I sigh and decide to give him what he wants. For Nebat's sake. "The Pishon, I think."

Zadok's eyes full moon. "How many days did it take the Egyptians to embalm Jacob?"

"Same as the flood. Forty."

"And the name of the pharaoh who challenged Moses?"

"The question is a trick. It's just Pharaoh."

"It's just Pharaoh." Zadok claps his hands and grins. "You're connected to that scroll, I knew it! It contains one of your favorite euphemisms for penetration, 'to lie with.' It's in there several times, and I had never heard anyone else use that expression. When a young girl mentions a phrase like that, it sticks with you."

"I've heard a lot of people use that phrase. Raddai uses it. The man who shared my cell was charged with 'lying with a man.'"

"We both know that those three words have only been in circulation since the reading of the scroll, not before." He snorts. "Anyway, there are too many stories in *The Chronicles* about women—Sarah, Hagar, Rebekah, Tamar—headstrong wives who confront their husbands, and they're all so well-developed. Then there's Rachel—feigning having her monthly bleeding so her father won't look for his stolen idols underneath her in her riding blanket. I'm not sure a man, even Moses, has that kind of detailed eye for the feminine. And is it just a coincidence that your husband was the one who found the writing?"

"I just have a good ear and memory, that's all."

"Bullshit!" he shouts, shaking his head a little.

"Maybe I'm just using my witchcraft to find your answers," I say.

"I want to know how you did it."

"Did what?"

"Tell me," he smirks.

"Entered the Temple?"

"You know what I mean."

"Did what?" I ask to break his beaming.

"You know," he says, that cursed grin never leaving—that grin screaming like a herald that he knows. Clever Zadok knows.

"What?"

"How you wrote such a work. How you came up with your tales, your characters, what inspired you. I remember when you were a girl, telling your stories of the Nile before Solomon and the court, but nothing like this and on such an august scale."

"Wrote it? You must be making a joke. That's quite a leap from me simply reading it. Moses wrote it. In *The Chronicles*, it says, 'Moses wrote all of Yahweh's words.' The book ends with Moses' death—"

"Where it states, 'No man has ever seen his grave, to this day.' If Moses wrote the thing, how could he have written about his own death? But assuming he could, wouldn't he have written, 'No man has seen *my* grave, to this day.' And the words 'to this day,' are telling, are they not? Then there is the papyrus itself. Five hundred years old? Really?"

"Everyone knows Moses wrote it."

"If you explain it all, I promise I will get you out of here. The author of *The Chronicles* should not be stoned."

PART II
GENESIS

Chapter One

"Why don't you start at the beginning," Zadok says.

But it's not that simple. I just can't gather up the words. It's not so much that the crackling of incense distracts me. But I wonder just where to begin. Because memories are tricky things, especially the primal ones. How do I know those pieces of the past are not something drawn from imagination or a remnant left of a forgotten dream? I don't want to be led astray, as the lonely is to the charmer, and the gullible, the false prophet. I have this snippet of an image, that of a woman, who I believe to be my mother, smiling at me, her eyes full and tawny. But when I reach out and try to hold her, she's water seeping through knobby fingers.

If the recollection is true, that was the only time I ever saw her. Queen Makeda. I spent my childhood away from her, on an isolated cattle ranch downriver from Saba, the Shebite capital, living with my Aunt Daanja and my Uncle Hori. I asked my relatives many times about my parents, never satisfied with their responses.

"Why won't they see me?" My seven-year-old self asked my aunt, as she nervously readied our house for today's guest. Daanja circled the main area several times, making certain that every jar and ewer was in its proper location on the wicker tables, that every linen tapestry hung perfectly straight.

"Use the turquoise bowls, I want to match with them," Daanja said to our servant setting our eating table. "No, not that one, they're by the gold ones."

"Why won't they—"

"You know they live far away."

"I know, my father lives beyond where the river flows into the sea. But not my mother. If Irty can come, why can't she?"

"No!" she screamed to the servant. "Are you dim to color? That's hardly turquoise. The one with the dancers and the flute player. Yes, that one."

I had with me my doll Ruzu, made of brown leather and papyrus, with a little girl face and string for hair, beaten and worn, a victim of many childhood rampages.

"Hello, Keb, I missed you," I had Ruzu say in a high-pitched voice. "Saba was taken over by mean baboons. But I gave them a happy potion and now I have time to be with you. Come, give Mommy a hug."

"Child, you're in the way."

"What's a bastard?"

"A horrible word, now go play outside."

"Irty says—"

"Must I call your uncle back in here again?" Staring at herself in the polished bronze, Daanja adjusted the half-dozen ivory necklaces against her bare chest. "Go play and afterwards we'll have dinner. Your uncle's traded for some animals, including hartebeest, which I know is one of your favorites."

As my aunt shoved on her beloved earrings made from turquoise quarried from up in far off Sinai, I looked out the door and saw off into the distance one of my mother's men, a messenger, approach on muleback.

"I want to see my mother," I whimpered, my lower lip trembling, as I toyed a little with one of Daanja's ceramic beer jugs.

"Don't touch that, it's special, all the way from Memphis."

I had thought Sheba was a great kingdom, but Kemet, the Black Land to the north, what we Judahites call Egypt, captured the attention of my aunt and all her friends. They all seemingly wanted to be Egyptian. Maybe that's why Daanja married one.

Daanja and Hori had no children of their own, so except on those occasions when my sister Irty would visit, I played by myself. When I was punished, my aunt would have me sit for hours alone in our garden under the shade of a sprawling mesquite, which was fine by me. There I would gaze at our large cone-shaped thatched roof that reminded me of a coiled-up snake. I pretended it was a cobra that could talk and called him Semsem.

"Who's that coming into the house?" Semsem asked in a lower version of my voice.

"That's Daanja and Hori's friend," I told him.

"Do you think he'll want to play with us?" Semsem asked, as I imagined the snake slowly uncoiling his body from his perch on top of the house. Free of the mud and straw, he glided in the air and landed, gently wrapping his leathery skin around me.

"He has to spend time with my aunt and uncle," I said. "We're not supposed to talk to him, unless he talks to us."

"But he's from Saba and knows Mommy. We should talk to him." Semsem tickled my ear with his long snout.

"Stop that, Semsem. And, no, we won't talk to him. I've gotten into enough trouble today." I felt my behind, still sore from my uncle's hand.

A couple of times a year, Irty, a year junior to me, would come with her entourage, two or three of my mother's men, either on a boat down river or riding on donkeyback, staying for a day or two. I would always look forward to her visits, receiving notice sometimes days, sometimes weeks in advance. Never mind that we would often end our time fighting, and I would wind up running into the house in a fit of crying. Mad at the world, mad at the heavens, mad at everything.

"What does Mommy look like?" I asked my sister one day as we skipped into the garden.

"Like me, only bigger. See this?" Irty revealed a new gold bracelet. Engraved on it were pictures of scarabs and birds. "Mommy and my daddy gave it to me." I glared at the jewelry; sometimes Daanja and Hori would give me things, but never my mother. "Try to catch me."

I chased her around the mesquite tree. Running after her, I was happy again, but that feeling would be short lived. "Tell me again what Saba is like?" I asked as we both fell on the grass.

"It's so big and there are so many people. Elephants and leopards guard the city. The streets are gold. I have a hundred slaves, including a dozen talking apes."

"You do not." I said, staring at the mounted stuffed crocodile above my house's door, there to ward off evil spirits.

"I do, and I'm with Mommy and my daddy, the King, all the time. They love me."

"My father's a king too."

"My daddy's a real king." Irty rolled toward me. Her bracelet gleamed.

"So is mine."

"Like Daanja and Hori are really your auntie and uncle."

"What are you saying?"

Irty let out a smile. "You know they're just pretending."

"No, they're not."

"They are."

"No." I started to feel the wet around my eyes.

64

"Pretending, pretending, pretending. They pretend because my daddy wants you far away from him."

My crying became a full temper tantrum, abruptly ending our visit.

When I questioned Daanja on this she assured me that we were blood, that she and my mother were sisters, like Irty and me, that Irty was just teasing me again. And, of course, she would change the topic.

"Your uncle and I bartered for a leather skirt for you with ivory in it. You'll look so lovely wearing it."

"If Irty and I have different fathers, how can we be sisters?" I asked as she stopped sorting out her jewelry and went into her sleeping room.

"You have the same mother." I heard her call back.

"Why doesn't she come to see me?"

She came in holding out the leather skirt. "What do you think?"

"Why won't she see me?"

Daanja sighed, throwing the garment on the ostrich-skin chair. I started to sob and she left to get Hori to beat me.

I had crossed a month into my eighth year when Irty came next to see me. It would be the last time.

א

"You're going to behave," Daanja said as we watched Irty and her two guardians donkey toward us on the flat by the river. "For the gods' sakes, Child, you're older than she. Don't let her make you cry. Tell me you won't."

"I won't."

"This has to stop. If it doesn't . . . if it doesn't, I'll tell your mother, and Irty will never come here. Ever."

"You wouldn't tell her?"

"Don't sob and there'll be nothing to tell."

After Irty's driver helped my sister off the ass, she ran to me and we hugged.

"I have a surprise for you," she whispered.

"What is it?" I jumped up and down.

"Later."

"Tell me now."

"Later."

As the sun climbed, nearing its throne on top the sky, we were chasing each other around the garden. Irty stopped, looking at me with eyes large and bright like falcon eggs. "I have that surprise for you."

"What kind of surprise?"

"If I tell you, how can it be a surprise?"

"If you won't tell me, then how do I get it?"

"Come."

Irty took my hand and led me out of the garden, we ran near the cow pens and my uncle's slaughter yard—where Uncle Hori and his men were busying themselves on wrestling a heifer to the ground.

"What are you two up to?" my uncle shouted as he left his men, meeting us at the fence of tied-wooden stakes.

I looked to Irty. "Just playing," she said.

"Don't stray too far," he said looking at me. "Who knows what wild things may be out there."

"We won't," Irty said, her face filled with mischief.

He opened the gate. "Come here, Keb-fish." As I took a step, Hori put his hand to my ear. "Got it." It was some wild grass that had been wedged in there. He sweetly brushed my hair out with his fingers. Irty can talk all the lies she wants, but Hori wasn't pretending. He couldn't be.

"That cow looks like trouble," Irty said, pointing to the animal and the men still trying to subdue it.

My uncle said his goodbye and, as he strode toward his cow-hands, Irty grabbed my arm, taking me away, to a thicket of ferns surrounding an aging ebony at the Nile's ridge.

"Here's the surprise." She looked around and then finally straight at me, placing her hands on my shoulders. "Our mommy is coming."

"I don't believe you."

"She's coming," Irty said with convincing eyes.

"Really?"

"Yes, on ships from up river."

"Really? When?"

"Soon. But Mommy wanted you blindfolded first, so the surprise would be bigger."

While my sister grabbed some ferns and vines, my heart was exploding. After all these years, would I finally come to know a face that had been more ghost than real? Would every sinew of my mother clench me tight and never let go, taking me to the home I spent countless hours dreaming of?

Irty placed a makeshift mask over my eyes.

"I don't understand. Why the need for a blindfold?"

"I told you. Do you want to ruin it?"

After she was done, when I opened my lids, I could only see bits of light toying to be noticed behind the darkest green. Then I started feeling vines pinching against my body and I started to wrestle free. "What are you doing?" I asked.

"It's part of the surprise. Mommy will be the one to untie you. If you don't let me do this, she won't come." Obeying, I felt more vines wrapping and tugging. My legs and feet became bound.

"I think I see her, yes, she's coming."

"Let me see, let me see."

"I told you, she has to untie you. She's getting closer."

"This isn't fair. How come you get to see her and not me?"

"She's real close now," she said, her voice rolling in merriment. "Her boat has landed. My gods, she's coming. She's coming. Over here, Mommy! Over here! She sees us, she's coming up now. She's real close. Real close now. Almost here. Another few steps. Here she is."

I heard something like bushes rustling.

"Mommy are you there?"

I felt the plants around my eyes snap free. The blur gave way to Irty in a laughing fit. No motherly Queen of Sheba about to embrace me, no flotilla on the water.

"You're so stupid." More laughter. "Stupid, stupid, stupid." I tried to reach out to hit her, but my arms were shackled and useless. All I could do was to wobble on the grass, my mind consumed in crying out every tear I had in me. "I'll come back to get you later, Stupid."

Irty ran away in uncontrollable laughter.

I don't know how long I lay there, sorry for myself, sobbing to an audience of no one. After the emotion had drained, I collected myself. Rolling over to the ebony tree, I rubbed my wrists on the rough bark, back and forth several times, until the vines broke. Using both the tree and my hands, I removed the rest. Free, I went to give my sister some hurt.

א

Running back toward the house, I stopped at the slaughter yard. My uncle and his men were gone, probably eating their lunch. I was alone. The now dead heifer was hanging upside down, oozing blood, flies circling around it. Staring at the carcass, I hit upon a new plan of revenge. I tried the gate, shook it, but it was locked. After climbing the tall fence, I removed my leather skirt, the one my aunt had used to try to redirect my attention, the one she had me wear that day, the one with the embedded ivory that kept digging into my thighs. Standing naked, I brushed it against the corpse of a cow, soaking the thing red. I took the ruddy garment back to the ebony tree and left it there among the torn vines.

In the neighboring grassland by the river, I hid for four days, living off berries and fallen dates, waiting for them to be done with their search, waiting for Irty to donkey back to Saba. Hiding behind the acacias and baobab, I watched my sister clumsily mount her ass, noticing for once she was the one sobbing.

As I trudged into our house, my relatives were in disbelief.

"Child, we took you for dead," Daanja said, hugging me. "What happened?"

"I was attacked by a wild monkey." I said, stuttering.

Hori then took his turn to hold me. Then he knelt down and looked me in the eyes. "How horrible, little Keb-fish. Show me where it hurt you and I'll make it better."

After thinking of possible locations, I held out my unblemished right arm.

"Where, Child?" Daanja asked. "Where are the marks?"

I stared crying.

"What really happened?" she asked.

"Irty," I said, confessing.

"What about Irty?"

My relatives forced me to recount it all. And after the telling, my aunt was livid. I was unsure what she was mad at most. Pick a reason: that because of my trickery she had thought I died; that my uncle and his men had to stop work to look for me; that I had ruined a most expensive skirt.

"Spank her," my aunt said.

"Daanja—" Hori started to say.

"Spank her, Hori. Spank her so she remembers for a long, long time."

"No!" I screamed.

After a moment of hesitation, my uncle hit me as hard as he ever had.

We traded few words in the weeks that followed. I played by myself in the garden and did as I was told. I didn't raise any grief to my aunt about visiting my mother. We sat and ate our meals mostly in silence. Occasionally, Hori would begin a conversation with me, but Daanja looked at him to stop. And no new dresses were needed to guarantee my obedience.

Then one day during breakfast, a towering, stern-looking man came to the door. He stood, unbending as a rigid palm whose playful fronds had long since fallen off.

"My name is Geddi. King Awawa and Queen Makeda sent me to collect the girl."

He didn't give me a lot of time, and I only grabbed a few of my skirts. I was sure so much more would be waiting for me in the palace. As my life-long dream was finally going to come to fruition, I sped to the anchored boats—it would be my first time setting foot on one—skidding down the short dirt bluff to the river. At the swampy bank, by the low water, I embraced my relatives goodbye, their bodies moist, already sweltering in the midmorning sun. Part of me was scared, as scared as those times I had witnessed a pounding rainstorm, when the river had somehow lifted up and began raging down from the skies, pummeling our roof, the straw and mud above us offering no resistance. And now I was leaving the only home known to me, never having strayed more than a mile or two from the ranch. Yet another part of me was overflowing with promise and joy. In little less than a day I would be in Saba with my mother. My mother, the Queen.

As the men loaded my clothes and readied the boats, Daanja and Hori drooped like lilies, my aunt exposing tears for the first time, tears indistinguishable from mine. Maybe we were related after all.

"I'm sure I'll see both of you soon. If Irty can come visit, I'm sure I'll be able to do the same."

"Keb . . ." Hori started to say.

"What is it?" I asked. Daanja looked sternly at him.

"The gods will protect you," he finally said. Then he held me for a good length. "My heart to you."

"Be good, Child," Daanja said. "Don't be so headstrong."

I gave them one last hug. Then Geddi picked me up and we boarded the first of three ships. My new captain handed me over to a husky man who I later learned was named T'kari; he held me I assumed to keep me balanced when the boats would turn to head upstream. But we didn't turn. After they raised the rock anchors, the ships just kept on heading downriver with the current. For the first time I noticed that my little ark was crammed with elephant tusks, animal skins, spices, obsidian, precious stones, rhinoceros' horns, fruit, jugs of water, and a caged ape. I didn't understand what was happening.

"Why aren't we hoisting the sail and turning around?" I asked Geddi, as I tried to adapt to the shake and jar of the boat, and T'kari's strong hold. "Saba is up the river."

"We're not going to Saba." Geddi said, walking over to me.

"Where, where are we going?" I asked whimpering.

"I'm taking you to your father."

"King Aw—"

"Your real father."

"No! I want to go to Saba!"

Geddi smacked me hard across the face and I swallowed blood—the first time I would know the flavor. Through walls of emotion, I think I heard him say, "That's from the King. You should have done a better job keeping watch over your sister."

CHAPTER TWO

As I tell my story now to Zadok, the cell door opens. It's his servant, carrying a tray of flat bread, vinegar, and olive oil, placing it in front of me. I forgo dunking, simply stuffing morsels in my mouth, gulping without tasting, a slave to the commands of my body, a rabid wild thing.

I glimpse the old man and remember I'm civilized, and start slowing down my chews.

"I can see where you got your inspiration for the Cain and Abel story," Zadok says. "And for Joseph's jealous brothers."

"Do you see the tie that threads the entire work?" I ask in between bites. "How the stories are linked?" His face is a blank. "You don't see it?"

"Yes, of course."

"Each deceiver in turn ends up deceived?" I respond, saving him the embarrassment.

"Of course," he repeats. But it's just feigned politeness, his face all lined as if knotting his features can undo the riddle. Of course, what's really telling is that he doesn't expand on his comment. I can only conclude that he doesn't grasp it. The one man in all of the Kingdoms, who figured out I was the author, doesn't see how the tales are connected. Is he not as clever as I think or could the problem rest with me, that I was too slight with the reed? If it's blind to him, then it must be so to everyone. But had I hit the listener with a brick and had my narrator provide an explanation, it would have called attention to my hand. Still, even if my thread was thin, it didn't lessen Zadok's enjoyment or anyone else's.

"Here's another tie." I say, dipping some bread into vinegar. "When the brothers show Joseph's bloody coat to Jacob and when Tamar shows her father-in-law, Judah, his staff and seal, they both announce, 'Recognize this?' An expression I borrowed from Raddai, something he would scream at me whenever he caught me with a writing." Zadok gives a sympathetic nod. "With each deception story, I used some sort of clothing as the means of deceit. There's Jacob's hairy goat skins to dupe his father and steal his blessing, Leah's veil to dupe Jacob into marrying her, Joseph's Egyptian garment that Potiphar's wife used to dupe Potiphar into believing that Joseph raped her."

"Looks like your childhood skirt lives on in spite of your best efforts."

Here he sees. After all these years, it still pokes at my skin.

א

To the rhythm of a flute player, our boat's ten oarsmen muscled us past the tans and ochres of the steppe, past the grassland sporting unruly vegetation with its gnarled-branched thorn trees. They rowed us by walled villages, their occupants rushing toward the river with waving hands.

Then the world started to die. Beyond the banks there was no life. Only endless granite and yellow sand. The Nile too had changed to something harder. We were nearing the Shebite border and soon we would be at the cataract. I had long ago been told about these dangerous falls over our meals. My uncle was the storyteller, and his spirit would always burn every time he recounted tales of navigating through these deadly rapids. *There are five cataracts, little Keb-fish, in the Land of the Bow where Cushite tribesman would war with each other for territory and gold.* Even recounting my uncle's vivid telling and retelling, I nevertheless was unprepared when I gazed at the beginnings of the first cataract. I froze, taking in an inlet packed with colossal black boulders protruding above the river, each irregular and pointed rock was surrounded by churning white foam, all of it begging for a fight.

Looking at the water swirling, I remembered my only time that I had been in the river. It had been the previous summer, when my uncle took a rare day off from his work, bringing my aunt and me to the bank for a picnic. After we ate, Hori carried me into a shallow. "Watch out for crocodiles," he had joked. When he was chest deep in water, he just threw me in, hoping that the action would somehow cause me to learn to swim. But I just splashed and sank, my world becoming water, water filling my nostrils, my mouth, my throat, the fear the same as I would later imagine Pharaoh's army would experience drowning in the Sea of Reeds as they chased after the fleeing Israelites. I wasn't in the murk for long as Hori picked me up and rushed me over to the grass while I coughed the Nile out. Looking out now at the swirling eddies clashing with the rocks, I pictured our boat sinking, carrying me with it, walls of water collapsing over me, and no guilt-ridden uncle coming to the rescue.

As we approached the cataract, Geddi ordered each boat to anchor, allowing the oarsmen to fix ropes to the vessels' sides. Then after sunset, the pulling began. To the shouts from Geddi and his two other captains, the three screaming out overlapping directions, the lower ranks towed each ship, pulling on the ropes from on top the cliffs, navigating the ships around the rocks. Meanwhile, I clung hard onto to the railing trying not to fall with each jerk and heave of the flax.

But not everyone was pulling. Each boat retained one or two bowmen to keep lookout for what I imagined might be bandits and other unsavories. I fixed my stare on the one in ours, a man reminding me of the lotus, his body a lean stem, his thick eyelashes were entrancing as the flower fully opened. When he caught me staring, I shyly turned my gaze to the haulers on the bank.

That evening, having survived the whip of the falls and blades of granite, the boats anchored on the other side of the cataract, in a land not Sheba. I slept nearly shoulder to shoulder with the men on the acacia deck. As he had done on the nights before, Geddi gave me a lion's skin to wrap myself in and left me to the constellations. Staring at the northern sky, I scanned the vulture, the hippopotamus, the crocodile, the frog until I finally rested on the serpent and wished to the gods that I were back in my garden with Semsem.

א

A week or two later, the river turned fully around, causing us to sail south, but still sweeping us with the current. For a moment my heart was racing, thinking we were going back home, but then I remembered my uncle had told me that the river would eventually reverse course again toward Egypt.

"Would you like some dried figs?" a voice asked as I stared at the olive-gray water. "We're rationing what's left of the undried until we can trade for more at Napata. It's all starting to rot anyway."

THE REED

It was the lotus man with the bow. He had such a kind face with a jaw as square as a baobab trunk. But it was his eyelashes that captured me; how I could have buried myself in those lashes. The ragged men who worked on Hori's ranch, the farmers who came to trade, and the ones who escorted Irty, the only men I had ever seen up until the boats, they were all so unfairly ordinary and plain in comparison. Right there I fell in love— whatever love is to an eight-year-old.

Accepting the food, I tried to speak, but could manage no words.

"Alright, then," he said with a smile. Then he left me. I felt wretched that he thought me dumb, all because my mouth had become useless.

During the next few days, I did my best to avoid the bowman, although it's difficult when the length of your world is little more than a hundred feet. At those moments when willpower had crumbled, I found myself uncontrollably drawn to him, hiding behind tied-down cargo, studying him waxing his weapon, wondering if he would have to use of it. But as soon as I noticed any flutter of his head toward me, I jerked my eyes away before he could catch me, a reflex that soon became an art.

I tried not to think about him by seeking distractions. I attempted to befriend the caged ape, but he was rather consumed with swinging and howling whenever the water roughed, which was now most of the time. I named him Miiki, which caught on with the rest of the crew. And I dwelled on how my relatives were busying themselves, picturing Hori and his men disemboweling a hartebeest and my aunt scolding her servant for breaking one of her precious turquoise bowls, their lives going on just as always. But were they doing it all listlessly, preoccupied on their memories of me? Had they kept my sleeping room as it was when I left? Or were my relatives living their lives with the same spirit, spending not a thought on their former ward? Or with even more vigor, glad to be rid of such a troublesome weed?

One morning I was at the stern again, concentrating on the simple and repetitive rhythms of the flute music, wishing for just the smallest variation, my eyes alternating from the thistle of the rocky land, to the whitecaps in the wake, the latter reminding me of water boiling on Daanja's hearth.

"I have more figs for you."

Behind me was the bowman.

"Thanks," was all I could blurt out while taking the fruit.

"We'll pass through the next cataract tonight and we could pull into Napata as early as tomorrow afternoon. We shall have more than figs for you then, I promise."

"Thanks." If only I could expand my vocabulary.

"My name is Pi."

"Keb." I giggled and shyly found comfort looking toward shore. That's when I gazed upon an out-of-place, large round-top rock protruding from the bank up ahead. As we got closer, it was apparent that this burnt-sienna stone was shaped by man and covered with strange chiseled markings.

"That's a stele," he said.

"A what?"

"A stele. That's where the King of Egypt would inscribe his deeds, victories, or warnings. We'll be seeing them along the way."

"Inscribe, what's that?"

"It's a way of carving knowledge on a rock. Those markings there are words." He pointed at the sandstone. "If we wanted to, we could chisel our conversation on a rock, using hieroglyphs."

"What's this one?" I asked, pointing to the Egyptian marker.

"What do you mean?"

"Deed, victory, or warning?"

His eyes rolled downwards. "It says, um, 'Welcome to Egypt.'" He wasn't a very good liar, not like Irty.

"What's it really say?"

He looked away for a moment, I suppose, weighing the amount of truth he should bestow on me. "Warning."

"What's the warning?"

"I'm sure you would prefer not to know."

"Tell me."

"It must have been erected a long, long time ago because Egypt now could never carry out such an ugly threat, even if it desired to. I am far more worried about the Cushites."

"Tell me."

"Promise me you won't be at all frightened?" I nodded yes. Sailing past it, I saw picture strings of owls, snakes, and vultures, along with some other drawings, which I couldn't identify. "It reads: this is Egypt's southern border," he said. "Enemies shall . . ."

"Shall what?"

"Shall have their heads cut off, their families murdered, they shall have no successors."

I forced a grin.

"If you stare at that rock close up," he continued, "it's weathered, cracked, must have been set there centuries ago. Egypt has retreated far down the river. If they ever did have invading armies, they don't have them anymore. Look around, there's no one around to lop off anyone's head."

I put on a fake smile, feigning strength to maintain the beginnings of our friendship. But inside, I was one big, horrible mess.

א

We stayed at Napata, Cush's largest city, for a day to trade and then continued downstream. But now with hyena meat, sweet melons, tangy oranges, and beer. I had never had honey before and, after spreading it on flat bread, my mouth was like Osiris, reborn and resurrected.

The river eventually curved, turning northward again, and the waters here were the worse I had experienced. Waves pounded our craft, tossing it about as if it were a toy boat made out of reeds. I felt a never-ending nausea, throwing up several times over the side. Once when some of my vomit landed inside the boat, Geddi shoved my face in it.

Late in the afternoon, on a day when sun was burning more than its usual, every head turned to the east, including mine. That's when I saw them. They must be gods. Or giants birthed by gods. Four huge enthroned deities coming out of a cliff, maybe seventy feet tall. All four warning us to approach no further. My chest became its own cataract as I wished I could have taken command right there to order our boats to come about, making those figures shrink back into the horizon.

"Those large statues are all the likeness of an old king by the name of Ramesses," Pi told me, taking custody of my hand. "They get to me too, every time we sail past."

"So, they aren't gods?"

"No, just carvings, made by men. These four stone kings must have been created to show Cush who's boss, to make the pharaoh seem like a god. See that second Ramesses? His head has fallen off and is resting on the ground there. So Egyptian power and magic can't be all that strong, right?"

"What could have caused him to lose his head?"

"Who knows? Maybe the gods sent an earthquake."

"So, the deities are watching out for us?"

"I hope so." I squeezed his hand a little. "Perhaps they were also mad at Ramesses' hubris, building something so grand, his images towering, touching the sky."

THE REED

I thought that maybe it's good to be small and unnoticed, just like Pi who was a simple bowman and me, a little girl. I smiled and grabbed tightly on Pi's hand, wondering if we could be married, like my aunt and uncle. To have a home under a cone-shaped roof and a garden with a large mesquite tree to play in.

He grinned at me as the boats took us downstream past the statues, destined for a place far away from Sheba, to where the river meets the sea.

CHAPTER THREE

A week and a half later, we beat the Nile's annual flooding. The great river's timing was off its usual perfection. We traversed the last cataract, unobstructed by what should have been a rising tide, able to navigate around the boulders in the shallow, and we entered Upper Egypt.

Greeting us were thriving villages and a calm Nile. By the banks were light-skinned fishermen in small reed rafts along with farmers sitting on the grassy strand, all looking upstream, waiting, waiting for the water to rise to flood the plain. But it didn't.

A few weeks later, as we approached the first mud-brick walls and houses of Thebes, the center of Upper Egypt and one of our major trading sites, I asked Pi how he became a bowman on a ship like this.

"My grandfather was a mercenary for the Egyptian army, rose through the military ranks. Managed to become an official to the King of Lower Egypt, until he fell out of favor. Then he brought our family back to Sheba. He taught me the bow and how to read. Both he and later my father became advisors to our Shebite kings."

"Have you met my mother?" I asked anxiously as the city seemed to sprawl forever on the east bank.

"A few times."

"What does she look like?"

"Quite striking. Although now in middle age, she's beautiful, no question about it. Deep-set eyes, her face full of intelligence and strength. She's dignified as any royal I've ever seen. How she loves her children." I pictured her kissing and hugging Irty in front of her courtiers. "My wife thinks the world—"

"What? You're, you, you have a wife?" For the first time in weeks, I tasted that familiar salty wet.

"Did I not tell you?"

I ran to the ship's center in a full cry. I found my lion skin and crawled into it.

"Keb."

"Go away!"

"Come on, Keb. Please, talk to me."

"Go away!"

"Keb."

"Pi, you're needed," I heard one of the men say. Then my bowman made quick footsteps.

I don't know how long I hid in there weeping, mad at Pi, mad at myself, mad at everything the heavens had created, as if I could even return home with him. They were sending me to the ends of the earth, how could we make house together? I was a fool. It all made me think how terribly alone I soon would be. I cried myself into a heavy nap. Later, when the midday heat was at its heaviest, I poked out of the skin. The ship had anchored and the crew was gone, except two bowmen. I remember thinking that I couldn't be here when Pi returned. So when the two watchers were in the midst of some discussion, I jumped ship and ran through the streets of the biggest city that I would ever come across.

Through dusty roads I ran past the mud brick, weaving between carts led by donkeys, by drovers and their cattle. Zipping through the kilted poor and the comfortably dressed in their finery, men and women in painted faces and black wigs, covered with linen oddly draped and wrapped, some sporting even odder capes, sashes, and headdresses. My feet wouldn't let up, eclipsing the rag-wearing cripples and the blind and the beggars, all with hands out and reaching. All the while, all of the city's odors, sights, noise, curiosities, all of it, all the queerness of Thebes, oiling on me.

After my legs gave in, I plopped down against a massive limestone wall. Behind it was an even more massive complex, filled with towering stone statues, colonnades, pylons, and obelisks, all painted in the most brilliant colors. I felt small. Then walking towards me, a dozen boys in long skirts, carrying palettes, their heads all shaved except for side locks reaching beyond their shoulders. They started laughing, and said hurtful things like, "miserable Cush," and "burnt face." (Their Egyptian was a language I knew, taught to me by Hori). One of the boys, cheered on by his friends, picked up a rock and threw it at me, missing my head by an inch. They laughed some more and raced off.

I sat and cried. But that ended when I noticed a parade of donkeys. Bald-headed men, holding leashes, lined them up one after another. I crept up from behind and petted an unattended ass, like I used to pet the donkeys Irty would ride.

"Careful."

Behind me and staring was a middle-aged man. He too was bald, but made quite an imposing figure—one who I would later use to imagine Joseph after Pharaoh promoted the patriarch for interpreting his dreams—the man's face painted, black kohl around his eyes, red ochre on his lips, robed in white linen, a gold pectoral around his shoulders. Hanging from his neck was an Eye of Horus amulet similar to the one that Hori would wear, although this man's was much bigger, bearing a fine ceramic glaze, the amulet attached to a plaited gold chain.

"She's pretty," I said, as I let the donkey be. Off in the distance, two armed soldiers stood watch over us.

"You remind me of my young daughter. She'll pet anything. Pet a wild sphinx if it were alive. Do you have a name?"

"Keb."

"Your eyes are all red, are you all right?" he asked, as he walked me away from the animals. "Are you lost?"

"I'm going on a trip far away to see my father."

"Ah," he said smiling just a little, trying to brighten me up.

"Why are all these donkeys lined up?"

"It's a secret."

"I can keep a secret."

"I'm sure you can. Have you been to Karnak before?"

"Karnak?" My eyes were resting more on the animals than him.

"This Temple. Largest in the world."

"No, just passing through." I pointed to the pictures of the kings on the pylons. "Are these the head loppers?"

"Why would you say that?"

"My friend pointed out a rock that said kings would lop off our heads."

"These are pharaohs, who had to ensure order in their kingdoms. They would have only executed someone who might have broken up that divine order and only if they had to. You have nothing to worry about."

86

"Kings are pharaohs?"

"They are indeed." I notice he wore a large signet ring; its seal was a gold scarab.

"My mother is a queen and my father a king. Maybe I can grow up to be a queen or pharaoh."

"Your parents are royalty," he said, laughing. "Well, to govern here, you would have to be a man. But there's a legend that tells that there was once a woman pharaoh who lived a long, long time ago."

"Was there?"

"Queen Hatshepsut. She wore a false beard, ruling over both Upper and Lower Egypt."

"Is there a picture of her here? I want to see her. Can you take me to her?"

"No, I'm sorry. Later pharaohs felt uneasy about her and removed her images from temple walls, chiseled out her name, so the legend goes."

"What do you mean chiseled out her name?"

"Wiped it away. All traces, gone."

"That's not fair." I wondered if the same thing could happen to my mother that her name too might be blotted out.

He pointed to the one of the pylons. "See these markings?"

"Yes."

I looked back at the asses, which had more power over me than paintings on stone of quails and owls.

"Well, that's writing, that's what they chiseled away," the man said leading me further away from the animals. "Your name is Keb?"

"It is Keb," I said looking back at the shrinking donkeys.

"Want to see your name in writing?"

Now he had me. He took his thin staff and with it made three pictures in the dirt: a basket, an arm, and a foot.

"That's your name. Keb. The basket is a 'k' sound, the arm an 'eh', and the foot a 'buh.' Keb."

"My name?" It was as if I were looking at magic.

Then he drew an oval around it. "This is a cartouche. If you were pharaoh, your name would be in this. See, this is you, Queen Keb." I studied my name for some moments, walked around the markings, and then my eight-year-old mind wandered back to the asses.

"So why are all these donkeys lined up?"

"The scribal students here would have to study years before they learn their name in hieroglyphs, and you just mastered yours."

"I want to know about the donkeys."

"Maybe we should look for your people."

"Tell me about the donkeys."

"Do you want to visit the Chapel of the Hearing Ear?"

"Donkeys."

"Donkeys?" he repeated and grunted. "It will just be between you and me?"

"Yes, I promise."

"And no one else."

"No one, I promise."

"You swear to Amun-Re?"

"I swear."

Looking around, he found not a soul in earshot. Then he leaned in and whispered his secret.

א

I sit staring at Zadok.

"Why were they lined up?" Zadok asked, his eyes burning.

"I made a promise. I swore on their sun god. Apologies."

My mouth begs to smile, and I spend considerable energy taming it. The power of a story building toward a resolution that is withheld. A small torment he richly deserves. Yet, while I am glad I toyed with him, truth is, I can't tell Zadok what the priest told me. How could I break such a promise to which the sun in the sky was an unwavering witness? But what the man told me was this: Egypt was not the power it once was. The country was split in two, a weak king in the north, the priests in Thebes ruling the south. Lawlessness was everywhere and the tombs were being robbed and desecrated. The pharaohs' immortal souls were imperiled and needed saving. Perhaps that is why the god Hapi was delaying the flooding of the Nile, but something had to be done. The donkeys would head by barge to the west bank, and once there they would carry some forty royal mummies from plundered tombs to a lone, secret location to find eternal peace.

א

After he told me his secret, the bald priest walked me along a wide and busy street, lined by stone sphinxes, to the river where Geddi and T'kari found us.

"We are the custodians of this girl," my ship's captain said to the priest. "We need to take her back."

"I am Paraemheb, the Second God Servant of Amun-Re and Vizier of Upper Egypt. Keb says she is on a journey to meet her father."

"She is. This child's father rules over the Hebrew kingdoms."

"Well then." He put his hand on his heart and then waved it toward me. "My heart to you."

He turned to Geddi. "You will treat her well?"

"We will."

They treated me well—to two lasting lashes on my back.

א

Two days later, my skin was still burning, the cracking whip producing pain so sharp and enduring that the memory would never completely dull, the balm on my wounds providing little if any healing magic. But what made things worse was Pi's return from the city. When I saw him jump the strand for our vessel, my pulse began snapping like a float of famished crocodiles.

He cornered me against the railing, leaving me only the open air to hide behind.

"Keb, I didn't like how we ended—" I turned toward the city. "Your back, what happened?"

"What happened to your back?" he asked again.

I found the courage to face him. "Geddi and T'kari."

"I'm sorry."

"I, I—"

He took my hand and smiled kindly, calming my turtle speech. I grinned back, and my stinging skin began to quiet. Funny how a mere gesture and a simple touch can have ten times the power of necromantic ointments. So we were as we once were, Pi and me—but not quite. Before I never had to stave off thoughts that there might be places for us beyond the hard and locked boundaries of friendship.

א

We were deep into summer, but the Nile still refused to rise. The river was not her usual punctual self. Hapi must have been either angry, like the vizier said, or had other things on his mind as gods do. There was talk now of a drought, something buried in the memories of old men.

After we left Thebes, I spent much time trying to befriend the ape and practicing my letters. I told Pi of my encounter with the priest and how he showed me my name in hieroglyphs; my friend gave me a cheap olive jar to write on, along with a writing reed and black ink. The literate bowman taught me new symbols on the days he was on board and, when he disembarked, I loved practicing on the jar, showing off my work upon his return. Spelling 'Pi' was easy, just two characters: a mat, which was really just a square, and a leaf; and I could tell he was uncomfortable with seeing his name repeatedly covering the vessel.

Several weeks later, on another day without a trace of cloud, I awoke to the crew screaming and jumping up and down. The drought was over. The river rose just high enough to begin seeping over its banks, taking the boats up with it, all from a crest of reddish-brown muddy water rushing toward us. The color and the gush through the bed reminding me of life's blood.

As we entered Lower Egypt, armies of frogs stared at us from the widening banks, while papyrus reeds and clumps of cypress sprouted everywhere. At times I didn't know whether we were on water or land, but in either event the current kept sweeping us closer to the Great Sea. When we docked at Pi-Ramesses, I was entertained by brick makers working on the bank. They were stomping clay and straw with their feet, pouring their mixtures into molds to let harden in the sun. Overseers looked on from a safe distance, none of whom wanted to dirty their white-starched kilts.

Drought, the Nile turning to blood, frogs, workers making clay bricks. All images I would later use.

After Pi-Ramesses, we continued sailing downriver to the city of Tjaru; there my life fell apart.

א

"You want off this boat?" Pi asked, finding me sitting on top of some linen-covered kegs, my legs dangling in the warm air.

"We're not going to end up in trouble?" My eyes darted around the craft for the captain, but he was nowhere in sight.

"There's an abandoned fort that I want to explore, thought you might want to come."

I searched for Geddi by the banks, but couldn't find him. Instead, I saw the river divide the world in two. Thickets of lotus and papyrus reeds filled the fens on the west bank, while, after a small strip of grass, unending sand dunes made up the east. It was on the east where we were moored.

"Come on," he said.

"What about Geddi?"

"If he finds us, I'll take responsibility. Come on." I felt my lash marks. "Keb, to send an arrow forward, you have to pull back the bow. You can do this."

He took my hand, helping me off the ship. My legs had trouble adjusting to the ground, struggling to keep balance. But after a few minutes on the steppe, I relearned how to walk.

"Have you thought about what it will be like to grow up in a court of a king?" he asked.

"You grew up in one and you attend my mother, what should I expect?"

"Music, dancing, fun and games."

"I don't know how to dance."

"You'll learn."

I stopped and twirled around him, stumbling a little before I managed to stand up straight. "How was that?" I asked, grinning.

"Miserable," he teased. "But with some long, hard work, you may actually become . . ."

"Become what?

"Something better than miserable."

"Teach me."

"To dance?"

"Teach me something."

"Here?"

I nodded.

"As you wish, one little step," he said. "I've seen dancers stand on one leg, then jump, bring their legs in together mid air, and then land."

We practiced that, he first and then I followed his movements.

"Let's do that again," I pleaded. And so we did. "One more time."

"Hey, see that old fort up there, let's look around. Race you to it."

We ran up the hill and I was winning, giddy that I was pulling several feet ahead. As I lunged into the pilfered mud-brick to claim victory, Geddi and T'kari stepped out from behind one of the ruined walls, along with a man wearing a wool tunic and a turban. On his face was the queerest thing: bushy, dark brown tufts growing from his cheeks and chin. His skin (the part not covered with hair) was tan, but beaten and leathery, perhaps fired too long in the steady kiln of the sun.

I ran back to Pi, hiding behind him.

"That's the one," Geddi said in Egyptian to the man with the whiskers.

"What's happening?" I asked Pi in between gasping breaths, clutching his hand tight.

Pi squatted, meeting my eyes. "This man is going to take you the rest of the way, to see your father."

"Why didn't you tell me back at the boat?" Tears began to blur my vision.

"The Captain thought it better this way. I'm sorry, Keb."

"You're not coming?" I asked, going into full cry.

"I can't, I have to stay with the boats."

"I want you to come!" I grabbed hard onto Pi's arm.

"You'll be all right. Soon you'll be dancing in front of your father."

"I want you to come!"

I started hitting Pi for refusing me, for deceiving me, for being near me. I screamed over and over that I hated him. But that ended when Geddi walked over and slapped me hard in the face.

"Stop your clamoring or, I swear, I'll sell you into slavery."

Then with Geddi's nod, T'kari grabbed me. Against my struggle and screams, he carried me over to the strange man (who I would learn was called Reuel, the Ishmaelite) standing behind the fort, attending to a humped, drooling creature, lying on the ground. I was handed over like trade goods.

I witnessed through the spaces in the walls Pi motionless and staring, becoming just another silent monument littering the landscape. Then he turned and hiked with Geddi and T'kari down to the boats, never once looking back.

I never saw my bowman again.

How incredibly cruel of Pi to be my closest friend and then, without the slightest hesitation, to take it all away. I've experienced many horrible things in my life, and apart from losing Ariah, that was one of the worst. Like my sister, aunt, and uncle, he ceased being part of my world and became one of the stumbling memories in my heart, intruding more than most.

CHAPTER FOUR

Reuel and his Ishmaelite caravan carried me (and Miiki the ape) across the Shur desert and into Judah, until we reached my father's city. There stood Jerusalem. Like an invading army, my eye scaled the earthen ramparts. My vision then jumped to the high city wall to the mud-brick houses that filled the hill, hooking onto David's old residence, vaulting to the top of Mount Moriah, where stood the mostly-completed palace and the scaffolding surrounding the Temple in the midst of construction.

But before all that there was the Jerusalem gate to contend with. And all those wretches out in front. I felt scared. I'd never seen such a lawless mob.

"Stay close, don't wander," Reuel said to me as we approached the chaos.

There was no line, no rules on queuing in, just guesswork and swarming bodies, all waiting their turn to be interrogated by the guard before being granted the privilege of entry. Flanking those of us wishing admittance were lepers and cripples in raggedy wool (if anything), begging for handouts. Worse yet were the vendors—from children to old men—selling trinkets, such as poor-man's jewelry and junk pottery. Except for an Egyptian word bubbling up here and there, their overlapping Hebrew was just ear babble, all of it making a horrible racket.

A man put a doll in my hand and left his open, waiting, I suppose, for some silver. When neither the Ishmaelites nor I gave him metal, he lurched at me, grabbing the toy.

"Reuel, he took my doll. Get it back for me!"

"Forget it," he said shouting into my ear as he brought me in closer. "It was never yours to begin with."

I cried, but that didn't get the doll back nor stop the plague of merchants from crushing us. Reuel and the nomads did their best to shove them away, but what can one really do when attacked by a locust cloud?

We finally made our way to the gate, and the Ishmaelites gave the right answers to the guards, allowing us to pull our camels past the thick stone walls, by the elders sitting on their benches, all of them unsympathetic to the plight we just went through. Once inside, I could breathe and, while the market continued, it was calmer and less chaotic. Here the vendors for the most part stood behind display stands or had their wares laid out on wool blankets and woven mats; while most would shout at the passersby, at least they kept mainly to their spaces. Merchants weighed metal for anything you could think of: nuts, lentils, kindling wood, idols of clay and stone. On tabletops were ceramic jars, which I would later learn contained specialty goods such as Arabian frankincense and Sidonian perfumes. The bazaar lined the street for a couple hundred yards until yielding to the residential area. We climbed up the foul-smelling, fly-thick, dusty thoroughfare, past the terraced houses, all the way up the hill to the palace.

The Ishmaelites brought me into the large, drafty, cedar-paneled Hall of Throne. There I found courtiers in opulent linen tunics circled around two dwarfs in ribbon loincloths, greased from crown to foot in olive oil, lobbing punches at each other. When the diminutive wrestlers slipped and fell on the hard mosaic, they continued their punching, but did so horizontally, with some added ear biting and kicking. Noblemen and their wives were screaming at the now bloody fighters, seemingly hoping that their man would pummel the other to the point of taking him into the underworld, the elders' bodies twisting and contorting as if that could somehow summon their household gods to lay the final blow.

I glanced up and that's when I saw him.

From a gold and ivory throne such as one I had imagined my mother might sit on, a middle-aged man was relishing the moment, going back at forth from an occasional shout out at the wrestlers to savoring his wine. The King's dark brown hair was long, nearly reaching his shoulders. He had a potbelly, and on the whole, his build and height were average compared with those in the court, possibly smaller as the raised platform he was on had to have given him an extra inch or two. He wore a well-cropped beard, earring, amulet, and a fine linen robe displaying lots of gold and purple lions. His soft and gentle hands were swimming about, almost lost on the huge lion-carved armrests. His manner, almost effeminate. I tried to imagine him leading a bloodthirsty army, a warrior pharaoh painted on temple walls, about to smite his enemy, raising a mace with one hand and grabbing the hair of his kneeling captive with the other. But no, that was not this man.

An official whispered something to Solomon, who gazed down at me. Jumping off the throne, the King rushed over but skirted past me to Miiki, the caged ape, which the Ishmaelites had brought in. My father's eyes burned, and his smile, well, that could have stretched the length of both Kingdoms. I don't know how long he stared beaming, fascinated by the creature, even imitating some of Miiki's gestures. Then his official whispered something else to him, and the King eventually faced me.

"Keb, is it?" he said in flawless Egyptian.

I nodded.

"Queen Makeda, she is your mother?" He smelled of sweet myrrh.

Again, I nodded.

"How is she?"

"I, I hear she's well."

"You hear? Hmm. Come." He brought me up to the throne. By this time an Egyptian woman, black kohl lining her eyes, had occupied the seat next to him. With no chair for me, he sat me on his lap. "You must be tired and confounded. Well, there's no need to fear anymore. In fact, the best way to conquer that emotion is to learn. We must fetch someone to teach you."

He looked at the Egyptian woman, "Nebetah—"

She shook her head no, turning toward the wrestling still going on (one dwarf was gouging out the eyes of the other). After surveying the room, the King stared straight ahead for a minute or two. Then he said something in Hebrew to his official, who nodded and ran off. We sat there and Solomon just smiled. I tried to see my face in his; maybe our mouths were similar, I wasn't sure. While I had glimpsed my image dozens of times in my relatives' polished bronze, that seemed ages ago, a sketchy memory. I had looked monstrous in the distortion of the flowing Nile on the way here, as ugly as snout-headed Seth. So you can imagine that I was having difficulty reconstructing my features in my heart's eye. Maybe we had the same mouth and lips, I thought, who knew? The steward poured me some pomegranate juice, interrupting the awkwardness of whatever we were waiting for.

"His name is Miiki," I said, after taking a few sips.

"Whose?" Solomon asked.

"The ape."

"Is it?"

He continued grinning, but I wasn't sure how genuine the act. Then a man, whose endless beard was just beginning to gray, came stumbling and cowering toward the platform, slowly meeting the King's stare. This man was unlike any of the others in attendance. He was dressed in a courtier's tunic, but it was simple and plain, missing the tassels, sashes, and belts worn by everyone else. Also, he smelled of sweat, but it wasn't horrid; he could just use a bath or a little myrrh. His nails were in desperate need of a trim, one of his sandals straps was broken, and his long stringy hair was unkempt, as if his head never knew the experience of interacting with a comb.

"Ah Talus. This is Keb, my daughter and your new ward. We want you to teach her Hebrew, our history and customs. Oh, and music. It would be fitting for her to learn the lyre and the harp. Yes, I think that would be a good womanly thing."

"Um, I— " Talus started to say.

"Excellent. Keb, this is Talus, the royal librarian. He will be a most fine tutor. You will stay with him in his palace apartment."

"Sire?" asked the official who I later learned was Ahishar, Master of the Palace, and who was also speaking in Egyptian, perhaps following the King's lead. "Shouldn't she be brought up by a woman?"

"What woman here, who would have her, knows Egyptian?"

I sat with Solomon for a while longer, finishing my juice. He tried to reassure me with terse words and a leather-thin smile, but his eyes stared off, thinking of matters that only the gods could glean.

אֲ

"Cush cunt," "monkey girl," "burnt face." How I wish I never started picking up my new language, or at least its dark parts. I'd reminisce on life several months back when I had only snickering and unintelligible sounds to try to translate. Now passing my half-siblings and the courtiers in the hall, there could be no misunderstanding. So I would hide in Talus' apartment unless summoned by my father to appear at court. Years later, as an adult I would try to identify with them: how I must have seemed so different and strange, with my accent, my nose ring, my skin. Even now, since I've lived Jerusalem, I've come across perhaps only a dozen Cush traders at the market, and I haven't even seen a single black-faced slave. Yes, I must have looked quite peculiar. Plus my father would single me out, giving me favors that he seldom granted others, like sitting with him on the throne. Why me? What made me so special? I had no idea at the time and thought it arbitrary. While part of me enjoyed his attention, another part felt uncomfortable; it couldn't have sat well with Solomon's other children, for the hurt they put on me was unbearable. And Talus, for all his knowledge of languages and poetry, had little instruction on how an outsider could find acceptance by the meanest of children.

I spent a period where I would arrive early at the banquet hall, grabbing whatever they were serving, only to snake it back to the apartment to eat by myself. And when my guardian was at the library, I would remain in my solitude practicing the harp and lyre, and I'd work on my singing. There was a fragment of a harp song, "Help, O Yahweh," where the melody moved over only a few notes and was centered in my range. Performing it, I almost sounded pleasant:

The words of Yahweh are pure,
His words are silver purged in an earthen crucible,
So refined.

I pretended I was singing to Semsem and Ruzu. To my aunt and uncle. To Irty and Pi. And when I was finished, I would curtsey and they would applaud and throw bread in appreciation. Maybe I was starting to forfeit my childhood imagination, but I found I could only maintain that image of admirers for so long until it was just empty mats and furniture before me. If my voice and lyre were heard at all, it was in the ears of palace flies and mice.

א

"Ahishar tells me you haven't been at court," Talus said when I made a rare appearance in the library. His head was buried in a scroll, his fingers clutching a writing reed.

"Working on your poetry?" I said in Hebrew, my Egyptian barred by my Tyrian tutor.

"No one in the Kingdoms would want to hear that."

Whether anyone would was uncertain, but what was true was, apart from me, Talus never had an audience. What made this all the sadder was that my guardian would spend all his free time—what little there was left after schooling me—composing poetry, poetry that was never sung at court. Sometimes he would sing me snippets, but his wavering voice was grating, and he knew it. After making several unsuccessful attempts to have the Yubal Guild singers perform his works, he gave up, writing only for himself. Had he bribed them sufficiently, he might have met with some success.

"I'm cataloging," he said. "So why aren't you at court?"

"You're never there either."

"I'm not the King's daughter."

"I have to practice my harp."

I examined dusty shelves supporting clay tablets with wedge-shaped markings. In another section, my fingers lightly brushed against old rolled up papyri and leather scrolls, some just lying there unorganized, some in pigeonholes.

"You're too shy. You need to go, how else are you going to make friends and develop any chutzpah?"

"Chutzpah?" I asked with a mouthful of spit.

"It means audacity. And don't pronounce it as hard; it's a softer 'ch.' Chutzpah. And the more you're around people the better you can practice your Hebrew. And you should go for another reason. The King has ordered you."

"What's this?" I asked, picking up a papyrus scroll, covered with angular markings, changing the subject.

"You should be there." Talus' head was still down, his hair and beard were almost resting on top of the text he was working on. "You should obey your father. The King has exiled many of his children for less."

I just stroked the scroll I had found. Then I trudged up to him. "What's this?" I asked again, waiving the papyrus in front of him.

He finally looked up. "Something you shouldn't be playing with."

"What is it?"

"It's rare and expensive. Put it down."

I started dancing with it. "La da da, la da da. Oh, who is my partner?"

"*The Book of Jashar,* now put that down and give it to me." He started chasing me around the room.

"What is it?" I asked.

"Give it here, it's poetry."

"Someone else's, but not yours." I said, finally complying with his request. "What are these markings in it?"

"Hebrew." Talus placed it on a shelf, far out of reach. I found another scroll, but this one was awash with hieroglyphs, and I remembered my letters, the few words Pi taught me, and my name in a cartouche.

"This." I said, showing it to my tutor. "I want to learn this."

"You want me to recite it to you, and for you to recite it back?"

"I want to read it. I want to learn how to write hieroglyphs."

"I think not." He was back at his reed.

"Please."

He shook his head no and grunted. "Writing is not for women."

"Please."

"Scribing is for men."

"Teach me."

"Your father wants you to learn womanly arts, as if I can instruct you on that."

"He didn't say no to reading. I can learn arts of both sexes."

He put down his writing instrument and met my stare. "I'm also supposed to teach you Judahite customs, and a major one is that you don't mix things that shouldn't be mixed. Women's things are for women, men for men. That's how it is."

"Is that how it is in Tyre?" My tutor started organizing some tablets. "We don't have to tell anyone," I said to his back.

"And if someone catches you, I'll be blamed. And punished. And so will you. Anyway, I have too much to do, thanks to someone. Before I was just Talus the librarian. Now I'm Talus the librarian, Talus the tutor, Talus the guardian."

"You can teach me just a little."

"You need to concentrate on Hebrew, not Egyptian. This is a case where it's best not to water down your wine."

"So teach me how to read Hebrew then. We can start with the Jashar book."

"The Jashar book. Your father said he wants you to speak Hebrew, not read it."

"He said for you to teach me Hebrew, that includes writing."

"Semantics."

"Please, Talus." I was on knees now, my hands clasping.

"No."

"Talus."

"You heard what I said or are you missing ears?"

"Please, Talus, please."

"It's a thing that will never happen."

"If you teach me to read Hebrew, I could read all your poetry and let you know what I think."

CHAPTER FIVE

Learning how to write was a way to remember Pi, and I made it my mission to eventually read every scroll and tablet in the library—well, with the exception of all those dry tax and census records, and the inventory lists of palace supplies that hoggishly took up half the shelves. I remember the first time I held the writing reed, an imported juncus plant from Egypt. Like most of the ones used by Jerusalem scribes, it was stiff and thick and unbending, and my small right hand kept trying to conquer it.

After I learned the twenty-two letters, we started with Talus' poetry. His verse had lines of real beauty, but also contained Nile-long stretches of awful blandness, apparently breaking the rule of mixing the inappropriate. But I was kind and told him how lovely all his words were. Then we looked at some of the harp songs, especially the ones that doubled as writing aids for scribal students—such as "Happy Are Those Whose Way Is Blameless," in which each stanza follows the alphabet, all eight lines of the first stanza starting with an alef, the next stanza, a bet, and so on. It wasn't long before I consumed Judahite poetry that filled up entire scrolls such as *Samuel the Seer* and *The Wars of Yahweh.*

Once I mastered the Hebrew script, I learned the related language of Aramaic and the more distant Akkadian. The latter gave me a few headaches learning its wedged script, all of it on burnt-clay tablets containing groupings of tiny darkened triangles and brooms. I remember reading one Akkadian poem about a king, Sargon, whose mother abandoned him when he was a baby, cruelly placing him in a reed basket to drift down the river. A story far too similar to my own.

After enough begging, Talus taught me Egyptian hieroglyphs. I even attempted some Mycenaean and made it through most of a scroll about one of their gods who disobeyed his fellow deities by stealing fire and gifting it to the first humans. When the divine beings discovered his crime of making men more godlike, the fire stealer faced a horrible punishment of forever being chained to a rock, exposed to liver-picking vultures. It would be a theme I would use later, about someone doing something she was told not to do, resulting in both blessings and curses.

א

In my eleventh year, I sat with my Tyrian guardian in our makeshift tent of tree branches and goatskins, our shelter standing alongside a hundred others, all squeezed together on the roof of the palace for the annual Feast of Tents. Looking down at the courtyard and Mount Moriah, I glimpsed tents on top of every house and tents overflowing into the thoroughfare and narrow alleyways. Tents were even pitched outside the city walls. As always, the thousands of celebrants were gorging themselves on the free wine and food, shaking tambourines and dancing to the singers retelling of the importance of the temporary tent, protector of the nation, and a gift from Yahweh.

But this year was different. Solomon and the priests used the Feast to dedicate the just completed Temple of Yahweh, the sanctuary sitting parallel to the palace. Our national god was mentioned in almost every harp song, but, up until this point, to me Yahweh had been mere lyric. Not so on that dedication day. I remember the priests carrying the Ark of the Covenant, the gold chest containing the Commandments, from the old Tent to the new Temple, passing the towering flames on the Altar of Sacrifice. All the while listening to the choir sing of Yahweh's miracles, voices were rising from the top of the hill, as if the whole world and Yahweh's Divine Council could hear us and were singing along.

I felt him then in a way I have never felt any of the other gods. A god so mighty and so unlike the others that he needed no earthly guise as an idol to be worshipped. I imagined his face filling the sky in front of me and beyond, a face translucent yet present, a mountain of a face that was serious, strong, but with nursing eyes, staring right back at me. As my spine shivered, I could almost swear that I heard him say that he would always be with me, words so important for a young girl to hear, a girl who had spent her life until then passed around, a clump of loose river reed floating with the current.

א

"You feel him now?" says Zadok to me now as he shifts on his stool.

"There have been lapses. Since Ariah's death . . . until I was inside the Temple. When I stared at the purple and blue curtain, such a thin space separating me from him. Suddenly, it was old times."

"I think it was right after the dedication that Solomon brought you to me."

"He wanted me to learn from you. He thought what most of us thought, that Talus only believed in the Phoenician pantheon, if that."

"What would *The Chronicles* have turned out to be had you been a student of the Cult of Talus? Maybe Moses would have delivered us from Pharaoh with argument and poetry alone, or maybe he would have received help from the outstretched arm of the Phoenician god of war—what's his name?" Zadok's pupils corner up, trying to retrieve.

"Her name. Anath. She's also their goddess of love."

"Right, Anath, goddess of war and love. War and love: two labels, seemingly opposite, but that share the same struggle, don't you think? In both are centers of power, dominance, and submissiveness."

He chuckles over his own observation.

"The weaker party, the vassal," I add.

Zadok snorts, just a little. "Well, at least we saved you from Talus' deviation."

I let the incense fill my nostrils, while the burn and crackle of frankincense warms me. "Did I tell you back then I wanted to be a priest?"

"Did you?"

"I would spend hours watching the sacrifices." I close my eyes and see it in my mind like I'm back on the palace roof. A farmer cutting his animal's neck, giving the dying beast to the priest, who in turn would pour its blood around the brass, cutting it into pieces, placing the fat on the mesh, burning the pledge, a portion to Yahweh, the remainder taken by the priest and the farmer.

"Keb, are you all right?"

"I'm sorry, I was just thinking."

"I wish everyone employed in Yahweh's service would feel what you felt." Zadok says. "For some, it is a way to tap the divine, for many though, it is just mere occupation."

"I remember you explaining to me the meaning of the sacrifice, how it's a way to have communion with Yahweh. Do you still believe that?"

Zadok looks away. "Of course."

"But there are the other reasons, maybe?"

To this, the old man pores over the floor of unfinished, craggy limestone.

After a few moments of the incense snapping, I continue. "Back then my dream was to wear the white linen ephod and the papyrus sandals, but I couldn't."

"No, you couldn't."

"Women aren't pure enough for the task. Why do you think that is?"

"Why are men too inferior and impure to bear children?" I let my guard down to appreciate the comment.

"Is that almost a smile?" Zadok asks. "I didn't think you had it in you."

א

As my thirteenth year couldn't be put off, the age in which I could be wed and the first year after the perfect number, my father ordered me to the Lament, a ritual that twelve-year old royal Jerusalem girls had to ordeal. After an inordinate amount of useless protesting, I finally relented to leave the palace for the four days on the Mount of Olives. There I would reflect on the close of my virginity and childhood, and ready myself to marriage and motherhood, the epitome of life's fulfillment. So, escorted by a several soldiers, a cook, and our chaperone, Athaliah, the wife of one of my father's advisors, we left the city gate. There were a little more than two dozen of us, a mix of some of my half sisters and daughters of my father's officials. During the procession, everyone was grouped in twos and threes, laughing and joking. Except me. I walked alone.

Soon after we arrived, Athaliah would disappear for lengths of time and there was much gossip that she was with the commander of the guard. So with a near absence of supervision, we girls pretty much had the run of the hilltop to ourselves. Although we were supposed to chant dirges, reflect on transforming from daughters to wives, discuss our womanly duties, our so-called lamenting was a joke. The girls used the time to play games, dance, talk about the boys at court. There were a few who practiced kissing with each other, and maybe some who practiced more than just kissing. What was most disturbing though were the guards, a decade or more older than us, there supposedly to be our protectors, eyeing us first fruits. My half sister Zeruiah, flirty and curious, and with one of the more developed bodies, went off with a man into the woods to apparently experience that womanly transformation firsthand.

Hodiah and Reuma, along with several other girls, were giggling in conversation, and I inched toward their circle.

"I don't think this will be Zeruiah's first, in fact, I think she could teach that soldier boy a thing or two," Hodiah said, causing the group to snicker.

Thinking back on this now, while I can't blame the girls' amusement, it shouldn't have been a source of fun. If the two under discussion were found out, the soldier would have to marry Zeruiah. If he refused, he would still pay a full bride price for ruining her. But if they were to keep the affair a secret, it could be the end for Zeruiah when she eventually married another. She could be stoned or burned if, on the morning after her wedding night, her bed sheets weren't colored red.

Hodiah noticed me. "Ah, Keb, come join our court. We need a singer to entertain us."

"Where's your lyre?" Reuma asked. "Zeruiah could use some romantic plucking." She then pantomimed two in coupling. The whole circle broke down. I even grinned.

"Romantic plucking or fucking?" Hodiah blurted out, causing even more howling. When that died down, she turned to me with mischief in the eye. "So, Keb, have you ever kissed?" It was so easy for Hodiah to maintain her power over both the group and me.

I just shook my head no and looked shyly away.

"Maybe we can find you a handsome soldier, and you can have a foursome with Zeruiah." More giggling. "Who among the guard is handsome enough for you?"

I shrugged, wondering how to escape her torture.

"The very tall one, with the dark complexion, might be burnt enough for her," Reuma offered. Then Reuma turned to me. "You can teach him how they do it in Africa. Must be the same as the way sheep go at it."

"Her behind is too thin I'm afraid to handle the pounding," Hodiah added.

Everyone in a fit of hysteria. How alone I was, well, with the exception of my old friend, the salty paste around my eyes, which had disappeared for some time but now had come rushing back to visit. I ran off into the woods sobbing, and after a long bout of feeling sorry for myself, I decided I would spend as much of the time alone as I could. So I ended up exploring the grounds, stumbling upon a half a dozen burial tombs, and a few shrines my father had set up to gods venerated by his wives—altars for deities such as Dagon, Chemosh, and Molech. Encountering the shrines, I wanted to pray to my god, but of course, I couldn't be in my special place, on the roof of the palace, facing the Temple.

And even after much wandering around, I realized that on this part of the hill the olive trees were too many and too thick to allow me an unobstructed glimpse of Yahweh's house. Then I remembered my juglet of oil and what Zadok told me about praying, that I could do it anywhere, and if I wanted to, I could use a standing stone. I poked around and found a nice square of limestone, set it on end, poured oil on it, consecrating it as Zadok had done similarly on my father's head years before I was born. The rock wasn't an idol, but it was a sign of the sacred, reminding me of the rectangular Temple, a means to prayer that our forefathers had used in ancient days. I closed my eyes and started chanting.

"What are you doing?"

I opened my lids and there was Hodiah with Reuma and three other girls.

"I am, I'm praying."

"Praying?"

"Praying to Yahweh, the god, the god of Abraham and Isaac."

"Isaaccchh!" Hodiah said, imitating my over-pronunciation and spitting. "Well, K-K-Keb, we don't want to disturb you." Then she broke out in a fit of laughter.

"I can't k-k-keep from, from, from swallowing my, my, my spit!" Reuma said as I started sobbing. Then they took turns spitting on me. I crawled into a fetal position to hide.

"Cry, cry, cry! Black olive pie!" Hodiah screamed with delight.

The others joined in, "Cry, cry, cry! Black olive pie!"

I picked myself up, running—at times sliding—down the hill, hurling through the grazing fields, through the gate, back up the thoroughfare. I just hid in the apartment and waited for Talus to come back from the library. He could read me as well as any papyrus. As I warmed myself under wool blankets, he made me a nice lamb dinner.

א

"Your father sent me to give you lessons on womanly arts," a tall lady said after I opened the door. I suppose the first lesson is that it is all right to knock unexpectedly outside an apartment startling its occupant. Not that I was ungrateful, at least it wasn't another summons to perform at court. I didn't mind having instruction on the topic; there was only so much you can learn about being a fit wife and mother from epic poetry.

She must have been in her mid twenties, had queen-like beauty and, unlike the ladies who plaited their hair, her braids didn't stop at the neck, but extended down to her waist. She had great poise, which seemed to come without any effort. I thought it impossible for her back to be anything but straight, because even if she tried to slump, the rest of the room would somehow readjust itself to make her appear as upright as an obelisk. I recognized her from court, but, like so many wives of my father's officials and courtiers, I had never spoken to her.

"I'm Galit, Berah's wife."

"Berah? The one in charge of the harem? But isn't he a . . ."

"A eunuch, yes, but eunuchs can marry," Galit said with a just a hint of irritation. She studied me up and down, and then right to left.

"Are you here because of what happened at the Lament?" I asked.

"What happened at the Lament?"

"An incident that must have brought you to me."

"Berah didn't tell me. He didn't tell me much as he was busy with his shekels."

Galit had to be an Israelite or perhaps had lived even further north as she pronounced "sh" as an "s," and, even I, a foreign born, could hear the difference. Talus, when he was tired, would sometimes do the same.

"How long will these lessons last?"

"As long as you need them. Show me your dressing room."

She sat me down at my dressing table so we could both look at my face in the mirror.

"You have nice eyes, but we should accent them."

"I always thought of them as soft."

"What do you mean, soft?"

"Plain."

"I disagree. I'll bring you some kohl, we can make a thin black line around the rim of your eyes, and maybe . . ."

"Maybe?"

"Red henna on your lids and below your brows. I'd also like to try a sliver of malachite right under your eyes. The black, red, and green will make them pop, and will be a nice contrast to your dark skin. Trust me. See, look at me, I have a little malachite on my lids and just a touch of yellow ochre on my cheeks. Only a few ladies at court are coloring their faces—"

"The kohl, they do it in Egypt. Both men and women. To protect against the Evil Eye. My Uncle Hori would sometimes put it on."

"Like Nebetah up on the throne with your father."

"She hates me," I said.

"But you're both African."

"She looks down on anyone south of Thebes."

"And anyone east of Egypt." We both grinned. "Well, nobody likes her. Anyway, face coloring is just starting to

114

catch on and you can be among the first. Do you have any jewelry?"

I opened my little cedar box and she sifted through it, all my old bracelets, my turquoise from Sinai. She picked up my gold ring, and she felt the small gap in it.

"What is this? It's a little too large for your fingers."

"When I was young, back home, I'd wear it in my nose."

"You don't wear it now?"

"No one does here. I want to fit in."

She studied my image in the metal and fingered my hair. "I disagree. Flaunt your exotic nature, men will love it. Use these bracelets too. With these loopy rings, and perhaps an anklet, pectoral, and the nose, it'll tie your ensemble together, create a unified whole. Plus, you're a little thin—"

"Thin as a sandal strap," I offered.

"The jewelry will change that." She rummaged through the pieces. "But they are made of different materials. These should look similar, to maintain a consistency of style."

"Except for earrings, none of the women wear much jewelry."

"Being a little unique is good. But we need to have it all match. Also we should think of perfume.

"I use myrrh, sometimes."

"You should mix it with balsam. A little of that between your breasts is all you need.

"What breasts?"

"You have enough and you'll fill out, you'll see. Anyway, I'll take you to the market tomorrow."

"Thanks for helping me. I suppose when the King, or your husband even, orders you to do something, you must do it."

"It's no hardship. In fact, I'm glad to. You're a kind of younger me, well, you're maybe a tad shyer and lack a little confidence. But I come from Megiddo, in the North. I'm not quite as exotic as you, but I'm no Judahite." She played more with my hair. "We outsiders have to stick together, right?" I could see her smile touch mine in the mirror.

How rare it is to have found a friend.

א

Outside the palace, Talus was escorting me to one of the annex rooms in the Temple's outer courtyard for my lesson with Zadok, complaining as usual.

"A Haranite trader delivered fifty cuneiform tablets, and the court poet this past week was quite prolific, he came up with a dozen new harp songs I have to catalogue. All of them on the glory of your national god, as if there were no other topics."

"What is it about Yahweh you dislike?" I asked.

"Apart from the attention, it's the same problem I have with my own gods. He's too much like us."

"I don't understand."

"How to explain?" He paused for a moment. "You have a story where, at the beginning of time, Yahweh walked with men in Paradise."

"We do—"

Talus shushed me as several dozen initiates of the cult, young teenage Levites studying to become priests, came up from behind us. We stood and let them pass. They were carrying their writing palettes for their Temple lessons, their satchels strapped on their shoulders, chuckling, staring at me.

"I hope for lunch my mother packed some black olive pie," one said snickering, and the group burst out in laughter. Then they ran off ahead to the Temple grounds.

When they were far enough away, Talus spoke softly. "Are you all right?"

"I'm used to it."

Talus had that look of his, that face wishing he could make the sting go away, but what could he do?

"You were talking about Yahweh," I said.

Talus hesitated, but I nodded for him to continue. "I recall Yahweh had some fight with the men in Paradise and he threw them out," he said.

"Yes, the songs and legends don't tell us why they fought, only that, after Yahweh commanded the men to leave Paradise, he felt sorry that he did so and, as a kind of peace offering, made the men warm clothes for the harsh, cold world outside and put the garments on them."

"Exactly. Yahweh first becomes angry and then feels sorry. Such human emotions. Gods should be all knowing and have the highest virtue, not simply be petty creatures like us, only more powerful. Can't you see when Yahweh's flustered, then has regret—not to mention his designing garments—he comes down to our level and it makes him less powerful and godlike, I think."

"Less godlike? I don't understand. Gods shouldn't have emotions? They should be cold and stoic? That sounds frightening for the gods not to care about us."

"Why should they?"

"They made us."

"So?"

"If they're not involved with us, why would they need us to make sacrifices? What would our life's purpose be?"

"Can't we have a purpose other than to be their playthings? Can't they just create us, go on their way, and leave us alone?"

"A creator indifferent to his creation? That's horrible, like asking a mother not care about her child. I don't want to talk about this anymore." We trudged up the steps in silence.

א

Galit was curling my frizzy hair. She would grab small sections, dousing each with beeswax, which she had rubbed in her palms. Then she would wrap each waxed section for just a moment around a hearth-heated bronze cylinder.

"Now soon, your father will marry you off. It's possible you'll be in love with your husband, and he with you, but most of us are not that lucky." She pulled down hard on one of my locks. "Yet you do have options."

"Options? What options?"

"You could take a lover."

"Really," I said, giggling. Then I thought of Pi. If I were married to him, I wouldn't need any.

"Just don't get caught. Now to attract a man, besides beauty and personality, there are a couple of stratagems. There's the direct approach. Just go up to your potential lover, maintaining eye contact at all times, and say, 'Lie with me.'"

"I want him to rest with me?"

She laughed. "Up in Megiddo, we say that to mean penetrate. No one says that down here, but men will know what you mean and it is softer and more disarming than to just come right out and say penetrate."

"Lie with me." I laughed, and Galit seemed a little annoyed that I wasn't taking her seriously, but then she smiled.

"Another stratagem is to make them long for it. Make them go insane craving your charms. You're going to make them see you as some precious jewel that they can never obtain. If they become preoccupied thinking of you, you become that much more desirable."

"I don't think I could make any man go mad for me."

"Not that hard. Hook them first, make a big entrance. Beginnings are always important. Then once you have their attention, you tease and toy, making them excited. But you make them wait before you do any kind of touching. Maybe weeks or, better yet, months. Then, when it's time for the physical, you just give them a kiss. Hmm." She played with my hair, moving it this way and that. "Just a kiss mind you—still delaying what they really want, keeping up obstacles, dangling your affection in their sights. All the time you find a way to withhold it. But then you finally give them their reward. And when you do, make them see you in a whole new light, like they never imagined you would be when they first laid eyes on you. This ending part is critical, probably more important than the beginning. But you want to be the one in control, not being controlled."

She finished with my hair, draping some curls on the left side, covering up an imperfect mole along with some wild freckles.

"What do you think?" Galit asked.

"It's sublime, I can't believe it's me." Still, my charcoal skin, black as papyrus ink, stared back, telling me that no matter what enhancements Galit made to my appearance, I was still a burnt face living far away from the blazing African sun.

Galit continued. "On the make-them-long-for-it stratagem, I heard of a story where a woman dragged out the courtship, going so far as secretly having her plain-looking sister marry her potential husband—"

"Truly?"

"Then the groom was forced to contract with her father for a second marriage with her. I think he was too drunk at the wedding to know whom he was marrying."

A grin flooded her face.

"That reminds me of a Babylonian text with—"

"You can read?" she asked, sounding troubled. And me, carelessly breaking my promise to Talus. I just stared into the mirror. "If you have made that horrible mistake," Galit said, "never let your husband or lover know."

אָ

"There's only eleven here, there should be twelve," Talus said after he finished his counting. He reexamined the tablets, reading a little of the cuneiform on each of the clay. "The penultimate's missing. Where were you reading them last?"

"In my sleeping room," I answered, now feeling bad that I failed to return something back to the library in less volume than when I removed it.

"Aren't sleeping rooms for sleeping?" Rolling his eyes, he started stowing the tablets on a shelf behind his desk. "Never mind, let's go find it."

We walked the long corridor, and I could sense a mix of things stirring in him. Besides writing poetry for a following of only me, what was it that kept him going? All these years I have meditated on that. He had no family, which was unheard of, no sons, which meant no source of pride, no legacy for the future. For with fathering no children, he was cheating his duty to thinly populated Judah. Then again, as a foreigner, did he even have such a duty? Perhaps he did and this would explain why several years later Yahweh took his life.

As we approached our apartment, Talus' face shifted about, I imagine checking to see if anyone was in earshot. No one was. So as Talus put his hand through the keyhole to unlock the apartment, a more forgiving voice tried for comfort. "It's not like anyone besides you or me would know it's missing; still the Gilgamesh collection should be complete."

"What's the missing tablet?" I asked.

"The one that contains the flood story. Tell me, after reading it, what did you think?"

"About the whole poem or their flood story?"

"Either."

I didn't respond, gathering my thoughts as I stepped inside, knowing that a lesson was about to begin.

"Well, we can discuss the flood," Talus said. "In our song, Yahweh destroys the world but saves, um . . ." He snapped his fingers, trying to recall.

"Noah," I said as I followed him to the upstairs steps.

"Noah, that's correct, but on the missing tablet Enlil, Deluge, and the other Babylonian gods cause a flood and save Utnapishtim and his wife. Why are there two different flood accounts?"

"There were two floods." I said, as he let me jump in front of him to climb the stairs.

"Maybe—"

"Yahweh destroys the world here and Enlil destroys the world over there.

"Or the Babylonians got it wrong."

"Why?" I asked, reaching the second floor. "You think they just stole our story?"

"Maybe, or we stole—"

"The Babylonians knew Yahweh was responsible for the destruction and they want to pretend it was their gods?"

"Alright, why not? Let's assume that. Now why would the Babylonians write it down the way they did?"

"We just agreed that they wanted to pretend that Enlil and their pantheon are more powerful than Yahweh, right?"

"If that's the case, there must be something behind them writing *this* story down in *this* particular way."

"Well, a flood did happen."

"Yes, of course a flood did happen. But why these details told in this way? I mean the Noah song is pretty short, a couple of verses: he gathers some animals, it rains, the rains stop. They all leave the ark. End of song. Applause and bread crusts from the court." We stood at the threshold of my room, yet Talus seemed not to care, wanting to explore the lesson. "But in the Babylonian tablet, there is quite a lot of detail. Gilgamesh searches for immortality with Enkidu, has lots of adventures, runs into Utnapishtim, who tells Gilgamesh about the flood that happened, that Utnapishtim and his wife were the lone survivors. There's a lot of attention given on how they built their boat, such as it having no rudder, that the boat lands on a mountaintop, Utnapishtim sends out birds, makes sacrifice to the gods, that Utnapishtim and his wife were granted immortality. Then Utnapishtim tells Gilgamesh about the plant in the ocean that, while it won't give him eternal life, will rejuvenate him, and our hero finds the watery weed. But Gilgamesh falls asleep before he can eat it, and the snake takes it. That's the Babylonian flood story. It's pretty long. The Babylonians could have written the story down in some other way and not combine Gilgamesh's adventures with Utnapishtim's. Why not keep it short and tidy like the Noah song?"

I shrugged. "Your point is?"

"To show not only that there was a flood, but also to teach a lesson to the Babylonian subjects that searching for immortality for yourself is a waste of time. But you can find eternity in your city, Uruk, which will go on forever." I followed Talus into my sleeping room. "Where did you say you read it last?"

"Over there, by the bed."

"A story needs to have some sort of purpose. Now, as an exercise, if you were a scribe sitting in a Babylonian ziggurat, and you wanted to expand on some ancient story of your choosing, what lesson would you want to write about? Remember, all stories worth telling have to be about gods, or gods and men."

"Talus, you don't even believe in the gods."

"I believe in them. And I must have offended them because this is my eternal torture, searching for cuneiform under a child's bed."

"Why can't a story only be about men?" We both were on hands and knees.

"You have a point, why not? But we, the listener, always expect the gods to meddle in our affairs. Didn't you tell me that the world would be a lonely place if the gods didn't interfere?"

"I did."

"Anyway, it's expected and that's that. So, what's your story going to be? You like to recount stories, well, create something totally out of new wool. Say you're the gods, and you want to send a message to your people about something, what would your message be and what would you have your gods do about it?"

I thought for a moment. "I'd have all parents hug their children, and if they didn't, I guess I would just destroy the world," I said laughing.

"With no survivors?"

"Yes, everyone dies. I just remembered; I was reading it in the chamber closet." We both picked ourselves up and started for the room.

"You can't do that," he said.

"I can so. If I'm the gods, and if everyone got me angry."

"That story could never happen and everyone knows it. Even Ea saved Utnapishtim and his wife. In the Judahite flood song, Noah and his sons survive. If you just kill everyone and that's the end, it wouldn't make sense to anyone and no one would want to listen to it."

"They would 'cause I'm singing it!"

"No, there are conventions you need to follow, expectations that must be met. You need the story to be about gods, or gods and men, and if there are men in it, some must survive, because if they don't, it wouldn't make sense that their descendents would be around today to hear the tale. And there's got to be a point, some kind of lesson. And the men in the poem must be interesting ones or your poem won't be entertaining."

"Entertaining?"

"The whole thing comes down to a lesson camouflaged by distraction. It's like taking your labdanum with a lot of date honey."

"What about women?"

"What about them?"

"The story should have interesting women too, right?"

"Women? No. They're incidental. You just read Gilgamesh, what women are there? Enkidu's prostitute who shows up for a few lines and Utnapishtim's wife who barely receives a mention. Women in poems are there to act as foibles for the hero, or love interests, but that's it. They have tiny roles and then they leave the tablet."

"I don't understand, why can't you have interesting women?"

"Why? Your audience consists of men, and, more importantly, men who count. Oh, maybe there are women at court listening too, but they don't matter. What matters is the King. His elders. They would only want to hear about themselves."

"If there were interesting women, who sounded real, like—"

"Nonsense. We men just want to—ah, found it!" Talus said upon opening the closet door. The middle-aged librarian marveled at the clay square lying on the floor as if it were a plant about to bring him eternal life.

א

My tutor on the feminine and I were grinding grain to flour. I had milled several times before, and there wasn't anything new I could learn, but it was fun doing this with my new big sister, as I started to call her. Galit had decided to give me all her cooking expertise, skills that were atrophying ever since her arrival in Jerusalem, skills which she now left to her servants and the palace cooks. That and a little dressmaking were about the limits of her domestic abilities. If I wanted to learn shepherding, harvesting, or the thrashing arts, I would have to find it elsewhere.

"Now, once you have a husband, it's important to know how to keep a conversation going. Men love to talk about their work, so ask questions about that. You tell stories. I heard a few of yours at court."

"My father . . ." I trailed off.

"I know. Anyway, it's good that you can tell tales; men also love to be entertained. I can tell a couple. You know what I like to do before I give the story the big twist at the end?"

"What?"

She just smiled.

"What?" I asked again.

"See, I'm teasing you. Pausing or even saying nothing is good. Keeps their interest. When you pause, they want to know what's going to follow. Now there's also adult playing."

"What do you mean?"

"Pretend to be something you're not. Men love to see another kind of woman in you, and maybe another kind of man in them."

"Pretend I'm not me?"

"You could dress up like a harlot. Veil up your face, just leave the eyes showing. I did that—I mean, I heard someone did that with her husband." Galit said, grinning. "Even went to a well outside of the city where prostitutes gather and pretended to be one. He was in on it so he pretended to proposition her there, played a shepherd and gave her a sheep for a chance to know her—"

There was hurried banging at the door. A soldier. It had to be another summons. What song would the King force me to practice and then have me decimate in public as if it were a burnt offering? Up until a year ago, when I was called, it was just for lap-sitting sessions, which I actually enjoyed, except for the accompanying jealous eyes and malicious whispers. But now I had to perform in front of the entire congregation. Sometimes he would make me retell over and over portions of my Sheba-to-Jerusalem adventure, but lately it was to sing, harp and lyre. For my life I couldn't understand why. The Yubal Guild's pipe and harp players were so much better.

"The king wants you there for tomorrow's evening banquet," the soldier said while having a hard time keeping his eyes focused on me and not Galit, still grinding at the hand mill. Galit, for her part, wasn't helping, offering him an enticing smile.

"And?" I asked.

"And what?"

"Well, what song does he want me to perform?"

"I know of no song."

The guard bowed and left. As I returned to Galit, I dwelled on tomorrow's retelling, and whether, for the fun of it, I should give the Nile a sixth cataract.

CHAPTER SIX

"Ah, Keb, come here," my father shouted as I entered through the banquet hall, his words spearing unimpeded through the air's thick odors of cooked gazelle, roebuck and fatted geese. As I stepped up to the platform, Solomon presented me with a white linen dress. On it was a pattern of little purple lions, set inside vertical gold stripes, matching my father's robe. While the fabric must have been expensive, what must have really set Solomon back was the purple dye. I learned from Galit that the color was highly sought by the affluent as it could only be found in Phoenicia. While Judahite nobles felt a purse pinch from Tyrian traders when haggling for the item, to them it was worth it, as their oxen and cattle were not always visible to the world. Now the dye—that was a statement for all to see.

Along with the dress, Solomon also gave me my lion amulet, which I've always worn to this day. Again, I had to ask myself: why? Why did he single me out from all my siblings, lavish such attention, even in lieu of my older brothers in line for the throne? It seemed so arbitrary, to be chosen and handpicked.

How could a burnt-face like me deserve it? I didn't know the answer then, but I soon would.

"For your birthday," he said. My thirteenth had actually passed more than two months ago, but I found no need to correct. "I want you to go to your room, put it on, and hurry back."

I did, but I stole a few moments to peek into the mirror. It was quite the finest fabric I had ever donned, and for a moment, I was back in Sheba, in my ivory dress being scrutinized by my aunt—at an age where I learned all of jealousy's awful pangs, of a time when pernicious sisters would show off their gold bracelets. But this now was a different kind of awkwardness, trying to accept that I should somehow be worthy above others to be ensconced in the softest of material.

"We are giving Keb these fine presents because she is loving, inquisitive, generous, giving, hard working," Solomon said to his courtiers, but eyeing me as I goated back into the hall. "All these traits, we so do admire. Never once does she carp or complain that her burden is too heavy." He lifted his face from me, staring at a section of the court where stood several elders and officials, who I think were from the Northern tribes, and his smile blotted out. "Neither is she lazy. There are some in the realm who are too lazy to put food in their mouths. Those who pull their weight will find themselves in the finest of linen, those who don't will wear the slave's loincloth." He turned back to me, his warmth returning. "Please, Keb, walk around. Let everyone see you in your present."

As I paraded, no divine magic was necessary to turn the court into a cobra nest. All the little lions on my dress too changing into seething eyes. Everyone was livid—except for Solomon and Galit. She gave me an encouraging smile, but that faded into seriousness. We talked about this afterwards. At the time she was thinking about where in the city we were going to find matching purple lip dye.

אַ

I was summoned to court the next day, still not asked to sing, but required to wear the dress. I was hoping that the newness of my gift would become dulled, registering blank in my siblings' minds, that I would become an insignificant blur, like the tired palace frescoes or, better yet, the sycamores surrounding the city. But that was not to be. It was as before. Hissing and whispering. And their glares—sharp and dangerous as elan horns.

My father spotted me and waved me over. As Nebetah was absent, I was allowed to sit in her chair by my father on the dais. While I got myself as comfortable as I could on that large and ornate seat, Ahishar rushed up to the King with the court recorder, who was carrying a blank scroll, his writing board, and an inkwell.

"Jehohaphat is up here why?" Solomon asked, his eyes coveting an attractive teenage wife of a new courtier.

"Sire, we have a legal dispute that—"

"Legal dispute?" he asked. "Why aren't the tribal or city elders handling the matter?"

"Because of the two involved. They're not from a single tribe. One is from Dan, the other—"

"Is Levite, I suppose?"

"Most correct, Sire." Solomon chortled as if pleased with his own intuition. "Plus, you're always asking us to keep an eye out for interesting cases—"

"And this is about?"

"A question of ownership. We have two prostitutes claiming the same child."

Ahishar motioned the women before the King to plead their case.

"Nissah is mine, isn't he beautiful," one of them said, cradling the baby.

"This the Levite or the Danite?" Solomon asked his Master of the Palace.

"That would be the Levite."

Solomon just looked impatiently at the two. "I'm not going to wait forever, one of you start."

The Danite cleared her throat. "Your Majesty, we both live in the same house. I gave birth to the boy. His name is Ishbaal, by the way. Larel here gave birth to her child a week after mine, but killed it in the night by carelessly rolling on top of him in bed. She's such an imbecile. But she stole this one from me and laid her dead baby by my side thinking when I woke up, I wouldn't recognize my own."

Sitting cross-legged, with his board across his lap, Jehohaphat wrote it all down quickly on his papyrus, seemingly getting it all in a kind of shorthand that looked foreign. I remember thinking I should ask Talus about this script.

Solomon turned back to the Levite. "Say you, this true? Or is your account different?"

"Nissah's mine." The Levite said, keeping her eyes on the sleeping infant.

After waiting a few moments and hearing nothing more from the second prostitute, he turned to me. "You heard these women, as a teller of tales, what do you think?" Pulled away from studying the recorder's writing, I tried to find something—anything—intelligible out of my mouth. It was almost cruel the way he would elevate importance on me.

"I, I—"

"Don't worry, we just want your opinion. We'll make the verdict."

"I am, I'm unsure. The first, the Danite, well, she tells a very factual account. The details, they make it believable. But she seems a little cold and matter of fact about it all, the other, the other cares so much."

"So you think the Levite is the mother?"

"No, My Lord. I am at a loss."

"Pose questions then."

"You want me to, to examine them?"

"Proceed."

My mind scrambled, as if I were halfway down the hill and only given a minute to reassemble a once beautiful urn from every broken shard littering the thoroughfare.

"Umm, woman from Dan, why, why did you name your son Ishbaal?"

"My grandfather's name. It is tradition among my tribe to name a child after a grandfather."

"You, Levite, why Nissah?"

"Because I thought the name beautiful."

"Do either of you have any witnesses to support your account?"

"A tanner named Abijel, I'm sure is the father," the Danite said. "Apart from him, I found no work when I was pregnant. The baby has his eyes."

"Where is this Abijel, can he be produced?"

"He died a few weeks ago. But before, when I showed him Ishbaal, he said, 'That's my child.'"

"You, Levite, any witness for you?"

She shook her head and just rocked the baby.

"Uh huh," I said.

"What do you think?" my king asked me.

"I would like to have the supposed father here to confirm."

"How's your witchcraft?" He asked, smirking.

I just shrugged, finding the lightness of the remark wanting humor.

"When Abijel allegedly said, 'That's my child,' did he raise his voice on *child,* and form a query or did he leave it flat and make a statement?" Solomon asked.

"That is a problem with retelling." I couldn't think of any other questions to ask and tugged my hair. "My Lord, I honestly don't know who the mother is."

The baby started crying.

"Then what should be done?" He asked as if he had buried the answer in the sand long before I was born and was now waiting for me to dig it up.

I shrugged. Over the baby's sobs, I heard them snickering now, enjoying my defeat. I glanced at the assembly. Hodiah and Reuma couldn't have on big enough grins.

"We must do something." Solomon looked to the source of the escalating noise. "Calm him." He directed his attention back on me, waiting.

"I suppose you could cast a die," I finally said.

"Then one would be happy and one would not, and we'd be no closer to finding who the real mother is." He glared at the screaming newborn and the women. "Can someone stop that clamor? It's causing my head to throb." He turned back at me, his face a disappointment. "Have you no suggestion?"

I shrugged. *I'm displeasing him so. I know it.*

"If only we had access to sorcery that could satisfy both," he said, and then lowered his voice for only me to hear, "and somehow give them"—he paused—"each . . ."

"What?" I asked. "A baby for each?"

"Louder. No one heard you over the wailing."

"A baby for each?" I bellowed, trying to carry my voice over the infant's.

My father stared at some distant point and then journeyed back. "Why not?" He stood up, turned to the Ahishar, "Fetch my sword!" Solomon loosened up his right arm, moving it in circles.

The court erupted, causing the baby to double his racket.

"Your Majesty!" I said.

Solomon nodded to Ahishar while holding my wrist sternly, as if to say, *I heard you.* Voices from the main hall crescendoed. I had never seen the court this alive and insubordinate.

"At least I'll put an end to that gods' awful noise," Solomon shouted, his eyes on the hapless victim, still circling his arm.

"I beg you, don't do this thing!" said the Levite, her face awash in water.

"Silence!" shouted Ahishar to the assembly.

The courtiers complied and, with the exception of the baby and the now sobbing Levite, there was calm. After a few minutes, an attendant brought my father a gold saber with embedded rubies and diamonds. Solomon eyed it up and down and then slowly grasped the handle, as if this were the first time he handled the weapon or any weapon—I'm surprised he even knew where the handle was. As my father slowly, but gracefully, lifted the sword, I thought his arm might tremble. But it didn't, not the slightest twitch or jerk, not the slightest hesitation.

The Levite shielded her body over the fussing baby and looked up at the King. "Your Highness, please, I beg you! Give her the child! Give it to her. Please, please, please! If you need to take a life, take mine, not my Nissah!" the Levite screamed, sobbing.

I pictured my mother in a similar scene with her husband as he delivered the news that I would be exiled. Or was it more likely she just accepted that knowledge with the Danite's calm indifference?

My father exposed just the slightest hint of a smirk, lowered the sword, and gave the blade back to the Ahishar. "The mother of the child is this pleading Levite. Let her keep the boy."

"Thank you, My Liege, thank you," the mother said through her tears.

"So you're assuming—" I started to say.

"No one can hear you, speak up." My father interrupted, in a booming voice for all to hear. "You keep writing," he said looking down to Jehohaphat.

"You're assuming that only the true mother—that she would rather give up the child than to see it harmed?" I asked, trying to raise my volume to meet my father's.

"Exactly."

"My Lord, your premise is based on the assumption that only the true mother loves the child. What if the true mother didn't love her?"

"Assumptions, premises. I have to commend Talus. Anyway, clarify."

"What if the Danite were the true mother? It could be possible she doesn't love her baby, saw it as something of an inconvenience. I just don't think that in all cases love for a child is a given."

"Well, even if so, the Levite woman who pleaded for us to save the infant *should* be the mother, even if she wasn't the natural one. Love is better than blood, don't you agree?"

"What, what would you have done if neither woman begged you to stop? Would you have, would you have cut it?" I picture my father following through with his sword, veins and arteries gushing, sinew all over the dais, the women screaming, most of us wincing save for a few in the hall who couldn't thirst for enough blood.

The King simply grinned, then shouted to his cupbearer. "More pomegranate wine!"

From my vantage point high up on the dais, I couldn't believe what my eyes, the pathway to my heart, revealed. At first I thought it was my imagination, but it wasn't. As Ahishar showed the women the door, they were both nodding happily as he handed them something metallic. I'm almost positive it was silver.

And the baby, that was now nowhere to be seen.

I looked back at Solomon, falling into the abyss of his stare. I knew what had just happened. And he knew I knew.

On our adjoining armrests, I was unsure whether it was intentional or not, but his pinky stroked mine just a little.

אָ

I wrestled with the case of the prostitutes for some time, questioning how genuine my father was, obsessing on how he had used me with those two women who could have very well have been performers from the Guild. Then there was that time before when my father forced me to show off the linen dress. How with both situations I was a mere prop. I began having crippling thoughts that these weren't just aberrations, there must have been dozens of instances where I served as a vehicle for some ulterior purpose. Still, why me for all this?

A few weeks after the trial, I was in the library, and I stumbled upon the scroll of *The Annals of King Solomon*, a just completed poem by the Chief Scribe. The text was given to Talus to house until copies could be made and heralded throughout the Kingdoms (writings, like gods, can traverse both space and time). In *The Annals*, I read how, early in his reign, my gentle father had my Uncle Adonijah killed based solely on my grandmother Bathsheba's hearsay that Adonijah wanted to marry one of Solomon's concubines. If this were so, I could see how Solomon might take it as a threat—after all, Uncle Absalom started the Civil War with his father, David, by penetrating several of his. While the allegations of Adonijah's treason may have rung true, it seemed to me that they were fabricated based on two facts. First, the poem suggested that my uncle wasn't even given a chance to plead a defense before his execution. Second, Adonijah's days appeared numbered in any event from what happened years before during my father's accession. When David lay dying, my hapless uncle declared himself the new king, having the support of David's old guard. But a palace coup changed that, installing Solomon as monarch. (Lucky for Zadok, David's Priest at the time, he had chosen the right side.) My father let my uncle live, until the purported concubine incident. Killing Adonijah put an end to a former and a potential usurper.

But then, according to *The Annals*, my father executed all his remaining older brothers: Shammua, Shobab, and Nathan, also on similar-sounding charges. Were they trumped up? And a few of his younger brothers too. Each month would bring a new execution for treason. I suppose killing off your family is the price a king has to pay to secure his throne. Maybe that counts as wisdom. But it also makes you a monster.

For the next couple of months, every time the knock came, I would tell the soldier I was too ill to appear at court. I couldn't see my father, the thought made my stomach sour, which in a way turned my lie into truth. Sometimes I would stare at myself in the bronze, wondering how I could be the half product of such poison. Deep down, was I like him? If given a chance to succeed my mother, would I have had my sister Irty killed on some bogus grounds?

Searching for distraction, it was at this time I began my feeble attempts at writing poetry. In my first stab at it, I merged Pi with the Egyptian priest I had met. This new character grew up at the court of Pharaoh and, similar to my bowman's grandfather, was a foreigner who rose in the ranks until he eventually reached the high office of vizier. He saved his country from a great famine and a young woman from her cursed loneliness. I set my work aside for a couple months. When I picked it up later, I couldn't believe such dung came from my reed. The strained, awkward phrasing, the imperfect rhyming, the confusing thoughts, the unnatural dialogue—I burned it all.

א

Pounding at the door. The day before I had turned down the King's summons by once again feigning an illness. He had usually waited at least a week's interval to allow me to recover before the next attempt. So why the knocking? Had he now grown even more impatient? If not a summons, then what? Galit had no appointment, so who? Maybe Talus forgot his key again. I frantically hid my reed and papyrus in Talus' room as a precaution, and answered the door, half expecting a palace soldier. But it was no soldier.

"Your Majesty."

"I hear you are unwell." This was alarming; he had never come to the apartment before. And with no guard or servants accompanying him. Why was he here? Had he found a suitable husband, wanting to deliver the news personally?

"I am, I'm on the mend, please come in. Can I offer you some wine or honey water?"

"Wine." That made sense as his mouth smelled of it. He came into the central room as I went to get him his drink. "We haven't seen you in some time, what's wrong?"

"Probably a demon," I said, handing him a goblet. "I'm sorry I haven't been at court. Have I missed much entertainment?"

"Does Zadok know? I'll have him send over a priest to attend to you and have the old man himself say some prayers and make offerings."

"Thank you, but I think I'm recovering."

Looking around in each direction, Solomon was a cipher. "I thought the apartment larger. Maybe it's time you had your own quarters."

"Thank you, Sire, but I'm fine. This, this suits me."

"No, you should have your own place and servants. I think you would like that."

"I don't know how Talus would get by without me, but if that pleases Your Majesty." Now I was confused. If I were to be betrothed, then there would be no need for my own quarters, as I could simply stay put here until the wedding. Maybe I was to stay a maid a little while longer.

"Talus will be fine." He downed some of his wine and just gave me a most unsettling stare. "Come sit with Your Lord." As we plopped down, it was clear that he noticed the corner mat, and the harp standing there, along with an open scroll with lyrics and notations. Gods! How stupid I was to forget to hide that papyrus. He had to have known I could read, but said nothing.

Then his eyes gored into me for a few more moments. He took out a palm-sized box. "Here, maybe this will cure your sickness."

Golden earrings. Each braided metal chain held a small Judah lion, the animal standing on its hind legs, with its front paws up, striking the air.

"Quite the remedy, don't you agree?" he said.

"They're spectacular. Thank you. Should I put them on?"

"You know, you look just like your mother. More each day."

"Thank you, Sire. Um, what was she like? I never met her."

"She was my favorite. Had your dark eyes. Yes, they're bewitching."

He reached over, kissing me on the mouth. I recoiled.

"Please, Sire, don't, don't do this, I beg you."

He forced lips on me again. I pushed back, my cheeks sodden. *Yahweh, please stop him. Please!*

"Sire, please, I don't want to end up unsuitable for marriage."

I looked at his features, his obsessed, black eyes, throbbing veins, that horrible stinking mouth, everything distorted and gross. Possessed, he must be—taken over by the most demonic magic.

"Now who would want to take you as a wife?"

I kept trying to break free from his weight. But his arms kept gripping me, his body smothering. I turned my head, giving him my wet cheek, letting my cheek become my shield.

Yahweh, please come to my rescue, please! If you do, I will never desert you.

His hands, large now, found my head, held it in place. Solomon rammed those horrid, wine-smelling lips on me a third time.

"Please, please, I beg you," I screamed, both to Solomon and to Yahweh.

I tried for escape, but there was none—my father was too strong, holding my thin arms back, pinning me, breaking those thin arms if he wanted to.

The door creaked open.

Talus. It was Talus. Thank you, Yahweh, thank you.

CHAPTER SEVEN

Except for his appearances at the feasts, that was the last time I saw Solomon until he lay dying the night of my Temple trespass. I stopped coming to court and there were no more summonses. I suppose, had he wished, he could have had his way with me, putting me in the harem, doing unspeakable things. Or exiling me to some remote, illiterate town in the hill country, or sending me back to Sheba where my mother had wanted nothing of me. Or had his pleasure only to then toss me out of the palace, leaving me to either beg in the streets or prostitute for my life's remainder. But none of that had happened. He simply backed off when Talus barged in.

After the incident, the King left me alone to my clay and papyrus. Perhaps he wasn't a complete leviathan and had some human parts. When I look back on that horrid day, I knew wine was involved, and he might have easily been under the spell of the demon Azazel. Funny that after all these years I've become such an apologist. Am I wrong to forgive? Have I become too soft? Maybe like the prostitutes' baby, I can split the man—yes, there's that lecherous monster, but there's the other one who, at the time I was a young girl, alone and without companions, showed me kindness and something close to love.

I turned fourteen, then fifteen, sixteen, seventeen. Through those teenage years, my life consisted of Talus' apartment and the library. Once in a while I would venture with Galit to the market. Or make my way to the palace roof to gaze out at Yahweh's house to pray, often distracted by the wedding processions parading up and down the hill. Hodiah and Reuma and all my siblings I grew up with, every one of them were starting families. But not me. I remembered My Liege's words. *Who would want to take you as a wife?* Who would? I felt, at times, incredibly lonely. It made me think that Yahweh must have created the world if only to cure his own wretched loneliness.

א

"His name is Raddai," my father's advisor Jabesh said. Jabesh was a tall man who was easy to like, terminally optimistic, with arms that were long, expressive, and welcoming, like the golden walls of a fabled city. "He's twenty-three. He and his family live in Lachish. Let's see, what else? He's a scribe, his father scribes for the city elders. He's a distant cousin to His Majesty. His family traces their lineage to Obed."

"Have you seen him?" I asked, jumping up and down. "What does he look like?"

He beamed, contracting whatever joyous plague I was inflicted with. "I've heard reports that he's a fine young man. That's all I know, Keb."

"So, I'll be sent to Lachish?"

"Only for the wedding. Afterwards, you're to return to Jerusalem. For dowry, we are to find you and Raddai a suitable house here. Your new lord and master will be a junior scribe for the Temple. That is, if you want to marry him."

"I don't understand. My father is giving me a choice?"

"The King is most benevolent. You don't have to donkey to Lachish and drink the wine if you don't want to. It's completely up to you. Well, Keb, what's your answer?"

"How does one ride a donkey?"

A fine young man. Jabesh's announcement made that day one of my happiest. Not that my life was pure misery up until then. I had lived in a comfortable place surrounded by great scrolls and tablets from all the world. I could read and write, something few could admit to. I had Talus and Galit, and Yahweh of course. I didn't have to glean in the fields, beg for money, hide my leprosy in filthy rags. Yet grinded into me since the day I got here was my duty to bear sons. How I wanted a son, or even a daughter. A little boy or girl I could be there for, to love and to teach. And by being a good mother I would right every wrong done to me and all the omissions made in my own upbringing. Immediately, I started working on possible names for my child. Naming is the responsibility of the mother. A powerful act, only a fool or simpleton would undertake it lightly. Your child's character, his future, his very essence, all is affected by the name you choose. It's magic of the strongest kind.

I would travel southwest on the highway to Lachish, accompanied by two soldiers my father sent to protect me, and Jabesh to administer the contract, collect the bride-price, and transact other business with the city elders on my father's behalf. Also going were Talus and Galit, the two who cared for me most. As we assembled up our little caravan in the pre-dawn darkness, I became anxious leaving behind the safe and the knowing, from the tablet I had read, to the roof I had prayed on, to the apartment I had turned into a womb. Yet soon after I left the gate, the past dimmed. For how thrilling it was to experience the fresh, clean air of the hills, the shepherdess waving to us from the mount, the roll of the landscape, terrain often barren and harsh, but yielding the occasional barley farm and olive grove, all leading like an arrow to my life's culmination of becoming wife and mother.

At midday, with the heat beating down on us and my crotch sore from the ride, my stomach let me know it was empty. Fortunately, Jabesh was hungry too. "Let's rest at that well over there," Jabesh said, pointing. Then he guided my donkey off the road, as did one of the soldiers for Galit, both who had been trading looks since we started.

"How much is Keb worth?" Talus asked Jabesh.

"You talking bride price?" Jabesh responded as he helped me down. "That's really a matter between the groom's family and the King," Jabesh and I exchanged glances. "Raddai's father will forfeit his servant to Keb's new lord, and will give Keb some jewelry and the King a hundred and twenty shekels."

We neared the well, where a young man was attending to his flocks. "You there," Jabesh said to the shepherd, "we'll need water and so will our donkeys."

The young man grabbed our skins and went to work, either out of village hospitality or in fear of the soldiers' hammered iron. While under the shade of an oak, we sat eating bread and onions, and drinking cold well water. At the roadside keeping an eye out, the soldiers ate and joked by themselves, seemingly uninterested in the doings of our quartet.

"Narrate something for us, Keb," Jabesh said. "It's been years since we were privileged to your stories."

"Stories? You must have heard them all. But I can repeat, if that's what you want. I think my tales of my boat trip down the Nile have lost their freshness. Talus has some nice poetry."

"You know I can't sing." Talus said.

"I can sing it for you," I said, patting his hand.

"There's no need," Jabesh said, waving me off before I could even start. "I'm in no mood for music. Our ears will be filled with it soon enough when we get to Lachish."

"You could make something up," Galit said to me. "Could be good practice."

"Practice?" asked Talus. "Practice for what?"

"Something between us women," she said, smiling.

"Make something up? Right now?" I looked at them all, their faces collectively waiting for entertainment. I gave it some thought, shutting my eyes, but nothing came. "Sorry, I'm a blank. Apologies."

"You're going to give up that easily?" Talus asked. "How about something for the occasion, like a wedding story?"

"A wedding story? No, I don't think so."

"Try," Galit said, with her slight smile and wide dark browns egging me on.

Thinking of my own situation of leaving Jerusalem, my home, for this new city of Lachish, I had a flash of two of the patriarchs—of Abraham, who traveled from the land between the rivers to come here, and Isaac, who never left Canaan. Recalling the harp song that mentioned their wives, but not a grain of their lives, I came up with an idea, a fuzzy one, hoping it would clear with the telling.

"Alright, a wedding story," I said over the bleating of the shepherd's goats. "Abraham was in a bind. He didn't want his son Isaac to marry a local Canaanite girl, yet he didn't want Isaac to leave Canaan to find a wife elsewhere, which would have put in jeopardy Yahweh's plan of giving Abraham this land for his descendants. But Abraham came up with a solution. He sent one of his servants to Aram, the country of his former tribe, to find a suitable girl." Pausing briefly to come up with the next leg of the story, my gaze fell on our three donkeys chewing the grass. "The servant took ten camels, packed with gifts, to his master's ancestral home, and when he arrived, he prayed to his master's god, Yahweh." My eyes landed on the well where our shepherd friend went back to watering his herd. "Realizing he had stopped at a watering hole, the servant said, 'Yahweh, make something happen in front of me. Let the first girl who arrives and offers to water my camels be the one.' Then even before he finished speaking, there was Rebekah, Abraham's great-niece and a beautiful virgin. After the servant asked her for some water, she not only complied with his request, but at a dizzying pace she ran back and forth from the well, drawing water for his animals."

Thinking about what should come next, I scratched my upper lip and felt my ring. "Knowing that Yahweh had fulfilled his request, the servant gave the young woman arm bracelets and a nose ring. She ran back to her mother's house, and when her brother,"—I searched for a name—"Laban, saw her dressed in her new jewelry, he ran back to the spring, inviting the slave back to their house. The servant presented gifts to the girl's brother and mother, asking the two if Isaac could take the girl for his wife. They in turn asked Rebekah if she was willing to go with this man and she said, 'I will go.'"

I stared at the donkey packed with everyone's belongings, including the veil I would have to wear before entering Raddai's city. It's funny that that article of clothing meant one thing for Jerusalem's prostitutes and another for Lachish's betrothed. "When Rebekah arrived back at Isaac's camp in the Negev, she veiled herself, and Isaac brought her to his deceased mother's tent. She became his wife and he loved her. That's it, that's my impromptu wedding story."

My audience beamed, throwing pieces of their bread at me. Looking back, my story was rather short and not one of my best, and I know my friends were being polite. Nevertheless, I did relish the moment.

"Well done," Jabesh said. "Thank you."

"Can I add something to it?" Galit asked.

"Sure, and if anyone else wants to embellish my tale, please go right ahead."

"When the servant brought Rebekah to meet Isaac in his camp, her future master was out urinating in the field," Galit said, holding back a grin. "When she looked at his member and saw its size, she slid off her camel."

Everyone laughed and threw morsels at her.

"Galit, what caused her to fall exactly?" asked Jabesh. "Was the size too big or too small?"

The eunuch's wife just smiled, and the rest of us howled.

The four of us eating and laughing under the oak. Sometimes I feel I could almost relive that moment, not just to simply recall the blur of memory, but to actually resurrect it, seeing my friends as clear as I'm seeing Zadok now, tasting what I had tasted then, the bitter crunch of onions while dousing in the shady sun. When I would plunge into melancholy later in life, I would at times compare that happy afternoon at the well to my current misery, becoming even more despondent, finding the chasm between the past and present too big to scale.

I would reuse the Rebekah story, of course, in *The Chronicles*, including a slightly tamer version of Galit's addition. But none of my audience that day would be alive to listen to it a second time when the priests read my scroll at the Feast. Galit and her soldier guide would be stoned for adultery soon after our return from Lachish. Talus and Jabesh would

die in the plague that wiped out a fifth of Jerusalem's population six years later.

א

As the sun lay with the horizon, we arrived at the fortified city
high up in the hills. Lachish was one of the most important
strongholds in the realm, manned by soldiers whose job it was to
protect the Kingdoms from Edomites, Egyptians, Philistines, or
anyone else toying with idea of invading us from the south.
Before we entered the massive outer gate above the glacis, I lay-
ered on my additional wedding clothes, hiding my dark skin like
a leper, leaving only the browns and whites of my eyes for the
world to see.

After the guards allowed us inside the walls, by torchlight
and with Galit and I still on our donkeys, we proceeded to the
house of the groom's father, Obadiah, by a narrow, winding road
lined by Obadiah's many cheering friends and family. The
women celebrants, just like their Jerusalem counterparts, performed their traditional singing, dancing, and tambourine
playing. Now feeling awkward to be the subject of such lavish
attention, I escaped their gaze, looking up, focusing on the lit
temple at the city center, hoping the god or gods of Lachish
would, if not grant us favor, at least not cause us any harm. But
whether or not the deities had any interest at all between the
aspirations of two ordinary people about to become man and
wife, Jabesh did what he could, borrowing one of the soldier's
swords, using it to slash the air in front of me to ward off any
evil spirits.

At the door, the family greeted us: Obadiah, then his two
older sons, standing with their wives, followed by Obadiah's
young daughter. Obadiah's wife was not there to bless me, for

she had died in childbirth when delivering the girl. At the end of the line stood Raddai. He was a little taller than average and lanky, a curly dark brown mop of hair, his beard well trimmed, his ears pointed outwards—perhaps his weakest feature. His shirt had an olive-colored tassel hanging down from the bottom edge, emphasizing his privates. These linen chords had become fashionable at court for several years now, and the prevailing trend was the longer the better. But Raddai's was bordering on modest, as if his dress couldn't make up its mind on whether to be conservative or current. All in all, he was handsome and when he smiled, he seemed genuinely happy that the shy girl waiting under the robes and scarves would soon be part of his life.

Because I had no opportunity earlier to purify, they rushed me to the bath where I soaked myself with frankincense and myrrh. When I was done, a woman attendant anointed me with oil. I threw my linen back on. I was ready.

Back in the main room, I sat down to the wine that was waiting for us.

Raddai lifted up his goblet, declaring to the slits in my veil, "I take Keb as my wife, and I am her husband from this day forward." He drank it all and then looked to me to follow his lead, as did everyone. If I had wanted to, I suppose, I could have backed out by not touching my cup. But such a thing was never done, not when the betrothed had gotten this far. Every eye was on me.

I drank it all and quickly.

"Congratulations!" Jabesh shouted with the house erupting in ululating cries. Raddai took my quivering hand, led me to his room upstairs, and shut the door.

CHAPTER EIGHT

"Are you nervous?" he asked as he sat on his bed, "I am a little myself."

"A little." I just stood, my back merging with the wall, trying to ignore the shouts and music coming from below. "Maybe more than a little."

"You must be hot with all you have on. Do you want to take some off?"

I just continued standing, an unmoving block of stone, waiting to be chiseled.

"Do you want some wine or food? The room is well-stocked, and if you need anything else, you can just knock. My friends Jessie and Jehoiadah, who are taking turns outside, they can bring you something."

"I'm fine, thank you. I'm fine."

He paused; I suppose he was trying to figure the words to put me at ease, as every utterance a man makes is an act of manipulation. "Hmm, you are the King's daughter. Is he as wise as everyone says he is?"

"He has his moments."

Raddai came up to me. "Can I take this veil off you? Is it all right to gaze at my wife's face?"

"You're my lord and master."

He unwrapped the linen, slowly. For a moment he nearly grimaced, but then his smile returned.

"Have you come across anyone as dark, as dark as me?"

"Once at the main gate, we had some Cush traders. I don't mind the color. We all have our aberrations, look at my big ears." He wrapped my hand in his, trying to comfort me like heavy wool on the coldest of nights.

My husband then removed my outer garment leaving my dress and he started lightly kissing my exposed shoulder.

"My lord, can we, can we talk some?"

"Can we do so sitting?" He responded, slightly exasperated. He led me to the bed, positioning himself in the center and I sat at the edge. "Hmm, what would you like to talk about?"

"You're a scribe. What's a scribe's life like?"

He took a long breath, rubbing his face, but then let a small grin ripple across it. "I work for the priests in the chapel for funerary services, copying texts of contracts, inventory lists, salaries, fees, lists of offerings, things like that. I'd really like to take dictation, but that road seems blocked by my older brothers and by others from more important families. My hope is that I can eventually do that for your temple priests or for the King's court. My father and your father's people have arranged an apprenticeship for me in your temple."

"Who do your priests serve?"

"Are you asking what deity sits in our temple? Yahweh of Lachish."

"Is that the same Yahweh who is god over both Kingdoms?"

He took hold of my hand, giving it a gentle squeeze. "To be honest, I'm unsure," he said unrolling his grin further, trying to change the direction of our time together into something more profane. "Perhaps so."

He stroked my hair, and went back to making advances. How I parried with questions. That was until he kissed me on the lips, which brought up the memory of Solomon's wine-smelling breath. I jumped off the bed.

"What's wrong?"

"Maybe we need not rush, my lord. We have seven days."

"I can wait a few more hours, but they're expecting the sheets in the morning. We can't disappoint everyone."

"I could cut myself and redden them. We, we could pretend."

"Redden them? Pretend? You want to start off with a lie to my father?"

"We can say I got sick."

"Is it because of your imperfection? Are you afraid that down there you'll bleed black?"

"I, I . . ."

"The color doesn't matter, they just need to see blood."

"I just need a little time."

He rubbed his face again. "Or is it that you are no virgin?"

"I, I am my lord. I am."

He studied me. "Hmm. Yes. Yes, I believe you are. Tell you what." He glanced upward and then back at me. "Remove your dress, come to bed, and I'll just lay by your side for a long, long while, before we penetrate," he said, offering terms.

I slowly did as he ordered. I undressed and crept into the bed facing the door, trembling, and he lay behind me. His fingers pressed on my shoulder, then pricked my neck, my chest, the spine of my back. He took the liberty of feeling my behind; rubbing his hand in circles on it as the slave would wash the floor. Then he forced that hand between my tight legs, wedging them apart, commanding me to allow him entry to finger my pubic hair and then dig into my vagina. As his hand labored down there, I felt his tongue, a sticky and clammy muscle, invading my ear, licking it. His hands and his mouth were poking, prodding on this area and that; I found myself wincing and gritting my teeth to each new touch, to where this all would eventfully lead. I dreaded him inside me, feeling nauseated at the thought. And the *long, long while* he promised lasted only a few minutes, if that. He climbed on me and shoved it in, and did it. It wasn't the delight Galit had promised. A delight such as that wouldn't be racked with the gods' awful pain. At least he was finished quickly. I just faced the door, feeling the wet—not below as Galit had described, but above, bathing my cheeks.

א

The following morning, I awoke to a large breakfast waiting for me. But before I sat down to eat, I put on a change of clothing they'd brought up. Raddai grabbed the bed sheets—they were in fact red, not black—and handed them to his friend Jessie who had the day shift outside the door. He in turn passed them around for all to see and eventually to Jabesh for safekeeping on behalf of my father, should Raddai's family or Raddai himself later accuse me in front of the elders of lying about my virginity.

"You must be hungry," Raddai said, his face all smiles as we sat down at a low table that had been brought up, his volume raised a little to be heard over the celebratory music and chatter seeping through the walls. "We have nuts, breads, fruits, and plenty of milk to help it down. For our lunches and dinners this week, my father bought enough animals to allow him to leave his scribing work and become a goatherd."

"It looks lovely. Please thank your father for me."

154

"I will, but there's no need. So yesterday, you asked about me. Today I want to learn about you."

"Me?"

"Yes, I spent the last several years studying to be a scribe. This week I want to study you. And you can learn more about me, if you want."

Once again, I was at my father's court, telling my tales of Sheba and of the Nile (leaving out much of Pi), and Raddai couldn't hear enough. Whether he was feeling guilty about his conduct from the night before or whether he could relax now with everyone knowing that he had performed his connubial duties, I could only guess at.

That night he promised he would do nothing more than sleep beside me. He told me to go in first so that I would be behind him and he lay in front, his hands unable to fondle and pry. So we were on our sides, like rows of corn. When I touched his back once by accident, he turned his head a little, as if waiting for a signal that I was ready to go further. But of course, I withdrew. That was that, then we both went to sleep.

The next day as we were finishing our lunch, after I described for Raddai life in Jerusalem, he changed the topic.

"Have you started thinking about names for our first son?"

"A little. So far, I've come up with: David, Hezekiah, maybe Ariyahu."

"All fine names. Our son will grow up a pillar of strength, you'll see."

"Unless you—"

"Your eyes are remarkable," he said. I was taken aback with the compliment, so sudden and out of nowhere. "They're most dangerous," he said with a full smile. "I think I could gaze at them forever and never leave this room."

I looked down at my sandals.

"Now there you go taking them away from me. How unkind of you."

That night we got in our respective positions in the bed. Again, I just stayed behind him, staring at his back by the dim glow of a single lamp. He had several moles and I thought they looked a little like the hippopotamus constellation that I had gazed at countless times on Geddi's boat. The Egyptians believe those stars are the heavenly manifestation of Taweret, their goddess of childbirth—childbirth, my dream and my duty. But would I be so lucky? As I traced my finger in the air just above each of his moles, connecting them, I thought that unless I had become pregnant on our wedding night, I would never conceive. How could I if I'm too afraid to lie with my husband?

On the third day, Raddai's father allowed us a little breathing space from the room, and a chance to have the space cleaned and scrubbed. So, we both descended down the stairs to the shouts and cheers of the wedding guests. After each celebrant bestowed congratulations on us, Raddai left me in order to chat with his friends and family. Jabesh was at the city gate conducting business, but Galit and Talus were with me, giving me their smiles.

"Congratulations," Talus said, his beard now a lot grayer than the last time I had paid any attention to it. "You two are the perfect pair."

"Thanks, I hope you're enjoying yourself, that you're not missing cataloging your scrolls."

"I'll have plenty of time for that without having a ward to worry about."

"Yes, I'll miss your worrying."

"Everything's all right?" Galit asked.

"Everything is wonderful."

"It's good then?" For some reason Galit was not quite buying what I was trying to sell.

"Yes, very much so."

"Sounds like everything is sublime," Galit said. "Talus, can you excuse us girls for a moment?"

"But Keb just got here."

"Go." Talus was no god, just a mere mortal, and Galit's commanding beauty proved too much for him. When he left, Galit whispered, "If it is not everything you want it to be, give it time. Seldom are things perfect. I don't think such a thing exists."

"All is good, Galit. We're all good."

"Everything takes work. Even if you work at something hard, there are still things you can't control, like who you are given to as a wife. But the two of you are building something together; let's see what happens. Life can disappoint. But life can also surprise."

She squeezed my hand and kissed me on the cheek.

That afternoon, Raddai gave me a tour of his city. He showed me the gate where the elders held court, the city storage houses packed with oil and wheat, the city walls, high and protecting, the town square teeming with vendors, where the affluent would discuss politics and commerce, the alley where as a boy he would play soldier. He brought me close to the temple grounds, pointing out the annex where he did his copying. When we headed back, we passed a stream of professional mourners, the women singing a song of lament, their voices low and wavering, all slowly plodding out of the city for a burial before sunset. I felt it unfair that our wedding week was marred by such a bad omen. Yet Raddai tried to wash it all away for me; his face was nothing but happiness, his expression warm, genuine, and far more pleasing and valuable than any bride price. I soon forgot the mourners. As we walked the road to his father's house, Raddai held out his hand, asking for mine. I gave it.

By the fourth night I worked up the courage in bed to wrap my arms around him. It was nice to feel his heat until sleep took over. I did the same the next night. By the sixth night, Solomon's grouping lips had completely faded and I could be myself with him. I buried my body into his, hid myself in his scent, traversed his mouth, exploring, tasting everything, swallowing up his skin, heard his heart pound out for me. I danced in his warmth, finally letting our flesh merge into one. For the first time I forgot about that bowman I fell in love with among the cataracts.

א

On the eighth day, hung-over, tired, satiated, all of us weighing a couple pounds more than when we had arrived, we caravanned through the highlands back to Jerusalem. But we brought with us two more additions: my husband, and Eglail, Obadiah's servant and part of the bride price Jabesh had negotiated. Eglail's husband had been an engineer, but racked up gambling debts he couldn't pay, forcing him and Eglail into slavery. Obadiah had to buy both of them, for they were a package. The husband died shortly afterwards and Eglail, when she finished her sixth year of servitude, having no children or other relatives to take her, elected in lieu of freedom for the ear piercing, the sign of permanent ownership. Now since our third donkey carried our provisions, Eglail, though she was getting up in years, was forced to walk. As I held onto Raddai's waist from on top of the donkey, she stared coldly at me, her eyes darkly circled and bagged, reminding me of the god Horus. I have a habit of assuming people's contempt for me has to do with my skin or my birth status or both, and maybe that has played a part; but I have learned that Eglail just seems to feed on her inferiority, as if that gives her some kind of perverse pleasure.

"Eglail, please take my sandals," I said, starting to remove them.

"No, Mistress, your sandals are for you."

"You shouldn't have to walk thirty miles in your bare feet."

"The road is quite smooth."

"What use are they for me riding?" I held the sandals out, waving them, but she made no effort to grab them.

"Sandals are not for servants, Mistress."

"Take them."

"No, Mistress."

"I said take them!" I threw them at her.

"Let her be," Raddai said, ending it. "She doesn't want them."

Eglail picked each sandal off the ground and forced them back into my hands.

Once inside Jerusalem's walls, Jabesh directed us to our new house, an older mud brick, not far from the gate. There we said our goodbyes. I was troubled that my father may have forced a family from this house, but did he even care that much to be so heartless? I could see him caring about the hundred and twenty shekels he received from Obadiah. Yet had some family with small children been evicted because of me? And were now gleaning for the nothings in fields outside? Thinking that's what exactly had happened, it made me horribly sad, but not as sad as I would become.

Except for a few mats, some cookware, and pieces of pottery, the house was unfurnished. It wasn't large, two rooms in each of the two stories, perhaps just a little less space than Talus' apartment. The floor was uneven earth and we had to use a rickety ladder to reach the second level. Raddai grew quiet, as he often would do through the years. But at least this time he didn't erupt.

"With my job, we'll fill this place," he finally said to me, after gaining his composure and forcing a smile. "Not just with things, but with children. You'll see."

We did slowly fill the house with the plain and shabby. Yet children eluded me. It took me a few months to become pregnant, but that ended in a miscarriage. We couldn't afford to entomb the baby in a cave or even spare the shekel to lay it in the pits out in the Hinnom. So, we broke a law, burying it in our small garden.

A few months later I was pregnant again, but soon the garden had another visitor.

I withdrew from Raddai for nearly half a year, scared of trying again, yet he was intent on having a child as soon as possible, and it was obvious why. His line couldn't die with him. Being childless was a stigma. Moreover, he blamed his lack of promotion on it. Not only did his superiors look at him as peculiar for having produced no offspring, but the silver he had intended to save for bribes to rise within the scribal hierarchy had to be paid instead to the priests on fertility prayers.

"I'm taking an evening job with Sirah the trader, he's in need of a scribe," Raddai said after coming back from work one day as Eglail and I served him another meal of flat bread, olive oil, and the few vegetables we had picked earlier.

"Sirah? I don't think I know him."

"He exports olives and imports metal from . . ." Raddai paused trying to remember. "I don't know, somewhere far up north."

"Not in Israel."

"Farther."

"The metals, are they tin and copper?"

"That's right."

"Lydia, maybe?"

"How did you know?" He asked while chewing.

"You're keeping your Temple job?" He nodded yes and kept chewing. "Why then do you need to work for him on top of what you're already doing?"

"Isn't it obvious? Shekels for bribes and prayers. I thought my marriage connection to your father would mean something. Apparently, it means ox dung. How come we've never been invited to court?"

"I could talk to Ahishar."

"I don't think so."

"Really, it—"

"I said not to!" He dipped his bread in a plate of olive oil and cucumbers, took a bite, grimaced, then struck the table. "How I miss having meat!"

א

In order to ward off evil spirits and cure my affliction, I bartered off some of my jewelry and bought with it a series of healing herbs and remedies: black cumin, rose petals, clove flower, labdanum, juniper, fennel, myrrh, Salt Sea gourds, mice. I even had my abdomen tattooed.

And of course, I prayed. I prayed more times than I can remember. I'd offer Yahweh a drink of wine, milk, and honey all mixed together. I'd close my eyes, extending my arms, holding my palms out to him.

"Yahweh of Jerusalem and of the two Kingdoms, this is Keb, your faithful servant. You've helped me before, you brought me safely out of Cush, Egypt, and Shur. You saved me from my father's near rape. You gave me a husband. I beg of you, please help me once again, and let me have a son so that my husband's line may continue. Tiny Judah needs more sons to grow into men to defend us against your enemies. That is the reason you have given me a womb. Help me complete my life's role. Please!"

Remedies, herbs, libations. None of it worked.

א

It was right before the wheat harvest of my twenty-first year that my womb had become another burial cave. Then after more than a month of not leaving my bed, I finally had the energy to return to the market to hunt for another cure.

"Do you have anything else?" I asked the vendor.

"Come look at these. I just got them in last week." He pointed to the queerest-looking plants.

"What are they?"

"Mandrakes."

"I read, heard somewhere that it's an aphrodisiac."

"They're very fresh. Look here, the berries are still ripe."

The large green plant he held up bore a reddish fruit, but what caught the eye was the long, brown root. Almost a couple feet in length. It appeared nearly human, sporting outgrowths that looked like long, dangling arms and legs.

"They say it has magical qualities. A strong aphrodisiac, yes. But some say it is also a fertility cure. They were picked in moonlight so they're sure to work."

Perhaps it was because of the vendor's mention that the plant could induce lovesickness, but the more I stared at the root, the less it resembled a complete man, and more just his member.

"How do you take this? Am I eating the berries or the root?"

"Well, you could simply wear the root around your neck, but . . ."

"But what?"

"They say for the spell to really work, you should eat tiny portions of the fruit."

I inhaled the berries; they had quite a sweet spicy aroma and were most invigorating.

"Tiny portions, you say?"

"Tiny portions, yes, Mistress."

"What if you eat too much?"

א

Later I was staring at the berries, wondering if I should swallow. Maybe I should be cautious. So I took my carving knife and cut the fruit in half. The vendor had assured me that one berry would do me no permanent harm; only if I ate a few or more that the accumulated poison might kill.

"Recognize this?!"

Raddai. He was carrying a papyrus containing hieroglyphs in lines of red and black ink. It was an Egyptian text called *The Tale of Two Brothers*, a love triangle between siblings and the wife of one of them. I thought for a moment whether I should play dumb, but that would have made everything terribly worse.

"How did you find it?" I had hid the scroll in a large storage jar in the back of the pantry area of the kitchen.

My husband glanced at Eglail, then back to me. "What are you doing with this?"

"Talus, he gave it to me."

"Don't tell me you know how to read?"

I didn't know how to respond to his question, so I stood there, a silent letter. Eglail, meanwhile, seemed to be painfully holding in a grin.

"This is Egyptian. I can't even read this! What else?"

"What else, what, my lord?"

163

"What other languages, wife?"

"Just, just that." I cringed.

"Hebrew?"

"No, my lord. Only Egyptian."

"Are you hiding any more writings from me?"

"No, no my lord."

He waved the scroll in my face. "This ends. You hear me?"

"Yes, my lord. Of course."

"If Jotham or anyone at work knew. This on top of the fact the gods have chosen to curse you. Come here."

He dragged me to the table. And brought out another scroll, this one in Hebrew, thrusting the papyrus toward me. It was a writing I had not seen before.

"This. You see this? This is the marriage contract between my father and yours. You know what it says? I'll tell you. If you are barren after three years, I have the right to take any slaves of yours as concubines. Since we only have one, I will have Eglail tonight. Should that not work, I'll take another wife. Sirah has a nine, soon-to-be-ten-year-old daughter. Perhaps when she comes of age."

He waited for my words, for some acceptance of his decision, but I could only talk to him in tears.

"I'll tell you something else," he said. "I've tried for divorce, and you would think that would be no problem, but your fucking father won't allow it! Eglail, come."

"No!" I shouted and reached for him, sobbing, but he struck me hard on the side of my head.

"Never say no to me."

He took Eglail into our sleeping room, every line of the servant's face pronouncing joy, the slave a quite eager and willing participant. All the while I crawled into a fetal, rocking, shutting my eyes, my screams competing with Eglail's.

CHAPTER NINE

"These are for you." I turned from the hearth to find Raddai holding out an offering: bronze bracelets. As was his pattern after treating me harshly he would become the boy again that I had met in his father's house.

"Thank you, my lord, but can we afford these?"

"You can have something nice once in a while."

"But the prayers and bribes?"

"Prayers we have to pay, the bribes can wait."

Although I welcomed his kindness, the jewelry failed to wipe clear what had happened the night before with Eglail. She too had changed. When earlier that day I had asked her to go out to the garden to pick vegetables for the night's stew, she refused.

"I think it better for my child if I do not exert myself, Mistress."

Child? What were the odds? Eglail must have been forty or more. Now maybe Raddai did what he did thinking he might produce an heir through her, but I think it more that he went into her mostly as means of hurting me, to teach me a lesson upon discovering that I could read hieroglyphs. While my undertaking such a manly thing was bad in his eyes, perhaps what was worse was that I had withheld this information, making him the last to know about the goings on in his own house. He would be dishonored if my abilities became the subject of gossip, that underneath it all his colleagues might think he was a milksop who couldn't control his wife.

"If you can't pick any vegetables," I had said to Eglail, "then fetch us some water."

"There's all that commotion at the gate, Mistress, people shoving, pushing. What if someone were to accidentally hit my belly, the child could end up injured? I think it best I stay here and rest."

"You're flat as parched bread, Eglail. I'm sure that any child that might be in you now can take a little shoving and pushing."

My theory on my husband's joining with Eglail bore out. From this point until he married Sirah's daughter Hannah and stopped lying with our servant altogether, Raddai would lie with Eglail only after he had a fight with me. He would remind me how ugly he found her, even when she was in earshot. Raddai would always ensure that, of what little food was on our table, my portion would be more than hers. He always treated Eglail as a slave, whereas with me, I was always treated as a wife.

How I kept on trying to get pregnant. After Raddai warmed to me, I ate half a mandrake fruit. While the aroma was invigorating, the scent did nothing to prepare me for the taste, for the berry was far sweeter and tangier than the best-picked pomegranate. My mouth then decided to try the whole, but stopped there. After I had my next monthly bleeding, I gambled with my health, swallowing two berries all at once. I became bedridden with nausea for well over a month.

א

In the 29th year of Solomon's reign, Jerusalem was visited by the great plague. It was a gradual thing at first, hardly noticeable, but baby cubs soon become menacing bears. Talking with a few acquaintances at the Gihon, I learned that dozens of people throughout the city had come down with a fever and, at first, I didn't think much of it. But soon soldiers were donkeying bodies, corpses covered with boils, out of the city and dumping them into pits in the Hinnom. Burial processions to the tombs were happening several times a day, and I started hearing names for this new pestilence: "Arrows of Yahweh," "The Shears," and "Mot's Dance." Soon the dead were laying everywhere: in the thoroughfare, in the market, propped up against the city walls, at house doors. Along with the bodies came, of course, wretched smells, picking ravens, flies, and rats. Panic was ubiquitous, and there was gossip that the King himself had come down with Mot's Dance, but had battled back. We were all afraid of going outdoors in fear that the demon's work had an easier time out in the open. Still, there were vegetables that had to be gathered and water jugs that needed to be filled. So we did it all and quickly—nearly spilling everything when racing back from the spring.

To stop the disease, Temple priests were busy night and day praying to Yahweh, and the priests to the lesser gods were attending their shrines on the Mount of Olives, their altars lit far into the night. Solomon made several decrees to temporarily stop the brothels, public drunkenness, and other overly profane behavior. Men were not to lie with their wives. The King also ordered the entire population to make daily prayers to their household gods, and those of us who had access to the cistern were required to bathe twice a day. Even the Guild singers lent their voices with magical chants to force evil spirits out of the city.

The plague reigned a little more than four months and then it was over. But not before it took Talus' life. Ahishar bravely left the palace to venture to the slum so that he could deliver the news to me personally. I was in shock when he told me. "No, no, no!" I screamed. Through my wailing I heard Ahishar say that my old guardian had been found dead, collapsed at his desk in the library. Since Talus never acquired enough shekels to be entombed, the soldiers just gathered him up and threw him into the pit.

Like I had done when I learned the news of Galit's stoning for her adultery, I experienced full-fledged grief, in all of its miserable facets, spending much time in the coarse goat-hair sackcloth, grinding the earth deep into my scalp, crying until there was no cry left.

Galit gone and now Talus.

I was quickly running out of people to love.

א

As the harvests came and went, the gods continued to curse me. So, when Hannah came of age, Raddai took her as a wife, paying a steep price to do so. He agreed that Sirah would owe him no dowry. But that was not all. Raddai also agreed to pay Sirah a bride price of thirty shekels—shekels that would have gone to a year's worth of my fertility prayers—along with two years of free labor. Raddai's temple job alone would have to support all of us for a while. So, my husband converted our storage space into both a small shrine area for Hannah's household gods and a new sleeping room for me. I just stood there as the thirteen-year-old moved into his chamber. What could I do? I couldn't oppose his actions. It would be like a goat striking the shepherd.

I tried to adjust to our new living arrangements, but I found it onerous. When it came to preparing meals, weaving, and other household chores, I would tell the other two women I was sick and spent much of my time on my mat, sleeping a lot. When I lay awake, I'd try to understand why my life was so wretched, taking inventory of all that had ever happened, isolating my specific actions and inactions that somehow must have offended the gods. Yahweh's nonintervention was more than baffling; for on one hand he had no difficulty hearing my prayer to stop Solomon's rape, yet where was he now? Or was he watching me as clear as Eglail's spying eyes, but had become hardened because of something I did or didn't do? Still, a promise is a promise. I couldn't go back on my end of our deal. He had come to my rescue before; I had to believe he would eventually do so again. For better or for worse, we were stuck with each other.

When I heard my sister wife scream with delight through the open air and thin plaster, I searched for some way to be deaf to it. I would go to the roof whenever the weather allowed, where the noises muffled. And when it became too cold or rainy, I stayed in my room, enduring the tumbling and the grinding. Searching for distractions, I yearned to have something to read to take my heart away from it all. But of course, there was no scroll or tablet for me, assuming I had the courage to disobey my lord and master. The new librarian was a stranger, so where could I go for material? When my energy returned, I ventured down to the market, scouring the stalls in vain for writings, but there was nothing to buy, which made perfect sense. So very few Jerusalemites were literate, and if the palace wanted epic writings or courtly poetry composed in other nations, my father's officials would not deign to trek down to the vulgar city peddlers. No, such trading deals were made directly with their administrative counterparts in other lands. Even if the vendors were to carry texts painstakingly copied from originals or other copies, their prices would be exorbitant; I might as well try to buy a fleet of chariots.

But one day I came across a new tradesman selling various Phoenician trinkets and curiosities, and there on display on a wool blanket was a large blank papyrus roll.

"Made in Byblos," the trader said. "Very fine. Sixty sheets. Give it a feel."

Kneeling down, I stroked my fingertip against the mashed-up plant that became a writing surface. "How much?"

"A hundred shekels or if you want to pay in kind."

Almost what Raddai's father paid for me. Of course, even if the man came down from the asking price, any amount would be far out of reach, and where would I hide it from Eglail? The indent in the beaten earth of my room? Deep enough perhaps that I could put my mat over it. But no, what would I do with it? Go back to writing that embarrassing childhood poem about Pi marrying a young Shebite? Then what if Raddai were to find it? I stared at it some more, but realized how ridiculous and stupid the idea.

"Thank you, but I don't think so."

"I'll throw in a reed, ink well, and a board." I heard him say to my back as I headed to the gate. I had promised Hannah I would draw the water this morning. She was becoming round and I told her either Eglail or I would do the heavy chores from now until the baby.

"For you, eighty shekels or in kind," he echoed behind me, his voice falling farther from my ears.

I left him and waited in the queue to exit the city, thinking of that scroll. If it were mine, what would I write? My Rebekah story? Silliness. To what end would that accomplish? I told myself to forget about it. *Some things are just not meant to happen—* words that I had begun saying to myself with the force of a prayer.

A prick at my shoulder.

"I really like you, Mistress. For you, seventy shekels."

א

I slid the loom between the doorway and where I'd be sitting, while trying to make as little noise as possible. Should Raddai barge into my room, I would have a moment to slip the papyrus back in the floor crevice and yank the mat over it, and perhaps my disobedience might go unnoticed behind the partial wool weave. Yet with the lamplight daring me, I took the scroll out. I unraveled it at its beginning, feeling the weight of the sheets that followed. So many and unspoiled. As with all things new, flushed with promise and hope. Perhaps that is why virgins are so treasured.

Placing the writing board over my crossed legs, and the papyrus on top of it, I held the stiff juncus rush between my fingers. Then I dipped the reed in the well.

Now what?

I waited for my heart to pounce an idea. But there was nothing.

I sighed and put everything back in its hiding place, and moved the loom to where it had been. Lying down, I thought about what in the heavens I wanted to write and why I needed to write it, feeling sad that whatever would come out of my reed would be read by an audience of one. But what if I were to manufacture some story and then bury it, and hope that some future countrymen would then later make its discovery? Yet with my luck, before long a stray animal would sniff it out and tear at it, making the thing its meal. I exhaled a long breath, thinking it's a shame that Galit and Talus were dead, for I could have sung the work to them. I knew that they would have appreciated it, if only out of politeness. But they were long gone, and I didn't want to end up like Talus, writing unsung poetry. If it weren't for my eyes, his words would have been known to no one except him, taking them all down with him to the underworld. All that labor for naught. But at least Talus wasn't under the constant threat of being discovered by a husband who had no qualms of striking the face of a misbehaving wife.

Still, something in me needed to put ink to papyrus.

Then I thought of Solomon.

Who else living would appreciate a telling out of my own hand? I could give it to Ahishar to give to the King for a present. A reconciliation. I would just ask my father to say nothing to my husband. That day when Solomon came to the apartment, he had to have known I could at least read, if not write, so receiving the finished scroll would come as no shocking revelation. Now bedridden from the plague, my father I'm sure could use some entertainment. I thought it curious that I had traded the golden earrings, his present he had given me, for the papyrus. If I were in turn to give the completed writing back to the King, it would create a kind of cosmic circle.

The scroll would be for Solomon. But what would he want to read or have sung to him? At court he would call on me to tell my tales of Sheba and Egypt. So, should I write down my life story, save all the cursed parts like his attempted rape while under the demon's spell? How long a history would that be? No, the times of Keb weren't a fit subject for verse. And who writes of their own life anyway? This project required something more worthy. If not about me, then what? I suppose I could have regurgitated all the harp songs he relishes. But any musician could be summoned into his chamber for that. What would he enjoy that would be new?

I closed my eyes and slept on it, but when I awoke, my heart was as empty as the scroll.

א

Standing in front of the mirror, Hannah was examining her belly.

"I'm really ready for this, to have my life back. And to sleep. I'd give anything just for a little more. I wish I could rest as sound as Raddai. Any advice?"

"On sleeping? I've never gotten as far as you have, the most was seven months. You could ask Eglail, she had a boy and a girl, I believe."

"She never mentions them."

"The gods took them when they were young," I said.

Hannah stroked her midsection. "Well, I'm just ready. Raddai's a bit of puzzle about it."

"Is he?"

"Well, he caresses me here, saying how he can't wait for a son, but he doesn't want to go into me lately. I think he misses my former figure."

"Maybe he feels he might injure the child."

"Do you think I'll get it back?"

"Get what back?"

"My figure. They say that men like a bit of plumpness, still, you don't want to be too plump."

"Before it gets too late, I'll gather what I can for supper."

Escaping, I walked outside to the patch of earth that the four of us, soon to be five, relied so much on to scrape by. The problem was there was little sun to make many vegetables grow, the surrounding houses taking turns casting their ruinous shadows. Gritting my teeth, I found more weeds than anything edible, and the unwanted growth needed to be trimmed back and soon. If I were to wait much longer, the garden would be completely taken over. A project for tomorrow, perhaps. I thought if only I had the magic to just wish the unruly grass away, creating order out of this chaos like in the Babylonian creation poem, *When on High*. That's when it hit me—my mind whirling with a purpose. I knew the story I would write! It would be a creation poem, but one told from our point of view. Yet the Babylonian tale was seven tablets; I had room on the scroll for something larger, much larger. So why bind myself to simply the genesis of the world, why not a story of our people? The harp songs just had glimpses of our history; there was no epic tying it all together. This would be new. But how long? From the beginning until the people received the Commandments? Up until the Monarchy? To the present? No, not the present, this was a gift for Solomon, he was my audience, and if I were to write something about him that would shine a lamp badly. No, it would have to end before him. Still, exactly when? And how much scroll did I have to play with?

I started my work, but after only a couple nights, I had to put the juncus rush down. As my sister wife was now too big for Raddai, my husband invited me back into his chamber. How nice it was to once again feel the whirlwind of his warmth envelop and consume me, as I had remembered, and for a few moments to be taken far away from my haplessness. But that shot of warm rain came and went. After Hannah delivered her stillborn, he went back to her to try again, leaving me to ink my scroll. After some stops and starts, the words came; some more quickly than others, but come they did.

As with Raddai's unexpected affectation, life can occasionally surprise. And two things can grow at once.

CHAPTER TEN

"Push," I heard Eglail instruct over my cries. She and Hannah held me down on the birthing stool. On the two cold limestone slabs, over waves of tearing pain, I had my baby. Coming out, he was alive and crying, the most wondrous sound that ever fell on ears, both godly and human. If Yahweh had forgotten my prayers, they must have come roaring back like trumpets shattering ancient walls. Looking at him, I knew I would never be lonely ever again, not with my son—my son, my boy, this being that came out of me, warm and wet, so tiny, yet so perfect and so beautiful. His head and body movements were slow at first, but then moving and jerking, commanding attention. I had been debating between calling him Ariyahu, meaning 'lion of Yahweh,' or the shortened form of the name, Ariah. When I gazed at his brown, pudgy face, something in me said he was an Ariah.

"My lord, come and see your child," I heard Hannah shout to the main room, as I cradled my little boy. "Come, he's fine and healthy."

Raddai rushed in.

"Here, look at your son," I said, my voice rough and faint.

But he just stood there staring at the crying infant and then turned to me with the same kind of contempt as the day he discovered the Egyptian scroll I'd been hiding. The veil was lifted and I understood. To him, our Ariah was another burnt face, a black-skinned monster. Perhaps he always assumed his son would be a tan Judahite. That Raddai's superior color could never be minus to something as deformed as mine.

My eyes turned to the women for support. While Hannah came to my side, holding my hand, Eglail was hardly able to suppress her glee.

Ariah's father turned and walked out.

"What will you do?" I said to his back, straining my throat. But there was no response. I started sobbing as Raddai, lord and master over our household, could do plenty. If he chose, my husband could abandon Ariah on the Mount of Olives, leaving him to the jackals. A father had that right and there would be nothing I could do to stop it. I wept all night long thinking of that ghastly possibility.

The next day Raddai neared as close to us as the doorway, fixing his attention at this helpless, sleeping boy in my arms.

"I've named him Ariah. Do you want to hold him?"

"Not right now."

I couldn't decipher his thoughts and started having horrid thoughts of my own. I grabbed my boy tightly, and turned, shielding him from my husband. "You're not going to . . ." I said, trailing off, my eyes locked on Ariah's face, wrinkled and brown like a ripe date.

"I'm not going to do anything. I have a feeling we'll all soon be reduced to begging for scraps at the gate. With his color, he might help bring more in the bowl."

THE REED

Raddai squatted on my mat and touched his son's tiny fingers.

א

My boy was bathed, rubbed with salt, and wrapped in linen strips. Eight days after he entered this world, a priest circumcised him, cutting off his skin with a flint rock. As Ariah started growing, Raddai would at times show affection, such as patting his frizzy hair. Then there were times he would say the most hateful things.

"At least no one has to spit when they see him to distract the Evil Eye."

When my son turned three, we celebrated the end of his weaning. Raddai didn't want a large event; I think he was afraid to show off Ariah in front of a crowd. It was just the household, Raddai treating his son only slightly better than a leper. I tried hard to accept that my husband didn't have it in him to display any overwhelming love, that whatever he did express was conflicted: the gentle rubbing of his son's hair or the building of toys followed by the meanest of speech. I suppose he could never completely extinguish the notion that Ariah was a hideous mongrel, that our boy was an offense to the divine order, on par with the combining of wool with linen, of sowing two different kinds of seeds, of breeding a sheep with a goat.

And what of my writing? I felt no to need to obsess over it, as I had Ariah now. But when my son was sleeping soundly through the night and I lay awake, I would pick up the reed, piecing together a narrative from bits of legends and songs. Yet many of my sources were just story fragments and, worse, the patriarchs lacked motivations for their actions. So I had to fill in the blanks. Yahweh's motivations weren't always clear either.

Why, for example, did he choose one man to put on the ark from all the world? What made our survivor so special? None of the Noah songs or the flood epics from other peoples provided an adequate answer. And I needed an answer to understand why Yahweh did what he did.

But it occurred to me that since Yahweh is just, the reason had to be that Noah must have been the only righteous man in a very wicked world. But nobody could be too virtuous. Noah had to be blameless only up until Yahweh made his selection, but nothing required him to continue being a paragon after he was singled out. People's goodness waxes and wanes, and so must have his. As the rains started, I envisioned Noah lifting not a finger to save anyone, including the innocent animals and infants splashing in the waters. Noah was not Abraham, who I had negotiate with Yahweh—the patriarch using the acumen of a vendor at the market to spare Sodom if there were just a smattering of good living among the depraved, talking the deity down from finding fifty innocents to ten. Instead, my Noah said not a word to his god to rescue the screaming and drowning by the sides of the rising ark. After the Flood, Noah became a drunkard, and even cursed his blameless grandson. But might I not do the same? After witnessing the world's annihilation, how could anyone remain so steadfast and not be broken?

Some of my old tutor's lessons on writing were helpful, and I applied them. Some I ignored. Sorry, Talus, I did give my gender prominent roles in my epic. I figured my father, a lover of women, wouldn't mind our appearance. And I made many of my heroes (both men and women) tricksters similar to Solomon. If my father could stage a phony trial with those so-called prostitutes, he might appreciate reading that his ancestors similarly used their wits, not always their brawn, to outmaneuver their adversaries. I threw in puns and word games, knowing that would please him too. Finding that poetry was too confining for dialogue, I did without verse for most of the work, adopting a non-rhythmic writing style I had found in a few short stories from Egypt.

I heard from Ahishar that Solomon's condition had worsened; my father was starting to become forgetful. When Ahishar told me that the King found the strength to leave his bed, but then staggered into the banquet hall totally naked, unaware of his lack of decorum, I knew it was time for me to end the project.

I had just finished Moses' death and was debating whether I should fill up a few more sheets about the Conquest, when I couldn't find the scroll. My writing board, rush, and ink well were missing too. They were not in the dip in the floor under the mat. I yanked up the sheepskin to see if it somehow got moved to another section of the floor, but found nothing. I frantically searched all over my sleeping room, even scouring Ariah's crib.

Where the sheol could it have got to? I went back to the dip, finding nothing. I held up the lamp up to every object I could find, tossing my dresses out of my chest, rummaging through the idols, checking every square of the room again. Again nothing. Could Ariah have toyed with it? When morning finally came, and with the daylight attending me, several more searches proved just as fruitless. I had to accept that it was gone. But it wasn't difficult to determine who took possession. For if a drooling camel once pokes its wet nose in a tent, its body will soon follow.

א

"Have you been in my room?"

"No, Mistress." Eglail's eyes were down, but her mouth had that look like she was hiding her glee, just like the time with the Egyptian scroll, just like when Ariah was born.

"Is there something you want?" I asked.

"Something I want? I don't understand."

"You heard me, is there something you want?"

"No, Mistress, I only want to serve you and the family."

"If you want to serve me, why then were you snooping in my room?"

"Why would you think that?"

"Cause something's gone missing from it."

"Can I help you find it?"

"Yes, you can, you can give it back to me."

"Give what, Mistress?"

"You know very well what."

"The thing you think I took?" She clenched her teeth; how hard it must have been for her to not to unfurl a smile.

"Let's stop playing at these games. Is there something you want?"

"Mistress, are you accusing me of blackmail?"

"Is there something you want for it?"

"What could you possibly give me?"

"I have a little jewelry."

"What? Your golden earrings? I haven't seen those in a while." Eglail raised her head and looked up, her eyes planted in mine. "But if I did come across something unusual, I wouldn't hide it. Or use it for blackmail. I would let the right person know of its existence."

"What have I done to make you hate me?"

"How could a faithful servant hate her mistress?"

Eglail smirked. Her neck stiffened too, like an ox unwilling to be led.

א

I waited for Raddai's return from his night job, half playing with Ariah, half puttering around, trying at my chores, but preoccupied, my heart thinking about the beating or worse that was to come. While Eglail was preparing the evening's stew—holding in her grin mostly, but at times letting it go—questions raced across my mind. Had I been a more abusive mistress than most? Or was it my dark skin and my illegitimacy that she just couldn't accept? How demeaning it must have been for her all these years to have had to serve someone like me. I wondered if she had long ago cursed me, and if that curse had been the cause for my misery. But even if someday Eglail were to warm to me, she would have no power to take her words back. Even coming from a slave, what is said cannot be unsaid.

Later, I trembled when Raddai confronted me.

"The scroll had with it a writing board and ink. This writing comes from your own hand, does it not?"

"It does. It does, my lord."

"This is Hebrew, you told me before you only knew Egyptian. Another lie, wife?"

I just flinched, waiting for it. But he stayed his hand—for now.

"I don't recognize this work. Did you make a copy from another writing?"

"I did not, my lord. I made it."

"*You* made it?"

I didn't want to see his rage, so I kept my eyes shut.

"Look at me," he shouted and I heeded his command. "Answer me. You say you made it?"

"I did."

"You're telling me these are your stories?"

"They are."

"They are your invention?"

"I created, fleshed them out from the harp songs."

"I don't recall any harp songs on an Adam or an Eve, or a Cain or an Abel, or of a tower reaching the skies, or of a woman who turns to salt."

"Those, those came from me, from my imagination."

"That's most of the scroll." He started shaking his head as if it were a wadi filling up with raging water. "You promised me before that this nonsense would stop. And here we are again."

"Yes." I noticed his hand starting to clench. I threw myself at him, my stomach landing on the dirt floor, my hands clasping his knees, my neck stretched up, a supplicant in my own home. "This will be the end, I promise."

"Just like you promised the last time, wife?"

"I'm sorry, my lord, I'm sorry."

He raised his fist up to strike me.

"I beg you, my lord, please forgive me." Crying, I looked at his eyes, trying to find that boy from long ago. But he clenched his fist tighter, I gritted my teeth, waiting for it. Then a loud sobbing from behind me. Ariah. Raddai saw him too.

"Get away from me," he said, withdrawing his hand. "See to your son's racket."

I lunged, and hugged my boy, trying to quiet him. And Raddai, he just kept the papyrus and walked into his chamber with Hannah waiting for him.

Sixth months later, Raddai was promoted to Third Scribe, in charge of all scribal work in the Temple, hurdling over several dozens more senior. The household moved into a lavish palace apartment. From wool tatters to Sidonite linen, from one servant to three, from a tottering ladder to a staircase of the finest cedar, from a floor of beaten dirt to one covered in amethyst and topaz. And less than a year ago, when Elihoreph died, my husband took his place as Scribe for the Kingdoms, working hand in hand with the Prince Regent. Raddai never said a word to me about how he was able to tower from nothing to the top of the bureaucracy. The scroll never became a topic of discussion.

א

"He never told you in advance that it was going to be read at the Feast?" Zadok asks me now, as he shovels the last of the incense on the hearth.

"He didn't. I knew this year's would be different. There were rumors that my brother and the priests had changed the festival's purpose from that of celebrating the tent in the olive field to the tent in the desert wilderness. But I had no idea what was to come. So there I was, six months ago, with the household on top of the palace. I gazed down at the Temple and the city pilgrims, on their merriment, their eating and drinking, at the children running around and playing.

"Then, to my amazement, on the morning of the seventh day, Ahimaaz and the priests recited to the people *The Chronicles of Moses,* the newly discovered scroll that had been *found* in the Temple. Raddai must have put the entire scribal community to work making copies so that each priest would have a papyrus and could be stationed at points throughout the entire city to read the work simultaneously to the whole population. Ahimaaz of course read the original by the altar; only he could place his fingers onto something from the hand of Moses.

"There I was, along with thousands, hearing what I had written, knowing exactly how each story would unfold, anticipating like a prophetess the next word to be spoken. My husband, the priests, the scribes—none had altered a single letter. Funny that Raddai wouldn't look at me, the coward; he couldn't at least silently acknowledge what I had done for the Temple, for the celebrants, for his career. When the priests read about the ten plagues—that, after each one, Pharaoh would give in to Moses and Aaron, only for Yahweh to harden Pharaoh's heart—did Raddai realize that he was the source from which I drew my inspiration?

"Solomon, my intended audience, was in his bed witnessing not a thing. Although I was disappointed, the reaction from everyone else more than made up for it. Walking out of our tent, I toured the roof, looking around, stunned, staring at the multitude. Everyone, except the youngest of children, had quieted and was utterly mesmerized, even the Prince Regent. Their attention fixed, their hush broken now and then by their laughter from the wordplay, listening to stories by me, a foreigner, a burnt face, a woman. After it was over, the people started chanting and screaming for *The Chronicles* to be read again. And, as you know, it was.

"How can one articulate what utter joy is? I can't. But I know this: the reading was probably my second happiest memory, after the birth of my son. Ever since I had come to Jerusalem I had always longed to fit in, to be accepted, to be something other than different and looked down upon. Even though it wasn't Keb they were cheering for, it was something that came out of me. In those few hours, I no longer felt like a pariah, for how could a pariah give the people something that they loved, to touch them so. Not only did I finally feel welcomed, I felt important. I mattered."

I close my eyes, reliving the moment, remembering it all. Like when the priests spoke my words, how they made them come to life. Then I recall everything that happened afterwards, thinking the most horrible of thoughts.

Zadok takes on a glow beyond that given by the lamp. "Never before to my knowledge has anyone attempted what you've done. I mean the style. I've never known anything like it in storytelling. Your dialogue, it seems so real."

THE REED

I'm tired and question whether my act of vanity was a mistake. Yes, I enjoyed explaining to the old priest how it all came about, but I picture all my words, written and spoken, mixing like ores in the smelter, then cooling into hard stones . . .

"Another thing that works," Zadok continues, "is that, unlike some other people's narratives, here all the patriarchs have flaws. Abraham passes off his wife as his sister, Jacob dupes his father, Joseph's a tattletale."

. . . Stones packed high on donkeyback . . .

"Your wordplay. 'Jacob was cooking up some stew.' I love your double meaning like he's hatching a plan."

. . . The soldiers unloading the limestone chunks, handing them out to the priests, the priests grasping them tight, their arms raised, reaching back . . .

"What follows is one of my favorite parts, what Esau tells his father Isaac when he learns that his brother, Jacob, stole his blessing, 'Can it be that you have no blessing for me? Is the one blessing all you have, Father?' It sounds so true."

"It's easy to feel sorry for him," I say, halfway listening, halfway in the stoning field, wincing.

"Thinking about it now, your life and these stories mirror how the nation sees itself. No, rather how the nation wants to see itself now, after having *The Chronicles* read to them. Compared to Egypt and the Philistines, and the Canaanites here before us, Judah and Israel are the underdog. Winning by accepting Yahweh's help and by using our wits."

What is worse: being buried to your waist, gazing out at your executioners, waiting for the first rock, the anticipation of it all, or the act itself? One is a mental anguish, the other bodily, but what is truly more wretched?

"Is that what you intended?" Zadok asks.

"What? Intended?"

187

"That the stories show the tribes as the underdog?"

"I'm not sure, but I'm glad that's what you see in it."

"It's perfect, every word. Yahweh should strike down anyone who tries to change it." Zadok sits on the moment. "There is no question that you are the author of our beloved text, but that doesn't explain why you were in the Temple."

"I hope you don't mind, but I'm tired of talking."

"Of course. It's very late. I'll do what I can to get you out of this place." He crutches to the door and then bangs his staff on the oak. His servant, who had been waiting on the other side, creaks it open.

But the old man doesn't leave yet, for he's still not quite done with me. "What is this fourth river out of Eden, the Pishon?"

"A brook in Sheba that our ranch bordered on."

He laughs and nods to the servant to carry him out. As I crawl into wool blankets, my mind muses whether I did anything tonight to help save myself or whether I just quickened my execution. Did I just put at risk my doings in the Temple? Then again, maybe my worrying is an empty exercise. Perhaps Zadok is simply a tired fool, hanging around his son like an old, dented, tarnished breastplate, and we just wasted each other's time. But my internal debate is a fairly short as I quickly drift off into much needed sleep.

PART III
EXODUS

CHAPTER ONE

We must be story creatures, for what else on this earth can shape one's past into a great adventure, divine a future out of entrails, create meaning out of dreams? Especially dreams. As my eyes open, I remember mine from last night. I had dreamt of Ariah. In his room, I had built a tent out of blankets and coaxed my boy into coming inside it, to play sticks for swords. Though it took some doing to get him into the pretend fort.

"Put your sister's doll down and take this stick," I said.

"No!" he shouted back, holding tight onto a leather figure that looked a lot like my old Ruzu.

"The city is under attack by monsters. We need you." He just picked at the doll. "Everyone knows that you're the best monster killer in the Kingdoms. If you don't lead the attack, the city will be overrun by the beasts." I tickled him and he let out a howl. "Come on, Ariah, we need you."

I gently offered him the stick and this time he took it. He followed me into the fort and we banged our wooden swords together.

"Take that, Monster," he said.

But the sticks melted away and he cried. Then I awoke without him.

As sleep drains from me, I realize my surroundings have changed, because while I slept, fresh bread and water were brought in and the chamber pot cleaned. The pools of urine, mopped up as well. The small hearth remains and incense burns. Zadok's doing? It must be.

Although I welcome the improvements to my accommodations, it was a mistake, I think, sharing so much history with the old priest. Knowing too much about a person gives you a control over her and, apart from your father or husband, no one should have that kind of power.

I look over to the space once occupied by my former cellmate and brood on whether he's now in Sheol or if Zadok was able to do something. If the old priest was unsuccessful, then words, my words, the very same words that Zadok and the celebrants felt glee over, those words caused a man's life to end. How will I live with that if I do get out of here? I picture Nebat's frightened and scared face and I know I'll carry that image to the underworld.

What's happening back at my apartment? Raddai home yet from Edom? Does he even care that I'm missing? In that first month after Ariah's death, he went out of his way to care for me, comforting me with kind talk, a hug, a squeeze of the hand. He also broke down a few times, even asking for the sackcloth. But when that month of mourning was over, my husband was his old self, back to the time when he treated me as if I were just taking up unwanted space, no better than a storage jar of rotted olives. He has to know I'm confined down here. Ahimaaz must have told him. Someone so high must know. Yet with my death, his secret of the scroll's origin dies too. That works out quite nicely for him, doesn't it? I see him kissing Hannah's large belly, exploring her hill country. I take the bread I'm eating and throw it at the cell wall, aiming at that fat belly of hers.

A noisy creaking and echoing. The door. My chest starts its predictable pound, but then slowly quiets. Zadok's servant, still in the reddish loincloth. Although he's not a big man, maybe a couple of inches taller than me, his arms and chest are large with blue veins jetting out, a result, I assume, of carrying his master. He hasn't much of a beard, just scraggly whiskers of youth, the hair of someone in his early twenties, if that. Although a slave, he has a caravan of days in front of him.

"Come."

"I can just walk out of here?"

"We can," he says in an Ammonite accent.

"What about the guards?"

"Don't worry about them."

"You didn't fight them?"

"Me?" He laughs. "You know how many they have stationed here?"

"Then why are they no problem?"

He pantomimes dropping silver weights in someone's palm. "We have to walk back up the hill. I can carry you."

"That's all right. I can manage."

"As you wish, but you might want these then." Reaching into his large skin, he pulls out a pair of women's sandals and hands them to me. They fit perfectly, and it seems more than forever that my soles have felt every scrape and prick of the rough. Now if I could only wash and oil my feet, I could walk to Babylon and back.

"I hope you don't mind, Mistress, but Zadok wants you to cover your face and play the prostitute," he says, as he hands me a veil. I do as the slave commands, and for a moment I'm back in Lachish, a young girl waiting for her future to begin.

It's early. Stepping outside, I can just make the beginnings of blueness above the dark horizon. I'm cold, but nevertheless relieved to be out of that squalor. I hear the sting and clamor of the ram's horn and a voice bellowing, "The King is dead, long live the King." Silhouettes stream past, heading to what looks like a line queuing at the gate, waiting for it to open. Too early for women and slaves to be filling their jars at the spring. Where could they be going?

We reach our destination, the old palace, what had been David's residence terraced below the summit. The compound is small and plain compared to Solomon's palace above, and in truth it's just a collection of several mid-sized apartments. After leading me across an outdoor patio, the Ammonite brings me into one of the quarters. As I unwrap the veil and take in the center room, I'm struck at the splendor of fine imported Phoenician vases and tapestries. But what nets my gaze is a mural of the constellations at dusk. Commanding attention at the center, shining its brilliance, is the evening star.

"Cimon here made this," says Zadok hobbling with his crutch to a chair, motioning his head at the artwork.

"Cimon?"

"My servant."

I shake my head, smiling at the shirtless man. "You did this? I could swear I could be right outside looking over the west wall at sunset. It's that real."

"Thank you, Mistress."

"Where did you learn your art?"

"In his native land of Ammon." Zadok explains. "Cimon, your father was a craftsman, as I recall, until . . ."

"He was," the slave responds.

"Until?" I ask.

"He and the whole village were burned," Zadok says.

"I'm sorry," I say to the servant. "What happened?"

"A matter of some unpaid tribute, I'm afraid," Zadok answers.

"Nebat, my cellmate, were you able to save him?"

"He was executed right after they brought him out of your cell. I was too late, I'm sorry." *Nebat dead because of me, because of my words.* "Please sit. We have to discuss getting you out of here." He nods to Cimon, who leaves us.

"Out of where?" I ask, plopping down on a rug facing the old priest, still thinking of the young man I shared a space with, his face a collection cuts and bruises, that ruined face probably now decaying below the Hinnom soil.

"Somewhere where my son can't reach you."

I drink a few sips of cold honey water that has been laid out for me, but Zadok's words have taken away the taste. "You want me to leave Jerusalem?"

"Further than that I'm afraid."

"Where then? Somewhere in Southern Judah? In the Negev?"

"No—"

"Am I to hide in Israel?"

He shakes his head no. "I was thinking you should leave the Kingdoms."

Stunned, I just stare, my armpits becoming damp.

"My son is intent on your destruction for he sees your hand in Solomon's death. He's only hesitated so far in order to obtain the King's permission, you being a half-sister."

"So can't I just hide in some, in some small town?"

"He has a lot of resources, and you're someone whose skin . . ."

"Someone who stands out."

"I'm afraid so."

"You want me to leave the Kingdoms? To where?"

"Perhaps its best for you in Sheba."

I stir his words around. "Sheba? I don't think so."

"Hear me. Between your brother and my son, they have a reach that extends quite far, even to Phoenicia and Egypt. You can't stay here, they'll find you."

"I don't think so."

"If you have a better alternative, I'm willing to entertain it." Zadok's breath smells of too much labdanum and old age.

"What about my husband?"

"What of him?"

"Would he intervene with Ahimaaz?"

"Would he?"

I know the answer to that. Ruminating, I stare at the constellation mural. Judah and Sheba share these same stars, but so much else is different. "I knew three people back when I was a girl, my aunt and uncle, my sister, and who knows whether they're still living, whether they would have me. My mother. My mother threw me out of the country." Another worrying thought hits me. "What of Ariah?"

"Ariah?"

"Who will feed him?"

"Your husband, I would think." I wonder about this. Not once since Ariah's death has he or the servants performed the task. "And if he doesn't, I'll send Cimon."

"I appreciate that, but what should happen if your servant is freed—"

"I'll find someone, another slave or I'll hire someone."

"But what if . . ."

"What if what?"

I pause and then say it. "What if you should die?"

The old man smiles a little. "Even if you were to stay here and were intent on feeding him yourself, on your way to the tomb and back, you would eventually be discovered by the guards. Stay or go, you will have to let your son's hunger be abated by others. Take a bath and eat, and think on it. Meanwhile I'll make some preparations and we'll talk more in a little while. It's best you leave by first light tomorrow."

"I just pass through the gate tomorrow morning, then walk hundreds of miles. First through the desert, then to the Delta, where I turn south until I reach Sheba?"

"No, you'll head north first—"

"North?"

"It sounds counterintuitive, I know."

"North?" I ask again.

"Look, you're a little agitated at the moment. Cimon is drawing your bath. I want you to relax first and then I'll explain it all."

א

Lying in the stone tub, removing the stench and dank from my body, I relish the sensation of frankincense, myrrh, natron, all mixed in water collected from the old palace's cistern, heated by Cimon using Zadok's hearth. I splash water on me and recall the countless times these past months that I would wail in the tub for Ariah, letting the water wash away the tears, the tub the one place I could hide those tears from Raddai. I think of my little lion's smiling, innocent, puffy face, how happy he looked when he was alive and then after . . . when after the Feast, they . . . *how they gathered what was left of him and I saw his tiny, lifeless body.*

When my cry is done, my mind chews on why Zadok is helping me. Is it really because of my scroll? Or because of Ariah? I conclude it must be because of my son, but whatever the motive, I'm starting to accept he may be right. But Sheba? I try to remember some Shebian, yet except for some greetings and a few dozen words that are the same in Egyptian, I can barely recall anything. Struggling, I manage to string a dozen old words together to create meaning, but it's an ordeal. For as long as I can remember, I've been speaking in Hebrew, thinking in Hebrew, dreaming in Hebrew. Funny, I know several languages, but I lost my fluency in the one I learned first. And except for my skin color, at this stage of my life, I'm as much a Shebite as I am an Edomite. No, I'm probably more Edomite; I've heard that at least Yahweh is worshipped down there. I picture me bowing down before the Shebian pantheon, strange beings whose earthly guise is half animal and half human, sacrificing to them, burning incense, laying out cow meat and beer, asking for the deities' help, to gods whom I have ignored for a lifetime, whom I'm sure would turn not an ear to me. But if I anointed stones with oil down there and prayed to Yahweh? Could he even hear me in the depths of Africa, so far away from his house here on earth?

I think of Hori. He was loving to me when not under the spell of my aunt. Although well into his late fifties now, is he still wrestling heifers to the ground? I think of my bowman from my youth and his thick lashes. He was at least a decade older than me. Could he be a widower looking for a wife? But there's Raddai and I query: is adultery still a sin if my husband and my god are hundreds of miles away?

My fingertips have become wrinkly fruit. It's time to dry and then let Zadok persuade me that my salvation lies below the Fifth Cataract.

But that's something I already know.

CHAPTER TWO

Water just can't compare to wine. And the goat-and-vegetable stew is a welcome addition to the limited diet I've been on for the past few days. As the three of us sit sopping our bread, I wonder how comfortable Zadok can be reclining on the sheepskins, his flexibility lost a reign or two ago. Every now and then, Cimon adjusts his body to something more tolerable, but the old man's face racks with the pains of arthritis.

"Shechem?" I repeat.

"Your brother will be acclaimed there in three days."

"I thought he was already made King."

"Anointed here quickly in Jerusalem, but not yet acclaimed. Things are happening fast, but not that fast. Still, they want it done before the start of the harvest. Anyway, heralds have already been dispatched throughout the Kingdoms. It will be crowded there, very crowded, many will leave their farms and orchards to land a glimpse of Rehoboam, and where there are people—"

"There are traders."

"Traders, yes." He smiles, impressed that I have caught on. "Picture the vendors at the city market and then double that, then double that several more times. I imagine there'll be caravans from Egypt, Cush, and, who knows, possibly even Sheba."

"They'll just take me to Saba?"

"For enough shekels, men will do anything."

"Shekels?"

"A gift from me."

"That's very kind." I think on this. "But why wouldn't they just take the silver and sell me?"

"No doubt they might, but better to be a live slave than a dead freeman."

"They will sell me."

"As a child, you weren't sold by the Ishmaelites. Maybe there is some honor among thieves. Not to dismiss your value, but how much could they possibly obtain for a married, non-virgin African, close to the end of her childbearing years? Plus, in addition to paying them the silver, you'll promise them that your mother will reward them handsomely when you reach Sheba."

"If she doesn't?"

Zadok swallows his bread. "Then she doesn't."

"Ahimaaz will be in Shechem."

"The King can't be acclaimed without him. Raddai will be there too. While my son may still think you're languishing in the dungeon, best you stay under the veil."

"You wouldn't happen to have any En-Gedi henna? And maybe some red ochre?"

"I can send Cimon to the market, assuming there are still vendors at the gate. Why?"

"Some insurance."

"To better play the whore?"

"Not that." Then I see it in my heart's eye and I swallow. "Shechem. That's most curious."

"Curious?" Zadok asks.

"That's my story where Jacob's daughter Dinah went out to see the daughters of the land, and it ended poorly for her."

"Then let's hope you're a worse prophetess than a writer."

א

By light fueled from pressed olives, within perhaps an hour of starting my new life, I sit by the mirror Cimon bought and mix the henna and the ochre together on the palette into a pasty dye. I test a section on my hand. More ochre, I think, as the hue is darker than what I want. So I remove the stain with some sheep's oil on a linen strip. Another try and I think this is the best it'll be, so I start lightening my skin. Not all of it, just on my feet, my hands, and around my eyes—the parts my clothes won't conceal. I attempted dyeing myself once before, with Galit. *If it really bothers you, let's see if we can make you less dark.* Giving in to her argument, I ended up looking more Egyptian than Judahite, and even for an Egyptian my appearance looked rather unnatural—a little too red. I decided then to not hide my color. But now I don't have that luxury, not if my dark skin is exposed between the sandal and the wool.

I remember making henna tattoos with Ariah. I tried to draw a lion on his cheek. He drew a smiling sun on mine. And stick figures of Mommy, Daddy, and him on my other cheek.

"Playing with dyes?" Raddai asked, standing there, watching us. "Isn't it a touch feminine? Is this something you should be doing with a boy?"

"Do you want us to stop, my lord?"

He was about to say something when our boy called out to him. "Daddy, can I draw on you?"

When Raddai just walked away, Ariah started crying. I remember thinking that if you believe I am doing such a wretched job raising our boy, then perhaps you should spend more time with him and do it better. Raddai should have been there for Ariah. A boy looks to his father as the devotee does his god. Yet I was the one who brought up our lion, as if I were rearing a daughter. Apart from lobbing criticism, seldom would Raddai want involvement. In that department, he was as unchanging as an Egyptian. Fatherhood should be more than just making a toy horse and then deserting him to be with your teenage wife or working your two jobs. Had I been too much the shrew? Were my expectations unrealistic? Would most husbands do exactly what Raddai had done, start anew with a young wife to produce an unblemished son? Yes. Yes, they probably would.

Draping on a poor-woman's garment that Zadok left for me, I find the wool tickles and scratches, so I throw my linen back on, even though it still reeks a little from the foulness of the dungeon. Then I put the wool over it, something I would never have done in the past, because by mixing the two garments I'm breaking the sumptuary law. I'll probably be breaking several more before this is over.

I meet them downstairs for a breakfast of pomegranates, grapes, bread, olive oil, and yogurt.

"While Cimon will go with you, you can't be too careful. Stay on the central highway with the pilgrims. While many have already left, the roads should still be full."

"How will you make do without Cimon?"

"Oh, I'm well-supplied here. I can manage for a few days. I'm not that much of an invalid. Not yet. My daughter-in-law tends to visit when her husband is out of the city. When he's not trying to talk me into living with them, she is." He swallows a date and continues. "Keep with your fellow Judahites, stay away from the Israelites."

"How can I stay away? They're half of us."

"Keb, I just want you to be careful. I've lived a little longer than you and have spent time up there. I've found many, if not most, uncivilized, ignorant, and wayward. But it's their nature. The ones that aren't highwaymen or fleecing you, they're either gleaning in the fields or screwing their livestock. It's just a good idea not to mix with them."

"Don't mix with them. You talk of them as the farmer talks of disparate seeds."

"Have you been around many?"

"My friend Galit came from the North."

"It's just been my experience, that except for a few, they're just not as cultured as we are. I don't know how they'd survive without us. Anyway, lately there's some talk in the North of succession. There have even been a couple of riots that your brother had to put down. All small stuff, but still. That's why Rehoboam agreed to be acclaimed in their Shechem, as a gesture to them. Just be—"

"I'll stay to the highway, keep with the pilgrims, and I'll be careful."

He nods to Cimon who returns with a large skin.

"Open it," Zadok instructs.

I pull out a collapsible writing board set complete with reeds, sheets of papyri, a well, and a juglet of black ink.

"A present," he says.

"You're too kind."

He nods, beaming. "Cimon, come here."

"Do you want me to pick you up?"

"First, I want you to reach under my tunic and touch my testicles." After Cimon complies, he goes on. "Swear by Yahweh, god of the skies and of the earth, and by your god Moloch that you will protect Keb from all harm, that you will see her safely to the acclimation. Do as she says, as you would me, even laying down your life. Then come back to me."

"All this you say, Zadok, I swear," the Ammonite testifies, "I swear to Yahweh and I swear to Moloch."

"You can remove your hand and help me up now." As Cimon obeys, Zadok turns to me. "I'm also entrusting to Cimon my seal and chord in case you are questioned. Of course, if you are stopped by one of my son's agents, my insignia will not help, but there are some who may be ignorant of Ahimaaz's intentions toward you and who still may know the name Zadok. Cimon also carries my letter saying he's my property should anyone question who he belongs to, just in case my seal and chord are inadequate. The letter is more for his journey back after he delivers you to the traders. On your way there, you may want to pretend that he is your servant."

I look at Cimon, wondering if my life will truly depend on him. He took an oath to protect me, but does that mean anything to an Ammonite slave?

"Your skins are stuffed with water and milk," Zadok continues. "Cimon also has bread, olive oil, onions, cucumbers, grapes, figs, and dates. Cimon will also carry a change of clothing, a new linen garment we purchased for you to wear for your comfort when you leave the Kingdoms. And twenty shekels for the traders. I imagine that should be more than enough. You should leave now. The gate will open soon. Go while it is still twilight and you can blend into the crowd leaving the city."

As the slave and I head for the doorway and I veil up my face, the old man throws me some final words. "While you were washing yesterday, Cimon took me to the Temple where I made sacrifice and said prayers. I promise, Yahweh will be watching.

He got you out of the dungeon; he'll be with you now as he's always been."

א

There must be over a hundred of us, tightly packed, waiting for the Jerusalem gate to open. I feel no better than a conscript in the midst of battle, pressed inside a row, deep in formation, waiting for the man in front to fall. Then there's the city stink. If there's something I won't miss, it's the stink. That's the problem with defensive walls: how they're better at keeping odors in than out. Thank Yahweh we're in the month of Ziv, at least we're not in the season of picking summer fruit in the choking-hot, stuffy air, with neither wind to wisp it away nor rain to diffuse.

There's a restless girl, maybe ten or eleven, tugging at her mother's arm, wearing a nose ring. I take a quick census around me and I see a few more rings on noses. This is most amusing. Before the reading of the scroll, I'm certain that only one person in the city wore such adornments: me. Look at that, my fictional, ring-wearing Rebekah has started a novelty. Funny what a reed and a well of ink can do.

I take in one last look at the old palace, where I stayed last night and where Zadok must now manage alone for a little while. Finding the roof, I imagine my grandfather David strolling on it during an early-summer day, after taking an afternoon nap. It was then he spotted the married Bathsheba washing on a neighboring rooftop. I try to pick out which nearby house might have been my grandmother's, probably one of the ones terraced right below (I wish I had met her, but she died before I arrived here). Bathsheba had to have known she was in the King's sights up there. She must have planned it all along, having her servants haul up the limestone tub, showing off her nakedness when her husband was away at one of the many wars. When David took her—that was adultery for both of them. But of course, you don't get punished if the King is a co-conspirator. Well, not by the laws of the realm, but punished by Yahweh. He did take their baby.

Above David's old residence, perched on the summit, are the Temple and the King's palace. I see them anew just like I did when I was a little girl on that day I arrived here for the first time. Never glimpsing Yahweh's house again will be another hole in me that can't be filled. The palace, I'll miss that too, especially the memories of me as a child with Talus and Galit, and even with my father. But mostly those times later in life, of chasing a giddy Ariah down long hallways.

They open the gate and we have no problem getting past the guards. For one thing, there are too many of us for the soldiers to interview, assuming they're even looking for me. But, as always, their attention seems fixed on the people trying to get into the city, not out. After herding through, I take in for the last time the lower pool, the grazing and stoning fields, the sycamores and date palms out in the Hinnom, the trees all so firmly planted in the soil.

Go from your father's house to the land that I will show you.

Still, I'm not ready to venture out, not yet. There is something I need to do first. "Cimon, I want to visit my boy and feed him."

"You have a son?"

"He's in the Mount of Olives."

The servant scratches his neck. "Mistress, Zadok gave me instructions to have you at the acclimation on time."

"'Do as she says, as you would me.'"

"He also said we are to keep with the pilgrims, and they aren't going where you want to go. See them? They're all streaming right, to the highway."

"'Do as she says as you would me.' You took an oath."

"Your safety is paramount and that was part of the oath too. If Zadok asked me to do something that might injure him, say he said, 'Cimon, I think I can walk down the gate,' I would still carry him over his protests."

"This will be the last time I can visit my boy. If you want to stop me and carry me to Shechem, that will be your decision."

"Mistress, please."

"You can go to the right if you want, but I'm veering left." I take several steps and remove my shawl. Then I stop, finding him where I left him. "Coming?"

Trekking the field over to the twin hill, my sandals feel heavy slugging through the mud. It must have come down fairly hard last night, as quite a number of fallen fronds have landed in the muck. I'm ready for the season's rains to finally end, as they should have weeks ago. Then again, when I arrive at Sheba—if I arrive at Sheba—will I grow tired of one day of oppressive blue following another?

We reach the base of the hill. I see the two paths, one going to shrines and the place where I underwent my childhood rite until my sisters' taunts bullied me home. The other to the tombs. Naturally we take the latter, and I try to detect my former footprints, as I've made so many, but the recent rains must have ordered them away. While the traces of my steps may be gone, I don't need them to walk the hill, for I could do so with eyes veiled, sensing every rock and weed by heart.

"Can I help?" Cimon asks, as I momentarily lose my footing in the mush.

"I can manage."

Smelling the clean air, feeling the damp, the hurt in my knees, what has become a near daily ritual, I take it all in, holding it for as long as I can, like a dying man breathing in his last.

Leading Zadok's slave, I enter the beginnings of the cemetery, finding the hewn bedrock of family tombs planted side by side, food baskets and bowls in front of most. Only the well-off can afford these rock cuts; the poor are buried in pits out in the valley, as are a few of my stillborns. We come to the one with the large round flat stone sealing the front, the one with Raddai's name inscribed over it. Not wanting to be buried with his family in Lachish, my husband purchased this resting place for himself and his descendants, the line that will start anew with him, so each can lie with his father. Here is where my Ariah now rests. For the moment, Ariah lies on his rock bench alone.

I've been reliving that horrid day, over and over: tearing my clothes, the screaming and sobbing, grinding dirt in my hair, donning the coarse sackcloth, the goat hair digging into my skin, sitting in the ash, then rushing to entomb what was left of him before sundown, covering him in shrouds. Then all of us, Raddai, Hannah and her girls, the slaves, the mourners, everyone wailing, slowly traipsing the hill, rolling back the rock, lighting the lamps, burning incense, laying him on the bench, resting his head on the chiseled headrest, placing by his side his toys, changes of clothing, and juglets of food and milk. Then we close his eyes, leaving the lights burning so he won't stumble with Mot in the darkness on his way. We seal the cave. Then cry ourselves sick as Yahweh consigned him to the Gates.

"Give me the milk and some dates," I ask Cimon.

"As you wish, Mistress."

As Cimon hands the skins over, I can see his disapproval of what I am doing to our food supplies, but who knows when my boy will eat again. Even if Zadok is true to his word, it may be days before his Ammonite returns here to carry on the function. Some believe, unless the dead are continually fed, that they have the power to cause harm to the living. So after I leave the city for good, would my ravenous boy take his revenge out on me? Not my innocent Ariah, not him. But what if down there his sweetness has died, leaving just an angry, evil spirit. An angry, evil, and hungry spirit.

I'm sure Raddai tells himself it was enough for him to just buy the tomb, so why give our son any food? He took the family here a little over six months ago, to show us our resting place. Funny, our visit conveniently happened just weeks before my son died, as if Yahweh had just bestowed Raddai, of all men, with the gift of prophecy.

"Would you like to talk to your loved one?"

The voice creeps from a woman near my age, her face clothed in dirt, her body wrapped in a few wool rags that serve as a kind of garment. I have seen her up here a few times bothering other mourners, when the soldiers have been away from the tombs as they are today.

"I have a talent for peering into the netherworld," she continues.

"I think not." Cimon offers before I answer, trying to plant a seed of moving on.

"How much?" I ask.

"A shekel."

I tug on the slave's loincloth. "Come on, we better be going." The witch's price seems exorbitant and I have wasted too much time as it is. Plus, I'll need all we have for the traders.

"Don't you want to talk to your child?"

"How do you know my husband or my parents are not in there and that I would want to talk to one or all of them?"

"I know."

Does she? Is she legitimate or a charlatan? Whatever her nature, Cimon follows me as I start retracing our morning footprints. She attaches herself to us though like a pesky moth, but at a safe pace or two behind. Like the poor she is, she has no sandals, her feet are black sticks of mud.

"You're still with us? Better leave or I'll tell the soldiers at the bottom, and you'll know what they'll do to you when they find you."

"That would mean you would have to stay and witness, but the acclimation's waiting for you?"

How does she know? Because we're carrying skins and half the city is pilgrimaging up to Shechem? Or does she really have the gift of sight?

"Three quarters of a shekel, Mistress. He has so much to tell."

"A quarter," I say.

She shakes her head so we start our decline down the hill.

"Half," I hear her call out behind us. "I can't do it for charity. It will take a lot of milk for him to come near the surface, and I have to lay that out."

"I already gave him some food."

"I'm sorry to say that won't be near enough."

"Tell me, all the times I've been up here, have you been hiding in the woods over there waiting, and when I'm done, you go steal the food I've given Ariah?"

"Mistress, I would never tempt the wrath of the souls down in Sheol. I have my own goat for milk, I don't need yours."

"A quarter."

"A half. You won't regret it. When they come to the surface, I can hear them quite well."

Leaving her, I keep hiking down the path, expecting another call out to meet my price. But this time there is only the wind moaning through the sycamores. She must read I'm weakening, ready to swap the sword for the olive branch.

I stop, my feet frozen in the mix of mud and grass. But she probably knew that before I did.

CHAPTER THREE

Cimon is digging at the foot of the tomb. Every so often he looks up, glaring, signaling his discontent that we should not be doing this, that he's breaking his promise to his master. *Well, Keb, you better get use to this. He's not your slave. He's Zadok's.*

"What do you do exactly?" I ask the witch. "Do you bring him up onto the earth?"

"That would make him angry. He will get close to the surface, and if he wants to talk, I can hear."

"You'll let me know everything he says?"

"Naturally. He was taken at a young age?"

"He was close to seven."

She lets a moment or two pass. "There is something unusual about your journey north?"

"Unusual?" I repeat.

"Some people are excited about such a journey and welcome it." I just wasted a half a shekel on this fraud and poor Cimon is digging for nothing. "But you are not one of those people, are you?" she asks, as I weave my attention back on her. "I'm afraid you are not excited at all. Maybe what you are feeling is dread."

"Perhaps."

"There's trouble back home, isn't there?"

I say nothing, letting her do the work.

"You're running from something, aren't you?" she asks.

"What makes you say that?"

"I know." Again, what visible signs might she be using as crutches for insight? What does she see: a woman with a servant by a tomb. She must realize I have silver. Or had silver. I'm alone without a husband. But this absent husband could be busy, as mine is, or she may see me as a widow. My outer garment is wool, clothing of the poor, yet I wear sandals. A wealthy woman disguising herself. With strange henna circling her eyes. That's all the evidence she needs. Then again, some demon may have gifted her with prophecy, and she can divine. Perhaps she can.

"This is your first time with a necromancer, isn't it? You are unsure."

"I am."

"You have thought many times about going to one, but lacked the courage until now." Here she misses the mark, while Cimon's digging like a conscript. "But you have put more faith in traditional things. Things like prayer and the priests of the Temple?"

"Perhaps."

"The priests despise us. They feel we invade their territory. Why pay a priest when you can go to a necromancer. But if you're the priests and you can stone your competition, all the shekels will then come to you, don't you see?" She redirects her focus on Cimon. "That is deep enough, just round it and make as close to a perfect circle as you can." Her eyes then burn in mine. "There is a lot that is troubling you, Mistress. But I sense that it will work itself out."

"How so?"

"By letting things take their course. Sometimes it's best not to be at war with oneself. Be the pebble flowing with the current. To do the opposite only feeds the demons and Evil Eye. Is it your dark skin?"

I touch my veilless cheek, remembering I removed the fabric after we left the city. "What about my skin?"

"Some might think it's bad luck."

"It is bad luck."

"What's bad can change. I believe yours will change. Just give it time."

If she can truly glean the future, would I want to know it? If only I could be told of just the good and be deaf and blind to the rest.

The witch again examines Cimon's work. "You can stop now. Over there are my skins, place the milk in the hole and add to it yours that you laid out."

By her goatskins is a pushcart that seems to contain her few belongings: tattered rags, mainly, but sticking out of the wool, a small toy chariot, one that shows signs of age as the wood is chipped, stained, weathered, and the plaything is missing a wheel. So she had a son who was taken. Does she still grieve or has she somehow learned to be numb to it all?

Cimon grabs two sacks and starts reaching for a third. "Two's fine," she says, "that should be enough for Ariah."

She knows my son's name! Wait, I mentioned his name before, I think. Or maybe not. I can't remember. If I had blurted it out, have I unwittingly done something terrible? While my understanding of witchery is limited, I recall that a necromancer armed with that knowledge, along with the ability to summon demons, would have tremendous power over Ariah. Power to harm him and do the worst of things. The Gates of Sheol would offer no protection.

When the slave is done pouring, the woman sits on her knees by the pit, creaks her neck, then shuts her eyes, taking several long breaths as she holds out her palms, and starts chanting unfamiliar sounds. "Ama nama mea vu, ama nama mea vu . . ."

Cimon flashes a cold stare. Do they have witches in Ammon? They must.

"I see a small boy," she says with her lids still closed. "He's dark like you."

"That's him."

"I see him, I do. He comes for the milk. Ariah over here. We're here. It's all right. Drink a little, that's what the milk is for. It's all for you. Drink up, drink until your hunger is satisfied. That's right. It's good, isn't it? I see you are done for now. Is there something you would like to say to your mother?"

There is a long pause, and my heart churns inside and out.

"I love you Mommy," the witch says in a high-pitched voice.

I break down. "My gods. I love you too, my little lion."

"I miss you so much."

"I, I miss you too, I . . ." I can't finish, my voice becoming nothing but uncontrollable weeping.

"It's all right, please don't cry, Mommy. Please do not worry for me down here. I'm all right. You know me. I'm a lion. Not afraid of anything."

"You wretched fake!" I strike her hard across the face.

Leaving that witch with her head down in the milk, I trudge as fast as I can in the wet grass, with Cimon rushing behind me. Since my son's death, I can't remember being this angry, angry at the swindler, angry at myself for being swindled. My shy, timid Ariah, not afraid of anything. I'm sure one day he would have roared, but he wasn't roaring yet, not when he died. When her pain goes away, I'm sure she'll be laughing. Laughing like Hodiah and Reuma were laughing all those years ago on the other side of the hill.

"Is there anything I can do?" Cimon asks.

I should tell him he was right. The slave was right all along. We've wasted precious time and a half shekel that I needed. But I just remain silent, keeping my admission to myself. At least he is refraining from giving me an I-told-you look. Does he know that it was not just me, but his master too who had erred? For it's not the Israelites I have to worry about fleecing me; it's my fellow Judahites. Or maybe it's everyone. The witch tells you some words you want to hear, you start to believe, and then get taken in, as if shot by your own arrows.

When we reach the bottom and I veil up, I question for a moment whether I should say something to the guards about her, to let the elders punish her fully, but that I cannot do. She was right about one thing: I would have to remain in the city and witness, and then I would be back in the dungeon. So she'll live another day to dupe her next grieving victim.

I have no choice. Passing by the guards on duty outside the gate, I ignore them as we hurry, crossing the rain-soaked valley and incline up Mount Zion, the western hill that leads to the central road. We're now targets for thieves, a couple of hours behind the Jerusalem pilgrims. Two ripe grapes waiting for the press.

א

My eyes and Cimon's dart all over the landscape looking for signs of danger, whatever that could be. Occasionally we turn around to see if anyone is creeping up, our legs in a slight jog, trying to make up the time, trying to catch up to the celebrants whose company we should have never left.

I think of the witch. I punched her. Strange. I never hit anyone before. Not a slave, not even Ariah. Well, there was that

215

time a month ago I threatened Eglail with death when she was at it snooping again, but it was just a threat, I didn't have to act. But here I am slugging a woman. Could old Zadok be right, that outside the ramparts of civilized Jerusalem or any Judahite city, people turn into wolves?

Overlapping shrieks. I halt, tensing up, waiting for the highwaymen.

"There, see them, just a flock of birds," Cimon says as he points in the distance. "Quails, perhaps."

As I watch them fly off, sailing through whitish gray, I relax a little, but fret on whether I can take two or three days of this. Each step I take is one more step north, a step farther away from Jerusalem, a city as familiar and protecting as a child's lullaby. Glancing backwards, I can still see clearly the Temple and the palace on top of Mount Moriah. Yet I know we're already in the territory of Benjamin, in the beginnings of Kingdom of Israel, the kingdom that David's rival Saul cobbled together.

Ahead in the distance, there's a ritual bath, and looming beyond that, walls and defensive towers. My geography Talus taught me as a child comes back like a burgeoning vine. In front of me has to be Gibeah, Saul's old capital.

"So why don't you just run away?" I ask, hoping that prattling will calm me.

"What's that, Mistress?"

"Why don't you just flee, as I understand Zadok would have no recourse."

"Leave you here on the highway alone?"

"You could."

"I should just leave you? Who'd dig your pit then when you encounter the next spurious witch?" he asks, wearing something close to a smirk.

216

I ignore him, gazing out at the remaining oaks and sycamores on the hills, so many have been chopped down for needed
lumber and to clear soil.

"I swore on Moloch to get you to Shechem and for me to return back," he offers.

"It doesn't look like Moloch's done you much good. Your
town—"

"Like Yahweh's done for you?"

"Your town burned. You're a slave."

"I assume Moloch let my town burn for a reason. As for me,
I'm well in my fifth year. My freedom's near."

"No piercing of the ear for you then?"

"If I decide to do that, I'll be the one piercing it."

"And Zadok?"

"What of him?"

"He'll have to manage without you."

"I suppose he'll have to."

"Who will carry him to the Temple?"

"Maybe your god. Zadok can ride on the invisible shoulders
of your deity."

"You like to mock, don't you? First me, then—"

"Apologies. Mistress." He runs his fingers through his course
hair. "If you were me, you'd run?" he asks, circling the subject to
where it started.

"I'm not you."

"But if you were?"

"I'd owe a duty to my master and my god. But if I were the
type where that meant nothing, I guess it would depend if I had
a place to go to. You have no other kin? No other villages or cities for you in Ammon?"

"Not in Ammon. But there is a place on the other side of the
Jordan I have—" His mouth runs silent. Something robs him of

his thoughts. He points. "Up there. See them? They're leaving the city gate."

Pilgrims.

He looks at me, and I nod. And we both run.

But after just several steps, I grab his shoulder. "Cimon, stop."

"This will only take a moment," I say as I remove my cheap wool outer garment, leaving on my linen dress. He puts on that questioning look of his. "If we are to pretend that you are my slave, I need to look like I'm made of silver."

"But at Shechem—"

"At Shechem, I'll put it back on. Here." I hand him my scarf and the wool, and he stuffs it as best he can in one of the large skins.

"You understand you're making yourself more of a target."

"Not if they accept us and we blend in. Hand me that smaller skin there." In it, I find some olive oil. "I know, we could use this for eating, I'm just taking a little." What I really need is a cleansing cream of sheep's tail oil and powdered limestone, which I carelessly forgot to pack, but I rub what I have around my eyes. "Is the henna gone?"

He shakes his head. "You still look like a brown bear. But with everything in reverse."

Annoyed at him and at the dye, I place the oil juglet back in the pouch.

"They'll think it is just the latest way we Judahite women paint our faces. Come on."

We run and catch up to a dozen Benjaminites as they climb up the ridge. Cimon nudges me to speak.

"Are you going to the acclimation, going to Shechem?" I shout out. "If so, can we join your party?"

One of them waves us over and we become part of the pack. And soon enough, a few start singing:

I long, I yearn for the courts of Yahweh
My body and my soul shout to the highest god
Happy is the man who finds refuge in you
Whose mind is on the pilgrim highways

I know this one and join in. For a little while, I lose myself in the melody, trying to forget all my thorns and thistles: the looming bandits, Ahimaaz and his knife, my city and Temple that I'll never see again, my dead cellmate, that phony witch, Zadok's arrogant servant beside me, my Ariah, hungry and malignant, waiting to be fed, and my possible future as a slave, performing unspeakable acts with my master.

Stop it, Keb. Keep your mind from whirling. Breathe and relax, you're no longer in the cell about to be stoned. Feel the warmth from the sun jutting out its head, smell the unsullied air, enjoy the curve of the hill, and remember that Yahweh has come through for you time and time again. As Zadok said, he got you out of the dungeon—or was Yahweh then just a mere observer and it was all Zadok's doing? No, Yahweh had to have lifted a finger. So I try my hardest to concentrate on the song, raising my voice louder.

Happy is the man whose mind is on the highways.

א

A ram's horn blasts. We submissively jump off the trail, letting fifty soldiers overtake us, all of them carrying spears and bronze shields, their destination no doubt the same as ours. I don't attain a good study of the troops, for it's best to be unnoticed. I crunch down pretending to adjust one of my mud-soaked sandals, compressing my body as much as possible. After a safe interval has elapsed, I rise and see leather-coned helmets and body plates over white tunics grow small down the road.

We resume our journey, and with the warming sun climbing the sky come insects. With no incense to scare them off, the gnats and flies are as ubiquitous and thick as womanly gossip at a village well. Swatting them only leads to new pests circling around me, so I try a strategy of acceptance.

Our band grows as a few more celebrants join us. The cliquish Benjaminites have left Cimon and me alone, which is just what I want. Less questions means less fabrications. But soon one ends his beautiful aloofness.

"So you're from Judah?" asks a man with a beard that may never have been cut, extending down to his chest, overcompensating for his thinning crown hair. What little hair he has on top, he has tried to grow out, placing it in a way to try to cover what's gone missing, looking worse for the attempt.

"Yes," I respond. "We're from Jerusalem."

"Really? Do you run into the new King at all?"

"The King? I've seen him at the festivals."

"We've done a few of those," he says, pointing to his wife beside him. "We don't do a whole lot of traveling, but how many times in your life can you witness an acclimation? With the new King, well, we're hoping for a better life."

"I think everyone is." Does he know that Rehoboam has been running the Kingdoms as Prince Regent for almost three years now?

"Do you land opportunities to speak to him?" he asks, playing with his hair, which the wind keeps knocking out of place.

"Who?"

"The King."

"I just live there, I don't attend court." I speak in half-truths of course. I have passed my brother many times in palace hall-ways when I lived there as a child. In these latter years, Raddai has occasionally forced me to court and to the banquet hall, and I would have no choice but be in Rehoboam's company. My brother is like what Solomon was, only larger in stature, but smaller in kingliness: his spine poorer of posture, his voice thin-ner of authority, his eyes always darting about in search of his advisors, his skin looking uncomfortable in the purple as if he had a rash all over his body. But I have mostly kept my distance from my idiot brother, remaining in my apartment, breaking up the monotony with an occasional visit to the market and lately with several trips a week to the Mount of Olives. In fact, I've never exchanged any words with Rehoboam in my entire life.

"You don't keep company with him and the elders and such?" The Benjaminite asks.

"I don't."

"He doesn't stroll down the streets and take the air?"

"I haven't seen him do that. A few times I have seen him leave the city with his retinue and soldiers."

"Well, if you have an opportunity to petition the King, can you let him know something?"

"What would that be?"

"Our taxes. They're too high."

"Are they?"

"A tenth of what the tax collector thinks I should produce, and that's just to Judah. That's not including the other tenth I have to pay my elders. Failing that, it's three months of forced labor or be conscripted in the army. You Judahites, you get out of it, don't you?"

"Get out of what?"

"Paying taxes."

I shrug.

"That's what I heard," he says.

"I'm a woman, what would I know of such things?"

"Nothing, I suppose. Well, we may try to petition him if we make it close enough."

With nothing I can do for him, he goes back to his wife, leaving me alone.

"Three months of labor out of twelve would be quite a burden, indeed," Cimon whispers to me, smiling.

I point out at the eastern hills. "No one's stopping you, except Moloch."

He shakes his head, his grin not quitting.

We continue to walk the rocky landscape, although in patches, there are farms and orchards, a few more numerous now then when we started. We pass a field of violet flowers, and I wonder: are they mandrakes? Maybe it was here that the fruits I ate came from. Of course, at the moment these plants could provide me no benefit, even if I were to whirl down the ridge like a madman and steal them. There would be no divine smell, no tasty fruit, no love potion, no fertility remedy to conceive a son, and no opportunity, if I were ready, to speed my way to the Gates. Because it will be months from now when the red berries ripen and by then I'll be hundreds of miles from this field, with Shebite traders in Egypt or Cush, or even a sex slave in Edom for all I know.

Once, after Ariah died, I was thrown so far into despair, I went searching at the market for more mandrakes, to overeat them, wanting to end it. But this was during the early rains of the month of Bul, during the last grain planting, and of course there was none of the ripe berry to be had. Back at my palace apartment, thinking of an alternative, I stared at the cooking knives at length, even picking one up, wielding it, pressing my thumb against the sharp edge, then clutching the handle with both hands. But I couldn't do it. I felt then I was such a coward for postponing Sheol, even though that would be the only way I could speedily be with my lion. Crying and fetaling, I wanted so very much to see him, and thought how cruel and wretched it was that he was taken from me. That's when I stumbled upon my plan about trespassing into the Temple. The plan gave me purpose, weaning me away from the abyss, and as a consequence has placed me now in the central hills on a dirt path to Shechem.

אַ

Outside of Gibeon, we pick up a few more travelers. Our growing band continues northward. On a ridge overlooking us, two boys in a donkey race stop their animals to gaze down and wave big hellos, and most of us reciprocate, even haughty Cimon.

At midday, we stop for a rest. I find the skin of food, and offer some bread, oil, onions, and figs to my traveling companion.

"It's all right," he says, motioning me off. "I can go without."

"We have enough. Take it."

"I'm fine, Mistress, really."

"You're making me feel bad that I used some of our provisions for frivolities."

Indulging me, he takes a little bread and onion, something Eglail would never do. When he's finished, he finds a stick and starts rubbing it around in the dirt.

"What are you doing?" I ask.

Failing to answer, he just keeps scraping the branch around.

"Cimon?"

He looks up at me as I wait for his reply, but then he goes back to the cursed branch.

"Talk to me."

Trying to understand him, I recall my story of Lot's daughters. How after Sodom and Gomorrah, holed up in a desert cave, sure that was no one else was alive in all the world, desperate to preserve humanity's seed, the girls got their father drunk. Then they took turns penetrating with him. The two became pregnant and conceived sons who became the ancestors of the Ammonites and the Moabites. I look at this odd Ammonite and question just how far off I was in imagining he and his people are the product of some ancient incest, the offshoot of an abomination from long ago.

"I'm done," he says. "Come see from my point of view."

Wondering which one of us is the slave, I obey.

There's no question what I'm looking at: me. His portrait is quite good. As if he's captured every tired and sad line that collectively makes up my excuse of a face.

I gaze up at him and start to see his, maybe for the first time. Not deep angular features like Raddai or Pi, but softer and gentler, which had been masked over by his arrogance. Then there are his brown eyes with flecks of olive, eyes that may be deeper and wider than most to take in more of the world.

"You've captured me, the only thing missing is my dark skin. But a dirt outline I suppose has its limitations."

"When you look upon yourself in the mirror, it's your color you see first?"

"Apart from putting on the henna this morning, I haven't used a mirror in quite a while." I take in more of his earth art. "Too bad your work won't last."

"You've seen it and will hold onto it," he says, "no matter what happens to the ground."

"But will others have a chance to appreciate it? Still, it looks so real and a shame your drawing will eventually be no more."

"Should we just stay here, Mistress? Protect it from being run over by pilgrims and bandits?"

"I'd be more concerned about the next rains. Surely, that will see to its end."

"Then let's pray for a severe drought."

I offer him a full smile, maybe my first in a long time.

א

By late afternoon, as thick clouds take the sky, we stop a few miles from the Ephraim border, near Ba'al-hazor, a town known for its sheep shearing. About half the pilgrims go to find lodging among the villagers, the rest of us make camp by the road. Cimon takes out his idol, an oak figurine of Moloch. The god's face—solemn, serious, and watching. The Ammonite bustles up the hillside to place his deity under a sprawling cedar, then kneels and prays. I find an aged sycamore, its bark peeling, like flaking papyri, a victim of several thousand sunsets. Under it, I conse-crate a squarish stone with a few drops of oil from my juglet, praying to my god to both deliver me safely to Sheba and to feed Ariah in Sheol. When I'm done, I mull on whether I should keep the stone, but decide not to. If I were to make this rock my one symbol of the Temple, it would become more of an idol than I care to admit. Plus there have to be square stones in Sheba or wherever I end up. The world is full of square stones.

"Let's eat," I say taking out some fig cakes to share with the Ammonite. All this walking has turned my legs into limestone, causing my hunger to intensify, which in turn helps the taste of the cakes. Biting down on them, I could be eating curds and wild honey.

"This morning you mentioned that when you are freed you want to go to some place on the other side of the Jordan."

"Tishbe."

"Tishbe? Where's that?"

"They say it's in Gilead. Close to where I used to live in western Ammon."

"What's there for you?"

"I heard that Tishbe is a village of craftsmen, of artists and outcasts."

"Sounds sublime if it exists. But I've heard of no pottery, jewelry, tapestry or garment bearing that name."

"If the village is mere legend, then I will build it."

"Like Cain built Enoch."

"Cain?"

"Never mind."

"Cain of *The Chronicles*? I remember now from the Festival."

"You were there?"

"Zadok was there," he says.

"He was, yes."

"And where Zadok goes, so does his faithful servant." I start cleaning up and readying for bed, and the faithful servant lends a hand. "If this Cain who had so offended your god with a poor sacrifice can still find favor in his eyes and build a city, why not me?"

"Why not you?"

As I arrange a few of the goatskins and clothing to form something close to a sleeping mat, I wonder what it would be like to be Cimon, an ardent devotee of the Ammonite deity of second chances, a fervent believer of life after the flood.

CHAPTER FOUR

An incubus attacked me in the night! I wake up wet and feel my undertunic and loincloth, finding the latter damp. If I could see it in the pre-dawn dark, I'm sure I'd find it stained. I reach for the skin that I'm using as a headrest. In it, I have stowed my other loincloth (thank you Zadok for the change of undergarments). I find the clean linen and put it on. Fragments of my dream linger, planted in my heart by the night demon, and perhaps the full moon too was a co-conspirator. But what I would do to remove all traces of the nightmare from memory. Just like the way I imagined Potiphar's wife trying to seduce Joseph, and the way Galit would approach any man she wanted, I dreamt I went up to Cimon and said, "Lie with me." This was a command that he most willingly obeyed. There I was, caressing and kissing his large arms and chest, then descending down lower, to his member, starving for it like some ravenous animal. I put it deep inside me, committing adultery. Then I woke up as if it had all really happened.

It's not just acting on these desires, but merely coveting him that is a punishable by death. But I'm not coveting. It's not me, it's demonic forces taking control of my dreams and my body. It has to be. How can I have such feelings when I mourn so for my boy, when he's but six months in the tomb? If only I had a red garment to ward off the spirit.

"How did you sleep, Mistress?"

"I slept well enough, and you? Experience anything unusual in the night?"

"If you consider sleeping with a rock pressed up against your lower back unusual, then yes."

I sit cross-legged with Cimon, eating raisins and parched grain for breakfast, saying nothing more, trying to avoid looking at him, still working out the crimes I've committed. Over the past few days, I have amassed so many. But many of my acts and deeds are sins only because the priests have said they are, and I know firsthand that the priests can be wrong, horribly wrong. Just ask my friend in the dungeon. Maybe that so-called witch was right about one thing, why should they have exclusivity over knowing Yahweh's wishes, especially when they are now using my stories to steer them?

We pack up and walk with the travelers. By midmorning we leave the land of Benjamin and enter the tribal territory of Ephraim. Almost at the border, in the town of Beth-El, the terrain changes from a rocky and stubborn wilderness into a landscape with one fertile farm neighboring another. Growing on the terraced hillsides and the valley floor are high stalks of barley waiting for the sickle. In a few days, the grain will all be reaped, except for a tiny corner of each field, leaving that remnant to the gleaners.

"You all right, Mistress?"

"I'm fine."

"You seem rather quiet."

"I'm fine, Cimon."

I try not to dwell on last night's dream, of the consequences of acting on what the incubus placed in my heart, but
I think of little else. I had similar thoughts of Pi while bathing
in Zadok's tub two days ago, but that was just a fleeting notion, something that would have little chance of coming to
fruition. Even if adultery were to occur, it would be in a land
far away from Yahweh and the priests. But lying with Cimon? I
could just say the words or touch him, it could happen—
although if witnessed it would be death for us. I reflect on my
invented story of Jacob's first-born Reuben committing adultery with Jacob's concubine Bilhah. As a doting father to his
sons and the tribal chief, Jacob spared Reuben from a stoning,
and Bilhah too. But the act did eliminate Reuben from suc-
ceeding his father as heir.

I felt it important to ink the story, for the draconian penalty
for adultery should be mitigated. Take Galit. Was she supposed
to have remained celibate her whole life because a eunuch had
decided to take her as a wife? Isn't that too much to ask of any
woman? Then I remember the power of my writing. Assuming I
were to lie with Cimon and we were caught, would my Reuben
story now cause the priests to lessen my sentence and that of
Zadok's slave? But the question need not be answered if I can
remember that I'm still a married woman, that my duty and affection is to Raddai. For until he divorces me or dies, he's now
and forever my husband. Even if his passion for me has been
wanting for the longest time.

Is true romantic love even possible? Of any of my female
characters—Eve, Sarah, Rebekah, Rachel—did I ever have
them expressly think or state that they loved their husbands?
No, I didn't. Was that something I intended? Funny, I can't
remember my mindset at the time I picked up the juncus reed.
But they and the patriarchs must have been in love with each

other. Jacob was in love with Rachel. I recall the words I wrote, words that came from me. *So Jacob worked for Rachel for seven years. They seemed in his eyes only a few days, such was his love for her.*

In the beginning was I ever in love with Raddai? Not your ordinary love, mind you, but that Jacob kind of love. I think the answer is yes. But it's hard to know for sure as anything at that level or close to it was felt in another epoch, when the gods were less distant.

א

By midday we pick up a few more pilgrims at Shiloh, which had housed the ark before it was brought to Jerusalem. The town still contains a large Yahweh shrine that I've heard rivals his Temple in Jerusalem. As the ark resided here for hundreds of years, Yahweh's presence must still linger, and I try hard to feel him, but the profane thoughts I've been wrestling with all morning keep interfering. If our band were to stop, I would very much like to leave the highway and visit the sanctuary to make sacrifice. But nearly all in our troop want to push onward, anxious that we might arrive at Shechem in the dark. Then there's Cimon's grimace if I were to suggest we let them go on ahead. It's safer to keep with our company anyway.

We march on, leaving the city where the prophet Samuel grew up, passing more farms and orchards than I can count. It's warmer than it's been, and I spot not a raincloud in the blue. An unblemished sky is not only a most welcome sight but also a good omen, and I'm starting to think Zadok's plan may have a bowman's shot to work.

Not far from Shechem, our destination, we see a stream of people coming toward us.

"If you're planning to see the acclimation, and you're looking for accommodations, there's no room inside the gates," I hear one of the approachers say. "It's too crowded."

"No room at all?" one of our party asks.

"Well, you could try the field outside, but you'll be sharing it with well over a thousand, and they all look to be riff-raff and scoundrels. We're going to try our luck at Arumah, which is around here, somewhere."

I tug on Cimon's loincloth. "Should we try for the village?"

"Don't you think it's safer to be with the crowd in the grazing field?"

"A couple thousand or so people in a field? It must reek. If we go to the village center, someone will take us in." Of course, I don't really know this, but half our band had no problem finding shelter last night in Ba'al-hazor, and I've heard that it's an Israelite custom to take in strangers. "We should start while it's still light."

"Some here might camp on the road like last night. We should do likewise."

"You want another rock poking you? I myself could use a bed." To be honest, I prefer a little distance from Cimon tonight, and if we were in a house and separated, it would be for the best.

"What about Zadok's words to be wary of the Israelite?"

"What about them?"

Taking the lead, I stagger off the ridge highway with Cimon in tow and navigate the hill. We forge through a terraced field of golden barley, looking for any path that may lead to a village or at least a cluster of homes. After a while, we stumble across a small cemetery.

"There's a path." I barely register his words as I stare at the wood markers. Family members resting side by side, gathered together. At least no one's lying by himself alone. "Shall we take it?"

"What?"

"This path here, Mistress? I assume it leads to a village."

"Yes, why not."

The strip of walked-over grass takes us to four houses enclosed by a low, circular mud-brick wall, designed more to keep their animals in than an invading gang of miscreants out. A young girl comes down another path, opposite the compound, carrying a jug on her head.

"We're from Jerusalem and we're traveling to the acclimation," I shout. "Do you know anyone who could put us up for the night?"

She cradles the jug and runs into one of the houses.

I take in the shared yard. Scattered around are numerous jars and ewers, a dung-and-stick-fueled oven, an olive press, sickles, yokes, a variety of farm and animal equipment (only some of it looking familiar), four sheep and a goat, along with a trough for the livestock. I listen to the animal grunts, but it's in an undecipherable language. I stare at a tattered doll lying in the mud. Cimon nudges me.

"Do we just wait or should we try the other houses?"

Before I can speak, a man barges out with his wife and the girl, stopping a few feet from his door. Though in his thirties, his well-tanned face is cracked and creased and rough.

"You from Jerusalem, are you?"

"I am. Here for the acclimation."

"So my daughter, Athabaal, tells us." I see a boy Ariah's age take a step out from the doorway. It feels odd that the whole family is making us such a curiosity.

"I'm Keb and this is my servant, Cimon."

"I'm sorry, I'm being a poor host," he says rushing up to the wall, with his women following, the entire family in wool, threadbare, covered in stains. "Come inside, you

232

must be hungry." He motions us to an unlocked gate that leads into the enclosure. "My name is Nerel and this is my wife, Zibaal." Zibaal has a small nose and chin, ordinarily attractive features on most women, but oddly has the adverse effect of causing her large head to appear even larger.

"You're fortunate that Athabaal was a little late coming from the well or we would be in mid-meal by now," Zibaal says, looking disapprovingly at her daughter. We follow the three inside, but first I remove my sandals at the door. The windowless house is dusky, as the only light is the sinking sun poking its few remaining rays through the doorway.

"Sit, let me wash your feet," Zibaal shouts over the bleating of smelly goats crammed in the side stalls that flank the main area. Taking some of the water that the daughter had just brought in, Zibaal soaks a few wool rags that, by the look of them, could use a washing too. She strokes my legs with the wet fabric and, as she gets close, I realize that Zibaal hasn't fully bathed in some time. After two days without a bath, I must stink a bit myself.

"We really appreciate this," I say, not only because I do, but also to fill the air with much needed words. Zibaal gazes at Cimon and then back at me. I nod and she gives the Ammonite's feet and legs the same treatment.

"Daddy, is that a slave?" the boy asks.

"Yes, I am," Cimon says.

"Excuse my boy," Nerel tells me. "He hasn't seen any before, except the time we went to Jerusalem. Oh, let me grab my turban." Our host dashes upstairs and then comes back down, showing us his hat, resting it in his calloused hands. "We went to the Feast of Tents last year and I got this. First time we were in Jerusalem." The headwear has a linen Judah lion woven on it. I've seen this overpriced remembrance sold in the market.

"Nice," I say.

"We were thinking of going to the acclimation, but the harvest is almost here. Time is barley." He looks to his wife as if he were speaking her words.

They bring us upstairs to the table where sits a man, maybe sixty, who we learn is Nerel's father. After Nerel makes the introductions, the old man says not a word.

"It's all right if your slave eats with us?" the wife asks me.

"Quite all right."

"Apologies for not having any boiled goat. If we had advance notice, we would have had a pot waiting for you," Zibaal says. "Instead, we can only offer a stew of figs and olives."

"We're just glad to have anything cooked, and we can go without if there's not enough." Cimon and I sit on the mats and become comfortable around the low table.

"There'll be enough," says Zibaal as she brings two more wooden plates to add to the others. She serves us the stew from a plain, unadorned pot. Then she brings out dessert cakes in the shape of large-breasted Astarte—although with the family members' names ending in *el* and *baal*, I would have thought the dessert would be shaped differently.

"Blessed be the lord, your god, Astarte," I say so as not to offend.

"Thanks, but after going to the Feast last year, we're going to start offering sacrifices to Yahweh," Nerel says.

"You are? Really?"

"We've been making offerings all our lives to El, Astarte, and Ba'al—especially Ba'al since we're always concerned about having a productive harvest. Too much or too little rain and it can be a struggle. Before last summer, I'd never paid much attention to Yahweh, although I've heard he's popular in the South."

"We felt something new, something special for him when we listened to *The Chronicles*," Zibaal adds.

"I want to be Rebekah because she gave the camels water from the well," the girl Athabaal says. "Going from here to Haran must have made them very thirsty."

"She was very kind to them," I say, smiling.

"I like that one too, as it was Abraham's slave who pulled the caravan and played matchmaker." Cimon says, which causes me to shake my head at him.

"What about Noah?" the boy chimes in. "He saved *all* the animals."

"Noah probably had his sons do all the feeding," his sister argues.

"He didn't!" The boy starts to cry.

"Stop it, both of you," Nerel says, and then faces me. "My favorite part was the plagues," he says over the boy's sobbing.

"Take Eschbaal to his room," Zibaal directs the daughter while picking up another dessert cake to offer me. Warding her off, I turn my plate upside down.

"I see each plague as the defeat of a particular Egyptian god," I say. "Take the three days of darkness, that's Yahweh's triumph over Amun-Re, their sun god." I stop, catching myself, for I've been a fool. Why don't I just tell him I wrote the thing? And why stop there? I should add that your dinner guest is probably the most wanted fugitive in the Kingdoms. That Philistine mercenaries could be storming in at any moment.

"I don't know about that, but my other favorite part was when the sea collapsed over them Egyptians," Nerel says, "I enjoyed that one."

Behind this tale, Yahweh had forced the sea god Yam to do his bidding. But now I exercise more control, holding back my tongue.

"Since the Feast, the Chronicle stories are the only thing our children want to talk about," Nerel continues.

"We may go again to the festival this year to indulge them," the wife says, and then glares at her husband. "Just don't buy any more useless hats."

"See how she talks to me. Zibaal only started carping like this after she heard about Tamar of *The Chronicles* standing up to Judah, and those Hebrew midwives doing the same to Pharaoh."

"I've spoken my mind before."

"Not like this, I don't think."

"Because of Noah and Jacob, Eschbaal wants to shepherd to save animals," the old man says, talking for the first time, and then chuckles.

"Eschbaal loves playing Noah," Zibaal says.

"I don't think my grandson's quite figured it out that we herd the few goats we have not only to milk, but to eat if there's a shit crop, like this year."

"This year's been poor because of all the rain, but it's not a total catastrophe like it would be if we were in a drought," Nerel says. "Barley's pretty hardy—that's why I like it. Still, Adoram's men will ask for the same tenth that we would be producing under the best weather. That'll set us back."

"I'm sure our guest doesn't want to talk barley all night," Zibaal says. "So are you a widow or does your husband approve of you traveling alone with just your servant?"

"My husband died recently."

"Any children?"

"There was one."

"Sleeping with his father now, is he?"

"He is."

"How terribly sad for you."

א

Later, Cimon and I, along with the family, lie on mats on the roof. It is the first night of the summer warm enough to sleep up here, and Nerel unfortunately places me right next to Zadok's servant. Trying, but failing to cross the threshold into sleep, I stare at those large arms. At least by this time tomorrow, I'll be far away from them, on a caravan, I pray, heading south to the Negev or through Philistia and not to the harem of a Syrian prince.

As I turn on my back and stare up at Yahweh's celestial council, trying to associate each lesser god with his or her star, I manage to mostly take my mind off the Ammonite. Yet I have a full litany of other subjects to ponder: like whether my trespass in the Temple will do any good, like how best to negotiate with tomorrow's traders, like deserting Ariah to an untended tomb. But for some reason, I think most about our dinner tonight and how my stories have affected this Ephraimite family. How real these characters are for them, and how happy they are to recount my words. The very same words used to sentence the man from the dungeon to a cast of stones. And I dwell hard on why it is that both good and evil can spring from the same well of ink.

א

I awake, trying to shake my dream from last night, of Cimon again. Years ago, I had read an Egyptian scroll on dream interpretation. It said that if you dream of something twice, it is bound to happen.

The Ammonite and I pack our skins, say our goodbyes, and leave the compound, as the other residents come out of their houses to start their daily routines. I look back, watching Zibaal clean last night's dishes in the sand. Part of me wants to give her and the family one of our silver pieces for their hospitality, but as Galit told me many years ago, such a thing is not done. It is disrespectful and would rob your host of honor.

We retrace our steps back to the ridge highway and hike a couple miles north, eventually climbing steep Mount Gerizim. Stopping to don my wool and shawl my face, it dawns on me that, unlike yesterday when there was not a hint of cloud, the world above has turned gray, like ash from the altar, and there's now a kicking wind. Could the omens be changing? Reaching the summit and realizing I've never being this high up before, I try to squint hard enough to make out the northern pillar—one of the four holding up the sky—but see only countless hills and valleys. The world is that vast.

Unfolding below me is quite a marvel. Lodged between this peak and the next, Mount Ebal, sits the largest city I've seen outside Egypt. High walls and fortifications obscure much of it, but from this height I can view large patches of Shechem's houses, thin alleyways, and their temple, looking even bigger than Yahweh's in Jerusalem. On the grazing field filling up the narrow valley outside the city, several thousand are camped, more than the numbers at Jerusalem's feasts. The gates are closed, and I wonder if Rehoboam plans on just opening them, letting in the horde, allowing the rabble to plunder all that isn't nailed down.

Up until now, I had been convinced that my brother the King was nothing more than a hedonistic fool, only interested in grinding his harem for as long as his loins would allow, that he was born without a stitch of any political acumen. Yet quite surprisingly and out of character, he has made the astute move to be acclaimed here. As Zadok mentioned, it is a token to our Israelite brethren that Our Liege has come to their largest city. So much of the time the North seems to grudgingly bend to Judah's will, so why not toss them this conciliatory bone? Also, there's symbolism. I remember from a harp song that the twelve tribes long ago made a pact here with Yahweh to renew the covenant. So too will another oath be made today when Jacob's descendants submit to Rehoboam as king.

Shechem is the site where I placed Dinah's rape, another story drawn totally out of whole wool. In the tale, upon learning of his daughter's dishonor, Jacob was rather matter-of-fact about it, happily agreeing to a marriage between Dinah and the rapist, who was the prince of this city when it was in Canaanite hands. In contrast to the uncaring patriarch, I had Jacob's emotional sons, Simeon and Levi, livid about the prince's crime and scolding their father. *Shall he treat our sister like a whore?* Will I, too, end up enslaved to an uncaring master, receiving the same treatment or worse, my life's purpose to be raped over and over?

Signaling Cimon, I nod and we stagger downhill, then stir into the crowd.

"Be careful of your packs; hold them tight in your arms like this," he says, cradling one of his.

"And you be careful with the one with the silver."

"I plan to, Mistress."

"Good."

I recognize a Jerusalem face or two, but the rest are strangers. Many wear tunics in strange colors and patterns. Have they come from Israel's far reaches, cities and villages deep in the North and East, perhaps from the plain of Bashan or in Upper Galilee?

Under an evergreen oak by the main gate, there's a trader selling souvenir tapestries, one with Rehoboam's likeness, another with what I think is a scene of Jacob's sons about to massacre the Shechemites to avenge their sister's defilement. Perhaps it is vanity, but it is the picture on the second fabric that captures my attention. There are twelve men with swords drawn, but the weaver got it wrong. For in my story, it wasn't all the brothers, just Simeon and Levi who killed the entire male population of Shechem. The two were able to do this by first cunningly persuading the Shechemites to undergo circumcision, as a condition of a purported reconciliation between the brothers and the Shechemites in the aftermath of the prince's rape of Dinah. Then after all the Shechem men's members were cut, while the men were recovering from the ordeal and too weak to fight back, Simeon and Levi unsheathed their swords on them, including the prince.

I thought it clever to have the prince's member controlling him, leading him to rape throughout his life, and when part of the organ was removed, his life came to a fitting end. What shape would my story have taken had I not learned of a writing device from Talus, the one he called irony? My tutor showed me examples from songs of the island people of the Great Sea. I remember one in particular he sang concerning a king who mistakenly killed his father and, worse, married his mother. Then only after he had blinded himself was he able to see the truth.

With Cimon following me, I keep milling about, failing to find any Africans. Perhaps I should climb back up the mountain, allowing a better vantage point. Soon enough though, I spot three dark-skinned men selling ivory, wild skins, and other novelties found only south of Egypt. I swallow, mentally rehearse some Shebian, and gather my thoughts. But my thoughts only make things worse. *Keb, you think they will just take you to Sheba? No, they will steal your money and enslave you, you know that.*

Soon, some foreign prince will treat you like a whore, just like Dinah.

Still, I creep closer, hovering by their wares, waiting for the traders to start their barter, but they say nothing. I suppose they think that in my wool I have nothing of value to offer. Yet after a while, the tallest of the three waves a horn in my face.

"Elephant tusks from deep in Africa." He has one of those lazy eyes, seemingly looking slightly away at me when he talks, as if there is someone or something more interesting behind me, causing me to glance back too, finding only Cimon.

I pause, gathering old words. "From how far down there in Africa?" I say slowly in Shebian. The tongue's harder than I thought it would be, and unsure of my accuracy, I switch into a more familiar Egyptian. "From below the White River?" I pull back my wool sleeve a little and reveal my dark arm.

"You know some Shebian," he says in Egyptian. "You from there?"

"I am. You?"

"Kerma. In Cush. But you'd rather speak Egyptian?"

"For your benefit."

"My benefit?"

"Yes," I say, noticing his two friends standing a little too close.

"You're not here for trinkets, are you? What do you want?"

"I want passage back there."

"To Sheba?"

"How much?" I ask, sighing, knowing I'm no negotiator.

"How much do you have?"

"You name a price first."

"It will cost you."

"I didn't think it wouldn't." I shoot a glimpse at Cimon, who I know is finding all this gibberish.

"I mean really cost you. Have you been through Egypt lately?"

"Why don't you tell me what the country is like these days?"

"Egypt is strong now, united. They have heavy tariffs. How much do you have?"

"Cimon, give me the skin." I open it up, showing him the insides. "Nineteen and a half shekels. My mother Queen Makeda will give you more when I return."

"You're daughter to the Queen?"

"I am."

"How come you didn't say you're daughter to King Awawa?"

"I'm daughter to both. She handles these matters, that's all."

"She does?"

"Do we have a deal?"

"If you're royalty, why do you need us?"

"I was kidnapped."

"So now, hiding in this clothing, you're planning on escaping with our help."

I take a long breath. "Do we have a deal?"

"I could just turn you in and land a big reward."

"Do we have a deal?"

He stares at me for several moments, scratching his ear, and then glances at his comrades. "One condition."

"And that is?"

"This slave of yours leaves now."

I quickly throw a glance at Cimon and then return back to the Cushite. "Why?"

"I don't like the looks of him. I can see him stealing the silver back."

"He wouldn't do that. He's planning on staying to the end of the acclimation."

"We're not going to take both of you. He's going to have to leave you eventually."

I ponder this as I stare at the servant, wondering if I'm ready to let go of his company and protection, but conclude that I have little leverage.

"Cimon, we've reached an agreement. Thank you for all your help."

"Mistress, perhaps—"

"You can go back now." I hug him a moment longer than I should and I kiss him on the cheek. "Thanks for all you've done. My heart to you."

His legs remain rooted in the soil.

"Cimon, please."

"Perhaps I should stay for a little while more."

I gaze at the traders, wondering if I could renegotiate. But I know the answer. "Cimon, I want you to go. You did as you promised, you brought me here. Now you must honor the final part of your master's instructions: to return to him."

"Mistress—"

"You swore to your god."

He stays put as if my words were nothing more than the yakking of a fool, a murmur shrouded by the crowd noise.

"Please. Do this for me."

"You really think you'll be all right?"

"As Zadok said, I am in my god's hands."

He gathers in the traders, as if trying to decipher their intentions.

"If you're sure," he says, his voice still begging.

"I am."

"Mistress."

Cimon takes a few steps, then looks back for a final signal. With my last nod, I watch him leave, this time for good. Just like I watched Pi leave all those years ago. While part of me is relieved, for temptation is no longer today's problem, I am, for the most part, sad and anxious to no longer have him by my side. There was a lot to like in the Ammonite and in another time and place . . . *We could have been friends, or perhaps—yes, perhaps . . .*

So once again I'm handed off to strangers, wondering what's next, a new sheet of my life ready for the first line of wet ink. It begins by watching my fellow Africans joke among themselves, waiting for the ceremony to commence, eyeing the thickening crowd. After exchanging gold for silver with a wealthy couple, the traders welcome another Cushite into their ranks. He's new to the group, tall like Lazy Eye, wrapped in a lion skin.

"Underneath this wool is a Shebite woman," Lazy Eye says to the newcomer in a Cush dialect that I can, for the most part, make out. "She wants us to take her back home. She says she's a member of the Shebite ruling family."

"What ruling family?" he asks.

"Still, we should keep her," Lazy Eye mumbles. It hits me that the worst of everything has come true, and I look to see if I can run in this throng. Shuddering, my chest convulsing, my legs pulling me away, I only manage a step before one of them grabs me.

I keep struggling as Lion Skin half encircles me. But then my scattered thoughts coalesce.

"What do you mean 'what ruling family?'" I ask.

"What do you think?" Lazy Eye asks the lion-skin man, whom I assume is the leader.

Lion Skin pulls off my veil, scrutinizes my face, as I would fresh gourds at the market. "I think not."

"Why?" Lazy Eye asks.

"Where's the ruling family?" I ask. "Is Queen Makeda living?"

"I've never liked that business," says Lion Skin, ignoring me. "There's Shishak's duties, we'll lose any profit there, and then there's the cost of feeding her, keeping her alive."

"We could sell her in Shur."

"I think not. If she were younger." Lion Skin faces me. "You can go."

"What happened to my family?"

"The Puntites and their Napatan dogs warred with Sheba."

"And?"

"There's nothing left."

"What do you mean there's nothing left?"

"Just as I said."

"My family is dead?"

"The King and all the army were routed in the war several years ago. But there are rumors circulating that the King of Punt took the Queen and made her a royal wife. Prince Menelik may be with her in Punt too or he may have come to same end on the battlefield as his father. But these are just rumors, no one can say for sure."

"I have a sister Irty—"

"I've told you the sum of what I know. Saba is a wasteland, and so is much of the rest of the country. I've seen it."

I start welling. My aunt, uncle, Irty, everyone I knew. All gone? As an archer, Pi must have fought and probably died in that war. Will I never know my mother apart from a few shreds of story I heard from Irty, Pi, and my father?

"Can I have my silver back?"

"She paid us close to twenty pieces."

Lion Skin thinks for a moment. "Consider it payment for your freedom."

"I have some clothes and a writing board in that skin."

He examines the pouch, and then hands it to me. "Go now, go before I change my mind."

I stumble away, weaving aimlessly through the crowd, pushed and elbowed, pricked and bumped, weeping about

Sheba and the people I knew, that they're most likely gone from this earth. My cone-shaped roof is probably gone too. That where my house once stood sits a circle of burnt ground and ash, and perhaps laying there with it, the decaying bones of Daanja and Hori, all of it now a festival for celebratory ants.

I think of my garden, my teacher and playmate. My garden, a breast I suckled on for eight years, turned by the ravages into drooping steppe and sagging weeds.

Then I think of me. *Now what? Where do I go? What the sheol happens to me now?*

CHAPTER FIVE

The main gate opens, and Shechemites pour out, suggesting that the ceremony will take place outside the ramparts. After the city's residents fill the field, the army gushes like the Gihon to the sound of trumpets. Hundreds and hundreds of troops shout for us to make way, pushing us back with their shields, pressing us tight, creating a large, open space in the field's center. I'm thrown back too, holding tight to my skin, my legs kicked hard by something, aching miserably below, wondering how badly I'm bleeding down there, but managing to stay upright. And I wait. With no room to breathe, I wait. Then wait some more. I can't see anything, as there must be a dozen or so bodies, civilian and soldier, making a human wall between the clearing and me.

An uncomfortable span of time goes by. Then I feel waves surging against me, pushing me forward and then back, and I'm subjected to some loud, angry cursing directed at someone I can't see.

"Mistress," I hear in a familiar Ammonite accent behind me.

After he finds me, I wrap arms, nearly crying.

"Thank the heavens. But why? Why are you here?"

"I stuck around and thought I might watch the acclimation, but then thought it best to return back to Zadok. I was half way up the hill when I realized I didn't have his chord and seal."

I feel my skin. "I have it. I honestly don't know what I would have done if you hadn't come back."

He gives me a reassuring smile, but then that vanishes. "Why aren't you where I left you?"

I tell my story. When I'm done, I receive the widest of eyes. "I'm glad you're not harmed. But the silver, should we try to get it back?"

"Try to take it from them? They're not the kind to just hand it to us."

"Without it, Mistress, we won't be able to hire some honest traders to take you elsewhere."

"No, they're four big men. Let it be a hard lesson. I should have paid more attention to the trader's insistence for you to leave. There were other signs as well. But I was fixed more on his promise to take me to Sheba."

"When I paint, I often make the mistake of paying more attention to the subject than the background."

We're interrupted by another trumpet blast. The people in front of us bob and slide, trying to catch a glimpse.

"Would you like to follow what's happening?" he asks.

"How?"

He lifts me on top of his wide shoulders, allowing me to witness the spectacle. I have a more than adequate view, realizing I'm fairly close—maybe thirty, forty yards away—to what must be a recently installed platform by the now open gate. Behind the stage, the giant oak forms an impressive backdrop. I'm not on the slave's shoulders for long when, to the roar of horns, the King's royal guard, his runners, about fifty of them, storm out of the city carrying their wooden shields, clad in full uniform with their high boots and breastplates covered in iron scales, semi-circling behind the stage. Next, a dozen trumpeters, dressed in simple short tunics, follow suit, taking positions behind the runners. Following them, a couple of dozen horses gallop out, kicking up low clouds, making a god's racket, each horse tied to a clanking iron chariot. When they reach the middle of the field, half of the animal-driven contraptions go off to one side, half to the other, all abruptly halting at the pasture's edges. After them parade the tribal elders, in their finest linen and turbans, some of whom I recognize from court. The elders have a lengthy walk, as they have to situate past the chariots, then they turn around to face the stage. Then to more musical blasts, several palace officials (the King's mostly young advisors), including my husband, march out, setting themselves right behind the stage. I feel my shawl and duck a little behind a tall man right in front of me, hiding myself from my husband until I realize how impossible it is for him to find me disguised in the midst of all this. Raddai looks the same. I make out no extra wrinkles. But still, is he dwelling on his runaway wife, the one disgracing and shaming him when she set food in Yahweh's house, perhaps now jeopardizing his position as Scribe? Has he assembled the pieces to figure out why I was even in the Temple? He won't. His mind's not that fertile.

Then out strolls Ahimaaz, in full breastplate, first to set foot on the platform, causing me to again check and feel for my shawl. More notes of the horn, which signal the arrival of dozens and dozens of heralds who circulate along the borders of the clearing, facing the people. Finally, to swells of cheers that become near deafening, accompanied by several more runners, comes my brother the King. He's in so much purple to have cost the life of every sea snail in Tyre.

He bows to the crowd.

"Long live the King!" the heralds shout. The crowd picks up the line, and we scream along with them. "Long live the King!" Each repetition of the chant crescendos louder.

Rehoboam jumps on the dais with Ahimaaz, who motions for still and quiet. Ahimaaz signals the heralds, and together they cry out in near perfect unison, "Children of Jacob, this is Yahweh's anointed, King Rehoboam, son of Solomon, grandson of David! Shall we acclaim him King here today? If so, shout: we do!"

"We do!" everyone cries out, as do I.

A flourish of trumpets jumps intervals from the tonic to the fifth and back.

"Do we submit to him?"

"We do!"

More trumpet fanfare sets up Ahimaaz's next question.

"Do we pledge our lives to him?"

"We do!"

As we swear fealty, the heralds' hands clap, which we all mimic. Permitting this to go on for a little while, Ahimaaz eventually waves everyone to silence. But before he begins to speak again, a solo voice rises from the midst of the body, hollering words seemingly so out of place, a dissonant note in an otherwise perfectly harmonious composition.

"What of our taxes?"

Heads turn every which way, trying to identify the culprit.

"Judah, do you submit?" Ahimaaz asks.

"Judah submits," the Judah elders shout collectively from the middle of the field.

"Benjamin, do you submit?"

"Benjamin submits."

"What of our taxes?" the stubborn voice surfaces again. His question is then appropriated and repeated by dozens in the assembly, although it is changed to "Why tax us?"

THE REED

The tall man in front of me unfurls something: a linen tapestry. He holds it out, showing it to those across the field. Then he slowly turns around revealing it to me and the others behind him. Sewn on the linen is a picture of two men wrestling with each other, the two at each other throats. On the side of one of the fighters is an enormous lamb tied on the altar, on the other, a tiny bundle of grain. Cain and his brother Abel.

The bearer of the tapestry gives a wide, threatening smile, every brownish tooth on display.

The dozens shouting about their taxes become thousands. Then some sort of new chant ricochets through the crowd—at first, it's a blur to my ears, but then the blur becomes words. "To pay for ships in the south!" That dies, but a drone of "More Judah palaces!" takes its place. Listening to this and frowning, I recall court records on dusty library shelves that as a child I had read only after devouring more interesting materials. But from these writings I had gleaned that for every fortification built in Israel, there are ten in Judah. I know that my southern kingdom has to worry about Egypt and Edom and even Philistia, but the North has an awakening Phoenicia and Aram on its borders. And while our brother tribes have been paying crippling taxes for our defenses and theirs, Judahites pay nothing. And there's the subsidizing of my family's lavish lifestyle, all those daily provisions to the palace of oxen, sheep, goats, deer, gazelles, and roebucks. Could Israel been more mismanaged?

"Lighten our yoke! Lighten our yoke!" becomes the newest recitation making the rounds.

I spot several more Cain-and-Abel tapestries, all waving in the crowd.

Not liking the direction this is heading, my brother jumps off the podium and runs to his advisors.

I feel Cimon adjust his shoulders a little. "You all right?" I shout to him over the clamor. "Do you need to put me down?"

"My yoke's not that heavy."

"Think this is the time for levity?"

"I'll choose better words, Mistress."

"You can see what's going on?"

"I get a grasp."

"Lighten our yoke!" keeps reverberating.

"I'm worried," I say.

"If I were the King, I'd be worried too. I'm thinking it's not safe here for you. We need to leave."

"And go where?" I ask as my brother returns to the stage, motioning the crowd to stop their plea.

"Anywhere."

"Lighten our yoke! Lighten our yoke!"

The soldiers in the buffer march two steps back from the assembly and unsheathe their swords, shutting up the crowd.

"My father made your yoke heavy," Rehoboam shouts, both his pitch and hands quivering just slightly, his unrehearsed phrase picked up by the nearest herald who repeats it, which in turn is picked up by the next, creating a strange kind of echo throughout the pasture. "But I will add to it! My father flogged you with whips, but I will flog you with scorpions! My little finger is thicker than my father's cock!"

A rock is thrown at the King. It misses, but causes him to run and hide by his advisors. Whatever political astuteness I thought my ass of a brother showed by coming to Shechem, he just lost it in four sentences, reverting to his old form. If there were a man alive who could take back Judah's past injuries on Israel, putting the oil back in the olive, it is not my brother. In *The Chronicles of Moses*, I had the younger sons receive the blessing. Abel, Isaac, Jacob, Judah, Perez. Yes, part of it was because my younger sister Irty got everything. But also, I thought my father, a later born, would appreciate these junior siblings inheriting over the older, that underneath it all was the justification for his own ascendancy. But watching his oldest-born, Rehoboam, screw everything up, I ask myself why Solomon couldn't do what David did–choose a younger son for an heir, someone fit to preside over kingdoms.

If my father is watching all these mistakes and miscues from the depths of Sheol, how does he feel that this creation from his loins is doing such a wretched job clasping the scepter?

"Adoram, Adoram, Adoram," emanates from the multitude. They're shouting for my brother's chief of the tax collectors and the overseer of the forced labor. In a change of strategy, a less defiant Rehoboam orders two soldiers to seize the official, offering him up to the assembly, hoping to placate them. I almost slide off Cimon's shoulders, wincing at what I see—the mob grabbing and beating the man, devouring him like jackals. Several throw stones at what's left, until he's just a bloody thing on the grass. A few strip Adoram's body for his jewelry, breaking the corpse's fingers to get at tightly-fitted rings.

By the dais, the soldiers fall back to protect their sovereign, and a few of the congregation have the good sense to disperse. But most, like Cimon and I, stay on the field, too curious about what will happen next.

"Men of Manasseh," an elder hollers from the middle of the clearing, "come here!" After several long moments, one of the soldiers on the King's side runs over to his tribal leaders. Then a few more men in armor follow his steps. Hundreds from behind the King and around the field's perimeter pattern after.

"Men of Ephraim come here and join Manasseh!" A similar story, but this time there's no hesitation as hundreds desert at once. "Men of Gad, join Manasseh and Ephraim!" Brigades leave their king for the other end of the grazing field. And then the lesser tribes, the ones north of the Jezreel—Asher, Zebulon, Issachar, Naphtali, and Dan—mirror the first three, as they are all prone to do.

"No more House of David!" I hear someone cry out and this too becomes mimicked by thousands.

The large number of foreign mercenaries, the few hundred professional Judahite troops, the King's runners, the charioteers, and the Benjamin conscripts remain with the King who, flanked and protected by several soldiers, comes back to the podium.

"If you want a war, then we shan't disappoint!" shouts my brother over the din.

As more of the crowd flees before the swing and clash of metal, there's Rehoboam hovering by Ahimaaz, who is holding what looks like a sheep's liver, sizing it up, studying its every facet. As he does, I muddle over why Yahweh would let this happen, how he could permit his kingdoms to divide like this. But whatever the reason, I assume he must be waiting until the last moment to bring about a remedy. Waiting to show how great he is, to swoop in before it's too late, before the pillars fall and the sky crashes the earth.

"You can put me down." I shout to Cimon.

"We shouldn't stay here, it's not as if we can stop a battle," he says as my feet hit the grass.

"Where then?"

"We can't cross the field. Opposite then to the other hill." We start running hard, my pouches awkwardly jerking about. As we begin our climb, I think of that tall man smiling, the one with the tapestry. How he and the others turned my Cain story into a tool for rebellion.

I full stop. "Wait," I command Cimon.

"Why?"

I reach in my skin and yank out my writing set. Finding a relatively flat patch of ground, I squat, throwing the board on my lap. Then I whip out one of the papyrus sheets from the set, along with the well and reed. I'm about to put down ink, when I start to think this through.

"Mistress, we need to leave now."

"Zadok's letter, I need it."

"Mistress—"

"The letter!"

"The writing saying I'm his slave?"

"Yes. Hurry." He hands it to me and I break the seal. Unraveling it, I concentrate on Zadok's writing, how he shapes his letters. "Can you hold it in front of me? I need to free up my hands."

As Cimon complies, I set down my words; copying Zadok's style best I can, balancing the need for speed with accuracy. The old priest's strokes are light and unsteady, a casualty I suppose of his arthritis. Someone nearly barrels into me, yet fortunately my reed lingers above the page, sparing it from stray marks that ought not to be there.

"Can you tell me what you're doing?" Cimon asks over blasts of the shofar.

"Give me Zadok's chord and seal." Done scribing, I roll the sheet, tie it, stick some clay from my writing set on it, then press down with the seal cylinder. "Ahimaaz knows you?"

"He does."

"Give this to him. Tell him it's from your master and then leave while he's reading it. Before he can question you, disappear into the crowd. After you blend back in, put my linen over your loincloth to disguise yourself, and come back to me. Go now and hurry."

As Cimon chariots to the podium, I notice that the grazing pasture has transformed from one of ceremony into one preparing for war, for soldiers on both sides are now in clear lines with their swords drawn and shields up. I scan a mix of faces, some innocent and much too young, fresh out of their fathers' fields, some with teeth grinding, brows sweating, eyes darting nervously about, damp fingers clenching tightly onto grips, scared of turning into lifeless mounds or cripples lying forever by the beggar's bowl. Then there are the others who are foaming for a chance at glory, seeking to become heroes of stories they will repeatedly tell their children and grandchildren.

All of them waiting on the horns.

CHAPTER SIX

Judah's rams start blasting. Piercing high and grating. But
there's no battle, at least not yet. While soldiers stand and
wait, I make out Ahimaaz staring at the clouds marching
across the sky and the wind gusting through leafy treetops. His
focus on omens disturbed as a soldier leads the Ammonite to
the platform, Cimon approaching and bowing to the Priest,
on one knee with his head down, his arm extending the scroll.
Ahimaaz taking the papyrus, the slave then merging into the
chaos as instructed. And Yahweh's Priest, concentrating on
what now has been placed in his hands, pacing back and forth
on the dais. Then Ahimaaz rushing to Rehoboam, the two in
long discussion. *What holds their attention: my papyrus or the
leaves and sky?*

Cimon, in my tunic, finds me. "So what now?" he asks over
the racket of the horns.

"Let's see what happens."

Rehoboam waves over one of his generals, leading to more
talk. But then soon enough, the general sends a runner to the
horn players. The musicians, who until now had been making

nothing but long, sustained high-pitched blasts, blow a series of low staccato tones.

"Do you know what that means?" Cimon asks.

"Something either really good or really bad." More quick bursts of air through the shofar. Then, to my amazement, the King's men start to fall back, leaving the city by way of Mount Gerizim. "It must mean retreat. It means retreat." I hug him. "Thank you."

"What exactly did I do? This is because of your writing. What just happened?"

"Well, it may have been what I scribed, or it could have been omens, or an official simply advising the King on the right course of action. And Yahweh. Whatever happened, he must have had a hand."

"What was in the scroll?"

"I reminded him of the punishment that awaits when family kills family, by inking some words from *The Chronicles.*"

"You have *The Chronicles* memorized?"

"That's a long story." I smile.

"So what exactly did Ahimaaz read?"

"That Cain was more cursed than the ground, which opened its mouth to drink his brother's blood. Cain's crime was greater than he could bear."

א

Trumpets, flutes, drums. People screaming, but with joy, not insolence. Euphoria is in the air as we're caught in a groundswell of people. A mob, which was watching behind us on Mount Ebal streams down the slope and we end up tangled and smothered. We're running with them past the evergreen oak and the now wrecked and pummeled stage into the open gate. Inside the city, people are jumping up and down, dancing in the narrow walkways like lushes. As if participating in a wedding, the women of Shechem dash in and out of houses, grabbing their tambourines to sing songs of celebration.

"To the Temple!" I hear someone bellow. Similar to the chants earlier from the grazing field, this one too is picked up and shouted by hundreds. Then like everyone else in the human current, we hurry and jerk through city streets to the sanctuary—a huge building of mud brick and stone with two large pillars, like Yahweh's columns. But this is not a place of Yahweh. Above the uprights, on the façade, is carved, "Temple of El of the Covenant." But what covenant? Is this where the tribes made their oath? I thought it was with Judah's god, not this usurper.

A new call makes its sound heard. One syllable, roared over and over: "El. El. El. El." Guards unlock a temple granary and a storehouse of olive oil, and then toss skins of the stuff into the assembly for an impromptu feast. A storehouse of wine is also raided and Shechemites start gorging and drinking, like starving trough animals.

To the beating of drums and flutes, ephod-wearing priests roll out of the temple a ten-foot-high bronze bull into the courtyard. Around the idol, some of the male celebrants start stripping off their tunics and undergarments until naked, dancing in a frenzy around their molten god, the men resembling insects circling rotted food. Then about a dozen temple maids come rushing out of a smaller sanctuary for El's consort, Asherah, and, with the exception of their veils, disrobe as well. As the percussion beats and pounds out rhythms of intercourse, men quickly toss their shekels to a priest and start coupling with the prostitutes in an open area set aside for the practice behind the bull.

"El. El. El. El."

A young mother's right hand latches onto her boy, her left clutches her girl—both children near Ariah's age—so as to keep them from being sucked into the goings on, the children sobbing uncontrollably and trying, like me, to make sense best they can of why their father's out there, somewhere in the maelstrom, penetrating with a teenager.

"Cimon, pray to Moloch."

"Say what, Mistress?"

"Pray to him to stop this."

"To stop this? Why would Moloch want to meddle in something that is between El and Yahweh?"

"Do it. We'll use the wine that's left for a libation."

"Something like this might call for more than wine, we should sacrifice a—"

"There's no time. Pray."

He kneels down with me and chants, opening our wine skin to the skies.

I pray hard to Yahweh, as hard as I prayed during my father's attempted rape. But unlike then, there's no quick response. Instead, all around me bodies are wired puppets, operated by the foulest of demons, forcing the possessed to imbibe as much wine as their stomachs can hold, to dance until their legs can carry them no more, to penetrate until thwarted by their own exhaustion.

Is this because of me? Is Yahweh silent because he sees me as a practitioner to this apostasy, here attending this shrine of his rival? But whether it is me or not, his inaction makes him seem ineffectual. It's as if Yam and Leviathan were never defeated, and that the primordial waters and the sea monsters slithering in it now rule. Where is the god most high? The god of armies who smote the Egyptians? Is he where he was a short while ago when my brother lost Israel? Maybe preoccupied in the same remote corner of the heavens as he was the day when my Ariah was taken.

"Mistress, come."

Cimon picks me up off the ground for there's a frenzied mob rushing toward us.

And I see it.

Adoram's head. It's paraded around on a spike and handed off from one gleeful bearer to the next; there are even a few who fight over the privilege being the next keeper of the trophy. The drums keep hammering, causing my own head to ache, and I start feeling dizzy and nauseated, reaching for Cimon. But it is the taxman's severed head, bobbing to the percussion, which is the last thing I see as the wavy lines come and take my consciousness away.

PART IV
NUMBERS

CHAPTER ONE

My head aches something awful as I wake to a piercing gray dome, the sky unyielding on its choice of color. After a few moments, I realize that Cimon is carrying me.

"Where are we?"

"Back on the highway, heading to Jerusalem."

We're in the midst of a large company, some in high spirits, some not.

"You think that wise?" I ask.

"Where would you have me take you?"

"I don't know. But you must be tired. I'm sure I can walk."

"I'm fine, Mistress."

"Please." He puts me down and I gain my strength to become upright.

"I'm thinking that Zadok may have an alternative plan or at least more shekels to try again," he says.

"And getting past the guards at the gate? They'll be looking for me."

"We have a day and a half to figure that out, Mistress."

So much had happened at Shechem, yet I find no urge to ruminate to my traveling companion on what had just transpired. What words could add to such events, to help make sense of it? So we walk in silence. All around me, high rows of corn are strangely at peace. In fact, the whole earth is a docile lamb, waiting for the farmer's shears. I find it odd. As all of Ephraim readies for the harvest, it's as if nothing extraordinary occurred just a few miles north. The crops are just as tall, their color, the same hue as yesterday.

I think about tomorrow's homecoming. It's strange that in a way I do miss Jerusalem's miserable odors, Hannah's self-centeredness, Eglail's hostility. I miss it because the old and familiar is a siren. After what I just experienced, I'm not quite ready for more of the uncharted. Yet, when I'm back within the city ramparts—that is if I make it past the guards—in Zadok's charge for a day or two, my old routine will be something I can never return to. Still, how I would like to gaze at the Temple one last time and feed my hungry boy.

We sleep by the roadside in the mixed company of Ephraimites, Benjaminites, and Judahites. People stick to their tribes, but no one tries to start anything. Maybe we're all too exhausted or maybe it's just custom that pilgrims on their way forge a single identity. After all, we still share common threats, like the highwayman lurking beyond the hill or the next olive grove. Perhaps there's more that binds us than we think. We are all still Jacob's children.

It's a restless night. I wake up several times, but at least I don't dream of Cimon's massive arms or Ariah's decaying corpse. But what I remember is hardly better, and it's nothing coherent, none of the bizarre narratives that my heart often weaves. But flashes of mostly unpleasant things: the vines Irty tied me up with, Hodiah's and Reuma's taunts on the Mount of Olives, the

Shechem oak, the Astarte dessert cakes, the Cush traders, El in his earthly guise as a molten bull. Then I'm being cremated, fires surrounding me on the pyre, the flames swallowing my lifeless body and, because of that, the gods of the Gates denying me entry to join my little lion. Watching me burn is the tall man waving his tapestry of the warring Cain and Abel. With my last breath, I see that tall man smile that horrible smile.

For breakfast, Cimon and I try to ration what's left, having the few remaining grapes and a little bread. A short while later, we're on the highway with the sunrise illuminating the first day of the harvest: farmers cutting down tall stalks, tying the sheaves, throwing them in piles at the edges of their fields, their sons picking up the sickled barley and bundling it, stacking it all on donkeyback for delivery to the thrashing floor. Then, later over dinner, the telling on how the day went, with added exaggerations, culminating with much needed sleep so as to ready themselves to do it all over again. My witnessing the banalities of the fieldwork might suggest that the happenings in Shechem were only a product my mind had created. But I know it wasn't.

A Benjaminite family says their goodbyes, and they leave the road for their village in Mizpah. Mizpah? Where have I heard that name before?

Several Jerusalemites, including us, form a new contingent, leaving the remnant resting on the highway, picking up our pace, trying to reach the Jerusalem gate before sundown. As we hike through southern Benjamin and approach Gibeah, I remember the name Mizpah. Both that town and Gibeah were mentioned in a lengthy text called *The Levite and the Concubine*. As a child, I had read the account in a worn, flaking scroll in the library, the plot my inspiration for the story of Lot's daughters and the Sodomites. It was the most gruesome poem I had ever encountered, giving me vivid nightmares for a year, and I pray to the heavens that every word in that papyrus was a sham.

In the story, a concubine deserted her Levite master, leaving him in Ephraim for her father's house in Bethlehem. The Levite went after her, lodging five days with the father who fed and entertained him. Then the Levite and his concubine reconciled and headed home, and by nightfall, made it to Gibeah in Benjamin. They sat in the town square, hoping someone would offer them a roof for the night. While none of the native Gibeahites made any overtures, an old Ephraimite residing in the city came and took the wayfarers in, fed their donkeys, bathed their feet, and offered them food and drink. Then, as in my Sodom story, a mob gathered at the house, pounded at the door, demanding the Levite so they could know him carnally. The Ephraimite offered the rabble his virgin daughter instead, pleading not do this thing to his guest. But the Gibeahites wouldn't listen; they only grew in size and kept battering the door. In order to spare himself, the desperate Levite pushed his resisting and pleading concubine out of the house, abandoning her to the throng. All though the night, the men raped and abused her.

Toward daybreak, the woman came back, only to collapse at the entrance of the house. When it was time to go, the Levite found his concubine at the door, lying on the ground, her hands at the threshold. He shouted, "Get up." But there was no reply. So he strapped the corpse onto his donkey and headed home. There, he picked up a knife and, using all his priestly skills, cut her into twelve parts, sending one piece to each of the tribes.

In response, the entire community gathered at Mizpah and, upon hearing the Levite's retelling of the story, took an oath to wage war on Benjamin. With Judah the first to attack, the Benjaminites countered and leveled huge casualties. It was a stalemate until the tribes eventually lulled the enemy into an ambush and defeated them, save six-hundred Benjaminites who fled into the wilderness. Now as this was holy war, the tribes put the Benjaminite women and children to the sword, but after doing so, realized that they had all just doomed Benjamin to extinction, despite the six hundred male survivors. The reason for this is the Mizpah participants had agreed to a second oath that none of their daughters were to marry a Benjaminite. But the tribes hit upon a solution requiring adherence to a third vow made at Mizpah: to totally annihilate any city that failed to send soldiers for the war. And Jabesh-Gilead failed to do so. So the tribes killed off all of that city's inhabitants, except four hundred virgins who were given to the surviving Benjaminite soldiers. But there were still not enough girls for all the six hundred. The still unmarried Benjaminites were told to lie in wait in the vineyards outside Shiloh, to snatch maidens coming out to dance at the annual feast there, and to take them as wives. The war over and the survival of Benjamin assured, each man dispersed to his own tribe and clan.

Closing in at the Benjamin-Judah border, Cimon and I reach Gibeah, where much of this cursed story was set all those years ago. The city, like the hills surrounding it, seems as calm and at rest as a warm, scented bath. But now that Judah and Israel have broke into two, could such horrible things repeat? Could there really be holy war between the Kingdoms, causing brigades of soldiers to put innocents to death as in ancient times? I remember when I was traveling through Egypt as a young girl, the vizier (who I partly modeled my adult Joseph after) telling me that the there was so much lawlessness in the land that the royal tombs were being robbed, all because the country, once united and strong, had similarly become divided. Could that happen here? Will the treasures in the tomb of Solomon and David, and perhaps even the riches in the palace and Temple, one day be stolen, carried off, melted down, and then sold as trinkets in the market?

"We need to figure out how to sneak you in," Cimon says.

"I've been working on that. Here." I hand him my sandals. Then I take out the writing set, find another blank papyrus, and with the sheet and with Zadok's letter, I forge another document. Finished, I put on the veil, while hastily explaining to Cimon my plan. Seeing to its execution, the two of us scamper to the Jerusalem gate, in a race with the sun.

א

There is a huge line of returning celebrants waiting their turn to be inspected by the guard. In the queue, I wonder if we will make it in before the sunset when the soldiers shut the huge acacia. Extending my arm out, I can place the width of two fingers between the sun and a dip in the contour of Mount Zion and wonder how much time we have. Turning back to the line, I count well over a dozen ahead of us and I start getting nervous. If we can't get into the city, then it'll be another night sleeping unprotected on the cold roadside, only this time we will go to bed hungry, as we have exhausted our supplies. But Fortune appears—with less than a half a fingerbreadth of space remaining, we land our opportunity.

"State your business," the guard says to Cimon. I recognize this mercenary, seeing him several times here on my way to the Mount of Olives and back, exchanging a variety of words with him. He looks a little older than Cimon and, apart from his stubbly beard, his face is smooth and a little ruddy, like pomegranate skin. In my few dealings with him I had wondered what his life would be had he not donned the coned helmet? (What would my own life be like had Talus not shown me the writing reed?) But now there's no question that the guard will identify me without my disguise. Although he may have forgotten the flat of my nose or the smallness of my chin, I'm the only dark-skinned resident in the city.

"I am servant to Zadok ben Nathan, father to Ahimaaz ben Zadok, the Priest."

"Uh-huh. And she?"

"My master told me to go seek out a woman for his comfort. This is a letter explaining his instructions about procuring the maid."

"Why not one of the city prostitutes?"

"He wanted me to find a virgin, a clean girl. You see, my master was the

former—"

"Zadok, I know of him."

The guard stares at the seal then breaks open the document, his eyes clearly not understanding it. But he must see the impression bearing a shining star and the Judah lion. The feline is the symbol of the royal house; that's all that matters.

"I feel sorry for you," the mercenary says to me. "To have to join with him. I can only imagine what his breath must smell like." He turns to another guard standing next to him, one whom I don't recognize. The soldier's thick eyebrows are unruly and undisciplined, wrapping far around, almost joining his hair. "How can that old ash heap still get it up?"

"Maybe she's a witch who can spell his cock to rise," Eyebrows jokes to the ruddy guard. "Should we remove the veil and test her magic?" The question is uttered with more seriousness.

"Who are you?" the ruddy mercenary asks me. But I stay quiet, not letting my distinctive voice, with traces of a once-heavy Shebite accent, give me away. "Answer me, is what the slave speaks true? Are you a harlot for the old Priest?"

271

"Master, she's the daughter of an Aramean slave and does not understand our language," Cimon says, playing his part quite well. "My master wanted to purchase a girl who would be silent and not shrew at him in his remaining days."

The mercenary feels my scarf, as my chest ratchets up. I'm waiting for him to jerk it off, to see my blackness, leading him to ask why—why is the wife of Raddai the Scribe disguised as a whore? Knowing who I am, would the two really take me to one of the gate's chambers and do horrible things before throwing me back in the dungeon? His fingers glide slowly on the cloth.

"I say we examine her," Eyebrows says, snickering, then fixing his gaze hard as if I were a spoil of war, plucked and waiting.

"My master was very insistent that she be untouched. If she isn't, I am to procure another."

"Let's close up and take her—"

The ruddy mercenary swings a look to his colleague. "Astarte's cunt, you're an imbecile." He then pivots back on Cimon. "Go. Tell your master to have fun."

As we pass the vendors inside the gate, and I can swallow fields of air again, a flash of memory comes—of Ariah with Eglail last year. The two had come looking for me when, after I left Ariah to nap, I came down here looking for spices. My little one had woken, crying for me. At this very mat, showcasing as it does now various herbs, piled in colorful bowls, my boy came rushing toward me, sobbing uncontrollably, the crying finally ending when I picked him up in my arms.

"I thought you left me, Mommy," he said.

"I would never leave you, Lion. Never ever."

How he beamed at me as I spun around with him, our little dance watched on by angry vendors who were screaming at me with their arms out, protecting their wares.

The memory is taken from me when two soldiers ride brazenly by us on their mules, the gallop hoofing up dirt, some of it finding lodging in my gasping throat and irritated eyes.

Leaving the market, climbing the hill, we find Zadok outside the old palace, his profile to us, leaning on his crutch, gazing out at the western sky. A sliver of moon and the evening star. That's all that is visible. The former Priest will have to wait a little longer for the sun to fully die before Yahweh's court can fully assemble.

"Zadok!" shouts Cimon. The former priest turns and frowns, his black teeth hiding somewhere in those receding gums. The Ammonite rushes to the old man. "Master, what can I do?"

"Get her inside."

A little later, over a welcomed meal of roasted calf and mixed vegetables, we start to recap our adventure. I tell Zadok about the Cushite traders, but then I jump to the apostasy at Shechem.

"El is big up there, even bigger than his son Ba'al," Zadok says and then downs a little wine. "Unfortunately, that's the tradeoff for having the Temple in Jerusalem and all those El and Ba'al shrines in the North. While Judah can obtain more Yahweh worshippers for the feasts, if you don't want to pilgrim, there's the Israelite gods right there for you in your city. I had suggested that we demolish it all, every shrine and high place, every molten bull, and every idol, leaving only the Temple, but Solomon would have none of it. He was too afraid of angering the other gods."

"It's not just in the North," I answer. "Jerusalemites also venerate the lesser gods. Even the Levites."

"No one said you had to be a zealot to earn a living as a priest."

"To attempt divine favor in Judah, people try all the deities like they're shopping at the market. At Shechem it's worse, it's as if no one ever heard of Yahweh."

"If your father worships El, so most likely will you," Zadok says, and I'm back with him long ago in the annex, that little girl devouring his every word. "Israel, Jael, Rachael, Samuel. Notice anything in common? There are the *el* name endings, yes, but they also are all heroes in the North. It would be nice if they decided to call their kingdom Isra-yahweh, but they don't."

"Cimon and I stayed with an Ephraimite family. They'd been praying to Ba'al, Astarte, and El, but then they heard *The Chronicles*."

"Are you telling me that now they want to pray only to Yahweh?"

"I don't know if they want to exclusively, but they said they felt something special for him."

"Change one family, change the world. I would like to think that. But not all Israel has heard your words. Perhaps some in Benjamin and Ephraim. But it's too long a walk from Megiddo to Jerusalem. And it may be quite some time before they will—"

Banging at the door. We all turn our heads.

"Father, let me in!"

CHAPTER TWO

Zadok points upstairs, but before we manage a step, he grabs Cimon's arm, his head nodding at my bowl and goblet. The slave and I scoop up the extra pottery. Then the Ammonite leads me to the second floor, as I hear Zadok stumble to the door.

"Open up! Or must I use my key?"

"I'm coming."

Once on the higher level, the slave motions me to one of the sleeping rooms, but I shake him off, staying close to the end of the stairway to better hear the man who seems so threatened by me, a five-foot nothing of a girl.

"I heard you mumbling," Ahimaaz asks over the sound of steps thumping on limestone. "You're not talking to yourself, are you? This is what happens when you live alone."

"I was speaking to Cimon. How was your journey? I understand the acclimation could have gone a touch better. What did Rehoboam say to the crowd who came to acclaim him? Something about whipping them with scorpions?"

Crawling over, I gaze down the entryway, the top of Ahimaaz's balding crown coming into view. The son helps his father to his seat.

"Unfortunately, our new king listens too much to his young friends who put these things in his mouth. How did you know?"

"I receive information apart from you, Son."

"I mean, how did you know before it happened?"

"Before it happened?" Zadok asks.

"With your letter. How?"

My gods, I never got a chance to tell Zadok about my forgery.

"My letter?"

"The Cain quote you gave me stopped a war," Ahimaaz says. "What were the omens and signs you saw that I didn't?"

The old man pauses. "The Cain quote, yes. Well, I was Priest for a very long time. Yahweh sometimes calls to me." Well done, Zadok. Thank you for figuring it out.

"You hear his voice?"

"Sometimes."

"Apart from deciphering lots and gemstones, I haven't heard him speak to me."

"He will. Son, just give it some time. You just started. We should fill you with some wine. Cimon, come down here and hand my son a goblet." I roll so the Ammonite can maneuver around me to descend the stairs.

"Do I need to tell you about the North's new king, or has Yahweh mentioned that too?" Ahimaaz asks.

"New king? That was quick."

"Ah, something I know that you don't. Well, immediately after the Shechem disaster, your old friend, Ahijah of Shiloh—"

"Ahijah's not exactly a friend."

"Your old rival then. He anointed one of the Shechem elders as king, and he was acclaimed right there. The city's their new capital, and this elder has taken a similar throne name as ours: Jeroboam."

"Hmm . . . Jeroboam. Interesting."

"I assume he lacks imagination," Ahimaaz says.

"Or maybe he wants to sow confusion. If you think your king is Rehoboam and suddenly someone tells you it's really Jeroboam, it's an easy switch."

"Maybe. There are stories going around that, before Shechem, Ahijah tore off his garment, cut it into twelve pieces, giving this Jeroboam ten of them." Cimon brings in the goblet, pours, and hands it to the son.

"An imaginative tale." Zadok snorts. "Hmm. He keeps two pieces. What of Benjamin, then? I assume the tribe and ours are still united."

"The Benjaminites hate Ephraim and the new Northern Kingdom of Israel even more than they hate us. Yes, they're with us."

"Well, it also helped that David purged their elders and put in his own. I'm still questioning why Ahijah would do this? How would it land him your job? I mean, that's what he always wanted, to be Priest in the Temple."

"I don't know," Ahimaaz says.

"Unless he wants to make Shiloh the Jerusalem of Israel. To pretend that Yahweh's real house is up there, creating a rival to our Temple."

"If that's behind it, he lost, unless he wants to priest for El. My agents tell me that Jeroboam's first decrees included making El their national god, and he now plans on building a cult center housing a giant bull at Dan and rebuilding the one at Beth-El."

"At the two ends of his country. This Jeroboam's clever. You see what he's doing?"

"Father, why don't you just tell me?"

"If you're an Ephraimite or a Gadite, why pilgrim all the way down to Jerusalem for the feasts when the shorter walk now is to Beth-El, right there before the border? And if you're north of the

Jezreel, your traveling time is lessened dramatically with the Danite shrine right there. If only Jeroboam were a Yahwist. Yes, we could use someone clever like him on our throne."

"I'd take the idiot over the backstabber. A Yahweh priest anoints you king, and then you say, 'Thank you, now go away and stay in your little shrine in Shiloh.'"

Zadok bobs his head thinking this through. "Ahijah must be seething. With El as their national god, he and his Levites will receive even less offerings. And if Jeroboam turns all the Yahweh shrines into ones for El? The Levites, if they stay with Yahweh, could soon be starving."

"They're not the only ones in trouble. So is Judah."

"So is Judah."

As I watch the father and son sip their wine, I work this out, concurring with the older priest and the younger. Judah is indeed in trouble. Israel has more men than we, more fertile soil, more vineyards, more olive groves, orchards, farmland, more everything. We're landlocked steppe and desert. And the chariots that my father bought, the ones never used in wars (we never had a real war since David, just skirmishes), they're all housed up in the North's cities of Hazor and Megiddo, now probably confiscated by our new enemy. And how are we supposed to suzerain over Edom, Moab, and Ammon with only Philistine mercenaries whose salaries had been paid out of taxes levied on Israel? One day we could be at war on every front, including the one shared by our fellow sons of Jacob. Judah is in a sorry shape.

"We figured out how that black witch got into the Temple."

"Have you?"

"There's a tunnel leading into it that she accessed through the chamber closet. She apparently jumped through the hole. We know this because we found her sandals by the Temple entrance point. We've stoned the palace sentries that let her pass."

I wince hearing this. Dagonil, Plow Ox, Blue Eyes dead because of me. Just like my cellmate. Do I curse everyone I come near?

"If she just walked in, maybe she's no witch," Zadok says.

"Witch or not, she soiled the Temple. Did you hear me, she jumped through the shit hole."

"Yes, that would make her most unclean."

"Besides the chamber slaves, she was the last to see Solomon before he died. Yahweh says she killed him."

"You looked to the gemstones for divination, I take it? If that's what the stones say, then she killed him. Unless you read them wrong."

"I didn't misinterpret. Raddai has prepared her death warrant." Hearing this I shudder, but I force myself to keep listening to Ahimaaz speak his wretched words. "The moment I can call the King away from the harem, I'll have him put his seal on it. The only thing is . . ."

"The only thing is?"

"She escaped."

"Has she?"

"You wouldn't know anything about this?"

"Why would I know?"

"You tutored her, you're sort of fond of her." Ahimaaz leaves the table and circles the ground floor, looking around. "Then there's what happened at the festi—"

"You had to do what you had to. But I know nothing of her whereabouts. If she's a witch, then maybe she just vanished into thin air. What did her dungeon guards have to say?"

"They and their captain are gone as well."

"Mercenaries, I take it?" Zadok asks.

"Probably in Ashkelon or Gaza by now."

"Maybe they took her with them?"

"No one at the gate has reported seeing her pass, but they did report the mercenaries leaving. While maybe she got through undetected, I'm going to assume she's still here, maybe hiding under a veil. When the King's finished with his party—"

"You mean his orgy."

"I'm going have him order that all veiled women be searched." Ahimaaz's voice now hammers with all the power of a curse. "Door to door, brothel to brothel, if necessary. It's because of that witch that Yahweh caused Israel to rebel, I'm sure of it. The timing is too curious. I'm certain if she dies, Yahweh will forgive and bring Israel back to the fold. Finding her and punishing her is of the utmost importance."

"Yahweh could have torn the Kingdoms asunder for a hundred other reasons. Pick one." Zadok holds his hand up and finger counts. "Solomon's permitting worship of other gods, choosing his feeble son as a successor, Judah's flogging the North with whips and now scorpions, Yahweh keeping us from being too cocky—"

"You're always defending her."

"I'm not, but you seem obsessed."

"They're a plague. All those Cush. I remember when I was a boy, a runner in the Civil War. Joab sent me and a Cush messenger to deliver the news to David that we'd won over Absalom. When David asked if his son still lived, the idiot Cush blurted out the answer like it was just another report, and it broke the King. David kept moaning over and over how he wished that he'd be the one dead and that Absalom should live instead. His words still burn in me, 'If only I had died instead of you.' Can you imagine what it was like watching him cry and go on like that?"

"That's enough evidence to cast judgment on the lot of 'em?"

"I'm going to find that witch. She's the only dark African in a city of ten thousand. It can't be too difficult."

Zadok sighs. "Son, can I pour you some more wine?"

"My family is waiting. Your family is waiting. Why are you living here? This is an embarrassment to me and to you. Come live with us in the palace."

"In a tiny back room? You need the space for all my grandchildren and your slaves. I have elbow room here."

"I'll talk to Rehoboam. You'll have your own apartment next to mine. You'll have that elbow room."

"I like my independence. I've lived here all my life. I remember you playing on that spot right there."

"You could be playing with your grandchildren all the time, teaching them. You love to teach, and they could use your lessons. Independence. You don't hold my post anymore."

"When I free Cimon, I'll join you, I promise."

When Ahimaaz leaves, Zadok hobbles to the stairway. "You heard all that?"

"I heard," I answer. "What's to become of me?"

There's only silence below.

א

Even though I'm on a real bed for the first time in days, I fail to find sleep. I keep thinking of Raddai's hand, moving along the papyrus, gripping the reed tightly, carefully forming his letters, preparing my death warrant for my brother to stamp his seal. As my husband inked his words, could there have been any hesitation, remorse, or even tears? Or perhaps carrying out Ahimaaz's order was so onerous that he had an underling to perform the task. No, rather, I can see him doing his job almost with vigor, the chance to put an end to his incorrigible, deformed wife. The source of his ridicule, the burnt-face from wild Africa, that cursed woman who, when she did deliver, gave him a blemished son—the witch in league with demons.

While I'm tossing in clean linen sheets, I keep thinking on all that has happened since this started. Was it a week ago? No, it had to be longer. I was at the King's chamber persuading the guards to let me feed my father. I remember what we said as if it were sewn in my spine, their images made a part of me too and burning.

"Please let me see my father one last time," I had said.

Then Dagonil answered, "Ba'al's ass," as if to say what's the big fucking harm.

But Dagonil was wrong. Terribly wrong. I caused four deaths, his included. That's the big fucking harm. *Have I accomplished anything?* With kingdoms torn apart, who knows anything anymore?

At sunrise, I come down for the breakfast Cimon has prepared, fruits of all kinds, warm bread, olive oil, and yogurt. But I'm not hungry.

"Any ideas spur from sleep?" I ask Zadok. As he finishes his chew, I try to picture him as a naked boy playing in the thoroughfare when his shadow was much smaller. Or even as young man studying old texts. But I can't. Was he ever young?

"I'll go the Temple today, make sacrifices and say prayers. Maybe Yahweh will speak."

"Do you actually hear his voice?"

"In my way. So tell me about this letter I wrote that stopped a war?"

I review what we did at Shechem. "I hope you approve. Using your seal."

"Probably the best thing I ever put to papyrus," he says, smiling. His eyes twinkle. "You have the cunning of your father and grandfather."

282

I look down at my plate, unsure how to accept such praise. Then I feel a nudge on my arm. It's Cimon.

"Why don't you share with him the second letter you wrote on my master's behalf, the one that got us though the gate?"

I glare at him for stirring trouble. But I don't think Zadok heard, for his lids are shut, his head bobbing a little, his mouth chortling. Then after a moment the old man opens those calculating eyes and beams.

"What?" I ask. "You figure out my next move?"

He just grins like he did in the cell when I confessed authorship, his face a festival.

"What?" I ask again.

"How would you like to save the Kingdoms?"

"What?"

"How would you like to save the Kingdoms?" he asks again.

"Zadok, please just say what you mean."

"You could bring Israel back to Judah."

"And how would I do this?"

"By writing a new *Chronicles.*"

א

"A new one?" I ask as my throat parches and I search frantically for the goat milk.

"Hear me. Ahijah anointed this Jeroboam. Ahijah has power, he's persuasive, has a following. Although he's a Yahwist, the Israelites listen to him. But he's now disgruntled, perhaps realizing his mistake."

"I overheard all this last night. This is the priest that Jeroboam has dismissed, keeping him in his exile at Shiloh?"

"People listen to him, he's a maker of kings; why not a breaker of them as well."

"He just made Jeroboam El's anointed here on earth. Why would Israel desert their new liege?"

"If they left El for Yahweh."

"They'd do this with a new *Chronicles*?"

"Well, we'll have to make some changes, some rewriting. Or perhaps, no, we'll keep everything. It's all precious gems, but you'll make some additions, write some new stories I think we need. But the answer to your question is yes. If enough up there can be like that Ephraimite family, why not? With a scroll of stories that will make them see that we have more in common than they may think."

"Now you're saying we're alike? I thought the North was a bunch of uncivilized barbarians."

"I may have exaggerated out of concerns for your safety. But we're all children of Jacob, we were all once slaves in Egypt."

"New stories?"

"Well, *The Chronicles* are a bit Judah-heavy. You have most of your stories taking place here in the south, like in Hebron and Beersheba, not so much in Israel."

"That's not true. There's the Dinah story at Shechem."

"To avenge their sister's rape, Jacob's sons sack and kill all the inhabitants of a city that is now Israel's capital. No, you'll need happier stories taking place up there, oh, say, in places like Beth-El or . . ."

"Or?"

"Dothan. Why not Dothan? With stories about their heroes who you didn't use the first time."

"Heroes? Heroes like who?"

"Say Joshua."

"Who's Joshua?

"The leader of the Conquest."

"You mean Caleb?"

"Not to the North."

I play at my food. "I don't want to do this."

"Why?" he asks, his voice flustered.

I continue poking at my fruit as if that will somehow change the subject.

"Why not?" he asks again, but now louder and summoning an answer.

"I wrote the stories as an entertainment for Solomon. It was Raddai who made it into something more. Now you want me to purposely rewrite their history. It would be to deliberately set out a lie, to fool them. I won't do it."

"You told me how much you've improved the lives of that family in Ephraim, that Yahweh is now with them. Don't you want to do that for thousands more?"

"And what happened to them would happen to all Israel?" I say, laughing in disbelief, the way I imagined Abraham's Sarah doing at the flap of the tent.

"You underestimate the power of your reed. I've found that you can use the most brilliant logic on someone and still be preaching to the deaf. But when you wrap that logic in story, suddenly they hear."

"No, it would be wrong to create a fiction and pretend it's real. To put words in Yahweh's mouth that I know he didn't say."

"But you had done—"

"To make their past a forgery."

"You already did that with the original."

"But that was just to be read or listened to by one man, my father, and with him knowing that it all came out of my imagination."

"You want the nations to go their separate ways? We almost had a civil war on our hands and escaped it by the thinness of a sheet of papyrus. We may not be so lucky next time. You want to risk that happening again, when you could have prevented it?"

"Can I say something?" Cimon asks. I almost forgot he was sitting with us.

"What?" Zadok responds.

The Ammonite's eyes lance mine, shedding his usual playfulness. "I'm not taking sides, but I have a question. You say you wrote *The Chronicles* for the former king, that he would know it came from your reed."

"Yes, that's what I said."

"How do you know?"

"How do I know what, Cimon?"

"It wasn't your god."

"What do you mean?" I ask. Zadok too looks puzzled.

"Mistress, how do you know your Yahweh didn't write the thing, using you as his brush, that you're his reed?"

CHAPTER THREE

I sit in the bath, playing with the scented water, my hands pushing the surface, watching it wave. The disturbance takes over the placid liquid body that was there before. As the water grows lukewarm, I think about the twenty-two letters, and whether it was gods or men who created them. But whoever the originator, did they realize all the hurt their invention could do?

My kidneys tell me that Zadok's idea is wrong. Each new story I were to write could lead to a new misinterpretation. How many more unintended deaths would occur, like my friend in the dungeon? I write of Lot, of the Sodomites' attempted rape of the angels, about the city's destruction. I do it all in an attempt to illustrate the duty to be hospitable to your neighbor, to explain the barren plain around the Salt Sea, that you shouldn't mistreat your daughters. And now it's suddenly acceptable to stone any man who lies with another. That's too much responsibility. Who am I to try and change the fate of a kingdom?

Yet, after writing *The Chronicles* the first time, here I am, alive—yes, hunted by priests and mercenaries, my son taken from me—but alive. I haven't been struck dead by plague or an earthquake. If what I had been doing was a crime, surely, I would have been smitten by now. Could the slave be right, that I'm a mere conduit? Silliness. Why me? A foreigner, a woman. Why wouldn't Yahweh use the real Moses as his reed? It makes no sense. But when I wrote my scroll, often the words came easily, sometimes too easily. Then there were portions that, when I reread them, I questioned whether they were mine. Their origin, the inspiration of how it got on the page was a dead memory. Still, it's madness to think that the divine was acting through me. Yet, if Zadok had proposed the notion, I would have dismissed it right away as part of his machinations. That mind of his is more contraption than human, it never sleeps. *But there's something about the slave.* When he's not making his humor, there's the artist in him that seems to speak truths.

א

Cimon brings Zadok back from the Temple in the late afternoon, which is a welcome relief to boredom. For after bathing and dressing, through the warm hanging air, I must have toured Zadok's apartment a dozen times. I now know each room's contours nearly as well as the spaces of my own palace residence. Not only have I spent my time orienting myself to new surroundings, I have also tried to gain a better understanding of my host through a study of his possessions. The vividly colored Sidonite tapestries and Tyrian pottery tell me he has taste for the exotic and expensive, although some of his vases are chipped and nicked, making me wonder if it has been a while since Zadok had either the inclination or the means to acquire such imports. He has kept an old, small wooden rocking horse and a few spinning tops, also by their looks many years old. Are the toys for his grandchildren, or are they mementos from Ahimaaz's youth?

Checking all the rooms, I find no household gods, and the lack of idols makes perfect sense for Yahweh's former priest. Then there's Cimon's constellation mural. It's something I've never seen anywhere before. Did the idea of the star map spring from Zadok's mind or his slave's?

As the servant and I begin preparing dinner, Zadok shouts from his sitting chair. "Keb, let Cimon handle it all, I want to talk to you." So I join him. "My son tells me that the King's young advisors have convinced him to begin war preparations."

"To war against whom?"

"Whom do you think?"

"Why?" I ask. "What would he gain from doing that?"

"He now believes its best to attack first before being the one attacked."

"Has the King so soon forgotten what happened just days ago, when the threat of Cain's curse stopped him from starting a war?"

"Your brother now thinks it's safer to be Cain than Abel."

I grimace. How much of my brother Rehoboam's decision is based on distrusting Israel, and how much of it is that he now realizes he rules over a tiny little rump of just Judah and Benjamin? My brother may think he wears the crown, but vanity is his king.

"I assume you'll look to the omens, and if the signs say you should attack, then you should," I say.

"Omens can be misread. If it's holy war, you know what that means."

"I know."

"It won't be tomorrow; it will take some time. We don't have the numbers to match their forces, not with Philistine mercenaries and Benjamin troops alone. Rehoboam will have to persuade the elders to allow conscripts from Judah, and we will have to train them. But it will happen, perhaps in a year, at the start of the next campaigning season. Perhaps sooner."

He passes some wind, and his face tries to hide the embarrassment. When you become aged, the body, like an old harness, shows its wear; he need not be ashamed. Still, that mind of his is a blade, fresh off the whetstone.

"I've been mulling something over," Zadok says. I just hold eyes, waiting for his mull. "Do you think Yahweh intentionally caused you to stay in Shechem? Caused you to stay in the Kingdoms and come back to me for a reason?"

I begin to tire at his latest stratagem and his constant manipulations. Now I'm supposed to swallow that Yahweh engineered a war and the razing of Sheba just to keep me in Zadok's apartment to play scribe.

"Cimon could use a hand," I say as my legs pull me up. "I feel bad I'm not helping out."

Zadok grabs my arm, bringing me back down. "I have something for you. Reach into that skin there." I find it and pull out a large scroll. I don't have to open it to know it's exactly fifty-four sheets long.

"It's not the original, it's one of the copies for the priests to read. Go ahead and open it."

"I don't want to."

"When you were writing *The Chronicles*, what was the experience like?"

"What do you mean?"

"You must have enjoyed the process."

"I felt I had to put the words down."

"It was a chore then, no different from preparing dinner?"

"I wouldn't say that."

"I wish I could write this new work, and if I could, I wouldn't need you, but I do. I don't have your talent for composition. No one does. You have this skill, maybe the only one in the world with such inventiveness. If you weren't meant to write it, why are you blessed with such ability?"

I open the scribe's copy. The gimels' downward strokes are longer, the dalets look more triangle than circle, the mems are totally foreign. But the words are mine. Or Yahweh's.

"Why didn't Yahweh choose to work through you, when you were Priest?" I ask. "Or why not David or Solomon? It makes no sense for him to choose me, a nobody."

"I do not purport to know the mind of the deities, no one can, you know that. But I know this: you're not a nobody. You're the author of the greatest work ever written."

א

Zadok has Cimon clear a space for me to write in my sleeping room, as the former priest wants me to spend my time there should Ahimaaz barge in. In fact, my instruction from my host is to remain upstairs at all times whenever I'm alone (although if I'm hungry I can make any needed trips to the downstairs pantry). Under no circumstances, except perhaps an earthquake or a fire, am I permitted to leave the apartment. Tapestries and mosaics fill the walls, there are olives and nuts in storage jars, and of course I have my writing set, wine, incense, scented body oil, and the bath. It all amounts to a much nicer cell than the one in the dungeon. But it is still a cell.

Zadok teaches me all the northern heroes and lore that he knows, as well as some of the North's favorite expressions to pepper the work. He also promises to bring me Israelite scrolls that are beginning to drip into the library and the Temple. Already some newly out-of-work Levites from the North have left their former Yahweh shrines to journey across the border to beg for employment in Jerusalem. One has smuggled out a scroll, *The Acts of King Saul*, which, thanks to Zadok, is now in my hands. Gleaning it, I find nothing too helpful. The poetry claims that Saul was a foot taller and more handsome than anyone in his kingdom, even though—as the papyrus makes pains to repeatedly point out—Saul was from Benjamin, Israel's smallest tribe, and that his clan was the humblest of all the clans. There are several verses devoted to how Saul and his Benjaminites defeated the Ammonites and, by doing so, saved a town called Jabesh-Gilead. And not surprisingly, much of the poem becomes a long rant against Saul's main adversary, my grandfather David and his tribe of Judah. But worst of all, the author gives himself license to lazily stray from strict adherence to the meter, almost as often as keeping to it, allowing content to master over form when content should be its slave.

My first week on the project and I'm empty of how to proceed, wasting my time staring at the blank papyrus my keeper gave me, fretting that there is no divine Muse at work, that I'm nothing more than Zadok's game piece. But when I forfeit writing during the day and instead try weaving words in the late evening by the glow of a single small oil lamp, as I had done in the first go around, recreating the old conditions, ideas come. The first, and this is cardinal, is to give Yahweh a secondary name: El. Later in the work—I haven't figured out just where—I'll have Yahweh announce that men should only call him by his primary title. This is to suggest to our Northern brethren that, by worshipping El, they had been worshipping Yahweh all along, but just didn't know it. A very Zadokite stratagem.

So I begin. On a new scroll, I start copying down the duplicate Zadok gave me, the beginnings of *The Chronicles*: Adam and Eve, Cain, Noah, Abraham. Then I try to prepare myself for my first novelty, but before I do, like a sheep chewing its cud, I pause to reread and digest what I wrote. Talus once told me of a legend among the Sea Peoples of the son of a river god who could not tear himself away from the beauty of his own reflection in a pool of water. He died there, unable to walk away to take in nourishment. Realizing that I've been staring far too long at my own wordy pool, I dip the reed into the inkwell.

While I make exceptions here and there, I generally follow Zadok's advice to keep intact the earlier stories, so I mostly copy and insert. And one of my first insertions concerns expanding on Hagar, Sarah's Egyptian slave woman. While Judah's headstrong daughter-in-law Tamar and the young, energetic Rebekah are characters who I wish I could be, I identify more with my creation Hagar. In my story in the first Chronicles, Sarah, now in her old age, did not trust Yahweh's promise that she would ever bear Abraham a child, so she offered Abraham her servant, Hagar, as a wife. When Hagar became pregnant, she became unruly and Sarah found it hard to control her. So with Abraham's consent, Sarah abused her to such a degree that she ran away until Yahweh's angel convinced Hagar to return to suffer at her mistress' hands. But the angel also promised Hagar that she would have a son, who, like Abraham, would be the father of many descendents. Now comes my addition. Hagar has her child, Ishmael, a name I concoct from imagining him as the ancestor of the Ishmaelites. Writing the name out now and applying the El suffix seems so odd, as if my letters were going left to right, wrongly over the page.

After Sarah finally gives birth to Isaac, I have her try to convince Abraham to send Hagar and Ishmael away for good. But it takes Yahweh (in his guise as El) to do that, telling the patriarch to listen to his wife. So Abraham gives Hagar some bread and a skin, leaving her and her son to wander the desert alone. When the skin is empty, Hagar sends her Ishmael to rest under the shade of a bush, and she walks a bowshot away so she wouldn't be next to him when he dies. She sits, facing her little boy and cries. Cries like I have been doing these past six months. Cries like I'm doing now, my eyes becoming watery and red, my lids puffy, my mouth choking. How I would give anything to see his smiling, innocent face. His small hands playing with mine. I swipe the scroll off my lap, pick up the writing board, throw it, smashing it against the wall, then alternate between rubbing my hair hard and beating my chest.

"Are you all right?" a voice asks on the other side of the door. Yahweh, how could I be all right when you took my lion from me? How could you do that? I just don't understand. Use your power and explain it to me.

The voice of Yahweh kindles flames of fire.

"Mistress, answer me, are you all right?"

I try to compose myself to the slave who's breaking my lament. "Cimon, I'm all right," I say sobbing, rocking back and forth.

"You don't sound all right."

"I will be. Please let me be."

But I'm not all right. I can never be all right.

א

On the evening of the full moon, the three of us celebrate the first day of the Feast of Unleavened Bread, which I had called the Passover in the first *Chronicles*. Filling our table is recently harvested barley along with lamb, minus the votive offering of the grain and meat that earlier in the day Zadok brought to the Temple.

"In a few weeks' time, conscripts will start to drill out in the Hinnom," Zadok says as I pour him some wine. "And not just here, new recruits will start to train outside other Judah cities as well."

"Will they?" I respond.

"It won't be long before they will be ready."

I sop up my lamb.

"You hear me, it won't be long," Zadok says.

"I'm writing as fast as I can," I say.

"Write fast, but not so fast that you sacrifice quality."

To this I just swallow my food.

"So how is it going?" Zadok asks.

"Today I made Reuben a positive force." Zadok had told me at the project's beginning that many Israelites living east of the Jordan River have a tradition of belonging to the ancient tribe of Reuben and would want their tribal ancestor to have a larger role.

"You didn't alter the story of him sleeping with Bilhah?"

"You told me not to change anything."

"Well, if Reuben doesn't have penetration with Jacob's concubine, you have a problem with the succession."

"I don't have the problem, because he still lays with her."

"The succession?" Cimon asks.

"Keb needs to have *The Chronicles* make clear why it is that Judah ends up as Jacob's heir, and as a consequence why our tribe should rule over Israel. As the first born, Reuben would normally have taken the scepter, but Jacob discovering what his son did to his concubine rules him out. Simeon and Levi, the next in line, are eliminated because Jacob can't forgive them for going to war against Shechem. That leaves fourth-born Judah."

"What about Joseph? Lately I hear Keb reading a lot pages to you about him. He doesn't take over for the Hebrews?"

Zadok looks at me. "You're going to insert the harp song to make it clear it is Judah."

"I said I would." I turn to Cimon. *Those eyes of his.* "In this new text, we're building up Joseph, as he's one of the North's biggest heroes. He'll take over the patriarchal duties when Jacob gets old and the brothers end up in Egypt." I return to Zadok. "But the scepter will go to Judah. Getting back to my point, Reuben now tries to save Joseph from the well."

"Judah doesn't save him?" Zadok asks, as I spread some olives on the flat bread.

"Now they both do. You want Reuben to have some good qualities, don't you? I also have Reuben, as a boy, finding mandrakes in the wheat field, which he gives to his mother, Leah, to help her with her infertility. Leah, in turn, trades them to Rachel for the privilege of taking her sister's turn to go to bed with Jacob."

"So what happens without the magic of the fruit? Does Leah conceive?"

"You'll appreciate this. Yahweh, in his guise as El, eventually listens to Leah's prayers and she gives birth to Issachar, then quickly births Zebulon and then Dinah. See, I'm doing what you want, putting all the northern tribes in there. Proud?" I think how it took forever for Yahweh to hear my prayers, and when he did, he gave me the most loving boy who he then snatched up. Talus would have called that irony.

"I'm sensing that you're only writing this for my benefit," the old man says.

"Here, have some wine," Cimon says while filling my goblet using his large arms, hoping as always that his interruptions will turn Zadok's words and mine into ploughshares.

"But it's for their benefit." Zadok says. "It is for them."

I turn to Cimon. "Maybe your master wants more wine too."

"You're doing it for them. Just filling in the gaps of the North's history, that's all."

"And what history would that be? If there's anything real in these stories, it's as full and as wide as a lyre string."

"A history that they need. Everyone needs a glimpse of where they came from."

"Even if that glimpse comes from me?"

"You're just the reed."

I sigh. "I'm still puzzled on how this would reunite the Kingdoms."

"Ahijah will use it to rally the people behind him."

"How do you know that he won't just burn it?"

"This was a fine meal, don't you think?" Cimon interjects. "I don't know how I do it." He smiles, probably hoping we'll beget smiles too.

"Yes, the lamb was succulent," Zadok says. He raises his glass. "Next year in Jerusalem."

Cimon and I raise ours, then the three of us repeat an old custom to encourage pilgrims. "Next year in Jerusalem," we all say in unison. Yet perhaps Zadok made the toast in haste, as I fret on where I'll be then.

א

Helping Cimon with the dishes, I wash the plates and goblets in the cistern water, while he attends to the cooking pots. All the time, I'm staring at those large, Ammonite arms, then I make my way to his bare feet, which are large too, and I recall this is one of Galit's tests for surmising how big a man would be. She had other measures as well, such as the power of a suitor's eye contact, the slowness of his voice.

Has the incubus followed me across the Judahite border? Unafraid of patrolling mercenaries and attacking outlaws, sneaking past the soldiers at the gate, able to climb the hill?

"I've been overhearing snippets of the new work when Zadok reads it out loud." Cimon says. "It's so easy to see the stories unfold in my mind, as if your words are painting pictures."

I stare at those brown and olive eyes. "You'll have to do the rest. I'm sorry, I don't feel well."

I run up the stairs. Slam the door to my sleeping room. Bury my head face down in the linen sheets, trying to shed the image of the Ammonite, but his face and arms burn so. Then there's the picture he drew of me in the sand, capturing every detail, nothing escaping his uniquely colored eyes. I start imagining my lips pressed hard on his, then tasting his honey skin, enjoying it so. Tossing, I face the ceiling. Adultery is a grievous sin, you can't just go lie with another man outside your husband, even a husband with as many numbering faults as mine. If only I knew the right incantations to steer the incubus away. *Yahweh, how am I to write the thing with Zadok's servant under the same roof? And if it's not Cimon, then I'm dwelling on my boy, my thoughts grazing on a field of lust one minute and death the next.*

Finding a skin of wine, I drink it all, hoping that it will send me to sleep and clear my mind. But I just stare up, wishing the slave were upon me.

א

I mull over last night's dream, an awful variation of *The Levite and the Concubine*, and hope it doesn't come in pairs like Joseph's. Although much of it now is more blot than clarity, I recall I was Zadok's concubine, dressed in my veil and wool disguise. Zadok and I were arguing over something, the topic of which has left me, but I ran away to the palace, to Solomon. He took me in only to ram those horrid, wine-soaked lips back onto mine. Then I was in the stoning field, facing the Temple priests, the ones who had found me in the Sanctuary, hurling their rocks at me with Ahimaaz overseeing the execution. But I wasn't dead. Not yet. Cimon picked me up from the ground and carried me in those big arms back to Zadok. The last image that ruled me before I awoke was that of the old priest. He had my writing reed ready and was about to use it to cut me into twelve parts.

א

And with the wheat harvest comes our second festival of the year, the Feast of Weeks. After dining with Zadok and Cimon on grain that had once been tall stalks of golden corn only a week ago in the farmer's field, I go to my room and write. I have reached the part of this new *Chronicles* concerning the Hebrew slaves toiling in Egypt. It is here where I decide to merge El with Yahweh, and my setting is the burning bush. When Moses asks what his god's name is, after a little wordplay and a dramatic hesitation in which the deity says, *"I am who I am,"* our god relents and makes clear to Moses what the people shall refer to him as from this moment on:

> *You shall say this to the children of Israel: Yahweh, your father's god, Abraham's god, Isaac's god, and Jacob's god has sent me to you. This is my name forever, and this is how I am to be remembered for all eternity.*

In rewriting the story, it occurs to me now that Yahweh really could have gone under such monikers as El because he didn't want men to have magic over him. So perhaps this aspect of the new *Chronicles* is not too far afield. It also seems to me that Yahweh too must be a secondary name, his true identity unknown to all, save him. Knowing names is power. To the

Egyptians, only by knowing the names of the gatekeepers can you reach their underworld. Isis became powerful because she learned the secret names of her fellow deities. I'm sure our god most high wouldn't let himself fall into such a trap. He must have multiple disguises. Still, you cannot be too careful, and that's why there's that commandment on the tablet: *You shall not bring up the name Yahweh for a falsehood.* There to prevent his creations from controlling him.

I recall the witch at the Mount of Olives. I pray she was a sham. That she's not in league with dark spirits. The woman knows Ariah's name. *She knows it.* If vested in magic, she could have Isis' power over him. No, she's a charlatan, she has to be. She thought him something other than he was, and guessed wrong. Still, to be safe, maybe I should have done more to her than merely slapped her in the face. Something that is not done in the presence of witnesses.

Chapter Four

"Keb," I hear Cimon call from below.

Coming down the steps, I find the servant holding out a goatskin pouch.

"You're here early. Where's Zadok?"

"Still at the Temple, but he wanted me to cook these for you as soon as possible." He opens up the pouch. "Ox hearts." I just grimace. "Zadok says it's to help inspire creativity."

I stare at the bloody things. "I don't think so."

"He was most insistent," the Ammonite says with a slight smile. "I can cook these as they are or put them in a stew."

"I don't think so."

"You'd rather eat them raw?" Again, with that smile.

I close the skin up and take a step back toward the stairs.

"What are you reading?" Cimon asks, pointing to my papyrus I brought down with me in my haste.

"It's useless and a bleeder of time."

"You could indulge me. I have some time before I'm to go back and fetch Zadok."

I sigh. "Just keep those ox hearts away from me." I plop down on Zadok's chair, trying my best to not to take in the slave's chest and arms, but then finding his eyes just as dangerous. So, with some effort, I force my gaze downward into the scroll, to a safer place. "It's a text brought down by a refugee Levite priest from Tirzah." I hear my voice quiver and try to control it. "Tirzah's a town just to the north of Shechem, supposedly one of the greenest and most lovely in the realm. The scroll's poetry doesn't quite match the city though, as it's a gruesome story collection of the judges, various strongmen and one prophetess who ruled various parts of Israel before the monarchy."

"A woman up North ruled like a king?"

I take an ill-advised glance into those brown and olives, but then bury myself in the text. "In a way. Her name was Deborah. The culmination of her tale is when Yael, a simple wife, received the Canaanite general Sisera into her home, feigning hospitality with an offer of milk. When the enemy commander then took a nap, Yael pounded a tent peg into his head."

"He must have had some headache when he woke up."

I grin. "There're other stories in this too. There's an amazing tale of a Danite judge, Samson, who liked to pose riddles and whose long hair gave him godlike strength. He was so strong, in fact, that he was able to rip a lion apart. His love, Delilah, cut off his magic locks, making him weak, allowing the Philistines to blind him. But even without his sight, he destroyed a temple at Gaza, killing himself and three thousand of the enemy. Then there are many lines devoted to the Gileadian judge, Jephthah, who made the most horrid vow to El, 'If you deliver the enemy into my hands, then whatever comes out of the door of my house to meet me I will sacrifice . . .'" I breakdown, thinking about how it was his daughter who came rushing out.

"Mistress, are you ok? I'll get a cloth." He runs into the pantry.

I compose myself and shout out to him. "Funny thing is, that reading the scroll from one end to the other, I find a judge from every tribe *except* Judah. In fact, while many of the tribes would ban together to fight this foe or that, there's never a mention of us in the South. It's odd that our tribe, David's tribe, the most important, to be missing in the scroll like this."

Cimon returns with a linen strip, and he uses it to gently dry my eyes and cheek. Like a sudden dust storm, Cimon's presence overtakes me.

"Excuse me," I say and rush upstairs. I try to force myself to read, but the incubus' spell is too strong. I find my fingers holding no scrolls, but instead touching myself below.

א

"Why won't you eat the hearts?" I hear Zadok call out as he and Cimon stumble in at their normal late hour. I walk down the stairs, as I had done earlier.

"The words are coming. I don't think it necessary." Cimon mercifully leaves us to Zadok's hearth.

"Nonsense, the animal's mind can only help yours. Where are you in your writing?"

"The Israelites are between Pharaoh's chariots and the sea."

"Can I read?"

I hand him the scroll and he holds it out in front of him, extending his arms as far as they can go, squinting.

"Here was Egypt coming after them," Zadok reads out loud, "and the Israelites were greatly frightened. They said to Moses, 'Was it for lack of graves in Egypt that you took us to die in the wilderness?'" He puts down the work. "That sounds so real, so beautiful. I can picture them saying that. How did you hit on these words?"

"I don't know. I just heard them."

"Did you, now? Well, I'm glad you're writing more about Moses. Old Ahijah fancies himself a descendant of the prophet. More of this, and he can't but help fall in love with it."

"My writing is nothing more than making a savory meal and putting goat skins on hairless arms. Just something else to deceive old men."

"With your words, we will correct Rehoboam's mistakes. It's the edge we need to reunite the Kingdoms. Don't you want to witness both North and South pile in here, into Jerusalem for the feasts, sacrificing at your Temple?"

"My Temple?" The epiphany strikes like a battering ram. "I see it now. That's what this is about. What you mean is both North and South coming to *your* Temple."

"My Temple, your Temple. I meant our Temple, Yahweh's Temple."

"No, you meant your Temple."

"I can't fathom what you're implying."

"You do. More people worshipping Yahweh means more people coming to the Temple, and Ahimaaz is Priest over everybody, not just tiny little Judah."

"Don't be ridiculous. We're trying to stop a war."

"This is all for your indelible glory. The priesthood passed down from father to son until the end of time. That notion's great in theory; the only thing stopping your line from keeping the title is if a Zadok somewhere along the way produces no sons. Or if Egypt or Aram or Israel conquers Judah. Either way, no more Zadokites."

"This is not for my vanity."

"I want to be by myself."

I return to my sleeping room, thinking of Zadok's foolish quest for immortality. Zadok's motives, good or bad, shouldn't affect my decision on whether to continue. Still, it troubles me that the old man seems only in it for himself, and I've been his unwitting accomplice. Gilgamesh, like Zadok, wanted eternity too, but ultimately failed, accepting that he could only at most receive youth, but didn't even have the energy for that. The ancient king had to live with his mortality, learning that all of man's achievements are but puffs of wind. Eventually, it was enough for him to simply take pride in the massive city walls he built, walls that have long since been razed; the foundation stones now buried deep under grassy mounds.

As I drink some to numb my disgust, I muse that living forever is a myth, a fool's dream. Zadok and his line, like the rest of us, will end up dead in Sheol. Nothing lasts. Everything is earth's clay. We live and we die, and it all takes place within a moment. Lifespans that stretch centuries are things of earlier epochs. That is why I placed the Tree of Life in Eden, protected by the cherubim and the fiery, ever-turning sword.

א

This morning I'm playing with the dyes Cimon secretly purchased for me: En Gedi henna, yellow and red ochre, even a little red ink. I'm experimenting to find something closer to a more natural pigment, instead of the hideous color I had on during the acclimation. While doing this, I calculate I've been housed up here now for over three months. It must be the time of the grape harvest. Too long a time to be within these walls. Thankfully, Cimon has been making semiweekly feed-

ings to Ariah, but I need to get out and see my boy—and I'll
dress up as a man to do it. On the subject of colors, I chew on
what hues Zadok's face will become when he sees me transformed. Well, it's your fault Zadok, I'll tell him. With all your
adroit manipulations, you should have figured out a way to
convince your son to stop harassing veiled women in the
street. You should have persuaded him that I must have left
with the dungeon guards when all this began and am now
living in the Land of the Philistines. Who in their right mind
would confine a black witch under their roof for countless
months, sticking her in a small sleeping room, feeding her ox
hearts, with some mad notion that an arrangement of words
on a scroll would cause thousands of people to depose their
anointed?

Getting closer to an acceptable hue, I put down my palette
of dyes and rub the experiment off my hand with sheep oil and
powdered limestone. I go back to my reading. While eating a
plate of dried figs and almonds, I happen upon another scroll
just brought into the city from a northern refugee priest, this
one still sealed with the House of David lion. Tearing it open, I
see it is that horrible text of the Levite and his raped concubine,
the woman abused by the Benjaminites at Gibeah who the Levite
cut into parts, starting that long ago war with Benjamin. I've
noticed several copies of this work have arrived in Jerusalem
from various northern locations. Just like I've seen several scrolls
now of the harp song, "Jacob's Blessings." This is the song that
Zadok had me insert into my text, laying out the dying Jacob's
blessings and curses he gives to each of his twelve sons, the
founders of each tribe, and in which the patriarch hands the
scepter to Judah. Apart from those two ubiquitous writings, I've
found a third, too, that keeps popping up among the carried
refugee scrolls, the stories of *The Judges*, and a couple of these

scrolls were still sealed with the House of Saul/Benjaminite wolf until broken by me.

Realizing I still have a little dye still on me, I decide to take a bath. With a hot easterly wind, the summer heat has been unrelenting, so I don't trouble myself to warm the water; I just remove the block and let the cistern water fill the tub. I pour in the frankincense, myrrh, and natron. If I wanted to embalm myself, I'm halfway there. Jumping in, I submerge my head, letting the water press on my face. I think about my next lines. I'm going to make sure what happened at Shechem will never happen again—the parade of nakedness, the drinking to excess, the fornicating with temple prostitutes, all that abomination around the bull of El. A month ago, when I was writing of Jacob and his family leaving Shechem after the Dinah incident, I had Jacob bury some El idols by that sprawling oak outside the Shechem gate. You see by burying El, I had hoped to bury the cult as well.

But I realize now these lines of text are too subtle. The way I'll really stamp out the anathema is to have the Israelites panic when Moses goes up the mountain. Yes, I'll have them force Aaron to fashion a molten calf, one of El's guises, and then, when Moses returns, the prophet will break the tablets upon seeing their celebration, just like the Shechemites broke Yahweh's commandments to bow before no other gods. Then Yahweh will force the people to choose between him and the calf, and the ones who keep to the calf, the Levites will put to the sword.

I start formulating the dialogue. I'll have the yielding Aaron say, "Take off the gold rings that are on the ears of your wives, your sons, and your daughters." But as recent former slaves with mud still on their feet, would the Israelites own jewelry? No, they wouldn't. So now what? *Where would they obtain the gold for the calf?* They're in the desert. They could war with some tribe out there and plunder it or stumble across a mine. No, I don't think so. So what are you going to do, Keb? How do you have them find the gold? I toy with the water, and study how it waves. Alright, I'll go back and have Yahweh cast some sort of spell to make the Egyptians just hand over all their jewelry to the departing Israelites. Yes, that should work. It's funny that sometimes I feel like a kind of god to these characters as I author their fates. Still, I'm bound to the laws of logic and story, robbed of any true omnipotence. If Yahweh has his share of limitations as well, perhaps I have been too hard on him.

"*. . . rings that are on the ears of your wives, your sons, and your daughters.*"

When I write, I enjoy grouping things in threes, something I picked up in my reading of Egyptian and Akkadian texts, as in the *Descent of the Goddess Ishtar*, when the deity goes into the underworld, the bull, the ass, and maid stop penetrating. In *The Tale of the Shipwrecked Sailor*, three times the serpent asks the sailor, "Who brought you to the island?" So many things come in threes. Three parts to a temple, three feasts, three patriarchs, three days of hospitality, three fish devour Osiris' member.

In *The Levite and the Concubine* story, there are a couple of threes that surface too. The battle of Gibeah lasted three days and there were three vows made at Mizpah. *Gibeah—wasn't that Saul's capital? Mizpah where the tribes made the oath to attack Benjamin, that town also had a relationship to Saul too. What was it?* But it's not just Gibeah and Mizpah, the Levite story is teeming with Saul connections.

I dash out of the tub, leaving a trail of scented water behind, and reach for the scrolls. I grab the one with the Levite story along with *The Acts of King Saul*. Finding an empty papyrus sheet, I jot down the links:

Town	*The Levite and the Concubine*	*The Acts of King Saul*
Gibeah	Place of rape/battle	Saul's capital
Mizpah	Place of the oath	Place of Saul's anointing
Jabesh	Only town that didn't join the battle; all put to the sword, except virgins	Town Saul helped save

There's one more connection I find: Bethlehem, home of the concubine's father, who gave the Levite five days of hospitality, two more than the customary three. This tiny village in Judah, containing just a smattering of houses, coincidentally happens to be the birthplace of Saul's enemy, David. I give this some more thought. David's Bethlehem provided the Levite five days of food, drink, and a roof, while in Saul's Gibeah, there was no parallel hospitality by the Benjaminites. Rather, all of the native townsfolk wanted to rape the Levite and it was only the resident Ephraimite who took the Levite and his concubine in. This couldn't be mere accident that such a horrid piece of writing has all these anti-Saul/Benjamin, but pro-David/Judah sentiments.

And then there's *The Judges* scroll, with Saul's Benjaminite seal, poetry with no mention of Judah, only of the other tribes banding together. But there's a small mention of us in the South, I think: Samson tears apart a lion, the symbol of Judah and David.

I weave out a theory. When the houses of David and Saul were warring, could each have created a writing to help defeat the other? Saul's was *The Judges* scroll. David's was the *Levite and the Concubine* text. Saul could have made copies of *The Judges* and sent them to cities throughout the North to show that tribal cooperation leads to defeating a common foe, that going it alone leads to curses, and, by the way, please join Saul and Benjamin to war against David and Judah. David could have one-upped Saul by inking a fiction showing how nasty those raping Benjaminites are and by extension how ugly Saul's house is—all of it to try to rally the North to him.

So these two scrolls have fabricated stories showing that the other house is the enemy. But why then this third ubiquitous harp song, "Jacob's Blessings," portraying one large, mostly happy family, including the brothers Judah and Benjamin. Yet in *The Judges* scroll, *The Levite and the Concubine*, and *The Acts of King Saul*, there's nary a hint of any familial bond between the two warring tribes?

I confront Zadok. After some flimsy denials to my speculation, he eventually confesses.

"Yes, during the war of the great houses, each tried to rally the other tribes to his side with swords and scrolls. Then when David eventually won over Saul's remaining son Ishbaal, David wanted to unify the Kingdoms, so he invented a family relationship with each tribe becoming a son of Jacob and a brother to Judah. Except Ephraim and Manasseh—those two powerful tribes—David demoted to sons of Joseph for there to be twelve, not thirteen, brothers. He had the court composer write 'Jacob's Blessings,' and sent heralds and harpists throughout the land to sing it to the elders in their palaces and to ordinary people at the feasts. He also had devised 'The Song of Patriarchs,' concocting a lineage between Israel's hero Jacob and our two, Abraham and Isaac. The people came to believe the songs, and the songs held the Kingdoms together for over half a century until your brother so stupidly tore them asunder."

"Jacob didn't have twelve sons and the tribes aren't related by blood?"

"Oh, there's blood. I'm aware of many intermarriages." He chortles, but then catches himself.

"So you're saying my history is a lie?"

"Come closer." Zadok puts his wart-covered hands on my shoulders. "Hear me. You're the daughter of Solomon and the granddaughter of David. And maybe there was really a Judah, a Benjamin, and a Joseph, and they could have all been brothers. Who's to say they weren't? And once we all were slaves to Pharaoh."

As I grab a large skin of wine and head to my room, I think of our bondage in Egypt. How do I know that that isn't a lie too?

CHAPTER FIVE

I dye my face, arms, hands, and feet. After it dries, I find one of Zadok's tunics. It's too long on my legs, overtaking my sandals. I pin it up a few inches. The old man's turban is also a bit loose, but I manage to tie it so it doesn't swallow my face. I study myself in the bronze. I've just broken another law, so throw another javelin in the quiver box. But maybe wearing men's dress is more a crime concocted out of the hearts of mortals and less so of the gods. After all, I'm still standing.

The turban keeps slipping, so I tie it tighter. I smooth out some dye over one of my lids. So long as no one stares too hard, I should pass. But there's only one way to really test my disguise.

Stepping outside for the first time in months, the only thing I can do is squint at the bright. The smells are as horrible as I remember but still are a kind of welcome relief from the same musty incense burning for more days than I can count. I've never been penned up this long. I don't think anyone has.

As my eyes adjust, I notice the daily routine in the city is the same as it's always been, as if there never was a schism. A few women and palace slaves are queuing up at the gate for Gihon water, their jars on the tops of heads and shoulders. There's the market, alive and bustling as ever, and the everyday pilgrims are heading up the thoroughfare with their votive offerings. But there is one change. New makeshift shelters of shoddy wood and cheap wool are pitched against the inside walls, housing refugee Levite families, some with carts brimming with their household wares. Zadok told me that he had convinced Ahimaaz to persuade the King to harbor them here. The Tribe of Levi has always been in a precarious position. The Levites were never given a land of their own, but they're the only ones allowed to become priests for Yahweh. Trouble is that there are only so many priest jobs to be had, and even fewer now after Jeroboam has turned their northern shrines into ones for El. So my brother Rehoboam's charity is on full display.

Out of habit, my legs take me to the line at the gate. The numbers leaving are small, for there are not many now fetching water, as it is midday and most have filled their jars earlier and will wait to refill in the late afternoon. As I get in the queue, ahead of me the guards interrogate a veiled woman and then strip off her cloth. Three and a half months after my arrest, and they're still checking.

I remove myself from the line, for I feel unready to try my manly guise with the soldiers. Although they're letting men pass without much interview, there will be the examination upon my reentry. Still, I would like to visit with Ariah, even though Cimon fed him just yesterday. Of course, I could simply leave Jerusalem, never to return, taking my chances and begging for scraps outside the gate or gleaning in the hills. I'd return to the Mount of Olives every so often to feed my boy with what the reaper has left, providing Ariah with chaff and milk so he doesn't have to find sustenance from out of the dust down there. Would scrounging for handouts be any worse than staying here and working on my fabrication?

Funny, the actual writing itself I find high pleasure in, often serving as a distraction. Whether the words come from me or from Yahweh, the product on the sheet I know is good. No, it's more than good. And I don't need Zadok to tell me it is. Although it is quite satisfying hearing him celebrate each letter, as if it's a form of worship. If the new *Chronicles* were ever to be read at a feast, I would like to see the crowd's reaction as I did at last year's reading. A writer needs an audience like gods need men.

Yet I find that it's a struggle at times inking this hoax. After learning that I fell for believing that there really was a Benjamin and a Judah with the same intensity of knowing my own name, that a fiction out of David's mind became my identity, dare I now pull the same trick on others? What gives me the right to create such a thing with strokes of my hand? Am I a god? I reflect on all those deceivers I wrote about. Abraham, Rebekah, Jacob, Joseph's brothers, Tamar, Potiphar's wife. Each pulling wool over someone else. Now I'm just one more puller of the wool.

Zadok assures me that it's for a greater good, a linchpin to hold the Kingdoms together. But how do I know? Who are we to toy with people's notions of themselves? If this really is Yahweh's doing, if he's using me as a tool, why couldn't he be a tad clearer to me with his intentions? If not an annunciation from an angel, or sending a head-hitting revelation like the sun rising in the west or men giving birth, how about at least providing more subtle signs? Signs like appearing in a dream, sending flocks of ravens, or plumes of smoke? Anything.

Zadok telling me I am Yahweh's reed could be just another lie. For if my Judahite history is a lie, then what is true? I know I am true, and so are the people I loved: Talus, Galit, Ariah. My childhood, my sister, my traveling up the Nile and across Shur—that is all true. And of course, Yahweh. How many times has he come to my rescue? He saw me safely out of Egypt, saved me from Solomon's rape, gave me a boy, took me out of the dungeon, led Cimon back to me at Shechem, planted the seed in my mind to write the Cain passage that would stop the war. How do I account for the existence of all the world, but for him? Yes, I may not understand him at times, but Yahweh is the most real of anything. He has to be.

I turn around from the gate and take in the market. Same old junk, all of it looking like shoddy grave goods. There's a mat covered with dolls and toys, including a few spinning tops and blowing whistles, like the ones Ariah would play with. I glance at some pottery, wishing I had a shekel or something to barter for that cheap serving bowl, but I didn't steal anything from Zadok to trade. Yet if I had the clay, I would ink a curse for Ahimaaz, writing across the vessel's surface, placing a spell on his heart, his kidneys, his bladder, his legs. Then I'd find some out-of-the-way corridor to shatter the thing.

If I had more shekels for more curses, I do the same to Eglail and that witch.

A vendor sells mandrakes, but the fruits are few and shriveled, a month past being ripe. Still, they could be up to the task, if I wanted it. I'm sad, but not mandrake sad. Not now anyway.

I explore some of the narrow alleys on the west side of the city, and when the walkways end, I jump on roofs of houses to go farther, causing several stray cats to lunge. All my years I've stuck to the thoroughfare, never venturing into the city sides, to the homes of the less well-off. But I never had reason to do so, and really no reason now. An older woman beating down a woven mat looks at me as if I don't belong. She's right.

Turning back, I make my way to the central road and start climbing the hill. Coming toward me are two soldiers guiding a donkey laden with palm-size limestone chunks. They maneuver around two young boys who are setting fire to a colony of ants as well as a separate group of boys kicking around a goat's head. The soldiers must be heading for the stoning field.

"What's that for?" I overhear one of the young goat kickers ask the soldiers, the boy pointing to the piled rocks.

"We're executing a betrothed virgin and her rapist."

"What'd she do wrong?"

"Didn't call out for help."

At the top of Mount Moriah, I scan the palace exterior for the window of my apartment. There it is, it has that coveted view looking down the hill and onto the Hinnom. At this moment is Hannah or Eglail peering out? If so, I don't think they have the proper angle to make out the woman in the palace side yard, passing herself off as a man, dressed in a linen tunic that was once fashionable half a century ago. How does Eglail occupy herself now that she has one less person to poison? Has she turned all her scorn on my sister-wife? And what of her? I suppose Hannah is forcing Eglail to pay heed to all her complaints on the difficulties she had giving birth a fifth time.

I think of Raddai. Is he too in the apartment now, or is he off with the King surveying our new northern border with Israel? When Raddai returned home on his first trip a year ago, Ariah ran to him. "Daddy, why were you gone for seventeen days?" Hearing this, my husband actually broke down and held and kissed Ariah, as if it were the first time he was introduced to his boy.

I stare out into the valley and see them. Conscripts, some marching awkwardly and out of step, others drilling like they have been doing this all their lives. Maybe five hundred of them out there. Although they're too far away for me to make out their faces, Zadok tells me they're mostly teenagers. So young.

At the Temple courtyard, I watch the offerings on the altar for a few minutes until my stomach starts to ache, and I find a place in the shadows to throw up. After gaining my composure, I realize there's vomit all over Zadok's sash. Another chore for Cimon. Running out of places to visit, I'm wondering if the zoo is still functioning; maybe the animals and I can commiserate on our respective confinements. Zadok told me that Rehoboam was thinking of ending the menagerie, that the upkeep has been too expensive. Moreover, the King's been hankering for exotic animal meat. The gossip at court is that he's heard lion is quite the delicacy.

I find the near twenty cages that I had visited with Ariah have been turned into housing for refugee Levite families. Wool blankets drape over iron bars and children run in and out of the improvised lodgings, chasing each other without exhaustion until reigned in by their less-playful parents. The air sits heavy with a wretched stink, some smells coming out of excrement-filled pots, others from the now-emptied contents strewn on the open ground. As the sun is in decline, a few of the exiles have started fires. I find a spot on the rocky soil and sit. Zadok will be back soon, wondering where I am, perhaps thinking that his son's agents barged into the apartment and have me in their custody. Then he'll probably be sending Cimon to the city gate to find out what he can, while the old man concocts an excuse to meet with Ahimaaz to pry any information out of him. I shouldn't let that happen, more for Cimon's sake, but for the moment I'm just not ready to hurry back. There are too many things to walk through in my emotional wilderness.

"Do you want some bread?" a man asks, whose hair, on his once shaved crown, is heralding its reappearance. He and his family are camped next to me.

"I'm fine, thank you," I say in a low, manly voice, dwelling on how fake it sounds. I'm brought back in time when I would do my imaginary friend Semsem's in my deeper register.

"The soldiers came by earlier with the handouts. There won't be more until tomorrow." He waves a morsel in front of me.

"Thank you, but I'm not hungry."

"You can at least share our fire with us, it will get cold soon."

"Alright."

"I am Puah. This is my wife and daughter." We all nod.

"Keb. Where you from?"

"Samaria."

"You priest there?"

"I was."

"I take it your shrine or temple was converted to El's?"

"It wasn't. I was the third priest for the Temple for Yahweh of Samaria, and our same god still lives there."

"Then why you here?"

"Jeroboam removed a couple of us Levites and handed our jobs over to his Ephraimites. You?"

"Me?"

"Yes, what brought you here, if I may ask?"

"I'm having second thoughts on a task and need some time to think it through," I say.

"Considering whether to do it?"

"Whether to finish it."

"Is it onerous?"

It's just starting to cool down and Puah's fire has become a friend. "It's not the doing that gives me pause."

"Then why the hesitation, if I may ask?" Again, he offers me a morsel, and this time I take it so as to not offend.

"People could be hurt after I'm done."

"You'd feel responsible?" he asks.

319

I chew a little bread as I compose my next thoughts. "If someone asked you to pray for them at the expense of someone else, say he was competing for a position with another, and the prayer worked, wouldn't you feel accountable that the other man was denied the post?"

"It wasn't me that altered the state of things, it would be Yahweh. I'm just the messenger."

"But for your message, Yahweh wouldn't have acted. So if you said nothing, things would be unchanged."

"I suppose." he said.

"But what if your message wasn't clear? What if your prayer wasn't long enough, or precise enough, or you said your prayer to the wrong deity, or for whatever reason, Yahweh heard it wrong. And he acted differently from what you intended. You'd feel accountable?"

"I think that's a risk all priests take when serving their god. If the gods didn't want priests to act as intermediaries, they would let us know. Whom do you pray to?"

"Yahweh."

"So, on this matter, put your faith in him."

"But if I don't know what he wants?"

"I still have my gemstones. Do you want me to ask him?"

Then I see his little girl, a freckle face like the other . . .

The voice of Yahweh kindles flames of fire.

I leave him and stumble in the twilight to the thoroughfare. I spot Cimon's backside running toward the gate.

"Cimon!"

א

"Why did you do this?" Zadok screams, as I knew he would.

"I'm writing about, about the wandering Israelites in the desert. To know them, to really understand them, I need, I needed to wander too."

"Without so much as telling us? Do you know how worried we were? This can never happen again. Never! You'll need a lesson. Cimon, beat her." The slave's face has all the joy of a sackcloth. "Cimon, you heard me. Beat her."

"Zadok?" the servant asks.

"Do it." The old man commands just like my aunt did all those years ago, forcing Hori to spank me.

The Ammonite reluctantly steps toward me, his hands trembling.

"He beats me, I put it down, I put down the reed. Forever."

"In this house I'm your master. Cimon, beat her."

"You're my master? I thought I was your guest and you, my host."

"Guest? What kind of guest would steal someone's clothes, disappear for lengths of time without so much as a word?"

"Zadok—" the servant blurts out.

"What guest endangers her life, all our lives, puts our plan at risk? You are no guest. In this house I'm your master. Hear me? Cimon, beat her."

"I heard you. But did you hear me? He lays a finger, the writing stops." I say, surprised I was able to speak the words so forcefully.

The old man grunts. "You obstinate, ungrateful girl. I save you and this is your thanks. Fine, then just go and come as you please, and I'll keep worrying like a soldier's wife when you disappear." He hobbles away.

"Thank you, Mistress," Cimon whispers. "Thank you."

א

Zadok has imposed a new regime. Before the sun rises and while I'm still sleeping, Cimon carries the old man to the Temple grounds and then returns to the apartment as my dungeon guard. There will be no more unannounced strolls through the city and, worse, even my day trips into the pantry are now banned. Whenever Zadok is away, I am to remain upstairs at all times. Cimon, who has custody of the first floor, will leave my food at the top of the stairs. So my cell is now decreased by half.

For the last couple of weeks, I have been writing steadily, even a little during the middle of the day, scribing on the Israelite's wanderings through the desert. As I've become something of an expert on complaining, I have Yahweh complain about the Israelites, the Israelites complain to Moses, and Moses complain to Yahweh. When his people carp at him because they're tired of eating manna and want meat, Moses speaks some great lines to our god: *I did not conceive these people, I did not give birth to them. Must I carry them in my arms like a wet-nurse carries a baby?*

This is one of my better pieces of dialogue, and I know Zadok's smile will ripen when he reads this. Then I decide to add a subtle reference to our author or, if not our author, at least the holder of the reed. I give Moses a Cushite wife. Why not? Yes, I suppose my potential audience will be composed, in part, of men like Ahimaaz, men who hate my color. Yes, Zadok has instructed me that I'm writing a work to appeal to the masses and this Cushite story may be a gamble. But similar to what I had done before with my stories of fathers mistreating their daughters, I write her in as a lesson, because these men who dismiss us for our skin should learn that we are not leviathans. Yet while I could have made her Shebite, that would be too great a risk for a wanted fugitive. Yet it's enough that she's a dark African.

I have Miriam and Aaron speak out against the Cush, and in a kind of Talusian irony, Yahweh punishes Miriam. He turns her into a leper and her skin changes to the opposite of the dark wife she just verbally attacked, becoming hideously white.

"How goes the writing?" Cimon's at my doorway, breaking Zadok's arrangement that we keep to our respective territories. Yet it occurs to me now that, while Zadok has stationed me here, like some vindictive god meting out punishment to his disobeying plaything, Cimon's banishment from the top floor may have only been a construct in my mind.

"It's coming," I answer. "You're back from feeding Ariah?"

"Yes, and I have news. I saw your witch trying to steal more shekels and reported her to the guard. They came and took her. She won't be bothering anybody anymore."

"Thank you." I rush up and hug him, then place my hand up against his cheek until I realize how dangerous that is. "Thank you," I say again, this time backing away, feeling awkward and sad that I cannot truly express what I want to express.

He takes in my writing. "Can you teach me how to write my name?"

Am I that little girl again watching the Thebian priest write my cartouche in the sand? Only this time the student is the teacher.

"Alright," I say. I tear off a clean scrap of papyrus and get into position. "You'll have to sit beside me and see how I do it on the board." *He sits right there, so close.* "It's three letters. The first is a shin." I draw the four lines. "See, it's down, up, down, up. Do you want to take the board?"

"You can keep it. I can just reach over a little." I give him the rush and, with his hand over my lap, he does it exact; it's a simple letter. "Down, up, down, up," he says. "Looks like the outline of a bird in flight."

"Yes, like a bird." I breathe a little and focus my eyes on the sheet. "The other two letters are a mem and a nun. The mem is a little more difficult. Watch." I take the reed back, avoiding touching his hand, and draw it. "It's kind of like a tilted shin, but with a tail." Inspecting my work, I notice the ink on the page looks oddly crooked and misshapen, as if it came from someone else's arm. "Let me do it again."

This time he places his hand over mine as I draw, and his touch, his warmth, his scent, spreading and tingling throughout me like a burst of waters over arid earth. I drop the reed and gaze up, disappearing in those ebonies. I taste his lips, lips I have wanted for the longest interval, his joining mine, his mouth a forest of spices.

He scoops me up and takes me to the bed, carrying me in those huge arms. He gently lowers me, as if he were handling a fragile rose petal, undoing my tunic, softly kissing my chin, his hands lightly stroking my hair, his tongue exploring, meeting mine, tasting, and then back softly on my lips, discovering, resting for a moment on the hollow of my neck, kissing my ear, feeling his warm, hot breath, then his lips slowly moving below, almost toying, until he reaches my breasts, which seem to excite him, their smallness just fine to him.

As the tip of his tongue nears my hard nipples, I quiver and moan. As if to tease, he hovers around them, delaying the destination. Then his mouth finally finds that part of my breast, which I want so much for his tongue to touch, while his fingers rub against the other. "Yes, yes, right there," I find myself whispering, wanting him so much to linger there. Please linger there. And Cimon does. When he's finished, my fingers reach and grab onto his sides, squeezing hard, almost pinching. My mouth becoming an untamable beast, drinking in his sweat, his juices, his taste, so salty sweet. His scent ruling over me, a rich blanket to drape on forever. His smooth chest, so large, so inviting.

My blood tides and I moan when his tongue reaches below, finding a place, a sensation new to me. As I grab tight onto his thick hair, he stays there, thank the heavens, yes. A divine prelude of what's ahead. After a while he comes up and my hands reach for his member, hard and erect. My hands, stroking, caressing; my lips kissing it and more. How I want him—all of him. Then, as if he's reading my thoughts, he slips it inside me. Filling me. His rhythm is light and gentle, something almost taut and disciplined. Then . . . then, as my toes curl and as I feel the wet, *he's become a wild bird soaring through me: down, up, down, up, down, up, down, up . . . his heat, becoming my heat. His flesh, his flesh and mine . . .*

I tremble, experiencing all of him. All of his delight.

Afterwards, as his breaths match with mine, his fingers lightly brush my scars from Geddi's lash.

"These marks, it adds to your mystery, and your beauty."

"I'm not beautiful."

"Of course you are. You must know that men stare at you." His hand still plays and caresses.

"It's because of my odd color."

"It's much more than that." He kisses the scars. "How did you get these?"

"When I was a young girl, I disobeyed the captain who brought me from Sheba."

"You're no wilting flower, are you, Keb?" I start thinking that what I experienced just now with Cimon is kingdoms better than anything I ever had with Raddai. Then it hits me what we just did—gods, what I just did. I lay there shaking. "What's wrong?"

"I'm sorry." I run to the bath, removing the block, letting the water fill it and then submerge, trying to remove the dank of sin from my body. I scrub, really scrub, harder than I ever scrubbed before.

I see him at the threshold, his circumcised member—the price for being a foreign slave—unashamedly out there in the open.

"Tell me what's wrong?"

"We just committed adultery."

"Did we?"

"If we're found out, we'll be stoned. It's a sin with Yahweh. Isn't it a sin with Moloch?"

"Adultery? Your supposed husband wrote your death warrant."

I start sobbing, thinking whether Ariah from down below had witnessed his mother lying with a man who is not his father, fornicating while he walks alone, hungrily through Sheol, and I start sobbing more. By the tub, Cimon squats down on the limestone floor, holding me, stopping my fretful rocking. How many crimes have I committed since this began? Only Yahweh knows. I can't count anymore.

CHAPTER SIX

Revealing his plan, Zadok displays a pride in his invention rivaling his marvel toward my composition. When it is time to go north, I'll wear his tunic and turban and just pass through the gate. Then, escorted by Cimon, I'll travel up to Shiloh, carrying the two scrolls, for the new *Chronicles* will be too long to be contained on just one. I'll also be carrying the old man's letter explaining the scheme and 250 shekels. The silver, a good portion of Zadok's savings, will provide Ahijah with any needed expenses to depose Jeroboam. In reality, the silver is probably more a bribe to Ahijah to encourage him to execute the plot along with finding me a place to live. In his letter, Zadok will suggest that Ahijah proclaim that he found this copy of *The Chronicles* in his Shiloh shrine, a leftover from when the ark of covenant was housed there.

Only one question remains: when would be the best time to travel north? The answer boils down to two options, both driven by the timing of two competing festivals, our Feast of Tents in Jerusalem and Jeroboam's copycat festival a month later in Israel's Beth-El. Both will generate road companions for part of the way to protect Cimon and me from the highwayman. But the Beth-El festival takes place a month after ours. If we were to wait until then, we'd have one less month to stop the war, a month we might need. Who knows, it may already be too late.

A third possibility, one which Zadok has dismissed altogether, would be to go even earlier, using Zadok's shekels to pay for an armed escort. But Zadok would rather have all his weights fill the skin of the Priest of Shiloh.

I've finished a draft and am now rewriting. With luck I should meet the earlier deadline. The only thing that has been hindering my reed has been the awkwardness with Cimon. I avoid him like the Evil Eye, making excuses whenever he approaches. I find myself wasting time dwelling on how bad this makes me feel, on how much I want to inhale his scent and taste him once again.

I just have to work out whether we have committed a sin. If we have, how can I compound the error by continuing to lie with him? Yet I can't help myself imagining not only his flesh upon me, but of having a life with him. It would be a simple life, a life of undyed cloth. I'd wait it out until he's freed, then the two of us would live in that town Tishbe he quests for on the other side of the Jordan. He, a former piece of property, and I, a deformed bastard. He, crafting for local merchants, and I, attending to household matters. And should Yahweh lift my curse and choose to bless me, well, we could watch our children grow. They could perhaps become craftsmen and scribes like their parents. Yes, I could do that quite easily, so long as I'm not wife to another.

א

"Here it is," I hand Zadok the two scrolls. "Finished." He holds them gently in his fingers so as not to cause any damage, as if they really came from the hand of Moses. "As a reward, I want your clothes."

"Yes, they're yours in a week."

"I'm not referring to Shiloh. I'm referring to tomorrow."

"I don't understand."

"I'm going to the Mount of Olives."

"Cimon just attended to your boy this morning."

"I want to see him."

"That is not a good—"

"I've been here for six months, and except for the one day, caged up in this place."

"The Feast starts tomorrow; the city will be packed with miscreants of every kind."

"I've attended the festivals every year. I think I can manage trekking to the hill and back."

"What if they stop and examine you at the gate?"

"You're going to need Cimon to take you up to the court-yard so there'll be no one to guard me for at least part of the day. Then when you're both gone, I'm going out the door, either with a disguise or without. I'd rather be disguised."

"Insolent girl," Zadok says, and he stares off, fingering his beard, knowing he was just outmaneuvered again by his guest. How he must be fretting that his machinations suddenly keep losing out. And that's something that may not be good for any of us.

א

My face dyed, my body swimming in Zadok's garb, I squeeze through the crowded, busy thoroughfare. It's still early; the festivities won't begin until midday. Yet, the people already line the street in their makeshift lean-tos and tents, the early arrivals enjoying the use of the city-provided shelters, the later ones forced to construct their own or doing without, many squatting on simple mats. While Zadok thought there would be a drop in attendance, it's as full as it's ever been.

I have no difficulty passing through the gate; the soldiers are all focused on the entrants. If the numbers trying to enter the city maintain their consistency, when I return no one's going to be asking me a long list of questions. I hurry past the grazing field and ascend the hill. At least the witch won't be there to greet me, thank the heavens. After Cimon turned her in, she was stoned a week later. Since slaves can't testify, the grieving family that she had been harassing threw the first rocks.

Outside Ariah's tomb, I see my boy's dish. While Cimon filled it yesterday, it's now empty. I hope yesterday's milk and bread went to my son and not some beggar or stray. From Zadok's skins, I take out replenishment and refill it. Then my stomach starts to ache, I plop to the ground, leaning against the bedrock, the rough edges pressing against me, probably soiling the priest's linen. I think of my trespass in the Temple, of Yahweh behind the yarn, and also of Ariah now behind the sealing stone. So little separating me from the holy and the dead. Still, there's a separation.

How quickly a year has come and gone, and yet, it couldn't have elapsed soon enough. That seventh day of the Feast I was consumed with awe as they read *The Chronicles*. Twice they read it, taking much of the whole day to do so. Then the sunset came, ending the festival. As the celebrants abandoned their tents for the gate and their homes, the singers performed their closing song:

> *The voice of Yahweh is power,*
> *The voice of Yahweh is majesty,*
> *The voice of Yahweh breaks cedars,*
> *The voice of Yahweh kindles flames of fire.*

But the singers didn't stop as they had done every year before. No, this time they kept repeating the cursed song well into the darkness. To the melodic repetition, Ahimaaz had to perform two last sacrifices.

They snatched Ariah away from me, my helpless lion. And that girl. *Guards holding me back, dragging me as I kick and claw and bite, pulling me back into the palace. I'm screaming, my son screaming, all our household screaming, the girl and her family . . . bringing the pair down to the altar. Gods—I imagine them taking the knife . . . offering parts of them to Yahweh as they would a wretched animal.*

What would ever bewitch Ahimaaz into thinking that Yahweh could possibly approve of such madness? Was he possessed by the most vicious of demons? Or was he simply born wicked and corrupt, without kidneys, that breathing within him lies a most miserable soul lacking anything resembling goodness or compassion?

Now I run down the hill, run to clear those horrible images from my mind, run to wipe it away, as if something like this could be wiped away.

Finding myself in the line at the gate, I wait for my interview. I answer some questions, I think, and they let me pass. I'm weaving through the crowd up the thoroughfare, nearing the top of Mount Moriah. People singing, drinking and feasting on just-picked olives, emptying skins, indulging on the city handouts. Oblivious to all my miserable thoughts. I'm passing the soldiers keeping the peace, some of them indulging too. I make it to the courtyard grounds, crammed with families and tents, and little ones running, barreling into their neighbor's spaces, two small boys playing at war with sticks for swords. The people start to chant, "*Chron-i-cles, Chron-i-cles*," their voices swelling louder. Hurrying out of the annex, the priests with their scrolls oblige, taking their positions throughout the assembly. A ram's horn blasts and they start reading in unison, "When Yahweh made the

Earth and Heaven—" The celebrants erupt into booming applause.

As Yahweh's priests continue to recite, there are bursts of laughter that interrupt, causing the priests to pause and wait, and when the laughter dies, they recite some more. Hearing my words and seeing the crowd's reaction, I find my sadness a waning moon. There's Ahimaaz by the altar, reading the original, and Zadok on a chair beside him. Fighting my way through the masses and the tents, I get closer to Ahimaaz, but not too close. I have to see the younger Priest's expression when he gets there in the scroll, but there's too many blocking me. So I step back and find a spot on the parapet to stand on. Although I'm a little more distant, I'm raised up and can see him well enough.

Not long into the reading, Ahimaaz's face starts to puzzle, and Zadok too looks bewildered. The Chief Priest's mouth stops for a minute and then he resumes, but his lips are not in synch with the others, hurrying his telling of the new story in order to catch up. And while the son's face still seems astonished and riddled, the old man starts to glow, shaking his head, smiling. He's figured it out—

A tug at my shoulder.

Cimon.

"Zadok told me to search for you," he says, whispering in my ear so as to not disturb those around us. "When I find you, I'm to bring you back to the apartment."

"In a little while," I whisper back.

"I'm supposed to use force if necessary." He smirks.

"I'm going to hear a little more. Zadok has his vanity; I have mine. Let's pretend you're still hunting for me."

I stand and listen, allowing my words and the crowd's laughter and applause to fill me, losing myself in a thread of perfect moments, moments that could only be stitched by the hands of a being more powerful.

As the sun continues its jaunt across the sky, there's some shouting. There must be a fight. The crowd surges toward us and a tent behind me buckles, then collapses. We dive to avoid being swept under, escaping the wood and cloth. But somebody else trying to evade the mess collides with me, rolling.

My right ankle!

My hands reach for my poor, throbbing ankle. I scream to the heavens as Cimon picks me up and carries me away.

א

"You stupid girl!" Zadok says, as Cimon takes him over the threshold. "I told you not to leave this place! You stupid, insolent girl. What are we to do now?"

"I can carry her," Cimon says as he places the old man on his chair next to me. I lie stretched out, on a wool mat.

"From here to Shiloh?"

"What about a cart?" I ask.

"Hear me, whether it's a cart or Cimon carrying you, you might as well be shouting, 'Thieves, come and attack us!' Let me see it." I raise my foot out and he takes the heel. "Wiggle your toes, can you do that?" It hurts as if my foot's grinding in a millstone, but my toes heed Zadok's command.

"What do you think?" I ask, cringing as I feel the pain wave. "Broken?"

"When it happened, did you hear anything?"

"Like what?"

"A snapping sound?"

"Everything was so loud. I don't remember."

He massages my foot a little, and I moan and bite my lip. "How bad is it? Can you stand the pain?" I wince feeling it. "You're not in complete agony, you're not passing out. Try moving your foot in a circle." I move it just a little, before the pain rushes. He stares at me.

"Well?" I ask, my head pulsing and dizzy.

"I know a little of the healing arts, but I'm no specialist. I think it's a bad sprain. Maybe you'll be all right by the end of the week, we'll see." As he speaks, I think how tragic it will be when he dies, taking his vast lifetime of knowledge with him, as if another royal library had been sacked and plundered. "Stay off it, keep it raised, and bathe it, and I'll say prayers."

"And if my ankle's not all right?"

"Then we have a month until Beth-El. Cimon, take me to my pot. Stupid, insolent girl."

א

Each day I follow the old man's cures, keeping my needy foot either bathed or elevated. I'm concerned though that the bruised color seems to be traveling downward from my swelled-up ankle to my toes, and I'm unsure of whether that's a good omen. After asking around, Zadok's learned that bee's honey mixed with goose eggs is now touted as a sure remedy, so I have also been rubbing the concoction on my ankle twice a day.

By the end of the festival, I'm a little better, but it's still a torture to walk. As I hobble in front of the priest and wait for him to opine on whether we can join the departing pilgrims, Zadok's wrinkly brow has already pronounced judgment.

"Well, obviously, you and Cimon can't go, not now anyway. It will have to wait until next month. But the time ought not go to waste. You can spend from now until the Beth-El feast doing something for me."

"And what will be my new chore?"

"Making me a copy."

"Of the new *Chronicles*?"

"In case something should happen, we shouldn't lose what you wrote."

"That makes me feel confident."

"It's just a precaution."

My ankle reminds me it's still there, master of me, so I reach for a seat to calm it. "Tonight, at the conclusion of the Feast—"

"Nothing happened."

"Ahimaaz?" I ask.

"Believes it's Yahweh's doing. He had planned on another sacrifice, had the children picked out. My son had come to the conclusion that Yahweh was not pleased last year because he'd given the deity a blemished child. But both of the children this time round, according to my son, were perfect. Thankfully, because of you, they were spared—"

The pain overwhelms and I cry out.

"Why couldn't you have listened to me?" Zadok asks. "You stupid girl."

Later with my leg up on a chair, my ankle oily in eggs and honey, my writing board at an awkward angle, I begin to copy. Stroke by stroke, inking my legacy in case Cimon and I should falter somewhere between here and Shiloh. The writing goes well for short periods, until my foot tingles, then I start wiggling my toes. When that fails to cure the needles, I limp on one of Zadok's old crutches, placing just a tiny bit of weight on it to walk the numbness off, then I return to my scribing. Each day I try to exert more pressure, as I can't have Cimon carry me thirty miles. And when the pain flares, I grin and bear. Both Zadok and I agree that I should forgo drinking to excess or taking poppy seed and honey. While it would dull the ache, it would also dull my copying. The less nuns on the scroll that look like mems, the better.

Thinking of Cimon, I sigh. On the positive, I had my monthly bleeding so there'll be no expanding belly to evidence what we did. Still, what about further penetrations? Mercifully, I have a respite on that, at least until I heal. Maybe I should be thankful for my injury. While the slave is always around—running my bath, donkeying me about the house as he donkeys Zadok—my jealous ankle wouldn't permit any carnal acts. So my impairment affords me time to sort things out.

Toward this end, I think of my character, Tamar, the woman I wish I could be. As I wrote in *The Chronicles*, Tamar was married to Judah's first born, Er, but he died young. So in order to continue Er's line, Judah married Tamar to his second son, Onan. But whenever Onan joined his wife, he withheld his semen, as any child produced from the union would be considered Er's offspring; so by spilling his seed, Onan selfishly persevered his own inheritance. Yahweh took offense to that and took his life also. Judah then betrothed Tamar to his third son, Shelah. But fearing that Tamar was cursed, Judah had second thoughts and kept delaying the marriage, even after Shelah came of marital age. So in order to have a child, Tamar veiled herself up at a well, playing the harlot, tricking Judah, a widower, into going into her. When she later confronted Judah and admitted to what she had done, he acknowledged that, adultery or not, she was more in the right than he, for she did what she had to do to fulfill her duty to Yahweh to bear children. Judah decided not to stone her. That was the end of the matter as Judah was the tribal leader and his word was law. So how wrong would I be to lie with the slave again, to be able to conceive while once more tasting his spiced-filled lips? Then I remind myself that Tamar is only a creation out of my heart; she wasn't real. Judah may have been a fiction too. But if the words on the scroll came from Yahweh, and I am only the reed?

א

I wake to the clamor and pouncing of rain hitting the roof above my sleeping room, an annunciation of the beginnings of winter. As the day after tomorrow marks the start of Jeroboam's imitation festival, I have a week to free my ankle of enough pain to convince it to make it to Shiloh. Concentrating on my writing, I spend most of the day brushing ink on bronze-colored papyrus, turning it into something black and African. By late afternoon, I finish the Balaam story and only have a few lines of copying left, all from the original *Chronicles*, my ending in which Moses gives each tribe their allotment. Then I'm done. I'm sure the Balaam tale is my weakest (it features a silly talking mule) but one that Zadok believes is necessary bone throwing to the Gadities, building on part of their folklore and taking place in and around their territory, northeast of the Salt Sea.

Setting the papyrus aside, I stand and my ankle feels close to normal, just juncus stiff. After a little walking in circles, loosening it up, I brave the stairs for the first time since the accident. I make it to the first floor intact, upright, and with minimal discomfort.

"Keb, stay right there!" Cimon says as he rushes over to support me.

"It's all right," I say waving him off. "My foot is nearly healed. I should tell Zadok. Where is he?"

"I left him outside. After the rains had cleared, he wanted to stare at the sky."

I find Zadok on the patio, sitting, his back to me, his hand raising his goblet to the evening star, the light twinkling in a section of sky free of clouds.

"Heal her ankle, let her insolence be a tool to help her on her way," I hear him murmur. "Salom, hear my prayer, the most powerful of all the gods, the most—"

"Who is Salom?"

Startled, he turns quickly toward me, spilling his libation all over his tunic. "Shit!" he yells to his now empty goblet and then glares at me.

"Who is Salom?"

"Nobody. Let's get inside."

"Who is Salom?"

"Just some additional help. It's not important." Zadok examines his damp, stained clothes.

"I don't understand, you always told me that Yahweh is the only deity that should command our respect, that worshipping lower gods would incur his wrath, disrupt the order of the Kingdoms. I remember sitting in the annex as a young girl, hearing you say that."

Zadok limps into the apartment, trying to escape.

"Well?" I ask, my back stiff and bristling.

"Well, what?"

"Who is this Salom that you just made an offering to?"

"He was a god of Jerusalem, long ago."

"Yahweh's god over Jerusalem."

"Yes, he is."

"So, again, who is Salom?"

"Just a little additional help for you on your journey. What's it matter?" Zadok retreats into his reading chair, his fingers obsessing over his ruined linen.

"It matters a great deal. When my teacher of Yahweh does the opposite of what he instructs, I want to know why. Who is Salom?"

"I'm helping you, and this is how you answer me. I save you from the dungeon, from my son, give you my shekels, put food and wine in your stomach, talk you into writing an even greater work. And all I get in return is this insolence."

"For you shall not bow down to another god—because Yahweh, his name is jealous, he's a jealous god."

"I know what you wrote, Keb."

"I got that from you."

"Yes, I know you did."

"So, who's this Salom that's so great that we need his help?"

"I told you, and I'm tiring of this. Show some respect. You are in my house."

"And I walk outside of it to find you venerating a star."

"You anoint a stone with oil and pray to it. Look to your own hypocrisy."

"You were the one to suggest that, you suggested that to me when I was an impressionable girl and you were Yahweh's Priest."

"Is everyone all right?" Cimon rushes into the main room from his cooking. "Your tunic?"

"We're fine, Cimon, I have questions for Zadok, that's all." I take a glimpse of the evening star on the mural. "I want another lesson. Pretend we're back in the annex. I'm that little girl cleaving to your every word. Tell me about Salom."

"Later, when you're less agitated."

"Do you want me to finish copying the scrolls?"

"I said later."

"I should change you," Cimon says.

"After dinner. I want to eat first."

"Salom." I say.

"What of him?"

"Let's talk about him now, hypocrite."

"Fuck you. Who are you to judge me? What makes you so certain of what's right and wrong? You're just like my son who's certain as all sheol that Judah is doomed because *you* set foot in the Temple. You know he wasn't so absolute until he read *The Chronicles*. Anyway, how about some gratitude? Have you forgotten that when you were young, I was the one who introduced you to your god? You wouldn't know Yahweh, but for me."

"Star worshiper."

"I've treated you like a daughter, you ungrateful bitch."

"Master, Mistress—"

"You were the Chief Priest of Yahweh. Now you're Priest of Salom."

"You want to know about Salom? I'll tell you. Before David conquered Jerusalem, I was Priest of Salom. The god of us Jebusites back then. I only took the job as Priest to Yahweh because David needed me, and it beat losing everything I had, becoming a farm hand or worse. It was David's—your grandfather's—idea to take his favorite god, Yahweh of Hebron, and turn him into a national deity, creator of the cosmos, fighter and winner over Leviathan. It could have been Salom he chose, and if he did, that's who you'd be culting over."

"Liar—"

"Both of you, stop—"

"Before that, outside of Judah, Yahweh was just a minor god in El's pantheon. David needed my help to convince the Jebusites living here to worship Yahweh, so I helped him."

"You're just an opportunist. An opportunist who worships stars. Priest of Salom."

"Don't you remember what I told you? You don't have to be a zealot to earn a living as a priest."

"What does Salom think of you in Yahweh's Temple all these years? I don't believe David—"

"David worshiped Salom too. Why do you think he named one of his sons Absalom, Ab-Salom, 'Salom is my father.'"

"It means 'peace is my father.' Salom means 'peace.'"

Zadok sits there, chortling.

"What's so funny?" I ask.

"You want in on the joke? Solomon, who turned out more of a Yahwist than anything else, at least in his earlier years, as he started building the Temple and Yahweh was all the rage, Salom worship became passé, an embarrassment. So he then forced everyone to use 'salom' as another word for 'peace' to cover up the Salom in his own name. Kings can do that."

"No, no, Yahweh—"

"Yahweh, Yahweh. Salom has more power than Yahweh ever will."

"Liar. You want your son and your grandson to priest over a minor god?"

"Priesting over a minor god is better than irrelevance."

"Hypocrite!"

"Insolent girl!"

Cimon throws his body into the middle of the battle. "Master! Mistress! How can you ever hope to close the rift between Judah and Israel when you can't stop your own fighting!"

"Cimon, get our fucking dinner!" Zadok shouts.

"Yes, Cimon, see to the hypocrite's fucking dinner!"

Zadok burns his aged eyes into mine. "Want more news? Your beloved Temple, it was built on a threshing floor that had been used for cult prostitution."

"You wretched liar!"

"There was no ark of the covenant until we made it."

341

"You just stood there and let them take him."

"What?"

"Ariah. You did nothing, nothing as they grabbed him." My eyes start to water.

"I wasn't there, hear me! I had left before the sacrifice."

"You could have done something, you fucking shit."

"Look to yourself on that."

"What are you saying?"

He sits there silently, just staring off. I come around the chair to meet his eyes.

"What are you saying?" I ask, but my words are met without response. He's old, but he heard me, his hearing is still adequate, never once has he cupped his ear.

"What are you saying?" I ask again.

"Forget it."

"'Look to yourself on that.' What the sheol do you mean?"

"Calm down. We've got work to do."

"I'm not doing anything until you answer me."

"Cimon, why are you still here? The hearth calls and so does my stomach." Zadok sits, toying with his colorless beard.

"If you don't answer me, I'll give myself up to Ahimaaz, and I'll tell him you've been harboring me all this time, against his orders. You'll never get to pretend priest at the Temple."

"You wouldn't dare. He won't believe you."

"I'll repeat the conversations you two have had here as proof," I say, smelling his foul, cursed breath.

Cimon wedges in-between us again. "Zadok, Keb—"

I take a step to the door. "Goodbye, Zadok. I'm off to tell Ahimaaz you're a Cush lover. That you disobeyed him in order to lie with your black witch."

"You want to know, you insolent girl? Your story, that's what caused it."

"What are you saying?" I ask, my face merging with his.

"I've said too much."

"Tell me!"

The former priest buries his face in his hands, rubbing his forehead as if that act could somehow pull the sun back up in the sky to where it was ten minutes earlier.

"Zadok, tell me. Tell me, please."

"Alright," Zadok says, allowing his eyes to confront mine. "When my son read your story about Adam and Eve expulsed from the Garden because they ate the forbidden fruit, he had an idea. That the Kingdoms, plagued with a litany of problems inside and out, could return to paradise if we sacrificed a second Adam and Eve, giving back to Yahweh the two who disobeyed him. Then we would all be, as in the beginning, sharing in the Tree of Life."

"No." I mouth, my eyes in full tear.

"He went to Rehoboam with it. To find two innocents."

"Then why, why Ariah? Why would they take, take Raddai's son—"

"Ariah was the price Raddai had to pay to be Chief Scribe. If Judah sacrificed a child of such a high official, than Yahweh would be pleased, so my son thought."

"No, no, no, no . . ."

"Your story gave Ahimaaz the idea. I'm sorry."

I storm to my room, my eyes flushed with tears, my stomach gurgling and nauseated, the floor, walls, and ceiling swallowing me alive. Finding my pot, I fill it. Zadok has to be lying, just to hurt me, to hit back at my insolence. *Yahweh, a minor god? My scroll caused Ariah's death?* Lies heaped on a dung heap of lies. Oh no, not this on top of that. The wavy lines. Pulsing and taunting me. Taking over. Make my way to the bed before it happens. My vision now, nothing but the lines. Then the blackness creeping in, taking over . . .

א

By the glow of lamps, Cimon's and Zadok's faces cloud over me. I wake with my head hurting like a field of war. And I remember it all now.

Getting up, I struggle to the stairs.

"Where are you going?" Zadok asks.

"To Beth-El."

"Wait, you haven't eaten," I hear Zadok call behind me.

"I'm not hungry," I say, as I descend.

"You've been unconscious for a long time, it's early morning, you need to eat. We have to prepare you, you have to put on your dye, my clothes, we have to get the scrolls."

"The scrolls are useless," I shout up to them. "They won't bring the Kingdoms together. Nothing will."

"After all the work you've done, how can you say such a thing?"

"Because Yahweh told me."

PART V
DEUTERONOMY

CHAPTER ONE

This kind man is poisoning me, and I'm allowing him to do it. With each bite of lamb, I'm justifying Yahweh's sentence. If I were to vomit it all up, would it be as if it never happened? Whatever the answer, I keep swallowing the meat.

"Is it not cooked well?" Nihaamia asks from across his low, wooden table. "I have some salted fish if you prefer?'

I take in this middle-aged man, his face a parade of wrinkles, some perhaps sun-birthed and others spawned by age. Then there's his shepherd's crook of a chin and tending eyes. I then throw more food down my throat. The stew's hot, maybe too hot, the morsels singeing my insides.

"You have to eat," he says.

"I should have returned to Judah first."

"So you've been telling me. But still, you have to eat." I put down my bread, what I'm using to sop the stew, the morsel a co-conspirator to my undoing. "I said what I said to save you," he continues. "If I didn't lie, you would have died on the ground where I found you. You seem all right now. Perhaps you heard him wrong?"

"I heard it all correctly."

"Or maybe our god has forgiven you—"

"Why would he?" I ask, as I stare at the large cracks in the clay wall behind him. From the earthquake, no doubt.

"Why can't Yahweh forgive? Remember, I'm the one who tricked you. If anyone should be punished, incurring his sharp arrows, it ought to be me. Anyway, you're still here."

"For the moment."

"If you believe he's biding time, let's hope that he waits for a long, long while."

I pick up the bread and use it to gulp down more stew. What's done is done, I suppose, and I'm starving. Was it two days ago that I last ate, or was it longer? I can't remember, but what's the point? Soon I'll be with my boy in the underworld. Then I'll be forgotten, as if all my deeds were recorded down in the blowing sand.

"My sons were most impressed with you," he continues. "I wish I had been there to see it all. What led you there?"

"It's a long story."

"I have all the world's time, unless Yahweh takes you during your telling."

I sigh, then decide to account it all back to him, as if he's Noah, I'm the dove, and my story of the last few days, a plucked-off olive leaf. I decide to revisit everything that happened, the horrid and the wondrous, and my mood echoes that time in the dungeon when I recounted a different tale to an old priest.

I tell Nihaamia that two days ago, when I woke up from my affliction, Zadok called out to me as I was about to leave.

"If you don't want to eat now, why don't you at least bring some food with you? You say you're going to Beth-El. That will take you all day or more to walk there."

"Yahweh said that I'm neither to eat nor drink until I complete my task and return back to Judah."

"What is this task?" Zadok asked.

"To admonish Jeroboam. Goodbye, Zadok. Goodbye, Cimon."

"Wait, did Yahweh say you couldn't be disguised? How are you going to get past the guards at the gate?"

So I dyed my face, hands, and feet, and donned Zadok's clothes. Zadok didn't pressure me to reconsider bringing the scrolls to Shiloh. Perhaps he would have Cimon do it or send someone else, or perhaps he was too tired to continue pressing his argument.

In the queue out of the city, as I did when I went to Shechem, I turned back for one last glance. Then I saw them. Raddai and his monster, Eglail, several bodies behind. I spun my head away and felt my insides grind. Why were they following me?

I had no trouble with the guards. Outside the city, at the beginnings of Mount Zion, my trembling hands pretended to adjust my sandals in the muck. I peeked back. To my surprise, Raddai and Eglail headed opposite. Toward the tomb, I was sure of it. Watching them go, I broke down crying. Crying for the longest time.

Had Zadok been telling the truth, that Raddai got his coveted post at the expense of our boy? When the guards took Ariah, my husband was screaming like the rest of us, but I had always wondered whether it was all a show. He had bought the tomb just weeks before, how does one explain such a coincidence? He had to have known what was coming; he's one of the Judah's highest officials, so how could he not? Still, I was glad to see him now recognizing his obligations and bringing our boy nourishment. Whether Raddai sees Ariah as blemished or not, whether our child has caused him a world of dishonor and disgrace, he is still his son.

As I had done six months ago, I climbed the muddy hill, but this time my ankle was stiff and tender. While I scaled the slope, in my heart I calculated whether my Eden story was truly responsible for what happened to Ariah, whether I was truly responsible. How can I be blamed for such a gross misinterpretation? What was Ahimaaz thinking? Going back to Eden is like a child going back into the womb, like Judah thinking it can reunite with Israel, like me thinking I could ever return to a time when my son's hands grabbed tightly onto my cheeks, his nose pressed against mine, his voice howling innocently with delight. Ahimaaz, can't you see that destiny's arrow flies in only one direction: forward? That the history of the world is the history of Yahweh granting men their freedom, not retaking it? He pushed us out of paradise so that we could be free to follow him or cast him aside. Children can't stay children forever.

I stuck to the main road as the sun transformed puddles into steamy mist rising to the heavens, like some ancient tower trying to touch the divine. In the valley by Gibeah, a farmer guided his plow ox to plant wheat at the beginning of his season and, in a neighboring olive orchard, pickers were harvesting fruit at the end of theirs. I suppose I could have trespassed out there in the flat, perhaps be less of a target to the thief, but the field hands had to contend with their yoked animals and the gleaners. Why should I have added to their worries? In any event, if I wanted to return to Jerusalem, I would have to negotiate my travel through these very fields. All because when Yahweh spoke to me, one of his stipulations was to leave Beth-El on a different path from the one I would arrive on. But I'd have to worry about that when I came back—if I were able to come back.

Go to Beth-El.

I tried to summon Yahweh's timbre in my mind, but his actual voice eluded me. I remembered it was serious, slow, deliberate. But his pitch, his register, his tone: all a hazy, childhood song. His words, though, his exact commands: that I recalled to the alef. I was to admonish Jeroboam, but not eat, not take anything with me, and not take the same road returning home. The first command made the most sense of all, but his other conditions I assumed were part of a test. Yes, I knew I couldn't know the sacred mind. Still, haven't I been tested enough?

"Keb!" a voice with an Ammonite accent called out.

I kept walking, but the servant caught up, his legs were stronger than mine, his strides longer too. Nor did he have an ankle that buckled.

"Cimon, I have to do this by myself. Please go back to Zadok."

"Keb, Zadok told me—"

"Tell him you found me dead on the road, attacked by wolves."

"Why do this all alone?"

"He told me." I pointed upward.

"Your god told you not to let me help?"

"He said don't bring anything with you."

"I'm not a thing."

"I'm not parsing words with you or him," I said as my ankle started to throb. How many miles until I'm limping? How many yards, for that matter?

"You don't have to do this alone. Moses had Aaron."

"Don't throw my story at me."

We kept walking silently as I tried to form my next argument to convince him to hurry back. But he changed the subject.

"We really haven't talked since that day you showed me my name. Is this more running from that?"

"I've been sent on an errand, that's all that this is about."

"So what about what happened that day?"

"I told you, I have to sort that out."

"When will the sorting be done?"

"Now that Yahweh is speaking to me, maybe he will let me know about us."

"If he doesn't?"

"Let me concentrate on this first. Please go back. After this is done, I'll work night and day on it, on whether I'm still Raddai's wife. I promise."

"But Raddai was a partner in your son's death."

"If that's true—" My sentence is cut short by his brown and olive eyes not letting up on their pleading. "Look, I need to do this alone. If you don't let me, I know in my heart I'll fail. I need you to go home. Please, Cimon, please. Do this for me."

Surrendering, he sighed and then hugged me, and for a length of moments we were tangled vines. He placed just the sweetest kiss on my cheek.

"Give Jeroboam the admonishment of a lifetime."

"He won't know the tongue that lashed him."

I teared up as I lost him over the hill, all the time fretting that it might be the end of our shared histories. It wouldn't be, I concluded. If by chance not on earth, Ariah and I would wait patiently for him at the Gates.

א

There was Gibeon in the distance, just like several months ago, but then I had Cimon and the pilgrims. Now I had no one, and I started to feel that perhaps I didn't really have Yahweh either.

The commanding voice that spoke to me was already fading into the realm of memory. Becoming like he had been for periods of my life: lingering, but something distant and removed, like the nomad's remembrances of water before the dried-up wadi. I tried to pretend that my god was right beside me, watching my back, hovering over me. But it was just pretending; that's all it was. Pretending as I had done with Semsem and Ruzu. Pretending as I had done when I lied to my aunt and uncle about being attacked by a monkey. Pretending as I had done when I was writing my new *Chronicles*, as if the words on the scroll could make the smallest difference. Yet no matter what tricks my heart would employ, it was just me, alone in the Benjamin wilderness.

And Dinah, born to Jacob, went out to see the daughters of the land.

To the west, on terracing cut into the hill on the other side of the narrow valley, a farmer laboriously guided his ox so that his yoked plow could loosen the damp soil. As I watched this, I tried to ward off the jitters by thinking of what lay ahead, of what I would have to do at Beth-El. In my new *Chronicles* I used that city as a setting for a few stories concerning our third patriarch. It was at Beth-El that I had our god most high promise to watch over Jacob. There Jacob would dream of a ladder reaching the skies and would later build an altar. And now I was to chastise Jeroboam for doing the same. Odd. Well, perhaps more coincidental than odd. Jeroboam's shrine was built for sacrificing to El, the wrong god.

The hill highway zigged and zagged, to Ramah and to Mizpah. Just as I had felt when I was hunched and stumbling in that dark tunnel below the palace, I was all alone. More so with all my missteps. I found myself straying from the road, for wild grass would often usurp the trusty beaten path. I can't remember the number of times I found myself walking into a dead-end thicket of bushes, or into a pile of donkey dung, or occasionally leaving the hilltop altogether, veering off into the valley. Worse, another set of pains that had only begun to register before now fully competed with my ankle—unpleasantries emanating from my stomach and my head. All because I was starving.

Before I had left, Zadok tried to have me eat, but that was something I couldn't do. Not just because of what Yahweh had said, but also because I had grown to despise the old man, resisting his commands, and this was just one more act of disobedience heaped on the mound. That last argument we had before my affliction—about his Salom worship—was the culmination of a miserable six months. Living under his roof had been like vinegar on natron, everything exacerbated because I had refused to forgive him. Zadok and his manipulations had done absolutely nothing to save my boy from the cutting knife and the burning altar.

If it were true that Raddai was complicit, just to receive the office of Scribe, that just evidenced Yahweh's never-ending battles with the gods of chaos: Yam, Leviathan, and Tiamat, along with their minions, the demons and the Evil Eye; the lot of them planting notions of sin in the minds of men. Had Ariah had a chance to grow up, would he have sided with good or evil? Would my lion even have been given the opportunity to choose freely? Perhaps Solomon's and Raddai's hideous doings, along with my own, would have doomed my grown boy into his own wretched acts. If he were to commit evil, would I feel responsible for birthing such a monstrosity?

As I got close to the town of Ba'al-hazor, several soldiers down the road were in the midst of interviewing passersby in both directions. When a man with an ox-driven cart came up from behind me, I allowed him to pass, and with the traveler and his animal contraption as a shield, I spun unnoticed down the hillside.

At the valley floor, my foot in agony, I managed to limp and try my best to disappear into the partial cover of a large orchard of pomegranate trees, all naked as their fruit must have been picked clean a month or so ago during the summer harvest. On the muddy dirt lay a thick branch that could be used as a walking stick. Picking it up, I debated as to whether I was breaking Yahweh's command—he had said to bring nothing, but this I had found on the way. Yet here I was interpreting his words to suit me, and maybe doing no better than Ahimaaz when he had read my Eden and Sodom tales. I imagined I could have just left it untouched to play it safe, but my ankle would have none of it, selling to the rest of me that Yahweh had placed the wood there for a purpose. When times are desperate, you can convince yourself of every truth as well as every kind of lunacy.

So, with the crutch, I hobbled toward the Ephraimite border, paralleling the ridge route, with all the grace of old Zadok and the speed of an entombment. Each step an ordeal, my stomach constantly reminding me how neglected it felt. Still deep in the orchard, I sat down to rest on a felled tree. It was then, when I was about to stand and be on my way, that I heard the voices.

CHAPTER TWO

"Who's going to stop me if I up and go back to Gaza?" a voice asked over the sound snapping branches, as I lunged for the ground. "A man has to be compensated for his work. You understand what I'm saying?"

"Naboth thinks they've run out of silver," another said.

"They're silvered enough." Now flat on the ground, my lips pressed against the dirt, trying hard not to swallow, I saw the bottom halves of two mercenaries. Both pissing on the same trunk of a tree, their tops obstructed by thick branches.

"Naboth also thinks it's 'cause of lack of tribute," said a soldier whose calves were thinner than the other.

"They're shitting talents, and even if they're not, well, if it was me, I melt all that unnecessary refuse in front of their temple. A dozen silver basins to wash animals, you got to be—hey you."

As the thick-calved one spotted me, I considered for a moment about trying to hobble my way out of there, but gave in to reality.

"I fell and hurt myself," I said in my manly voice, looking away submissively. "Can you, could you help me up?"

He extended his arm, and I grabbed it. Pulling me in, he squeezed my hand hard as I imagined he would a sword. He smiled, but only the corners of his mouth were engaging me, his eyes were off on another front. As I got upright, he turned to the other. "Think he has any?" After his friend nodded, he turned back to me. "We want some payment for helping you. What are you carrying?"

"What?"

"You heard me."

"I, I don't have any skins."

"You don't mind if we check?" He took his fat hands and patted me, stopping at my chest, and then softly smacked his lips. "Take off the tunic and turban." I froze, shivering. As I shut my eyes, he flung off my headdress. Then he ripped off my robe.

"This is that witch they're looking for." His cold, clammy, grimy, fat hands were all over my small breasts, feeling them, poking them, invading them. "Bend over," he ordered.

I just stood there trembling. "You know, do you know what happens when you, uh, penetrate a witch?" I blurted out, with my eyes still closed.

"Bend over!"

"I, I . . ."

He struck me across my face. "Have you no ears? Bend!"

"I, I'll summon the Evil Eye."

He jammed my head downward. I heard him flap open his loose-fitting tunic.

Something rushing, a loud thump, and a cry. Opening my eyes, there was Cimon. He apparently had lunged at the other and was now smashing the soldier's head with a rock. Then he hurled himself at my would-be rapist, who was reaching for his sword. They were on the ground spinning, blood in their mid sections.

When they stopped rolling, they laid motionless. As I neared them, I detected no life in Cimon. The other was moaning. I staggered a few steps back and found Cimon's rock. And used it.

I reached over to Cimon. Waiting for his chest to move, waiting for life in his eyes. Nothing. He was just flesh, his breath, his spirit gone. I started sobbing uncontrollably, scooping up muddy dirt and grinding it in my hair. After a good length, I remembered Yahweh's instructions, how I had to admonish Jeroboam. Mourning would have to wait. But Cimon, he should be buried. He had to be buried. If not, how could he descend down to the Gates? In tears, I frantically started scooping up earth where he lay, removing what I could, digging, turning the flat into something of a pit. My hands were on him, to roll him into it, and I broke down again. I stared up at the heavens. *Yahweh, why? If you didn't cause this, couldn't you at least have prevented it? Is this the price to keep me alive to do your bidding?*

Some time went by, and I managed to collect myself and pushed Cimon into what I had dug. Then I covered him with dirt and grass. When I was done, it ended up more mound than grave. But at least he wasn't out in the open, to be food for jackals or picked at by ravens. I quickly prayed that nothing ever grow here again, that this patch of earth be barren and sterile forever. I asked that Yahweh instruct Mot to help Cimon find his way, as the Ammonite would be without a light or food for his journey.

How I must have hurt him these last months with my ceaseless deliberations about whether to pursue a future with him. No better than the goddess Ishtar, who in the poem loved the beautiful allallu bird, only to afterwards hit the creature, breaking his wings.

I couldn't languish at Cimon's grave, as more soldiers would be coming to search for these two dead pig eaters. Finding

Zadok's ripped tunic and turban strewn on the ground, I threw it on and gathered up my crutch. Then I turned and saw the tips, several yards away, as if they were begging me to take them. Cimon had brought a skin (now ripped and torn) to carry them, and the ends were sticking out.

The scrolls.

No, they should be left there. In my affliction, Yahweh said not to bring anything, that nothing I could carry would join the Kingdoms. There was too much misery and death attached to that collection of ink marks. Better to leave them be. And even if the papyri were to be swept up by the wind, carried off forever, or gnawed at by animals, Zadok had his duplicate.

So I hobbled north, once again following the contours of the hill. But after a hundred yards or so, I limped back and scooped up *The Chronicles*, breaking yet another of Yahweh's commands. Having birthed the papyri, I just couldn't abandon them to the wood.

א

The sun was dropping as I made my way through the orchard. When there were no more trees, I crossed a farmer's field, hoping that I was safe in Ephraim, away from Judah's mercenaries. And if I were across the border, would I ever set foot in my old kingdom again? Something told me I would never return, even though my god had instructed me to harken back after I complied with his instructions. Be it person or thing as the cause, I thought I was to die here in Israel.

I continued hugging the hill when I found a path up the ridge, leading back to the highway. Struggling the slope, my ankle in near agony, crutch in one hand, scrolls crunched in the other, I thought of my invention, Rachel, her corpse left and barely buried at the side of the road outside Bethlehem. But at least in my story, Jacob erected a pillar for her. Cimon had no marker to let the world witness he was there, except a dirt mound, a little earthy blanket that probably would disappear by the ravages of winter rains and summer winds, leaving just his rotting flesh.

At the top, I relaxed. There was no soldier to question me, no highwayman. Just the walled city of Beth-El up ahead. Although my foot was in misery, I tried to speed, worried that I would lose my contest to the sun, which was already being swallowed up by a western mountaintop. My fear proved correct: by the time I reached the fields outside, the gate was closed. Looking around, I expected tents, lots of them, like the ones outside Jerusalem during our feast. But there were none. I saw only a pasture full of beggars, cripples, gleaners, and stray cats, all of them hunting for food. I came across what looked like a somewhat well-off family camped by the gate.

"Is there a feast here?" I asked them in my manly voice.

"There better be. We just got here but not in time to gain entry," the husband said.

"Why no tents then?"

"Tents?"

"He means like the Feast in Jerusalem," his wife interjected.

"We're not celebrating the tent in the wilderness?" I asked.

"Not tents, but olives," the husband said. "Care to share our fire?"

I did, accepting no offerings of food, keeping my words and thoughts to myself, watching new arrivals swarm the field, a few setting up camps by us. All the while, the pains in my gut and foot, along with the writhing and knotting round my head, had become nearly unbearable. And my heart—that organ wrestled with so many cursed thoughts. Thoughts of that mercenary back there, the one I killed, the one I took a rock to. Striking the witch was one thing, but this was something else. Now maybe the soldier would have died anyway, but would Yahweh forgive me as I imagined he might have done when my Moses had killed the Egyptian and then hid his body in the sand? The prophet doing so after he witnessed the man striking a Hebrew. Of course, when I wrote the thing, I needed the sequence to occur; it was a fiction, a contraption to draw Moses out of Egypt and into Midian so he could meet Yahweh at the burning bush. But what if I am Yahweh's reed and what I wrote of Moses really happened?

That mercenary I killed was evil; he deserved to die. He was the kind that had no conscience, the kind that would not hesitate eating a kid boiled in its mother's milk. A beast. But the Judahite law codes didn't allow for me to act as executioner, unless there's a second witness and the elders or the King have decreed death. I thought of those stories I had read in the scroll about the Judges, how heroic women of yore killed their adversaries with tent pegs and millstones. But these were just stories. These women weren't real. Or were they? Still, one more sin for Keb. Yet shouldn't it be a sinless man who should admonish Jeroboam?

Who am I that I should go before Pharaoh?

In my story, I had Yahweh ban Moses from entering the promised land all because of one crime: when the prophet's anger flared because the people were harping on him for not alleviating their thirst in the wilderness, he struck the rock with his staff instead of trusting in our god and waiting for the deity to bring the water out. One mistake was enough. So again, why me for all this?

And what of Cimon? Had Yahweh answered my prayer and allowed Mot to escort him to the Gates? If not, would Cimon end up neither here nor down there, a lost and lonely spirit? I needed to mourn for him, but mourning had to wait.

My mind's meanderings kept swerving like a featherless arrow, trying to reach its final target. I dwelled on how my words—*my words*—*my Cain*—*how they had killed Ariah.* How I had regretted inking that first scroll, and if anything should be placed on an altar, it ought to be those writings and me for scribing them.

The last thing I fixated on before being subjugated by sleep was about my doings for tomorrow, on how exactly was I to admonish the Israelite king. Yahweh had never told me what to say. I assume I was to tell the King to worship Yahweh, not El, not any other god. But was that it or was there more? When facing Jeroboam, was I to shout out whatever banalities frolicked across my heart? Or would Yahweh be putting the words in my mouth, as I have been putting words in his?

CHAPTER THREE

I woke soaked with dew. As I became coherent, I watched the family pack up their cart of belongings to queue up in a huge line at the open gate. I followed them on my crutch, piling in the line, still cleaving to the scrolls, my ankle pulsing, my stomach and my throat signaling how poor I've been treating them. I nearly fell as I skidded on a palm leaf I had stepped on. But once I regained my footing, I notice that draped from the tops of the city walls were stacks of olive branches—enough to fill an orchard.

Inside the ramparts, olive branches were everywhere: affixed on house walls, dangled from roofs, clenched in people's hands, worn as wreaths and ear jewelry, and sewn on tunics. A few celebrants were walking around practically naked, clothed only in leaves and branches, some only wearing vegetable loincloths, all in appreciation of the harvest.

"Some olive branches for you?" a guard in charge of the handouts asked. Before I could answer, he was already plunging deep into his barrel. But I waved him off, pushing on.

Just like the Jerusalem festivals, soldiers were tossing skins of wine and olive oil into the human thicket. The elders unlocked and opened up the city storage houses to provide bread to go with it. As I made my way to the city temple, everywhere celebrants were dancing. It was to a song, both familiar and foreign. The version I knew was meant for Yahweh, but this composition was sung to another:

> *May the land yield its produce,*
> *May El, our El, bless us,*
> *May El bless us,*
> *And be revered to the ends of the earth.*

In the temple courtyard, horn players made their shrill and the priests shoveled incense onto perfume altars. Then, from out of their sanctuary, which was small but under construction to become something grander, the priests carried out the gold bull of El. They transported the molten statue similar to how I imagined the ark might have been in the wilderness: on a board affixed to two acacia poles, three men to a side, each shouldering a rod. The six brought the idol onto a large, columned platform. The platform was stepped and it was on the higher part that they placed the bull. They set it next to the main altar, which was attended to by a priest in a breastplate as ornate and polished as Ahimaaz's. As the priests laid the idol there to rest, I worked hard to weave through the crowd, advancing as close as possible to the stage, still waiting for Yahweh to announce his words. But instead of divine auditions, I heard only what I had written, in the voice of my thoughts.

Don't fear, Abraham, I'm a shield for you.

To the sound of trumpet fanfare, a group of nobles and runners marched out from the elders' palace and into the courtyard. Leading them was a crowned man of above average height, about the age of his Judahite rival. His headdress was a simple band of gold, nothing near as ornate as my brother's, no precious jewels ensconced in the metal. Perhaps this was because, like his new kingdom, his regalia was more improvisation than anything thought out. Unlike my brother, he looked relaxed and confident. The skies could tumble and wisps of clouds ignite and he would not so much as duck.

I had hoped that now would be a good time for Yahweh to help his would-be prophetess on what to say. But I heard nothing except the horns and the crowd roaring and my own scattered thoughts.

"Israel, this golden bull here is but one leg of El's throne," Jeroboam said after he jumped on the higher stage, next to his idol, silencing his congregation. The king's heralds echoed his words, each sentence punctuated by whoops and applause and yells from the crowd. "There is another bull that sits in Dan, the other pedestal. El sits on top of all Israel, enthroned from south to north. Israel, you have been walking to Jerusalem long enough for Judah's feasts, to pay homage to their king, praying to their god. This is your god most high. Right here, the one that bested theirs and allowed for our separation!"

As the crowd broke into another round of wild revelry, I wondered if now I should interrupt and admonish. Cimon had said that I could use an Aaron. But even without his mouthpiece, Moses—who I made like me, slow of speech—still had spoken plenty to Pharaoh. So if this was my moment, right here in front of the King, why hadn't Yahweh allowed me any water to renew my throat, turning it instead into cracked soil in the midst of drought?

"El, with his son Ba'al, lord of fertility, brought you the olive harvest. El, father of all men, bull of the gods, brought you out of Egypt. But at today's threshold, prior to our celebration, unfortunately, we must take care of some hard matters."

He signaled to someone far behind me. To the noise of shouting and sobbing, the guards brought three men and three women in shackles to the lower podium. Then after them, the soldiers marched eight children up, each one chained in iron to another.

"Long ago in Mitzpah, all Israel swore a pact to unite and to protect each other," he continued. "When one city in the land failed to join in the fight against the Benjamin wolf, the tribes put the city's inhabitants to the sword."

He's using the Levite and the Concubine story. But the story's a complete fabrication, a lie concocted by David.

"These are the elders and their families of Golan in Manasseh. They refused to swear fealty to El's anointed, your King, who was acclaimed by all of you. So now, as in ancient days, we will put the traitors to the sword."

Jeroboam pointed to one of the elders, dressed in a colorful tunic and sash. The man was unbending and proud, perhaps the leader. Two soldiers grabbed him.

"Golan is tired of kings," the man shouted. "And I'm ready for Mot."

One of the soldiers clenched onto the man's long, braided hair, pulling down on it, forcing him to kneel. The soldier then unsheathed his sword, jamming it straight down into the man's shoulder, close to the neck. After the Golanite cried out and collapsed, the King surveyed the rest of the elders and their wives in a game of who's next. This caused many of the victims to recoil, either because they were envisioning what was to come or perhaps, by flinching, that the blade might somehow pass over them to find another.

"Please, please, please forgive me, My Liege!" one of the Golanite women cried out, prostrating herself on the ground. "You are my king, my lord. My husband—he is the traitor. I wish to El that he never took me as a wife."

Jeroboam nodded to a soldier, who swung his sword carelessly at her neck. She screamed out as the blow failed to do the job. It took two more swings to finish it. I felt nauseated and whatever was left inside of me from three days ago climbed up toward my throat. The remaining Golanites, well, they closed their eyes, wincing and sobbing. They knew they were going to die, right there, right then. Except one man who tried to break free of the shackles, hoping that by sheer force he could somehow clear himself of the iron. But after a few moments of useless but painful struggle, his legs and twisting body were stopped by sharp metal cutting open his stomach.

And what to make of this Jeroboam? Was he a cruel madman, taken over by an evil spirit? Or was he as Solomon was, ordering the executions out of pure calculation, putting on a show to tell Israel that he was one not to be trifled with? I squinted, trying to read his eyes, eyes that were too far away from me. But if I could discern them, would they be suffused with a monstrous glee that his new realm was birthed in this kind of ugliness or filled with sadness over a hard but necessary chore? Yet whatever his motivation, the slaughtering continued, and each Golanite took their turn, falling to the soldier's plunging dagger. All of this was watched on by an audience that was a mix of booming applause and hushed voices, of jubilant laughter and horrified grimaces; not a one attempting to stay the slaughter—not the soldier, not the priest, the elder, the musician, the slave, not the celebrant peering out of an olive-branch costume.

And not me. I too stood and did nothing, still waiting for the words. Feeling impotent, useless, a coward. Wondering, if my god had truly deserted me, how was I to do this thing on my own, a nobody, a nothing? With no divine hand to the rescue, could I simply will the words into existence? No, I couldn't. For Jeroboam, he was the text, and I, the empty margins. Then as the last elder fell, I looked up at the clouds and sky and wondered: *Yahweh, how could you send me on my path, only to forget me at the juncture?*

If there is one witness that should be here, it should be you, Yahweh. Meddling, pained, caring. Caring about me, your supposed messenger. Caring about these people who are being killed. Caring about Jeroboam and the soldiers doing the slaughtering.

When they finished with the adults, left were the children chained to each other. I teared up, cringing at them, all so young, all helplessly screaming and sobbing, just like Ariah and that freckled-face girl . . .

"The three boys and five girls we will give to El!" Jeroboam shouted.

And then I knew what I had to say. Just like I knew what I had to do a year ago, culminating in that night I broke into the Temple. That was the night I replaced an old scroll with a new one. For after Ariah died, I came up with a plan to prevent the sacrificing of children in Jerusalem from ever happening again. I would insert a new story into *The Chronicles*. About Abraham taking his son, his favorite son, the son of his old age, the son that he loved to the top of Mount Moriah, placing him on an altar, just like Ahimaaz's had done. Then as Abraham was about to knife his bound child, an angel called to him from heaven to put the instrument down—to spare his boy, presenting Abraham a ram for the altar instead.

How I had to strain all those months to rewrite the entire *Chronicles*, word for word, but with this new addition. Inking and hiding the work as I had done before, only this time in the sleeve of one of my tunics. Eglail had suspected what I was up to and I caught her in my room one day, hunting for it. *Eglail, you come in here snooping again and I'll come to you in the middle of the night and pillow your face.*

That stopped her, and the Isaac story stopped Ahimaaz a month ago at the last feast. Now I had to stop Jeroboam. The Israelite king looked at the unsheathed soldier and pointed to the first shackled boy, a boy who a week ago could have been skipping blithely in his garden.

I threw down my crutch. "Do not do this thing!" I screamed, rushing the now ruddy podium, surprised at my burst of energy, at my agility, and how unimpeded my words came out. Still, I found my hands shaking as poorly as a leper's and hid them behind my back. "Do not do this!" I screamed again as I reached the stage, ensuring my words were heard this time in case my first shout out had disappeared in the babble.

"Seize him," Jeroboam said, lengthening his finger and pointing down at me, his sandals and lower part of his tunic spotted in blood.

"These are *The Chronicles of Moses!*"

I held up the scrolls, using them as a prop, like the prop I had been for my father. My writings, now an extension of my arm, caused a stir among the celebrants. The guards who were about to pounce became instead stone idols. Jeroboam, too, stood there, frozen and inert like his golden bull of El.

"They say do not do this thing!" I shouted.

"*The Chronicles* are Judah's lies," the King finally said.

"These are the complete *Chronicles*, not the redacted version that Judah made, the one that suits Judah's interest. These are from the hand of Moses," I said with all the guile of my characters. "Read and you will see the history of the Israelites in Israel, events that occurred in the North, and east of the Jordan. The happenings of the patriarchs in Shechem and Beth-El and Kiriath Huzoth and Peni-El. Your history in your cities."

"*The Chronicles* are about the Judah god—"

"Judah's god is your god, they are one in the same. El is Yahweh and Yahweh is El. Here, read it and you will see."

"Give it to me." He reached down from the dais, and I handed him the crumpled scrolls, the outsides dirtied with wet grass and muddy soil. He gave them to his breastplates, who began reading the contents and who would stop now and then to converse with the King. I was at Shechem again, trying to stop the war. *Please, Yahweh, please. Make the story unharden his heart.*

The deliberating over, the King's eyes found me. "Who are you? Where did you get this?"

"I, I stole it."

"From their temple? But you are no priest?"

"I had help."

"Who helped you?"

After hesitating, I shouted the only name that came to mind. "Zadok ben Nathan."

"Why would Judah's old Priest do this?"

"He would like, he wants you to have it. He feels that if you knew that Israel and Judah share the same god most high, the only god who should be worshipped, it might, it would bring the Kingdoms closer together." I said, my words becoming clumsy again.

"So Israel can once again be ruled, taxed, and forced into labor from Jerusalem?"

"Israel and Judah are broken shards; they can never go back. Our god has told me. Still, the Kingdoms are of the same pot; they are—they need not be enemies."

"I've had enough of your—"

"It was their fathers who were traitors, what harm did these children do? Read the part about how our god stayed Abraham from sacrificing Isaac. He would not have you do this thing you are planning. If you do, only wretched things will come to you and your kingdom."

Jeroboam turned to his guard. "Take him. We will give him to El after the other offerings."

Two soldiers grabbed me. Perhaps for the last time, my chest pounded out and my eyes were awash in water. But I soon stopped thinking about me and my hapless life and instead thought of the children. There they were, the little ones, sobbing, begging for their lives, begging for their dead parents. I couldn't believe that they were going to kill these innocents in front of everyone; at least Ahimaaz did the deed after the Jerusalem celebrants left, hiding it in the dark.

With the King's nod, a soldier unshackled the first boy—he was maybe Ariah's age—and then grabbed the child. With all the force the child could muster, with his every sinew doing what it could, the boy resisted, kicking, biting, screaming. But with an arm firmly squeezing against the boy's chest to hold him in place, the soldier slit the child's throat. Then he carried the small, bleeding corpse up the step, onto the altar. There, the priest of El took his carving knife and cut him up into parts, tossing the pieces on the hearth, cooking him like an animal, the smell, foul and noxious. The priest took his portion, feeding on the hot, cooked flesh.

Then they did the same to his sister. I winced. *Is this what had happened to my lion and his Eve? Had Ahimaaz eaten parts of them? No, no, he couldn't have, could he?*

The other children were screaming, their bellowing sounded like shrilling, out-of-tune trumpets, wailing so loudly that their harsh and sorry noise had to have sailed close to the heavens, if not beyond. I could barely watch, my head tilted away, vomiting on the soldiers and myself, realizing that my coming here had been a disaster. I had failed to adhere to the letter of my deity's instructions. Why did I pick up that stupid walking stick and those cursed scrolls? Or were those acts of no consequence? Was it simply that my god's sending me here was nothing but a cruel joke? Something for Yahweh and the lesser gods to snicker at in the Divine Council? Still, I kept on praying for him to appear. *Do something, anything. Act!* Throughout it all, trying my hardest to wrestle free from the soldiers' grasp, thinking that if I could just break away, I might somehow stop them. I finally escaped their clutches when the guards and I lost our balance, as everything was rumbling, and I realized the earth was shaking—hard.

Yahweh had finally arrived.

CHAPTER FOUR

In a few long moments it was over. The temple was mostly intact, but parts of the roof had fallen and rubble was all over. The temple scaffolding had crashed to the ground, one piece falling on top of the altar, smashing it. A few bodies were pinned under mud brick, and there were people lying in pain, bleeding and sobbing. Some were motionless lumps. But the vast majority of the celebrants seemed to have come out unscathed. Families, priests, and soldiers—all who were healthy—were busy attending the wounded.

I felt my forehead. It was bleeding, grazed by a piece of stone or something. But the pain was minimal, perhaps any sensations there lost out in competition to my throbbing ankle and queasy stomach.

"Are you all right?"

Jeroboam. Seeing him up close for the first time, his face was solemn and sad. He was no possessed leviathan. He was just a man, ruling over a realm of injured and confused subjects, his ears and eyes searching for answers.

"I'm all right, Sire."

"I could use a seer."

My pupils searched and found the surviving children, two boys and four girls, still shackled to each other. They were standing on the muddy grass, in front of the crushed platform, crying, hovering by the corpses of their parents, competing with the flies for their attention. Perhaps they were wondering if the dead were truly dead or if their parents' souls could somehow return inside their flesh so as to have them once again.

"So there will be no more offerings?" I asked.

"The altar's destroyed," the King said. "But we'll rebuild it, and when we do, we'll offer rams instead."

"What will happen to them?"

"Who? The children? I'll raise them as I would my own, in my palace at Shechem. Say you, would you accept the position?"

"I can't be your seer. Our god has told me to return to Judah."

"How about at least staying the night and dining with me? Let me learn from you."

"You have *The Chronicles*."

I left him and walked over to the children. "You're not going to die," I tried to reassure them. "You'll be all right." But my words had no effect, as they kept sobbing for their parents who would never hold them again.

I found one little girl, her chin small, her cheeks dimpled. I pictured her making bread with her mother, laughing, a once happy child, a future in front of her. I reached out to hug her, but she shied away.

For a moment I thought about staying with these little ones and to help with the wounded. But Yahweh had told me in my affliction that when I was done to immediately return to Jerusalem. There was Jeroboam, talking to his officials, ensuring that the injured were freed from the rubble, even removing a few stones himself. Still, the king would shoot an occasional glance over to the small woman disguising herself in a dirt-stained turban and a ripped tunic, who I imagined he thought had the power to summon the most horrible things on the grandest of scales.

So I made my way out of the city, walking southwest, to find a different route home. I don't remember how far I got when I collapsed.

א

"When I became conscious, that's when I saw you," I say to Nihaamia, finishing my story. As he brings me more bread and olive oil, I remember vaguely waking in his arms, him telling me that his sons had seen what I'd done, that they had reported it all to him and that he then hurried to find me. Nihaamia revived me enough to force his water skin into my mouth. At first, I re-sisted, muttering that Yahweh had commanded that I couldn't consume anything until I reached Judah. But then, like a cun-ning patriarch, he lied to me, informing me that he was a prophet and that Yahweh's angel had instructed him to have me drink and eat. I believed him, or wanted to believe him, sloppily guzzling the skin's contents. After I had my fill, he put me on his ass and brought me to his house a mile outside of Beth-El. When I downed the first piece of his bread, he confessed he was no prophet.

"You say your sons were at the festival," I say. "They wor-ship El?"

He chortles. "No, but we need the city's shekels, and they need our olive oil. My sons were there to make our daily delivery during the feast week. But Jonathan and Ahinoah told me what you said to the King. Do you really believe that Yahweh and El are the same?"

"What does it matter?"

"When a prophet says these things—"

"I'm no prophet."

"You heard his voice, that makes you—"

"Someone who he spoke to just once. And only once. That's all I am."

He washes the blood from my forehead and brings me to his sleeping room, my ankle still smarting like a difficult child clamoring for attention. He gives me his mat, and I collapse on it.

Later, I wake up to bright sunlight and find a robe waiting for me. I notice a lyre hanging on the wall. I limp up to the instrument, my index finger caresses the smooth olive wood decorated in pearls. For a moment, I think about removing it from its holder, putting it in my hands, but I leave it be. Then I stumble out, finding Nihaamia whittling a stick of some sort by the eating table.

He looks up. "Making a flute for my daughter," he says. "I see you're alive."

"Where in the day are we?"

"Almost the middle. My daughter-in-law and Deborah are downstairs making our meal. You hungry? How are you feeling?"

"Better, I think. Thank you for your bed. Did I inconvenience you?"

"It was warm enough for us to sleep on the roof."

"Could I trouble you for some sheep's oil and limestone, if you have any?"

Rubbing off the dye, I become dark again. Nihaamia gives me one of his wife's old dresses to make my transformation complete. Then I meet his family over a lunch of bread and cooked olives. Nihaamia has two sons, the older one is Jonathan, the younger, Ahinoah. Jonathan's pregnant wife is Haggith and they have a daughter around Ariah's age. Nihaamia also has a twelve-year old daughter Deborah. But at the table, I'm a spirit in my own netherworld, grunting out answers to questions until the questions stop, barely listening to their discussion (something about all the work they had to do cleaning up after the earthquake), half taking them in, their talk paling to the clash and clank of my mind's wretched noise.

When we are finished, Nihaamia squeezes my arm. "I want to show you something."

Placing me on his mule, he guides me outside the hamlet containing three other houses, past the community well, down a path to their family plot. The oak stick markers suggest Mot's fingers, grasping the dead in his hands.

"My wife and my children are here—there, there, there, and there," he says, pointing. "My sons added a new grave today." He motions to a freshly dug, unmarked patch of earth. "They found your friend's grave that you dug in the orchard across the border. We moved him here this morning so we can feed him and he can sleep with us."

I bend down, grind dirt in my hair, and sob like the Flood.

א

Today, the girl Deborah asked me to accompany her to help shepherd the family's animals. I agree as my thirty days of mourning for Cimon are over, and I want to be somewhat useful until I can plot my future, that is if I have a future— I'm still questioning whether Yahweh will mete out punishment or grant me pardon. So right after an early breakfast, eaten in the glow of lamps, I slip my sandals on for the first time in a month, my ankle cooperating as it is free of pain. I step outside with her, taking in the cold gray. Stopping first to water the sheep and goats at the well, I find some of the other young girls of the hamlet are there, too, staring at me. Is it because of my skin or because I'm a newcomer or both? It shouldn't be because I'm a stranger; I have walked past them nearly every day to the cemetery with my bowls of bread and milk.

Keeping to myself, I pet the family's sheepdog while staring at Deborah as she easily exchanges the gossip of the day with friends. I remember Galit. Part of me thinks she's still waiting for me back in the palace, dreaming up a new way for me to wear my hair and color my face.

Later, when the air has warmed and the sun shaken free from the overcast, we sit in the grazing field, eating bread and onions, listening to the animals bleat and whine. Deborah takes out her new flute and plays the melody of "Sing to Yahweh a New Song." I had performed that too when I was her age.

"I think that last note should be up higher," I say.

She tries again.

"Keep going up a little more."

This time she gets it right and grins. "You know something about music?"

"A little." I smile back. "I used to harp and lyre."

"Like Father?"

"It was a long, long time ago."

Deborah grows silent, then meets my gaze. "My father says that you know the stories of *The Chronicles*. The summer before this past one, I was in Jerusalem and heard them."

"Were you?"

"I didn't want to go at first, but I'm glad I was there."

"Did you enjoy them, the stories?"

She nods. "Tell me one."

The shadow on the sundial must have turned backwards, for I'm at the well again, concocting tales to my wedding guests. "Is there one you like most?"

"How about Joseph?" she asks as she throws a heavy twig in front of a goat straying too far from the herd, bringing it back in. "The dog is useless."

So I recount about Jacob's twelve sons, including his favorite Joseph. I retell how his jealous brothers threw him in a pit, then sold him into slavery, and how he ended up a servant to Potiphar, Pharaoh's chief steward. How he spurned Potiphar's wife's advances, which led her to fabricate a lie that Joseph raped her, and because of that, Potiphar threw Joseph into prison. But then the Hebrew slave later rose to vizier of all Egypt for successfully interpreting Pharaoh's dreams of seven years of plenty followed by seven years of famine. In his new post, Joseph had the Egyptians gather grain during the years of abundance to act as a reserve during the hard years to follow.

When the famine hit, Canaan was also affected, causing Jacob's other sons to travel to plentiful Egypt where they stood before Joseph, not knowing who he was, begging for food. While Joseph gave them what they asked for, he tested them by intentionally planting his divination cup in Benjamin's food sack, then had his men find it. As a supposed punishment, he told his brothers that he would let them go back to Canaan on condition that they leave the young, framed Benjamin behind. When the brothers refused because they knew that Jacob would die if the boy failed to return home, they passed Joseph's test, and Joseph revealed himself.

"Joseph told his brothers, 'Even though you intended to do harm to me, Yahweh intended it for good, in order to preserve a numerous people.'"

The girl lets the sun warm her face and then looks up. "Then because of these jealous brothers, I'm here with you now, in this field."

"I suppose so."

"So bad things happen to allow for the good." She finds another stray and this time throws a stone. "Get back here!"

Was it that simple? Was it there all along in my scroll? Did my own hand write the answer I've been seeking? Did Ariah die in order for me to ink the Isaac-on-the-altar story in order to prevent more Ariahs from the priest's knife? Still, why that particular path, when there were a thousand less wretched ones Yahweh could have taken?

א

I'm weaving wool with Nihaamia's daughter-in-law, Haggith, whose pleasing face is flanked by long locks, the color of ripe barley. I'm surprised she can even spin in her condition as she looks like she will soon burst with child.

"You're very good, did you weave a lot in Jerusalem?"

"When I was first married, before we moved into the palace."

"Your husband, he—"

"I have no husband."

I concentrate on my loom, while she concentrates on hers. We both work our bundles, facing each other.

"How are you faring these days?" she asks me.

"I'm all right."

"Still sad from your friend's death?"

"It comes and goes," I say, as I get into a good rhythm working the loom's warp. "It's not just his death. Sometimes it hits hard, sometimes . . . It helps if I'm concentrating on some task."

"Well, we have lots of wool yarn."

"Weaving is a good remedy then. I suppose that's why Yahweh invented clothing, to help mourners." I do my best to work a grin.

Haggith beams. "You're fun. Can you adjust that for me?" She points to one of her loom's clay weights, and as I fix it, she clears her throat. "What do you think of Nihaamia?"

"All of you have been wonderful." I say, getting back to my loom.

"He's older, but not too old."

I haven't thought of him in that way, he's more of a father figure, like Uncle Hori and Solomon, and I'm grateful that the incubus has not followed me into this hamlet. I say nothing and continue weaving until that silent awkwardness creeps in.

"Is there a Yahweh temple or shrine nearby?"

"There's a shrine few miles away, on a hilltop by a magnificent oak. Deborah or one of the boys will show you. You like to venerate?"

"I find it helps."

"I'm not much into prayer. I feel like . . ."

"Like what?"

"Oh, like I'm nagging." I smile to this. "Have you always have been a devotee of Yahweh?"

I recount to her that day as a young girl I first found Yahweh and what he's meant to me. Then it occurs to me that my zealotry may be boring her and I recall an old scroll from the library. "At the north end of the world, people worship the Phrygian mother goddess, Cybele."

"Cybele?"

"Her worshipers stand at the bottom of a pit only to be drenched in bull's blood and gore, and with it, receive the animal's strength and life. Priests of the cult castrate themselves, then dress as women, sew clothes, grind grain, cook and clean, hoping these feminine tasks would please the Great Mother."

"I don't think there'll ever be a temple for her down here."

"You don't?"

"I don't think eunuch priests would go over well in Israel. When it comes to shortening things down by the thighs, circumcision is as far as our males will go."

We break out in laughter, and Haggith's bawdy joke reminds me a little of Galit. Could I have found a new friend?

א

"I want you to have this." Nihaamia says, holding out his lyre. "I don't play it anymore, and none of my children want to try."

"Maybe your grandchildren will take it up. I can't accept. Thank you, though."

"Well, can you at least make it sound for us while you're here?"

I take the jeweled music box. Funny how I would dread fingering the one Solomon gave me, and I wonder now what happened to it. Holding Nihaamia's, I'm a child. I softly strum a few odd chords.

"Is that all you can do?" he teases.

And so I bring it with me on my next shepherd outing with Deborah. My fingers are clumsy. But my hands improve as I play "Sing Yahweh a New Song," and I add my voice to it. Deborah dances, then grabs her flute and plays along, and we two could give the Yubal Guild some weighty competition.

Playing duets with Deborah, I think of Ariah. How we invented games together, like our storytelling, each of us adding the next thread to come up with a plot. How he helped me find innocent wonder, wonder that has recently come back.

When we return back to the house, we find that Haggith has just given birth on the stool with the help of some women in the hamlet. It's a girl. Surviving the ordeal, Haggith rests in her bed, rocking the fussy infant, her room crowded with family and neighbors.

"Have you thought of a name?" a woman asks.

"Tamar," Haggith says weakly, but her face is a roaring ray of sun. "I want her to be as feisty and strong as Judah's daughter-in-law."

א

I count eleven children and five adults, including Nihaamia, Deborah, and Haggith and her baby. They've all gathered in the shared courtyard, listening to me recount the beginning of *The Chronicles*. Since it's the Sabbath, it's a day off from repairing cisterns and spinning wool. Nihaamia convinced me to give lessons and storytell to the hamlet's little ones. Most have heard that Yahweh spoke to me, and gossip has spread of my admonishing Jeroboam and the earthquake that followed. I suppose some think of me as a prophetess, but only Nihaamia knows of my hand in writing down *The Chronicles*. As I retell the Noah story in front of this small and mostly young congregation, I have their full attention. Gone are the palace murmurs and jeers from my childhood.

"After Noah offered sacrifices on the altar, Yahweh said to himself, 'Never again will I doom the earth because of man, since the inclinations of the human heart are bad from youth. Never again will I destroy every living being as I have done.' So what do you think? Why would Yahweh, after destroying the world once, promise never to destroy it again?"

"He's a believer in second chances," a girl calls out.

"Maybe," I say. "Then why wouldn't he simply just give a warning the first time around?"

"He felt bad about what he did, but didn't know just how bad until he did it." Deborah says.

"He believes that since Noah is righteous, his children and their children will all be righteous too," Nihaamia's second son, Ahinoah, says, his adolescent voice bleating high and low. "Now the world will be good."

"But to this day, there are still bad people in the world." I answer. "So how do you account for that?"

"But there are good people too," Ahinoah responds. "Why should they be harmed?"

"I agree, why should they?"

"Can't Yahweh change?" Deborah asks. "First time around, he couldn't let the world be with all the evil in it. But then afterwards, he accepted the bad, learning to live with it."

"I suppose that could be," I say, not really knowing. Then I think of Abraham negotiating with Yahweh to save Sodom, if the deity can find ten virtuous people; so our god most high seemed to be more forgiving only a little further down in the scroll. "Maybe all of us can keep on learning while accepting imperfections." I look over their faces so eager for a message to be drawn from the entertainment, and me flimsily trying to act the sage. "Perhaps you're right, Deborah, perhaps Yahweh can accept us, even learn from us."

As I think about a creator learning from his creations, I smile at Deborah and then at Haggith rocking her baby.

א

"I have some disturbing news," Nihaamia says as he finds me in the field with my congregation, now totaling close to a hundred, as many Beth-Elites as well as people in neighboring villages have come to hear the stories. Each time I lyre and perform oratory, the crowd keeps growing, especially now since the winter rains have stopped sooner than expected. Many are barley farmers trying to fill a lull before the harvest.

"What is it?" I ask my host.

"This I'll need to show you."

So I follow him back to the house, climbing the roof. Nihaamia's olive groves extend throughout the hillside, terracing down into the valley. And I see them and they're so close. A few thousand or more armed men, camped on a plain of jagged rocks and wild grasses, heads facing toward us, their chins angled up, eyes wide and staring. Archers, chariots, infantry, trumpeters, flag bearers. But there is no battle. Not yet. For all of them are sitting around and waiting until boredom becomes a monster. If only men could be satisfied with a good day of tilling—that they can't is why the world is as it is. But it was Yahweh who made men as they are. And Yahweh must live with that decision.

"There'll be a war soon," he says to break what has been a long quiet.

"Probably," I say, almost frozen, my gaze still fixed on the men. "You think it's best I leave?"

"They're still looking for you, aren't they?"

"I don't see why they wouldn't be."

"Though it's been near a year since you were taken into custody, maybe they've forgotten."

"I doubt it. I caused the Kingdoms to separate." Nihaamia looks confounded. "That's what they believe."

"While you could dye over your dark color, that won't be enough to hide you. Too many people know you're here. By this time tomorrow, this hamlet, my orchard could be in the Kingdom of Judah. It could even be all burned to the ground, these fields sown with salt."

"I'll be on my way then."

"You could go to Shechem. The King offered you a position."

"I have another place in mind. I'll be all right, but I worry for you." He takes my hand to reassure me. "But can I ask one last favor? Zadok's tunic, the one I came here in. Take it and douse it in blood. Tell them I was killed by an animal."

"A wild lion?"

I think on this for a moment. "If you like."

I stare off into the valley and then at the next row of high hills. Not far past that, on the other side, is Judah. I imagine Moses at the end of his life, gazing at a river he can never cross, at a land he can never enter.

I say my goodbyes and pack my belongings. Every time it seems I find a place to call home, I'm forced to find another. I save my biggest hugs and tears for Haggith and Deborah. Words, my trade tools, become blunt and pointless.

As I mount my mule that Nihaamia has given me, I'm not alone. Several of my students have decided to join me. Perhaps they're frightened of the upcoming war, perhaps they're ones who can't inherit, like pimply-faced Ahinoah, or maybe they think I can help them find some meaning. But no matter their motive, I take their company. We can find meaning together.

"Where we going?" asks Ahinoah.

"Tishbe."

"Where's that?"

"On the other side of the Jordan."

"I haven't heard of it."

"If it's not there, we'll build it. I owe that much to a friend."

But before we head north on the central highway, we stop first at the Yahweh shrine Haggith told me about. I have always been leery of oracles, often thinking that not knowing is safer than knowing, that illiteracy of the future can be a kind of medicine to the mind. But I have compiled questions that need answering. The shrine is up on one of southern Ephraim's highest hills, close to the heavens, under a sprawling oak. I leave my flock at the base, climbing the steep steps alone to the high place.

Catching my breath at the top, I find the sanctuary. It's built into the bedrock and brightly painted. Above the entrance is a large outer ear, the ear of Yahweh.

A bald man in a loincloth comes out and shovels incense onto a perfume altar.

"Morning," he says.

"Morning to you, too."

"I don't see any animals or grain so I assume you're not here to make a sacrifice."

"I'm here for an oracle. This is a shrine for Yahweh, is it not?"

"It is."

"What do I do?"

"Most people who want an oracle provide a communal sacrifice. But as the shrine is in need of constant upkeep, I'll take a donation of at least a half shekel."

I find the metal in my skin, one of the pieces Nihaamia gave me for the journey, and I pay him. "Please ask Yahweh if he's forgiven me," I say as he weighs the silver.

"Let me first prepare to capture his attention."

On the main altar, he gives Yahweh a grain offering and recites a few prayers. While I watch him, a funny thought hits. What if what I had said to Jeroboam was no lie? What if Yahweh is El? And what if Yahweh had other divine names, names like Moloch, Salom, Amun-Re, Dagon, Marduk, and Zeus? *What if everyone's god most high was the same? Could we all be worshiping the same single deity and not know it?*

The priest reaches into his ephod. My heart quickens, hoping for what I need to see. He pulls out a ruby. Sparkling red, the color of Yahweh's protection, and Ariah's favorite.

"Yahweh has forgiven you."

I breathe and relax. Yahweh forgave the sinner Cain, I guess he can forgive me too.

"You can ask a few more questions, if you like."

I give it some thought, trying the priest's patience. "What is waiting for me on the other side of the Jordan?"

"You have to ask a yes or no question."

"Of course. Will I find fulfillment across the Jordan river?"

Another ruby. "Yahweh says you will find fulfillment."

"Does Tishbe exist?"

This time he pulls out an emerald. "Yahweh says it does not exist."

"Can I be like Cain and build it?"

He pulls out a ruby and nods.

"Can I marry again or is Raddai still my husband?"

"That's two questions. The oracle only works if you ask one at a time."

"Right, um, is Raddai still my husband?"

An emerald and the answer is negative.

"Will my stories live on, long after I die, into faraway days?"

This time his fingers seem to struggle to pull out the gem. But it is the ruby again. "Yahweh says your stories will live on. You can ask one more. Seven questions per half shekel. If you want to ask more on top of that, I'll require another donation."

I have no more pieces to spare; we will need the rest for the way. So I must make my last question count. I think for a minute, and more topics come, like whether I'll ever hear Yahweh's voice again, and whether the stories' origins rest with me or whether I'm simply the reed. But I think of something else that I must know.

I ask my question and he gives me Yahweh's answer.

"You will have another child."

"Thank you and may Yahweh bless you."

As I walk down the steps, I'm lost in thought. A child? In my mid-thirties? A woman with a history of miscarriages? How fanciful. Was it a mistake coming to the shrine? Did I just get taken as before with the spurious witch? Ever since Ariah's death, I've lost my confidence in priests—could the oracle have been just another kind of fraud? But since that day in Beth-El, when the earth shook and my words were heard and I made a difference, I've regained my faith and felt redeemed. So if Yahweh sees fit to give me a son, why not? It's possible; he's Yahweh after all. I can put my trust in him, just as Noah and his family did on the ark, allowing Yahweh to shut the door, protecting them from the rain.

I will always have a hole in me because of Ariah. But while part of my boy is in Sheol, part of him is here with me. "Ariah," I say out loud. What is that Egyptian saying? I remember: *to speak the name of the dead is to make them live again.* Ariah's death still hurts, but it's not crippling anymore. Not when I sense the warmth of Yahweh's sun.

As I bounce in a gentle rhythm on muleback, riding with my companions, I think about the possibility of having another child. Some of my imagined heroes—Sarah, Leah, Rebekah, Rachel—they had difficulty conceiving, but prevailed, even into old age. Why can't I? Why not me? So what would I call my new baby? Naming a child, like writing *The Chronicles*, is a powerful, creative act. Like Adam naming the animals, something that could even impose a future. So what to call him, what to call him? I want a name that hasn't been used before. If a boy, how about Eliyahu? Meaning El is Yahweh. Eliyahu. Hmm... Maybe shorten it to Elijah. Yes, Elijah. I like the sound of that.

א

As it's the Sabbath in our new Tishbe, we take a break from laying foundation stones. The steppe here doesn't look promising, and I question how productive this land will be. But it is an uninhabited patch, and it's ours. Sitting with my back resting against the side of a sycamore, the tree reminding me of that sprawling mesquite from my childhood, I take out Nihaamia's lyre. He'd planted it in one of our food sacks just as Joseph did to Benjamin.

I've been working on an original song. As far as putting my reed to prose, I'm unsure whether I will ever pick up the juncus again. But sometimes I think I could write down stories of the history of our people after Moses, stories of the conquest, of the prophets and judges, of David and Solomon. The problem is, I'm unsure how these writings would be interpreted or misinterpreted, for who can say whether marks on the sheet will make people perform wonders or wretched, horrible things? Still, I'm proud of what I wrote, and whether the stories originated from my mind or not, the stories came out of me. I held the reed and gave birth to it. I held it still as the narrative matured and took its shape, from the first black letter to inkwells of indelible lines.

Yet for the time being, I'll write songs of love to Yahweh—for who could find evil in love—though this particular composition I'm writing is not for him. I strum a little and hum, forging a melody. A set of dissonant notes struggles, but the tension eventually resolves, and the melody finds its home on the root chord. It is the combination of the struggling tones and their resting place that is magic to my ear. Each part meaningless and empty were it not for the other.

I peer out at the horizon. The day is warm and the valley goes on forever.

So much to create. The Garden's right in front of me.

"I am dark, but beautiful," I sing. No, make that, "I am dark *and* beautiful. Oh daughters of Jerusalem . . ."

I have to admit—this composition, these words, are right up there with anything played on the harp or lyre in Solomon's court. Even better. But what shall I call it? What shall I name this song—this song of songs?

Acknowledgements

Many thanks to those who gave their thoughtful suggestions and encouragement: Jim Brooks, Krisserin Canary, Kathy Cockerill, Laura Colker, Beth Figuls, Youngsong Martin, Amy Mintzer, Ken Musen, Kyra Oser, Mark Savas, Andrea Seigel, Sarah Skiles, Matt Stainer, Nicole Tsai, Stephen Williams. And a special shout out to Sapphira and Seth Edgarde who made this happen.

About the Author

Jordan Musen is an attorney and author who lives in Los Angeles.

To see our other great titles,
visit us at:

BLACKBIRD BOOKS
www.bbirdbooks.com

Made in United States
Orlando, FL
19 March 2025